THE BIRDS OF WINTER

A HARRY BROCK MYSTERY

THE BIRDS OF WINTER

KINLEY ROBY

FIVE STAR
A part of Gale, Cengage Learning

GALE
CENGAGE Learning·

Detroit • New York • San Francisco • New Haven, Conn • Waterville, Maine • London

GALE
CENGAGE Learning·

LIBRARY OF CONGRESS CATALOGING-IN-PUBLICATION DATA

Roby, Kinley E.
   The birds of winter : a Harry Brock mystery / By Kinley Roby.
   — 1st ed.
      p. cm.
   ISBN 978-1-4328-2599-7 (hardcover) — ISBN 1-4328-2599-2
(hardcover)
   1. Brock, Harry (Fictitious character : Roby)—Fiction. 2. Private
investigators—Florida—Fiction. I. Title.
PS3618.O3385B57 2012
813'.6—dc23   2012019933

First Edition. First Printing: November 2012.
Published in conjunction with Tekno Books and Ed Gorman.
Find us on Facebook– https://www.facebook.com/FiveStarCengage
Visit our website– http://www.gale.cengage.com/fivestar/
Contact Five Star™ Publishing at FiveStar@cengage.com

Printed in Mexico
1 2 3 4 5 6 7 16 15 14 13 12

To my beloved parents, Margaret and George Roby

When the Tao is lost, there is goodness.
When goodness is lost, there is morality.
When morality is lost, there is ritual.
When ritual is lost, there is justice.

—The *Tao Te Ching*
Lao Tzu, translated by Anon.

1

Early one May morning, a green Jaguar, racing a cloud of white dust, braked to a stop in front of Harry Brock's house on Bartram's Hammock, startling into clamorous flight a flock of white ibis that had been feeding in Puc Puggy Creek. Located in the northeast corner of Tequesta County, Southwest Florida, the Hammock was connected to the Everglades by the Stickpen Nature Reserve, several thousand acres of cypress swamp, inhabited by deer, wild pigs, black bear, alligators, wading birds, woodpeckers, snakes, and the occasional cougar.

Although only a little after nine, the sun had already burned the mist off Puc Puggy Creek and set the locust and katydid orchestras sawing and fiddling in the oaks surrounding the house and sandy patch of parched grass that separated the house from the road.

The sound of the car brought Harry out of his office onto the lanai. He watched through the screen with interest as a white-haired, heavyset man, wearing a long-sleeved tattersall shirt, maroon tie, and dark trousers, eased himself out of the car and after a brief hesitation walked briskly across the grass toward the house.

Harry took in the car and man from his brown oxfords to his silk necktie, tanned face, and perfectly trimmed and shaped hair, and wondered what had brought him to County Road 19 and the Hammock's narrow, white sand track.

"You must be lost," Harry said when the man paused at the

stone step, trying to peer through the screen and thwarted by the glare of the sun.

Harry was accustomed to finding an occasional bewildered and sometimes frightened stranger at his door. Some people found the near-tropical green density of the crowding trees, lianas, blooming vines, thorny brush, and the belling frog choruses fascinating. Others found it terrifying. For Harry, it was home and a source of endless interest.

"Not yet, but I may be on my way," the man said. "Are you Harry Brock?"

"That's right. Come in out of the sun," he added with a welcoming smile as he pushed open the door.

The man looked down at the doorstep, then stamped hard on it.

"Solid," he said, pausing for a second look before stepping into the welcoming shade of the lanai.

"Maine granite," Harry said. "I had it shipped down here. I wanted something that wouldn't blow away in a hurricane or crack and peel in the Florida sun."

"A philosopher," the man said, extending his hand. "The name's Gregory Breckenridge."

Harry took it and instantly found Breckenridge trying to pull him off balance and grind his knuckles.

"And strong," Breckenridge said with a thin smile, having failed at both attempts. "Why the hell are you living out here in this swamp?"

Harry was an inch or two shorter than Breckenridge. He had a lot less hair and what he did have was cropped short and more silver than white. Thickset and fit, he was physically more than a match for Breckenridge, who looked and felt to him like a man who enjoyed grinding knuckles when he could.

"It's not a swamp," he said, curbing his dislike. "It's a hammock, an Indian word that means a piece of land a foot or two higher than the wetlands surrounding it. Because it's covered with trees, it's a lot cooler than the wetter and more open areas. Speaking of the heat, you look warm. Do you want a glass of cold water?"

While Harry was talking, Breckenridge had been struggling to loosen his tie and unbutton his limp shirt collar. His face was redder from his efforts and streaked with sweat.

"Unless you've got something stronger," he said.

"Beer?"

"It's better than water. No glass."

"Have a seat," Harry said, gesturing toward a trio of white wooden lounge chairs. He went and fetched the beer.

"You *are* the private investigator Jeff Smolkin told me to talk to?" Breckenridge asked, taking the beer without thanking Harry.

Harry concluded that this man either had the social skills of a water moccasin or was being deliberately obnoxious. He also thought of several things he might do to Smolkin the next time he saw him.

"He's a friend of mine and a good lawyer," Harry said, and before Breckenridge could make some nasty comment added, "I've known him a long time. Why do you need a private investigator?"

"Why do you live in this god-forsaken wilderness?" Breckenridge asked, as if there was some connection between the two questions.

"Why do you live wherever you do?" Harry fired back, fed up with his guest's mouth.

Breckenridge emptied his can of beer and set it on the low table beside him. "Two reasons," he said, shooting out his feet and stretching. "I can afford to, and I like it."

"Same here," Harry said. "Do you want another beer?"

Breckenridge laughed, then shook his head. "You'd have to

pay me to live this far from town."

"That's another reason," Harry said, determined not to be outdone.

"You're joking," Breckenridge said, turning and looking at Harry as if he didn't believe what he had just heard.

"No, I'm a game warden, as well as a private investigator. The State of Florida pays me to look after this hammock and as much of the Stickpen Preserve as I can, but I make my living as a P.I. Why are you here?"

"Hold on a minute," Breckenridge said. "What's the Stickpen Preserve?"

"Bartram's Hammock and the Stickpen both belong to the State of Florida," Harry said, deciding the quickest way to get rid of this man was to answer his questions, get him back into his Jaguar and back on County Road 19. "They are nature reserves. The Stickpen reaches north from here about twenty miles and east to the edge of the Everglades, a good chunk of which is Indian reservation."

Breckenridge whistled and got out of his chair, shoved his hands into his pockets, and stared out at the surrounding forest.

"A lot of country," he said. "What are you supposed to do with it?"

"Take animal counts, water samples, monitor the health of the system, try to keep the orchid and alligator hide hunters out of the place, and make sure, starting usually in March, that people don't disturb the wood stork rookery in the Stickpen."

"I need someone who knows what he's doing to look for my wife," Breckenridge said, as if suddenly losing interest in his own questions and Harry's answers.

Harry waited.

"Well, are you that man?" Breckenridge finally demanded.

"To answer that, I'd have to know a lot more than I know now."

"You're not going to find her in a swamp, that's for god-damned sure," Breckenridge said in a hard voice, scowling at the pileated woodpecker that was hopping around the bole of one of the live oaks, alternately hammering the bark and calling loudly. "Listen to that bird!"

"You have a choice," Harry said, finally out of patience. "Tell me what I need to know to decide whether or not I can help you, or leave."

Breckenridge glared at Harry as if he might be going to take a swing at him. Harry stared back, but the next moment Breckenridge blew out his cheeks and shoved his hands back into his pockets.

"I'm about at the end of my tether," he said.

The shift surprised Harry, who thought for a moment that he was listening to another man. The loudmouth had been replaced by an obviously educated, soft-spoken Virginian.

"I'm a pretty good listener," Harry said. "Let's sit down."

"She's just disappeared!" Breckenridge said, dropping back onto the lounge chair. "It's as if she turned into smoke and blew away."

He seemed stuck, as if he'd lost track of what he was saying.

"You'd better start at the beginning," Harry said quietly.

Over the years, he had seen enough clients in a similar state of helplessness to know that if he could get Breckenridge talking, he would tell his story, which he obviously wanted and needed to do if Harry was to be any use to him. Apparently, Harry thought, Jeff Smolkin had either failed, or hadn't tried, to coax it out of him.

"I need the search to be out of sight," Breckenridge said in a tight voice. "No one can know I'm searching for her."

"Why?" Harry asked.

"Before I answer that, I've got to know for certain that we're having a confidential conversation."

Harry was interested enough by what he'd heard to keep Breckenridge talking. "Wait a minute," he said. He left the lanai and came back with a piece of paper that he passed to Breckenridge. "I'm a Florida licensed private investigator. Read the bold print. If you sign that paper, what you tell me is privileged unless you say you're going to commit a crime. If you do that, the police hear about it."

"How much will it cost me to sign it?"

"Nothing. If we come to an agreement, you'll pay me a per diem and expenses. If not, I'll tear up that paper."

Breckenridge had been reading while Harry spoke.

"My pen's in my jacket, and my jacket's in the car," he said.

Harry passed him a pen. Breckenridge signed the paper and passed it to Harry, who tossed it onto the low table between their chairs.

"Now," Harry said, "why the need for secrecy?"

"I'm the general partner of a hedge fund, Dominion Investments. The fund survives on two things, trust and performance. It's cruising now on about two and a half billion. Any scandal attaching itself to me would put the entire enterprise at serious risk. A man who doesn't know where his wife is may not know where his investors' money is, either."

"Good point," Harry said, impressed with the clarity and forthrightness of Breckenridge's answer. "Do you run this fund all by yourself?"

"Hell, no." Breckenridge grinned. "I've got thirty people divided between offices in Washington and Richmond. They turn the cranks. I think and sweat."

"Fair exchange," Harry said, returning the grin. "What was going on just before Mrs. Breckenridge disappeared?"

"That would take us back to December," he answered. "She left Greenfields—that's our home in James County, central Virginia—shortly before Christmas and came down here to our place on Oyster Drive in South Avola. The house looks out onto Snook Pass. Do you know the area?"

Harry said he did, recalling that you couldn't buy a bait shack on that stretch of the Seminole River for under a couple of million dollars.

"She stayed there until April eighteenth and then disappeared."

"Where were you when she left?"

"In Virginia. Usually I come down with her, but this year business kept me up north."

All this, rolling off Breckenridge's tongue slick as silk, Harry thought, sounded too pat. But he set his doubts aside for the time being and focused on listening to what he was being told and what he wasn't. "How did you learn she was gone?"

"Two weeks ago I called her, to say I would be coming down. Ernan, our butler, answered the phone and told me she had left that morning to visit friends in Miami. She had left a phone number."

"When did you last talk with your wife?" Harry asked.

"I think it was sometime in March."

"And the purpose of the call?"

"Our son Randall is studying in Italy. His birthday was coming up. She called me to ask if I would be in Rome that day, and if I were, would I make an effort to see him."

"Were you in Rome?"

"Yes, but unfortunately, I was busy and settled for calling him."

"Did you and your wife quarrel just before Christmas?" Harry asked.

Breckenridge had leaned forward, resting his elbows on his knees, and now sat staring at his folded hands as if they were a mystery to him.

The long pause puzzled Harry because when Breckenridge

15

looked at him, he said, "No, we never quarreled."

Harry doubted that was true, but if Breckenridge thought it was, Harry had learned something.

"And to your knowledge nothing has occurred that might have upset or frightened or angered her," Harry said.

The silence extended itself, and this time Harry let it grow until suddenly Breckenridge jumped up and said, "I've been wasting my time and yours."

"You mean your wife's not missing? She hasn't disappeared?" Harry asked, having just learned something more about Breckenridge.

"Don't be an idiot!" Breckenridge shouted, glaring down at Harry. "Of course she's missing. Do you think I'd be out in this damned mosquito farm looking for you if she wasn't?"

"I've reached the place," Harry said, leaning back in his chair as if he and Breckenridge had been having a quiet conversation, "where what people do and don't do no longer surprises me."

Then he made a point of looking at his watch as he got to his feet and went on talking. "But it's reaching that time of day when I usually have a cup of coffee and something to eat. As a rule, I get up around five, and by this time in the morning, my stomach begins to growl. How would coffee and crullers sound?"

From the expression on his listener's face, Harry thought he'd done what he set out to do. Breckenridge stared at Harry as if Harry had begun speaking Swahili.

"Let's go into the kitchen," Harry said, as if Breckenridge had answered in the affirmative.

Breckenridge hesitated and then followed him, still wearing a puzzled look.

"There are mugs in the cupboard over the sink," Harry said, plugging in the coffee maker. "The crullers are in that bread box beside the window. You might put them on the table."

When Harry had poured the coffee, and brought plates for

the crullers, the two men sat down, facing one another across the table.

"Do you live here alone?" Breckenridge asked. He had been looking around the sunny room and apparently listening to the mockingbird singing in the wisteria vine that covered the south end of the lanai.

"Yes."

"Never married?"

"Twice."

"Children?"

"Five, all grown. How's the coffee?"

"Terrible."

Harry sighed. "I've gotten used to it, but it's been hard."

Breckenridge nodded. "Like my marriage," he said, "only I gave up trying."

Then Breckenridge began talking. Harry listened but heard nothing about the other woman.

2

"And you've taken the job?" Tucker asked.

"Not yet," Harry said, leaning on his hoe.

"Don't get too comfortable back there," Tucker said. "We've got three more rows of these beans to go, and you've fallen behind."

It was true, and Harry found the fact amusing. He watched his old friend with interest and affection. A small man in his eighties, Tucker was dressed in a collarless, long-sleeved shirt, heron-white and scrupulously ironed. In his tattered straw hat and bib overalls, he moved freely along the row, his hoe making a satisfying crunch as its blade cut into the dark soil, uprooting weeds around the strong, green bean plants.

"I don't hear your hoe," Tucker said without turning his head, stirring Harry out of his ruminations.

"Right," Harry said with a smile.

When they were finished, Harry pulled off his battered Tilley hat and used it to wipe the sweat from his face.

"Let's put these hoes away and have some lemonade," Tucker said, regarding his companion with a critical eye. "I made a fresh batch earlier this morning. You look as if you could use some."

Harry had been hurrying to catch up and, being somewhat winded, tried to cover up his condition with a nod rather than a spoken response. It was embarrassing to be out-hoed by a man in his eighties.

"What do you know about this Breckenridge?" Tucker asked after they came out of the cedar-shingled tool shed attached to the barn.

"For starters," Harry said, "he owns a three or four million dollar house in South Avola on the Seminole River just north of where it empties through Snook Pass into the Gulf. He's got another place in James County in central Virginia."

"Horse country," Tucker said as they left the barn.

"Money country too, from what I've heard from Breckenridge," Harry added.

"They go together," Tucker said, grinning. "Have you been there?"

"Many years ago. It's in the eastern foothills of the Blue Ridge and has some of the most beautiful, rolling farmland I've ever seen. Many of the estates date back to royal land patents, granted in the late seventeenth and early eighteenth centuries."

Their sandy path led them to a henhouse with a hen run constructed of hurricane fence. As soon as he saw the two men, Longstreet, Tucker's large Plymouth Rock rooster, began to crow and flap his wings, scattering his flock of hens into squawking flight.

"Longstreet and his harem look to be healthy and happy," Harry said, gripping the fencing and giving it a shake. "What about the coyotes?"

Tucker tossed cracked corn from one of his capacious pockets into the run, causing the hens to forget they were frightened and come running to the feast while Longstreet strutted and crowed more lustily than ever.

"Longstreet's taking credit for the corn," Tucker said. "It's a weakness, but none of us has mentioned it to him. As for your question, Oh, Brother! says he's seen them on the henhouse roof on a couple occasions, and a few days ago I found evidence of their trying to dig under the fence, but you'll remember we buried that wire deep."

"Speaking of Oh, Brother!" Harry said when they went on toward the house, "where are he and Sanchez?"

"I think they're down in the citrus orchard," Tucker said as he and Harry stepped onto the back stoop.

The low, brown-stained, lapstrake house looked and felt to Harry as if it had grown out of the earth as naturally as the grass and flowering shrubs half burying it. Fifteen or twenty yards beyond the stoop, the woods began in a deeply shadowed, soaring tangle of ficus, bitterwood, laurel oaks, magnolia, and cabbage palms with strangler figs and a host of other vines twisting down from the canopy toward the cool, feathery growth of the forest understory.

While Tucker was in the kitchen, Harry stood on the stoop, studying the wall of trees and undergrowth, listening to the symphony of locusts, katydids, and tree frogs, thinking as he looked and listened that old-growth forest like the one in front of him was growing increasingly rare in Florida. Even though the Hammock was protected by the state, Harry often wondered how long it would escape the developers' bulldozers and power saws. His gloomy reflections were disturbed by a crackle of small branches, accompanied by the swaying tops of the smaller scrub nearest him.

"Speaking of the devil," he said as Tucker came out of his kitchen, carrying a tray with two glasses and a pitcher of iced pink lemonade that clinked enticingly.

A tall, black mule, wearing a straw hat with a red-shouldered hawk feather in its band, plowed out of the underbrush, followed by a big blue tick hound with his tongue lolling. Both animals were wet and splashed liberally with mud. They came straight up to Harry, Sanchez barking a greeting as he loped ahead of Oh, Brother!

"What have you been up to?" Harry asked, bending over to

grip the hound by the loose skin behind his ears. He gave Sanchez a good shake, treatment that caused the dog to show all his formidable teeth and respond with a deep rumbling growl.

"I'm glad to see you, too," Harry said, shaking the broad head a little harder.

Then he greeted the big mule, who pushed his nose into Harry's chest and blew softly while Harry stroked his neck.

"It gives me a lot of pleasure," Tucker said, setting the lemonade tray on the bentwood table, "to see how much Oh, Brother! likes you. He's fussy when it comes to people and a little puritanical, which probably comes from his being such a good judge of character."

Tucker came over to stand beside Harry, looking closely at the animals.

"Pour the lemonade," he said to Harry, "while I find out what took them into the woods. I thought you were going to the citrus grove, to visit with the new woodchuck family," he said to the two animals.

Harry grinned back at Sanchez, stroked Oh, Brother!'s nose, and left them to pour the lemonade. He drank one glass and was giving himself a refill when Tucker came back and eased himself into one of the rockers. Harry passed him a brimming glass and sat down in the other rocker.

"What did you find out?" he asked.

Harry was never sure whether or not he really believed Tucker's summaries of his conversations with his animals, but he was so accustomed to listening to them that they had become part of being Tucker's friend.

"That female cougar's back on the Hammock," Tucker said as he put down his glass with a sigh. "Oh, Brother! thinks she's come back to have some young ones. I think it's likely. Nothing but the coyotes have troubled the deer herd since Alfreda left. She'll have easy pickings."

Alfreda was a young bear Tucker adopted and finished raising several years ago, an arrangement that ended with the State Fish and Game Department's darting her and trucking her away to the northern part of the state, to Tucker's disgust. Harry recalled the Alfreda episode with lively amusement but managed not to laugh at the recollection.

News of the big cat's return concerned Harry. Having a panther on the Hammock was likely to complicate his life. The big animals were seriously endangered and had a penchant for getting run over. County Road 19 ran just to the west of the Hammock, and Harry knew that if the female was pregnant and on the Hammock to have her kittens, she would cross the road often when she hunted.

"Look at the bright side," Tucker said. "Our coyotes may come to feel a little crowded with that young lady on the Hammock and decide to move on. I don't think she'd hesitate to kill and eat them if they make any mistakes around her, especially once her cubs are born."

Harry added that he'd have to worry a little more about poachers; or, if word got out, about people wandering onto the Hammock trying to get a look at her. "Given space," he said, "she's not very dangerous, but stumbling onto one of her fresh kills or getting too near her kittens could make her mad, something it's better not to do."

"You're right," Tucker said, getting his rocker into motion, "but that's not all of it."

"How so?"

"Those two Nosy Parkers," he answered, nodding at Sanchez and Oh, Brother!, "have already been out there. Trying to get a look at her. Now, she doesn't like dogs at all and eats horses, but that's not going to stop these two from poking their noses in. Do you remember what happened with the bobcat and her kittens?"

Oh, Brother!, who had been dozing, brought up his head and pricked his ears when Tucker mentioned horses. Sanchez, sleeping spread out on the grass as if he'd been shot, was beyond making a response.

"They both got chewed, if I remember correctly," Harry said, amused by Oh, Brother!'s attentive gaze.

"That's right," Tucker said, frowning at the mule. "That was only a bobcat. Imagine what that panther could do to you. Well, don't say you weren't warned." Tucker turned his attention back to Harry. "The problem is, they think that just because they don't mean her any harm, she's going to become their friend."

Harry couldn't help laughing. Oh, Brother!, apparently insulted, stalked off around the house.

"What about Breckenridge?" Tucker asked. "I don't get much of a feel for him from what you've told me so far."

"Neither do I," Harry said. "He can be a real horse's ass; but when he forgets to play his tough guy game, he strikes me as being an intelligent man. But I don't think he was altogether honest with me, and that makes me uncertain whether or not to work for him."

"What about the vanishing wife?"

"Afton remains a mystery," Harry said. "Getting Breckenridge to talk about her is like pulling teeth."

"And he hasn't notified the police?"

"No."

"Why not?"

"What I said earlier, with the following addenda, he's afraid of the publicity, and either he knows she's alive, or he knows she's dead."

"Early impressions?" Tucker asked.

"Possibilities more than impressions," Harry said. "They may have had a quarrel, and she decided to take a vacation from

23

him. She may have skipped with another man. Or, turning to a darker page, she may have been kidnapped. At this point, I can't even make a partially informed guess." He paused, then said, "I'm sure of this, so far, I haven't gotten even an outline of the whole story."

"Are you tempted to take the job?"

"I hope to be able to answer that question once I've talked with Jeff Smolkin."

3

Harry stepped out of his silver Land Rover, into the shade enveloping the parking area to the side of Jeff Smolkin's five-story, cream-colored office building in downtown Avola. The leaves on the huge ficus trees providing the shade were stirring and rustling in the breeze from the Gulf, located a few blocks west. Harry couldn't hear the surf, but he could feel the breeze, though after taking his first full breath he lost most of his pleasure by the presence of a sharply acrid odor in the air.

Red tide, he thought sourly, and walked up the marble steps and into the building, adding to his dissatisfaction by reminding himself that the growing pollution in the bay was increasing the blooms of red tide, killing more fish and degrading the marine ecosystem in a serious way, not to mention spoiling days at the beach for hundreds of visitors.

"It's not my fault," Smolkin protested when Harry complained angrily about the smell as soon as he walked into the lawyer's office.

"Anyone owning a five-story building in this part of Avola," Harry said, dropping into a leather chair that he estimated cost more than all his kitchen furniture, "ought to be held generally responsible for everything."

Smolkin, a short round man with a face incapable of retaining a frown, gave a shout of laughter. He sat down beside Harry, then got up again to punch in several numbers on his phone. "Are you going to talk to me, or are you going to keep bobbing up and down like a whistle buoy?" Harry said.

"Just making sure we're not interrupted," Smolkin said cheerfully, hurrying back to his chair. He dropped into it, shoved his feet out, and folded his hands across his expanding stomach. "What brings you out of the forest primeval? Shouldn't you be hunting down poachers or something?"

They were interrupted by a beautiful but worried-looking young woman, wearing a lavender suit that failed to subdue the swelling curves beneath it. She took two long strides into the room, looked up from the papers she was carrying, and froze, long, dark hair framing her look of alarm at seeing that Jeff was not alone.

"Oh, Mr. Smolkin," she said. "I'm so sorry."

"Bernadette," Smolkin said, leaping to his feet, "this is Harry Brock. You can't work here long without finding him trailing through the corridors. He's poorly socialized, but he is a reasonably competent private investigator."

"West Texas," Harry said, already on his feet, shaking Bernadette's hand and finding her grip surprisingly strong, "and you grew up riding horses."

The look of concern vanished from Bernadette's face, replaced by a heart-stopping smile. "How did you know?" she asked. In her high heels she had two or three inches on Harry and considerably more on Smolkin.

"It had something to do with your accent and your grip," he answered, unable to limit the breadth of his own smile.

"I surely do miss it," she said, "but Mr. Smolkin has done all that he could to make me feel at home in Avola."

As she bent her smile on Smolkin, who turned pink in its radiance, Harry thought ungenerously that he bet he had.

"I'll just go along now," she said. "It was nice meeting you, Mr. Brock."

The two men watched her walk out of the room as if they

had been turned to stone.

"Mother of God," Harry said when the door closed behind her. "Where do you find them?"

Smolkin sighed deeply. "Think what she's going to do to a jury when she becomes a litigator," he said, as if he had invented her. "She's even brighter than she is beautiful."

"How many do you have now?" Harry asked.

"Five in this office and three in Sarasota," Smolkin said. "I suppose I should take a partner, but . . ."

His voice trailed off as if he had been considering the move and then remembered all eight reasons why he wasn't going to do it.

"You're insane," Harry said. "You're going to kill yourself."

"But think what a contribution I'm making to the profession," Smolkin said, assuming a beatific expression. "They're with me two or three years and then into law school."

"Except for Renata," Harry said.

"Right," he said, then continued without a pause, "they all graduate at or near the top of their class and then go anywhere they want. I'm betting it gets me into heaven."

"Maybe," Harry said, breaking down and grinning, "but you're killing yourself, and don't tell me it's a good way to die."

"Okay, I won't. What are you doing in my office? Want some coffee?"

He was on his feet again, after having just sat down. Harry, who remained seated, reached out and grasped Smolkin by the arm.

"No," he said. "Sit down. I'm trying to talk to you."

"I'm surprised you don't wander around in a robe with a hank of rope for a belt and stand on corners preaching abstinence."

"I just practice it," Harry said, more grimly than he intended, the vision of Bernadette drifting behind his eyes. "Gregory

Breckenridge came to see me. He said he wanted to hire me."

"I sent him," Smolkin said, having sat down with obvious reluctance.

"Why? I'm not a skip chaser."

"They're called skip tracers, and I'm not one either, but I know a few of them. They're scary people."

"Is Breckenridge for real? Has his wife really skipped, or have they had a fight, leading to Afton taking a little vacation?"

Smolkin squirmed around in his chair, threw a leg over an arm, and began scowling and swinging his foot. "It would take more time than I've got to find out," he said, sounding irritated just from thinking of Breckenridge.

"I take it your meeting with him didn't go all that well."

"That's right. Between his attitude and his terror that word of her departure would get to the media, I couldn't get enough information from him to find out."

"Why did he come to you in the first place? He must have a gaggle of lawyers working for him."

"Right, but he doesn't want them to know she's missing."

"And he hasn't told the police."

"God, no! He's way too worried about attracting attention to do that."

"Then why send him to me?"

"Seriously now, Harry," Smolkin said, getting both feet back on the floor and leaning forward, his elbows braced on his knees, "he may get to the point that he needs a lawyer, but he's not there yet. After talking with him for half an hour, I decided there was an even chance that his wife really has skipped or been carried off. He's got money enough to make him a target. I decided that what he does need is someone like you, who has the time to find out what happened to her."

"Did it occur to you that he might have killed her?" Harry asked.

"And was using us for cover? Yes, I thought of it, but I couldn't convince myself it was true, even though he's not easy to like. In fact, I thought he was a double-wide horse's ass."

Harry said he had thought so too at the beginning of their conversation, but that after a while Breckenridge had sounded like a man in need of help.

"That's the real reason I sent him to you," Smolkin said, jumping up and escaping to his desk before Harry could grab him. "Are you going to take the case?"

"Probably," Harry said.

Smolkin was already punching a button as Harry spoke. Before he was back around his desk, Renata, another brunette, pushed open the door. She was wearing rimless glasses, her hair in a chignon, and was dressed in a narrow black skirt, a long-sleeved white blouse with a bow at the throat, and black high-heeled pumps.

Harry had never seen her dressed like anything other than a schoolmarm, but she had the kind of beauty that made him feel slightly weak in the knees whenever he saw her. She was not going to see forty again and had been Smolkin's administrative assistant and strong right arm for years, but Harry thought that for brains, looks, and character she was halfway around the track while the fillies in Smolkin's stable were just getting out of the gate.

In the recent past, Harry had spent several months sorting out a series of killings and maimings on a stock farm, and the racing imagery still popped up every now and then.

"Hello, Harry," Renata said in a no-nonsense contralto. "What is it, Jeff?"

"Last winter we had occasion to hire someone who traced lost people. Harry needs to know who it was. Can you remember the name?"

"No, but I'll find it," she said. "Stop by my office on the way

29

out, Harry. I'll have it for you."

"If you don't come to your senses, Jeff, and marry that woman," Harry said when she was gone, "I'm going to."

"You can't have her," Smolkin protested, bouncing around on his chair. "This ship would go aground in a week without her. She's the partner I don't have. She's in court as much as I am."

"You're warned," Harry said.

"If you do take on Breckenridge," Smolkin said with sudden seriousness, "you're going to need some help. The outfit Renata's looking up for you was the best of its kind."

"That's not saying much, is it?" Harry asked.

"No. So what do you think?"

"I'm going to do some more work, and then I'll let you know."

Bruce, Renata's assistant, a faultlessly dressed young man with the shadow of a beard and polished nails, ushered Harry into Renata's office. The room was bright with yellow sunlight broken into brilliant bars and shafts by the leaves of a giant variegated philodendron that swarmed over the window wall behind Renata's desk, which was piled with blue briefs and similar lawyerly folders.

"You've been a stranger, my friend," she said, having waved Bruce out of the room and come around the desk to grasp both of Harry's hands.

It irritated Harry when women did that. He always suspected it was being done to ward off an unwanted advance and invariably felt insulted. But he found it easy to forgive Renata Holland, whatever she did. She stepped back to draw him toward the chairs in front of her desk.

"Want to stay a while?" she asked. "What's happening with that lovely old farmer friend of yours? Did he recover from his fall?"

"Has it been that long since I've been in here?" Harry asked.

"Yes, he's fine."

"And that cat?"

"Jane Bunting," Harry said with a laugh. "She's doing fine too. Look, I can't stay. There's a slew of work waiting for me out there."

Talking to her made Harry feel so good that he considered breaking a rule of *non licet* he had set for himself regarding Renata and asking her to dinner, then squelched it. She had worked for Smolkin for years, and despite the fact he was married and had three kids, her having stayed with him this long meant there was something more than dependence and a paycheck holding them together.

That, at least, was what he told himself.

At his hesitation, the reason for which he thought she had guessed, her smile slid ever so slightly and was instantly put back in place. Harry saw what she had done but pretended he hadn't and refused to allow himself to consider the meaning of it.

She turned to the desk, picked up a card, and passed it to him. "You're on your own with this one," she told him.

Harry glanced at the card and dropped it in his pocket.

"Thanks," he said. "You know about Breckenridge."

"Oh, yes," she said, making a face. "A nasty piece of work if you ask me, despite the handmade boots—or maybe because of them. Whatever his wife's done to him, count on it, he had it coming."

"Don't we all," Harry said, with a trace of bitterness mixed with loss.

That his dip in mood had anything to do with not asking her if she would like to go out with him was not something he was willing to think about.

4

He was almost back to the Hammock before he remembered the card in his shirt pocket.

His lapse had been prompted by Renata's comment that Breckenridge deserved whatever his wife was doing to him. It wasn't her assumption that Afton had done something to her husband that focused his thinking. It was the implication that just by being her husband, he automatically deserved punishment. That had led to his "Don't we all" remark, which, in turn, had emanated from painful personal experience, the wounds from which were not fully healed and had probably been more influential than his sense of honor in deciding against asking Renata out to dinner.

With Harry and women, it was a case of twice bitten, thrice shy. Two years before, he'd been deeply involved with Soñadora Asturias, a Mayan/Belgian woman from northern Guatemala who ran *Salvamento*, a rescue program dedicated to finding, freeing, and rehabilitating victims of human trafficking. Soñadora had been cared for by a priest after the death of her mother, and shortly before his death Soñadora learned that the priest was also her father. For a time she had been distressed and angry that he had kept the truth from her for so long. Despite her concern, she returned to help her father's replacement establish himself among the Indians. A year later she had written Harry, saying she intended to remain in Guatemala, devoting her life to Indian causes.

Harry was not surprised by her decision, but it had hurt him deeply. Perhaps more serious was his failed attempt to persuade his ex-wife Katherine to return to the Hammock. Six months ago she had remarried, ending their on-again, off-again attempts to live together, and also ending all chance of restoring their relationship.

Since coming to Florida, Harry had gradually acquired a reputation as something of a hermit, living on the Hammock with only Tucker for a neighbor and finding whatever he could of inner peace among the wild things in his forest world. Since Katherine's marriage, he had scarcely left the Hammock and had decided that after two failed marriages and with his five children grown and scattered, he had seen the elephant and would henceforth avoid the circus, which meant he intended to forgo the company of women. It was not a decision easily taken because Harry liked women. He enjoyed their company and the pleasure and fulfillment of loving them, but the cost had been too high, and he was damned if he was going to go on paying just to get a stick in the eye.

"I believe you've said that before," was Tucker's comment when Harry revealed his plans for the future.

"This time I mean it," Harry had replied.

"I advise you to sleep on it before committing yourself any further," Tucker said, irritating Harry by his insistence on always having the last word, which more often than not when Harry's plans for revamping his life were under discussion, was derogatory.

Harry had turned off CR 19 and onto the narrow wooden humpbacked bridge that connected the Hammock with the world in general when he plucked the card Renata had given him out of his shirt pocket. The perpetually loose plank in the bridge thumped and bumped under the Rover's wheels as he read the off-white card, on which was printed the name *Caedmon Rivers* in bold maroon letters, followed by the jarring boast *You Lose Them, I Find Them.* After that, another line: *Twelve Years of Experience.* Two telephone numbers and a fax number completed the card's information.

Harry jammed the card back into his pocket and almost over-ran his house because he was so busy trying to figure out why the card offended him, which forced him to yank the Rover out of the road at the last second and actually ding his fender on the huge live oak at the corner of his front lawn. He plowed to a stop in a cloud of dust.

Having had several previous Rovers, one of which was forced off the road and into Puc Puggy Creek, another blown up, and a third shot full of holes by people trying to kill him, he had become very particular about this one. Swearing fervently, he jumped out of the Rover and ran around its front to see how much damage he had done. Fortunately, he hadn't done any harm. There was no bark on the fender or paint on the tree.

He coughed a little from the dust and then went into the house, determined that whatever he did, he would not be call-ing Caedmon Rivers. He settled himself in front of his computer and began a serious search for information about Afton Breck-enridge. At the end of an hour, he had found her address and phone number in Avola and in James County, Virginia, and that she had no record of arrests, not even a traffic violation. Through the good offices of Lieutenant Maureen O'Reilly in the Tequesta County Sheriff's Department, he had run Afton Breckenridge's name through FBI records and found nothing.

Groaning with frustration, Harry pushed back from the computer to regroup, and walked into the kitchen on his way to the lanai just as the phone rang.

"Hello, Harry, I called to see if you were still above ground."

"Hello, Rowena. Is that any way for a priest to talk?"

Harry immediately felt better. Rowena Farnham was a close friend and rector of St. Jude's Episcopal Church, one of the richest churches in Avola. It was a mystery to Harry how her congregation tolerated her. Large and fiery and politically to the left of the I.W.W., he had once heard her preach on John Wesley's *Thoughts on the Present Scarcity of Provisions* and pretty well take the hide off anyone listening who had more than three dollars in the bank and wasn't planning to give them to charity. When it was over, he wanted to applaud but contained himself. He also thought she had probably deeply offended most of the congregation, but after the benediction, he was obliged to reconsider the effect of her talk. He found himself behind a very well-dressed, middle-aged couple as progress out of the church was slowed by the crush in the narthex. He overheard the woman ask her husband a bit huffily, "Well, what did you think of the sermon?"

"Excellent," the man said in an approving voice, "it's always good to be reminded that Episcopalians are better off than most people."

"You're right," the woman said, obviously relieved. "I hadn't thought of that."

Harry had been momentarily disoriented, wondering if he and the man had heard the same sermon.

"Since I seldom see you at church, you'd better drop by," Rowena said.

Harry glanced at his watch. "How about half an hour from now?"

"Fine. We'll have an early tea."

Harry considered St. Jude's one of Avola's finest small churches. It was a white clapboard structure with a graceful white spire that would have settled in a New England village without the risk of being pulled down. Of course, in Avola it was shaded by ficus rather than maple trees, and its Bermuda grass lawns were green all year round. For Harry it was a bittersweet reminder of his years as a Maine game warden, a career that ended disastrously when he was tried and acquitted for killing a man in self-defense.

He had tried to arrest the man for shooting a deer out of season, and the man had shot at and wounded him. Harry then tried to disable his attacker, but killed him when the bullet struck a bone and exploded, sending a sliver of lead through his heart. Harry's wife Jennifer, tired of living in backwoods Maine and furious that Harry had nearly been killed over a stupid deer, left him, taking their two young children with her.

Rowena's office was in the parish hall, located across the street from the church. The single-story building was surrounded by pink and white oleander bushes that in places nearly smothered the sprawling structure. Ring-neck doves in the ficus over the part of the building where Rowena's office was located were burbling peacefully. The sound of their voices and the sea breeze in the leaves held Harry in the sun-flecked shade until Rowena threw open her door.

"Come in here before you're arrested for loitering," she boomed in her best preaching voice, and added as he stepped past her into the chaos of her office, "most people around here don't look as if their clothes had been gifted by a Goodwill that was going out of business. How are you, Harry? Where have you been hiding? More important, why have you been hiding?"

Rowena Farnham was an imposing woman, tall and heavy, white hair cut short and with a round, smiling face that had in it a dignity that did not invite nonsense.

"You're in no position to cast stones," Harry said while he lifted books off a chair in order to have a place to sit down, "dressed in dungarees out at the knees, a Red Sox sweatshirt, and black sneakers that have seen better days."

"It's too hot for a cassock, and in a surplice I look like a hot air balloon, but I suppose you think they would be more in keeping with my calling," she replied, clearing another chair for herself close to his.

"I think you look just fine," Harry said. "I haven't been hiding. In fact, I've been busy as a one-armed paper hanger."

Rowena laughed. When she laughed, she put herself into it, leaning back a little and letting herself go. It was infectious, and Harry, who had not arrived in a humorous mood, found himself laughing with her.

"Why do you want to see me?" he asked, supposing she would say she wanted help with one of her projects among the minorities in the county. She busied herself at a side table, taking cloths off plates of scones and cookies and pouring tea into Spode cups from a silver service.

"Let's have these scones while they're still hot enough to melt the butter or warm the strawberry jam, as the case may be," she replied. "I began work at six this morning, and I'm famished. This idea of missing a meal is not the best notion I've ever chosen to act on."

She set up two folding side tables beside their chairs and lifted butter, jam, tea, and plates of scones onto the tables from a brilliantly lacquered tray. Harry wore a simple smile as he closed his eyes and breathed in the ambrosial aroma rising beside him.

"If God had a sense of smell," he told her, "I wouldn't give a handful of sand for your chances of living until sunset."

"All the more reason to eat now," she said cheerfully.

For a few minutes Harry gave his attention to buttering, spreading jam, eating, and drinking the Indian tea, which was black as raisins and, in his view, delicious. It passed through his mind that if he was to settle down and marry, he might be able to eat like this every day, but he let the thought go as quickly as it had come.

"There," Rowena said at last, wiping her mouth with a linen napkin. "You go first."

Harry fell back from eating his second scone, on which he had spread both butter and jam, and said after accepting a refill of tea, "Do you know Afton Breckenridge?"

"How interesting you should ask," she said. "I haven't seen her in church for a while, and she's usually a regular visitor when she's down here. Is she back in Virginia?"

"Quaker meeting has begun," Harry said.

"Right," she said, immediately serious.

"Her husband doesn't know where she is. Two weeks ago, she left her house, saying she was going to visit friends in Miami. Her husband and her house staffs haven't heard from her since."

"Troubling," Rowena said, brushing crumbs off her front before giving him her full attention. "And the police haven't found her?"

"They haven't been told she's missing—if she is."

"How about the people she went to visit?"

"There were no people. The number she left was for the Miami Seaquarium on Biscayne Bay. Breckenridge was not amused."

"No trace of her car?"

"No, I've only talked once with her husband, and I'm far from convinced her absence is anything more than a gambit in some marital squabble. You said that when she's here in Avola, she attends church regularly."

"Has Gregory hired you to find her?"

"He offered me the job, and I'll probably take it, but I'm not sure anything he told me is more than an approximation of the truth. How well do you know Afton Breckenridge?"

"As a parishioner, she's observant and generous to a fault," Rowena said, clearing away their dishes and piling them on the sideboard. "As an individual, she's pretty much a blank slate. She's friendly, a good conversationalist, informed, engaged, but she reveals nothing about herself, at least in the conversations I've had with her."

"What do you make of that?"

"Not necessarily anything," Rowena said a bit tartly. "She is, I would say, a woman who values her privacy." Rowena hesitated a moment and then said, with more of her usual animation, "I don't like speculating about people, especially if the speculation is negative. We're all in this thing together, and we ought to give one another the benefit of the doubt."

"Which means you're not all that satisfied with what you've said about her so far."

Rowena didn't respond until she had returned to her chair. That accomplished, she avoided looking at Harry, as if she was thinking hard. "There are people," she began finally, and rather slowly, "who have buried pain so deep that it almost never registers in their face or voice. But if you know what to look for—that is, if you've seen it often enough and had it validated— the eyes convey the heart's suffering whether the person wants them to or not."

Harry had known Rowena a long time. Over that time he had come to respect her compassion, her grasp of reality, and, most of all, her knowledge of people. He knew that awareness had come from her training and her pastoral work as a therapist, but more profoundly, she had accumulated it from her exposure to the suffering of those who came to Haven House, the church's sanctuary for battered women and anyone else in extremis. He also knew it was knowledge that had brought its own pain with it, and Harry respected her for the way she had also turned that into a tool for healing.

"And you saw something other than an insistence on privacy in her eyes?" he asked.

"I would go so far as to say this. I do not think Afton Breckenridge is a happy woman. I can say that," Rowena added
quickly, "because she never came to me for help with anything."

"Have you left something unsaid?" he asked.

She was sitting with her hands folded in her lap, staring out
the window closest to her. Harry did not think she was looking
at anything outside the room.

"Yes," she said at last. She turned to Harry, her voice harden-
ing. "Occasionally what looks out is not sadness, but something
far more frightening."

"Despair?"

"Despair is fairly easy to deal with. Fury is not."

5

"There are a lot of angry people around," Harry said. "Most of them don't disappear."

"True," Rowena said, with a sudden smile as if she had shaken off something unpleasant.

"Do you need some help with something?" he asked, ready to move on.

"Perhaps, and by the way, for the record, I am not consulting you in your professional capacity but talking to you in the strictest confidence as a friend."

"Understood," Harry said, slightly startled to realize that she had made it possible to speak to him about knowledge of a crime or the intention to commit one without forcing him to report it to the police.

"Do you know Peter Ogilvie?"

"Not personally, but I've heard you mention him and his wife off and on over the years, and I see or hear them mentioned in the local media almost as often as reports on the weather. They're very rich, and they spread their wealth around, mostly in places that ensure a media report. Avola's new Visitor Center is named after him."

"The sneer is not justified," Rowena said with some heat. "I have known Peter and Gwen for almost twenty years. They are fine people, generous and caring to a fault."

"If you say so."

"I do say so. He and Gwen are communicants. They've done

an enormous amount of work for the church. Aside from the direct financial support they have given us and Haven House, Peter has been and continues to be a financial advisor to the vestry and has increased the returns on our investments, despite the downturn—which, by the way, he shielded us from almost entirely—by thirty percent."

"I'm impressed."

"At a time when our pledging has dropped precipitously," she continued, "it has been possible, thanks to him, for us to continue our outreach at a level that is almost unchanged. As you can understand, that has been very reassuring, especially when the community need for our help is increasing at an alarming rate."

Harry listened closely to Rowena. When she stopped speaking and turned away to stare out the window again, he took the moment to think about what was troubling her. Her voice, the strained way in which she was sitting, and the vacancy of her gaze told their own story. Whatever it was, it was causing her a lot of discomfort.

Hoping to lighten her mood enough to persuade her to go on, he said, "Rowena, reengage."

"Sorry, Harry," she said. "This thing is keeping me up nights, and I sleep undisturbed through thunderstorms."

"You'd better tell me," he said.

"Yes, but I had no idea it would be so difficult." She paused again, and then, with an obvious effort, went on. "Gwen and Peter are serious art collectors. They have a world-class collection of seventeenth-century Dutch genre paintings." Rowena jumped up, crossed to the sideboard, and switched on the electric kettle. "More tea, Harry?" she asked, interrupting herself.

Harry declined, saying he was already afloat.

"Their collection is so extensive and important that they are constantly shipping pieces around the world to museums and sponsored exhibitions," Rowena continued, working diligently as she spoke, as if the activity made it possible for her to talk.

Harry saw that all this narrative and tea-making was a way of avoiding coming to the point. He wanted to urge her to stop dithering and tell him what was troubling her, but was afraid that if he did press her, he might shut her down entirely.

"These paintings have to be packed very carefully," she said, returning with her tea. "Roswell and Hart, the art dealers on Scissorbill Street, do all of that for them. I expect they make a tidy sum of money every year from the contract."

"Rowena," Harry said, losing patience, "I know where Roswell and Hart are located. I didn't think they wrapped and mailed Ogilvies' paintings for fun."

"Oh, they're not mailed," she countered.

"Just tell me," Harry said. "We'll both survive."

Rowena got a bit red and straightened her back ominously, but in the end she put the cup and saucer on the table beside her and sighed deeply.

"I have been told it's not just the sent pictures that are being returned."

It took Harry several seconds to grasp the implications of her comment.

"Are they smuggling drugs?" he asked, naming the first thing that came to his mind. In fact, he thought the idea preposterous and was even a little annoyed with Rowena for making a fuss about nothing.

"Be serious," Rowena said angrily. "It's unframed paintings."

She had finally said it, and Harry was astonished by the revelation.

"Stolen paintings," he said when he had recovered from his surprise.

"Yes."

"Who sold you this cock and bull story?" Harry demanded, his disbelief surfacing again.

"I'm not at liberty to say."

Then it was someone in the congregation who had come to her, because she couldn't go anywhere else. The situation took instant shape in Harry's mind.

"Has this person told anyone else?"

Ignoring the question, Rowena made both hands into fists and began pounding the arms of her chair. "I don't see how it could be true," she said loudly. "It defies all reason, and I have tried very hard not to believe it."

"Why hasn't your informant taken this to the police?"

"The reasons are personal," Rowena said, looking more pained than ever.

"Which means whoever it is has a close connection with the Ogilvies and probably works for them, needs the job, and wants to keep it. This person is probably a woman attending this church and turned to you for advice."

"I can't respond to that," she said, her expression changing to one of alarm.

Harry kept himself from smiling. This was obviously no laughing matter for Rowena, but Harry thought that had the congregation been seated in front of him, he could probably point to her.

"What made you decide to tell me?" Harry asked, deciding not to pursue that subject any further, at least not for the present.

"Because I know I can trust you," Rowena said, "because you know about these things, and because I'm about at the end of my tether. The Ogilvies are my friends. They're members of my congregation. I don't see how it's possible . . ."

"Art theft is a common enough crime," Harry said, interrupting her in the hope of reducing her anxiety, "and no different from any other criminal act, except it occurs in places and with people we don't often associate in our minds with thieves."

Rowena appeared to be verging on either fury or tears, and it was the first time he had seen her this upset. It unnerved him.

"I suppose you mean I don't expect to be mugged in a museum," she said harshly, glaring at him.

"But you'd better not leave your bag on the settee while you wander around, gazing at the Millets," Harry said, trying to quiet her mind.

"I feel like that worm in the rhyme," she said with slightly less ferocity, "stretched between two birds of equal strength."

"I'm not seeing the problem," Harry said, pretending to understand less than he did. "The woman's job may be at risk, but you know as well as I do that unless she wishes to become a co-conspirator, she must report it to the police. Unless she's undocumented, in which case she needs help in striking a deal that will protect her from arrest for another crime."

"I never said it was a woman," Rowena snapped.

"You didn't have to," Harry replied.

Rowena's shoulders slumped. "I might have known," she complained. "What kind of deal?"

"They take her testimony without turning her or her name over to Immigration."

"Would Jim Snyder do that?" she asked in surprise.

"Yes," Harry said, "there's no love lost between Jim and the Immigration people."

Jim Snyder was the captain of the Tequesta County Sheriff's Department and a close friend of Harry's, although they occasionally fell out because as a private investigator working on a client's behalf, he had been known to cross the frontiers of legality. When that happened, they found themselves working at cross purposes. Jim, being the man he was, suffered deeply when required to look the other way, even when he knew that what Harry was doing would in the end benefit both of them.

"It may be a solution," Rowena said, brightening slightly, "but will she do it? I'm not at all sure she will." Rowena stood up. "Harry, can I persuade you to go to Jim with this mess?"

"No," he said. "She needs a lawyer to protect her adequately in this situation."

"Do you have a name?"

"Jeff Smolkin."

"A good man," Rowena agreed.

"Do you want me to speak to Jeff first?" he asked. Mentioning Smolkin reminded him of Renata. It was a pleasant thought, but he pushed it away.

"That would help," Rowena said with obvious relief. "You know him, and I would prefer to remain at a distance."

"I agree, and be very careful," he said. "Remember what Fitzgerald said about the rich. The Ogilvies are very, very rich. If they are engaged in art theft, they are also dangerous."

"I've already thought of that," Rowena said. "I've also thought of consequences if they are not."

"It's not pleasant, and I'm sorry," Harry said. "But don't forget what I've said about the danger. Keep as far away from this as you can."

"What if I were to go to Peter and Gwen and tell them what I've been told?" Rowena said with sudden enthusiasm. "If they were involved in something illegal, wouldn't they stop it at once? And if they weren't, we could all have a good laugh over it. Of course, I wouldn't let on how I'd come to suspect them."

Rowena was walking Harry to the door when she made the suggestion, and on hearing it Harry thought his legs might give way. He rounded on Rowena in alarm. "Don't even think such a thing!" he said, grasping her by the arms.

He had never touched Rowena. She was not a person who

46

invited such liberties, but Harry was so distressed by what she had said, he leaped all the barriers and came very near to shaking her, or trying to. She might, he thought, coming to his senses, very well shake him. But he hung onto her as if he feared she might run straight into the tiger's den.

"What's come over you!" he demanded. "Have you lost your mind?"

"Harry," Rowena said, alarmed or astonished, placing her hands firmly on his chest, "let go of me."

Harry jumped back as if he had put both hands on a hot stove.

"I'm sorry. Don't go near the Ogilvies. Don't let your informant do it either. Until their innocence is established, you must assume they are criminals. You must also assume they're very dangerous."

"That's nonsense."

"Rowena, accept the reality of what you've stumbled into. If they're engaged in art theft, they're part of a criminal network involving dozens of people, and some of *them* will be dangerous."

"Don't be silly, Harry. The Ogilvies would never hurt me. It's unthinkable."

"No, of course they wouldn't. Someone else would do it for them."

"You've let your imagination run away with you," Rowena protested, obviously angry.

Harry paused to give himself time to think, then tried another approach. "You said that I knew about such things. Do you really think I do?"

"You're trying to maneuver me into agreeing with you, and I refuse to do that."

"Do you trust me?"

"I refuse to believe the Ogilvies would harm either me or . . . Never mind the name."

"Then you would be willing to trust your life to the Ogilvies and all their associates if you knew they were engaged in a criminal conspiracy involving the theft and resale of objects of art with a collective value, in all probability, of millions of dollars?"

Harry saw from her change of expression that he had dented her resistance. She started to speak, but he pressed his point. "What do you think will be the reaction of these people when they learn that you and your informant have broken through their shell of secrecy and are threatening to expose them to arrest and years and years in prison? If you were they, what would you do?"

"Try to silence us, but what if we have already told the police what we know or think we know? What would they gain?"

"There's still the trial. If you're not there to testify, what then?"

Rowena's gaze wavered.

"No conviction?"

"Most likely."

"With their wealth, why would the Ogilvies become involved in criminal activity in the first place?" Rowena demanded, doing a sudden about-face.

"Greed and excitement are two reasons," Harry said. "A third would be that in the past they knowingly or unknowingly bought something carrying a bogus provenance and were then blackmailed into doing what you think they may be doing, to avoid being exposed."

"Yes," she said with obvious reluctance, "I suppose something like that could account for their involvement, if they are involved."

"The police will have to decide whether or not they are," Harry said, "and you must not, absolutely must not, say a word to them about any of this. Promise me that you won't."

Rowena sighed and nodded, apparently too dejected to speak.

6

Harry left Rowena feeling very uncertain as to whether she would actually adhere to her unspoken promise, or that he had done the right thing in urging her to persuade the woman to talk to a lawyer. He was even less comfortable with the idea of her going to Jim Snyder. Once Jim had been told that the Ogilvies were art thieves, the cat would be out of the bag, and the informant and Rowena would become potential targets.

He knew well enough that it was an imperfect world in which *not nearly good enough* was as close as things usually got to perfect. But knowing it to be true and knowing that he had given Rowena the best advice he could give, short of advising her to forget what she'd heard and to tell her informant to forget what she'd seen, provided Harry with little comfort.

It was in these moments that Harry felt most sharply his solitary state. True, he could have taken his concern to Tucker and would have found in the old farmer a sympathetic, intelligent listener, whose comments would be measured and to some degree helpful. Pushing that lapse of control into a dusty closet in a remote corner of his mind and forcefully closing the door, Harry called Smolkin, leaving word with Renata that Jeff should expect a call from one of Rowena Farnham's parishioners and that he should interview the woman himself and listen carefully to what she had to say. Having made the call, Harry decided that for his own peace of mind he needed to talk with

Jim Snyder about his conversation with Rowena.

"Where have you been hiding?" Jim demanded when Harry walked into his office, unfolding his tall frame from behind his desk and reaching across it to shake Harry's hand. He added, "As if I didn't know. You and Tucker are turning into hermits."

"Exaggeration," Harry said, pleased to be in the lawman's company.

Jim was born and raised in Eastern Tennessee, and with his lanky body, long face, and short, pale hair, he looked and sounded like a mountain man. His father had been a preacher on Sunday and a farmer and manufacturer and distributor of white lightning the rest of the week. Frank Hodges, Jim's sergeant and support system, claimed that growing up with a man who was a preacher and a bootlegger had muddled the captain's head, making him too hard on himself and too sympathetic when it came to crooks.

"How are Kathleen and the baby?" Harry asked.

Kathleen Towers was the medical examiner for Tequesta County. She and Jim had stayed engaged so long that when they married, everyone who knew them was shocked. Harry felt that something immutable had suddenly changed. It was as if the world had moved a little, leaving him feeling squeamish.

"You're forgetting that time passes," Jim said. "Clara's two now and has added a whole chapter to the tale of terrible twos. Praise the Lord for day care. I think we're past the bad times. Kathleen seems better. Being back at work has helped."

"I'm glad to hear it," Harry said, hurrying past the recollection of the wall of anger she'd built around herself when she found herself pregnant at thirty-nine.

Harry caught the cloud that passed over Jim's face and quickly changed the subject. "I've got something to talk over with you," he said. "Have you got a few minutes?"

It was a reasonable question, and the stacks of folders on Jim's desk proved it.

"Sit," Jim said. "I'm listening."

"This has to be between us for the time being," Harry said, the worn folding chair creaking miserably as he settled onto it.

Like the rest of the county's public offices, the Sheriff's Department was strapped for money and its furnishings were primitive. When something wore out, it was replaced by something cheaper and often older.

"A woman came to Rowena Farnham and told her that the Ogilvies are smuggling artworks, probably stolen, into the country inside the cases in which their loaned pieces are being returned."

Harry stopped. Jim looked at him for a moment as if he hadn't heard what Harry said. Then he studied the pencil he was holding as if it was a wholly foreign object.

"Not the best news of the day," he said, putting the pencil down very carefully. "Any truth in it?"

"Rowena thinks there is and doesn't want to. The Ogilvies are valued members of St. Jude's."

Harry went on to summarize his conversation with Rowena and concluded by saying that he wasn't supposed to have mentioned this to anyone, but thought Jim should know that at least one person in Avola thought the Ogilvies were crooks.

"And I think something's afoot," Harry said, "although it might be nothing more than one of the Ogilvies' employees trying to put the stick into them."

"I'll tell the people out front not to ask her any questions when she shows up until she's seen me," Jim said.

It was as far as Harry expected his friend to go. As he got up to leave, he said, "Where's Frank?"

Sergeant Frank Hodges had been Jim's unofficial assistant for as long as Harry had known them. He was a true backwoods

Floridian, sandy-haired and red-faced, built along the lines of a refrigerator, irrepressibly cheerful, and a source of endless anecdotes, Jim Snyder's opposite in every way. But Frank Hodges knew all there was to know about being a lawman in Tequesta County. Jim had once told Harry that God had given him Frank Hodges to test his Christian charity.

"Home, recuperating," Jim said, shaking his head sorrowfully.

"Is he ill?" Harry asked, concerned because he had never known Frank to be sick.

"No, he's working on a broken arm and three cracked ribs."

"Are you planning to tell me what happened?"

"Don't get aerated! I'll get to it," Jim said, pausing to glance at the file he had been working on.

Harry stifled his impulse to say, *not by reading another arrest report.*

"Frank was responding to a complaint about what looked like a breaking and entering on Locust Lane in North Avola," Jim said, coming around the desk. "You know the area between Route 40 and the beach?"

Harry said he did. It was an area of small, low-cost houses where a staggering number of bank foreclosures had decimated the community, leaving those who remained in their houses feeling as if they were under siege. Realtors were running buses filled with potential speculators and a few house hunters through the associations, pushing hard to make sales, increasing the residents' sense of threat.

"I was through there last week," Harry said, "and it's beginning to look like a dead zone. No one's mowing the lawns on the foreclosed properties, and I thought many of the houses looked as if they were being rented to migrant workers."

"You're right," Jim said. "They're coming all the way from Immokalee. One family will rent one of the places from the bank. Then two more families will move in with them to reduce the cost. The banks look the other way and take the money."

"Further lowering house values," Harry said. "What happened to Frank?"

"He found the address and, seeing the curtains had been drawn and the front door left open, he decided to take a look inside."

"And found it was occupied."

"That's right. A man was standing against the wall, beside the door, waiting. When Frank stepped out of the sun into the dark room, he was partially blinded. Before his eyes adjusted to the reduced light, his assailant struck his right forearm with a crowbar—Frank had drawn his weapon—breaking it, then hit him on the back of the head as he stumbled forward."

"And when Frank came to, his attacker and the gun were gone," Harry said.

"We've talked with the woman who called in the complaint, but she claims she didn't see anyone leave the house, which is possible because the back door was also open."

"How is he?" Harry asked.

"Still in the hospital," Jim said. "That crowbar did quite a lot of damage to his skull. Fortunately, none of his mental functions seem to be impaired. Of course, he blames himself."

"He would, wouldn't he?" Harry said. "I'll look in on him."

A few minutes later, Harry was back on the road on his way to Caedmon Rivers' office on River Street.

His GPS took him into Ashbury Gardens, an association in North Avola he couldn't recall having been in before. It was a neighborhood of single-story stuccoes, bright with pastel colors. As he drove slowly along the streets, he saw only two properties with foreclosure notices on their doors, and the lawns on both were mowed.

The address he was seeking turned out to be a pale orange

house, its front half buried in a riotous bloom of blue plumbago bushes. A wide-spreading Canary Island palm surrounded by white wax begonias, its dark green fronds swaying in the gentle wind from the Gulf, dominated the small, neatly mowed lawn. Harry parked the Rover at the curb and stood assessing the house, the palm tree, and the BMW Z4 in the driveway and thought something was out of whack. Was it the car that was worth at least a quarter of the house? Maybe, maybe not.

He had to force himself to arrange this meeting with Rivers, possibly because he didn't know much about skip tracers except that he was sure he didn't like what they did. And he didn't expect to like this man. There was something repellent about hacking into every aspect of a person's life, not to mention hunting someone, hounding the person, running him—in this case, her—down like an animal. Harry braced himself and walked quickly up the white, crushed stone driveway and along the carefully swept, curving flagstone path to the door.

A woman answered the bell and stopped Harry from asking for Caedmon Rivers by saying, "Come in, Mr. Brock. You're on time. Thank you. My office is on your right."

Readjusting, Harry went into what he guessed had been intended by the builders as the living room but was now Rivers' work space. It was a large, high-ceilinged room (clearly an upgrade), painted off-white with red Mexican tiles on the floor. The paired windows on the front and side walls were curtained top to bottom with a thin, white fabric that shielded the room from the sun's heat while letting in a soft, diffused light.

"Let's sit down over here," she said, crossing in front of him and leading the way to a large, white sofa and three brown leather barrel chairs, arranged in a small arc in front of the sofa.

Following her, Harry took in the room. Much of it was occupied by metal files along the walls, two large desks each saddled with a desktop computer, and low cherry wood bookcases between and around the desks, filled with thick books of varying sizes and colors that looked like telephone directories, but Harry saw as he passed that two were not.

She seated herself on the couch and crossed her legs, her hands folded in her lap. Her skirt fell away from the exact top of her knee, whether by accident or design he wasn't sure. But having noticed that detail, he was reminded of an old puzzle. How could women sit for such long periods with one leg crossed over the other without changing position? It was a small but pleasant mystery, like the way finches and pine siskins could perch upside down on a bird feeder, eating seeds for long periods of time, without becoming dizzy.

"A very interesting room," he said, turning his attention to her.

"I like it," she said in a north of Maryland voice, well modulated but stripped of emotion.

Her voice brought him back to the problem at hand. What he saw looking at him with large dark eyes was a very self-possessed woman, somewhere in her forties, with thick auburn hair. Of medium height and a rather regal bearing, she was wearing a burgundy-colored suit. From its drape, texture, and tailoring, Harry guessed it was top of the line, like the car in the driveway.

He found the curve of her mouth and full lips appealing, thinking they softened her rather angular features. She was not smiling or, he thought, making any particular effort to make him feel comfortable. Her expression was not hostile. In fact, it seemed to him that there was nothing personal in it. She might have been looking at a painting she did not particularly like. It crossed Harry's mind that if he was a dog and she a cat, he might be in trouble.

Strangely enough, he did not feel uneasy under that unblinking gaze. Her eyes really were lovely, but being unable to read their message troubled him. For a reason he didn't explore, he decided not to speak first. The silence lasted quite a while, and she finally glanced at her watch.

"Are you having trouble telling me why you're here?" she asked in a businesslike voice.

"Yes," Harry said. "I'm a member of that adulterous generation seeking a sign."

It was bad, and he knew it. It was showing off, and he knew that too, but there was something about her that made him feel slightly reckless. Perhaps he didn't like her any more than she appeared to like him.

For a moment, her expression remained fixed. Then she smiled as one might smile at a tiresome child. "You said you were looking for someone and might need my help."

Feeling that he had already lost several points in this game, if that's what it was, he decided to try very hard not to be any more stupid than he had to be. "That's right, and before we get to that, I have to reach an agreement with you about confidentiality."

"I understand," she said. "Because you're a private investigator, I assume you're an intermediary and the principal will remain, at least for the present, anonymous. Is the assumption correct?"

"Yes."

Harry almost asked her how she knew he was a private investigator and stopped himself before he gave up more points. She probably knew his shoe size and what he put on his cereal.

"No surprises there then," she said, leaning forward slightly. "By the way, I'm impressed by your bio as well as your reputation."

"I don't have a bio," Harry protested.

The smile appeared again.

"Everyone has a bio," she told him, "and before I work with anyone, I make certain I know it, to insure clarity, and not to waste time. If I begin searching for this person, and if it's someone close to the person who's hired you, I'll have the name of the person you're working for within forty-eight hours and probably sooner."

Harry let his mind chase that assertion for a moment.

"I'm not boasting or attempting to impress you, if that's what you're thinking," she told him.

He had been exploring those possibilities and felt his face burn at being found out.

"Don't be embarrassed," she said. "This takes a little getting used to."

He thought she should have said, "I take a little getting used to."

"It's a difficult situation," he told her. "I usually sign an initial contract that makes it impossible legally to reveal anything my client and I discuss unless he tells me he's engaged in criminal activity or intends to commit a crime. I'd like to do something like that with you."

"I'm not bound as you are by the law to maintain confidentiality, but how long do you think I'd last in this business if telling me whatever I need to know isn't as safe as telling a tombstone?"

"Probably not long," Harry replied, "but it's not good enough. If you begin this search and word of it leaks, my client and potentially many others stand to lose a huge amount of money."

"Mr. Brock," she said after a moment's hesitation.

"Harry," he said.

"All right, call me Caedmon. I'll draw up a confidentiality agreement not to knowingly reveal the name or names of the people I'm working for, but I won't promise that someone, somewhere in the course of my investigation, won't pick up something and guess what's happening."

"How serious is the risk?"

"The risk is, of course, very serious, as you've suggested, but the statistical probability of it happening is vanishingly small," she told him. "Nevertheless, we've all heard the story of the married woman who flies from New York to the Twin Cities for a rendezvous with another woman's husband only to meet a common friend in the first restaurant they enter."

Harry laughed. Caedmon smiled, but Harry noticed the amusement didn't reach her eyes. At the recognition, he suddenly felt a sharp twist of sympathy that he experienced as something close to pain. He did not dislike this woman, and he had no right to feel sorry for her, but in that moment he became fully aware of her. It was as if all the superficial thoughts he had about her fell away and an altogether different person was sitting there looking at him out of those dark eyes.

"It's a pretty common experience," he said, resisting, even resenting, being pulled closer to her.

He had no interest in her. Period. Why should he care whether or not she laughed at her own jokes? *Get a grip, Brock.*

"So, Harry, do we go for the agreement or do we call this off?" she asked in that persistently neutral voice.

She was starting to get up and, almost mechanically, Harry stood with her. It was a further annoyance for him to find he didn't want their conversation to end. It was ridiculous.

Looking at her standing in front of him, fingers joined loosely in front of her, Harry saw that she possessed a natural grace he had not noticed before. She stood the way he had seen athletes stand, unselfconsciously, relaxed yet perfectly balanced. And she had a lovely body.

"Harry?" she said, her voice coming briefly alive. "Is anything wrong?"

"No, no!" he said. "Nothing. Let's draw up the agreement."

7

While Caedmon was opening a file beside the nearer desk, Harry took advantage of the pause to survey his feelings while giving himself a bracing lecture on his idiocies regarding women, a précis of the dolorous history of his past relationships, and a five-second refresher course in his determination to live without immersing himself in the ephemeral fires of emotional entanglements.

"I think this will serve our purpose," Caedmon said, handing him a sheet of paper.

Harry started. He had not noticed her return.

"Are you sure you're all right?" Caedmon asked, looking at him with a slight frown. "Can I get you a glass of water? What about some soda? I noticed you weren't wearing a hat when you came in. It's not wise, you know, in this sun, to go without one."

The sudden flood of comment, analysis, and advice rattled Harry.

"I'm really all right," he said hurriedly, taking the paper without looking at it. "Thanks for your concern, but I don't have sunstroke and I'm not expecting a seizure of any kind. I was thinking, and the novelty of the experience absorbed all my attention."

He had done it again, but she was actually smiling at him.

"You have a very odd sense of humor," she said. "I like it, but it takes a little getting used to. Does it have anything to do with your coming from Maine?"

"Oh, you know about that," he said, his heart sinking.

"Yes," she said, becoming serious. "It must have been a terrible thing to go through."

"What? Living in Maine?"

"No, nearly being jailed for murder," she said, frowning again.

Good God, Harry thought, *she knows about the trial. How in hell . . . ?* "It was a long time ago. I've pretty well forgotten it," he lied, thinking that if she could count, she knew how old he was.

"And I don't break out in all the really bad places if I even walk close to poison ivy," she responded.

"A pretty good comparison," Harry admitted. "It cost me my job, my wife, and two children. The truth is I haven't forgotten any of it. But I long ago stopped letting it ruin my life."

To Harry's further discomfiture, she gave him another of her what he now regarded as "weighed in the balance and found wanting" looks, her smile having vanished.

"I'm glad to hear it," she said. "Read the agreement."

"It will have to do," he said when he finished.

"Shall we sit down again and talk further?"

"Or we can stay on our feet and do some calisthenics. What do you think?"

It was all out of his mouth before he could stop himself. What was wrong with him?

"Let's sit down," she said. "I've already run three miles this morning."

With that she walked back to the couch, Harry following, some lines of poetry popping into his head.

"Do you talk to yourself a lot?" she asked, waiting for him to settle.

"I was reciting a poem," he said.

"Do you do this kind of thing often?"

"On occasion."

"What was the poem?"

" 'Upon Julia's Clothes,' by Robert Herrick," he answered, figuring he'd made such a fool of himself already that it was way too late to repair the damage.

"Recite it for me?"

Harry hesitated, then said, "Sure. It's an old poem, seventeenth century. Are you sure you want me to?"

He was getting cold feet.

"Yes, go ahead. I love poetry."

Harry cleared his throat and plunged in. "When as in silks my Julia goes,/ Then, then (methinks) how sweetly flows/ The liquefaction of her clothes./ Next when I cast mine eyes, and see/ That brave vibration each way free,/ O how that glittering taketh me!"

"Harry Brock," she said after a considerable pause, during which Harry saw her face growing pink and concluded that he had sailed right onto a reef, "you were watching my ass."

"No, of course I wasn't . . . it was just that . . . *glittering* seemed the right . . ." He gave up and slumped back in his chair. "Yes, I was."

"Good," she said, to his astonishment. "There are lots of men around these days who wouldn't give it a glance. Now, let's get to this other thing."

Her fee. Harry whistled when he heard it.

"And I'll want ten up front," she said. "My expenses are heavy," she added, following his musical reaction. "The rest is due when she's found."

"And if she's not?"

"She will be. Sooner if she's an ordinary skipper, later if she's not. I haven't lost one yet."

"Impressive," he said. "You're all right with Breckenridge's request that you and he meet as infrequently as possible and your exchanges take place through me?"

"Yes. Husbands and wives can be a heavy cross to bear," she said, turning down her mouth after making the comment. "Also, you're going to find," she told him as they were winding down, "that he's not going to want to give you the information I've asked for. No matter how loudly he squeals, screw it out of him. I need everything on the list I've given you, and once I've begun working, probably more."

She stopped to consider something, then said, "B. and I won't need to talk much, but I do need access to his staff both here and in Virginia. It's non-negotiable. Another thing: Don't be surprised if he becomes furious with you—and me too. It's almost certain he will."

"OK," Harry said, thinking that Breckenridge would certainly object to having his staff questioned. As for the warning, he thought her concern was exaggerated. They were at the front door by this time, and Caedmon had opened it halfway, then paused to speak.

"Just to review," she said, stopping Harry as he was stepping past her.

He turned, facing her with their toes almost touching, which she did not seem to mind as she went on talking and looking steadily and seriously at him. She wasn't wearing perfume, but close as he was her scent enveloped him. The effect was like having put his finger in a light socket. He closed his eyes to steady himself and pray that his nostrils hadn't flared.

"One," she continued, "get that contract signed and back to me yesterday. Time is money. Two, stay in touch. I want to talk with you often. Daily would be best. I'll have a new basket of questions every day once I'm launched."

"All right," Harry said, opening his eyes and forcing himself to stop trying to inhale her. He was listening to what she said, but he was also looking into her eyes and saw that they were sprinkled with gold flecks. Like stars in a night sky, he thought, wanting to go on drifting among them for as long as time lasted.

"You're doing it again," she said and finished opening the door.

"What?" he asked.

"Staring. Is there something weird about my eyes?"

"No, they're beautiful."

She shook her head. "I look as if I have a thyroid problem."

"Then I look like Quasimodo."

"I wasn't going to mention it. Now go, and thanks for the poem. Do you know more of them?"

"Not on that particular subject."

He was outside by this time.

"Too bad," she said, smiling, and closed the door.

"Dear God," Harry said, casting his eyes upward toward the cloudless sky, "please don't let this happen to me."

But before the prayer could be delivered, he revised it to, "Please let me be sensible."

He walked to the Rover, feeling as if he was striding in ten-league boots.

Harry had arranged to see Breckenridge after his talk with Rivers. He drove out of Ashbury Gardens, then turned south toward the Seminole River. The distance from Ashbury Gardens to the river was only about five miles, but once through the center of Avola and beyond the Tamiami Trail turnoff, the four-lane highway with its flowered islands contracted to a wide, two-lane avenue, shaded by huge ficus trees. Behind them, the stores and office buildings gave way to large and ornate multistory houses, surrounded by acres of lawns and gardens, most of them fenced and gated.

The closer Harry came to the Seminole River, the larger the houses became and the more extensive their gardens. Breckenridge's house, like the rest, was gated. Harry pressed the button on the communication box and a strongly accented male voice said, "This is the Breckenridge residence. How may I help?"

Harry gave the man his name, and the iron gates swung open on well-oiled hinges. When Harry drove under the porte-cochère, a man dressed in black trousers and a short-sleeved white shirt hurried to open his door.

"Good day, Mr. Brock," he said with a smile. "Mr. Breckenridge is expecting you. Please leave your keys in the car, and Serge will park it in the garage where it will be kept cool until you need it again."

Harry stepped onto the gravel.

"I am Ernan," the man said, extending his hand. He was slim and dark-haired, quick and elegant in his movements. Harry shook his hand while wondering if all Breckenridge's servants were Filipino.

"If you will follow me," he said with a slight bow and led Harry up the wide marble steps and into the house.

Harry followed him through a cathedral-ceilinged foyer with a gleaming black marble floor that opened into a larger space beyond, filled with light from tall windows opening onto the river. Crossing the glinting space, Harry felt as if he was walking on water. Ernan paused when they reached a freestanding marble staircase, made from a lighter stone but still shot through with black, that curved up to the second floor.

"Mr. Breckenridge is on the balcony," he said. "I'm afraid we have some stairs to climb. Would you prefer to take the elevator?"

"I'll risk the climb," Harry said.

"Certainly, sir," Ernan said with commendable restraint.

Breckenridge was sitting at a glass and wrought-iron table poring over an open file, the remains of his lunch pushed aside. The table was set near the front of a long, wide balcony, thrusting out from the house like the blunt prow of a ship. Stepping through the double glass doors Ernan had opened for him, Harry was able to look down the river to his right and see Snook Pass and half a mile up the river to his left. The house itself was separated from the river by fifty yards of manicured lawn. Gulls and pelicans, solitary and in flocks, were passing up and down the river, and above them vultures circled patiently, confident their vigils would be rewarded.

Ernan stopped Harry and went forward to speak to Breckenridge, who tossed his file onto the pile at his elbow and then stood up and waved Harry toward him.

"How did the meeting go?" he demanded, then said, "Sit down. Are you hungry?"

"No," Harry said, pulling out a chair.

"Take this away," Breckenridge said to Ernan, who vanished and then returned pushing a trolley. He quickly cleared the table and left.

In keeping with local practice, Harry and Breckenridge were dressed in sandals, shorts, and short-sleeved shirts. It was as close to the Avola men's casual dress uniform as one was likely to find. Male white-collar workers wore black trousers and evangelical-inspired, long-sleeved white shirts buttoned at the wrist, another uniform. In both cases the dress varied only in the cost of the items worn, including wrist watches.

"She'd better be damned good," Breckenridge said, glowering at Rivers' fee, which Harry decided to deal with first, including the ten up front.

"She has to be," Harry said. "She claims she's never failed to find a skipper yet. I'm inclined to believe her. Here's a preliminary list of the information about Mrs. Breckenridge that she wants from you. She wants it as soon as possible."

"Absolutely not," Breckenridge said, slamming the list down on the table. "Neither she nor anyone else gets to see anything that has to do with Afton's financial affairs. They are nobody's business but my wife's and mine."

Harry glimpsed through the bluster a viral fear and recalled what Caedmon had predicted would be Breckenridge's reaction.

"It's your call," Harry said, pulling his feet under him as if preparing to leave. "But if you won't cooperate, you'll lose Rivers. To find Mrs. Breckenridge, Rivers has to know everything there is to know about her."

"People like her are a dime a dozen. Find someone else."

"I could probably do that for you, but anyone you hired that was honest would demand the same things."

"What do my wife's financial affairs have to do with finding her, for Christ's sake?" Breckenridge barked, his chin thrust out aggressively.

"A great deal," Harry said. "For example, it will help Rivers decide whether your wife has planned this disappearance."

"Of course she didn't plan it!" Breckenridge shouted, jumping to his feet and upending his chair with a crash. "Don't be a damned fool!"

"It's a constant struggle," Harry said, getting his own temper under control as he rose more slowly, reminding himself again of Caedmon's warning.

"What?"

Breckenridge's face was so inflamed that Harry was afraid he might do himself an injury.

"She probably didn't plan this," Harry continued in a calm voice, "but it has to be eliminated as a possibility."

"Is everything all right, Mr. Breckenridge?" Ernan said behind Harry. "May I deal with the chair?"

"Yes, go ahead," he said. "Sit down, Brock. Sorry I shouted at you. Got carried away."

While that was going on, Ernan righted the chair, rearranged the cushions, and got Breckenridge seated.

"Did you and Rivers discuss the possibility that Afton might have done this deliberately?" Breckenridge asked when Ernan had left.

He sat with his elbows on the table, holding his head in his hands.

"No, we didn't discuss it. She simply broached it as a possibility," Harry said, sympathy for the man replacing the dregs of his anger.

"I suppose I can't know for certain that she hasn't left me," he said in a voice gravelly with whatever emotion he was struggling with.

And it was clear to Harry that something more was gnawing at him than the insult of having it thought that his wife might have left him. He looked like a man seriously conflicted, but about what, Harry had no idea.

"Would you rather we finished this another time?" Harry asked.

Breckenridge shook his head and sat back in his chair. "No, let's get it over with. Let me see the contract."

Harry put it on the table in front of him. "Signing that will commit you to cooperating on all the items on that list I gave you."

"You're sure I can trust her?"

"I've known Jeff Smolkin for a very long time," Harry said, "years, really, and he says she's absolutely reliable. I don't see how anyone in her line of work could stay in business as long as she has and not be trustworthy."

"Better the devil you know . . ." Breckenridge muttered, picking up the contract. "I'll have Smolkin look at it. If it's right, I'll sign it."

"My guess is, it's gold plated," Harry said with a relieved smile.

"At her prices it should be," Breckenridge said, still looking and sounding like a man in trouble.

8

Two days later, Harry had a call from Jeff Smolkin's office.

"Can you stop by?" Renata Holland asked in her office voice.

"Do you sing?" Harry asked.

"Just because my voice is lower than yours, you don't have to be nasty."

"I'm paying you a compliment. You have a lovely voice, dark and rich. I suppose you don't know that."

"Great save," she said. "Number One has something for you."

"I'll be along."

There had not been many waking hours since leaving Ashbury Gardens that Harry had not thought of Caedmon Rivers. He tried to tell himself it was only because he also had Gregory and Afton Breckenridge on his mind, but in those moments when he was not obsessed with trying to recover every moment they had spent together, he knew his explanation was drivel. He must face the truth.

He had fallen in love with the woman, a woman he had spent less than an hour with, a woman he knew almost nothing about. Wrong, he knew everything he needed to know and desired her above all things. Unless someone roped him to one of his oaks, he would soon throw himself off the Hammock and swim to Ashbury Gardens.

It was, of course, ridiculous. He was not sixteen—very far from it—and knew what misery awaited him were he to persist in this folly. Shakespeare had said it best: "Th' expense of spirit in a waste of shame/ Is lust in action . . ." And so he prated on until he was sick of himself, and when he was finished, his lacerating urge to be with her was diminished by neither a jot nor a tittle. Something drastic had to be done.

What that *something* was came to him when he walked into Renata's office.

"Would you look kindly on my asking you out to dinner?" he said without any preliminary greeting, inquiries about her health, or comments on the Red Sox's performance.

"Did you just ask me out to dinner?" she asked, wide-eyed as if she feared for her or his sanity.

"I did."

"Is this some sort of joke?" she demanded. "Because if it is . . ."

"You may be moved to laughter," Harry said, "but I'm not joking. Perhaps I'm going to wish I had been."

Her expression was one that led him to think so.

"If I've insulted you or stepped over some line here . . ." he began, but she stopped him.

"As long as it's not McGinty's Crab Shack," she said, "you're on."

"I'm thinking Waterside. Is that tacky enough, since you've ruled out the fancy places?" Waterside was one of Avola's best restaurants.

"I'm willing to give it a try," she said with a straight face.

"Would tomorrow night or the next be too soon?"

"Have you got a better deal for tonight?" she asked.

"Not if I can get a reservation."

She picked up her phone, punched in a number, and passed Harry the phone.

"Is seven all right?" he asked her. "I was thinking that if I picked you up at six we could have a drink at Lafitte's first."

"It's cutting it close," she said, "and Number One will fake a

71

breakdown if I leave here at five, but I'll make sure Bernadette is around to give him mouth-to-mouth resuscitation."

They both laughed at that, but Harry thought there was as much bitterness as humor in the remark.

A red light flashed on her phone.

"He's back in his office," she said, springing up from her desk. "Let's go. He's due in court in forty-five minutes."

"Here's the contract, Harry, along with a lot of other stuff," Smolkin said when Harry was ushered into his office.

"I thought he might back out," Harry said, taking the envelope.

"So did I, but he seems eager to get the search started."

"So is Caedmon."

"Who?"

"Caedmon Rivers, the skip chaser you recommended."

"Oh, yes. What do you think of her?" Smolkin's smile was mischievous.

"She's a smart woman," Harry said, wondering what lay behind it, "very businesslike."

"Not bad looking either," Smolkin said. "Or didn't you notice?"

"I noticed."

Smolkin's smile widened.

"Just watch yourself," he said. "I'd hate to lose you."

"I don't know what you're getting at," Harry protested with more feeling than he intended.

"Nothing!" Smolkin protested at once, "just teasing you. Rumor has it, she's got a temper."

Harry started to insist that he'd seen no evidence of it, but Smolkin turned suddenly serious.

"When I was in court yesterday," he said with poorly concealed pleasure, "Malvern Johnson, the bailiff, dropped a hint that something unusual had come in over Harley's transom that has put the stick into the assistant state's attorney and his people."

"I would have thought that Harley Dillard, as the ASA for the Twenty-first District, would have seen just about everything," Harry answered, still ruffled over Smolkin's prodding him about Caedmon.

"I gather this is a little different," Smolkin said. "I wouldn't have bothered you with it, but Breckenridge's name was mentioned. You might want to drop in at Harley's office."

Before he left Smolkin, the lawyer had decided there was probably nothing to the rumor. Harry pretended he didn't think there was, either. But both men knew that Malvern Johnson, odd as he was, usually knew before anyone else in the court when something unusual was afoot.

"Wear shoes tonight," Renata said without looking up from her work as Harry passed her door on the way out.

"Remember to take the pencil out of your hair," Harry replied, the exchange crowding Malvern Johnson's rumor temporarily out of his mind.

That and the fact that once he was on the way to Ashbury Gardens with Caedmon's contract, he began to feel guilty about having asked Renata Holland out to dinner. Not, he told himself, that there was anything in and of itself wrong with having dinner with Renata. She was after all an old friend, a bright, attractive woman. She was sure to make a pleasant companion for the evening.

None of his rationalizing did any good, however. Its wide-eyed innocence was exposed as disingenuous by the slouching truth, which was that he was taking her out in an effort to get his mind off Caedmon Rivers.

"Come in," Caedmon said, giving Harry a bright smile, "I've got a client on Skype. I'll be done with him in a minute. Is that the signed contract?"

He was trailing after her into her study. Today, she was dressed in sandals, white shorts, and a sleeveless green top with a deep V neck. All of which set off her tan, auburn hair, and luminous dark eyes to perfection. At least that's what Harry thought, if the racing of his heart, the dryness in his mouth, and a sort of general physical disturbance that in another setting might have suggested the onset of a serious illness could be called thinking.

"Have a seat," she said, pointing in the general direction of the couch as she swung off toward one of the computers.

While watching her go, Harry fell over one of the chairs in front of the couch.

Caedmon laughed and, glancing back, asked, "Where's your white stick?" Then she sat down and picked up her conversation. When she was finished, she came and stopped beside Harry, who had righted the chair he had knocked over and sat down on it. She dropped a hand on his shoulder and said, "Let's look at that contract."

Harry gave it to her, and she carried it to the couch. When she had read as much of it as she needed to and glanced through the pages of answers to the questions she had sent Breckenridge, she nodded in approval and put down the papers.

"We're in business, Harry," she said, bouncing up to offer him her hand.

She reached him before he had even begun to get out of his chair and leaned forward, hand outstretched. She was quite close to him, her breasts about even with his head. Harry tried not to look, but of course he failed, saw when he dragged his eyes up that she was grinning at him and felt his face burn.

"It's OK, partner," she said. Then, still holding his hand, she added, "I want to show you what I've found out so far."

She led him to the nearer desk and clicked on the computer. Typing much faster than Harry could count, she finished with a flourish and asked, "What do you see?"

A white rectangle with *Breckenridge, Afton,* typed at the top left-hand corner.

"Nothing but her name," Harry said, puzzled.

"Right," Caedmon said cheerfully.

"Why are you pleased?"

"Because I think we've got a skipper who's been erasing her tracks as she departed."

"You're sure of this?"

"No, but I think I will be by tomorrow. If I'm right, this is going to be fun."

"I don't get it," Harry said, wondering why she should be pleased if her work had been made more difficult.

She jumped up, dancing like a child, her eyes bright, her smile shining.

"The chase, Harry!" she said. "The chase!"

With that she flung herself on him, wrapped her arms around his neck, and gave him a force-ten hug. To keep from being knocked off his feet, he grabbed her as he staggered backward, recovering his balance with difficulty.

"Jesus!" he gasped.

"Did I hurt you?" she demanded, her voice full of alarm.

They were still in one another's arms, and she was looking up at him from a distance of about four inches. With her body pressed against his, his eyes locked on hers, his nostrils full of her scent, Harry, whose appeal to a Higher Power had nothing to do with fear or religious fervor but with an emotion far more primitive, broke through the last cobweb of restraint and kissed her on the mouth.

It was a deep dive and they did not breathe for a long time. Then they surfaced, gasping, and drew apart slowly, still clinging to one another, fighting for air. Caedmon recovered first.

"Wow!" she said, eyes wide, "did looking at the tops of my

75

tits do that?"

Desperate for an exculpatory explanation, Harry without thinking said hoarsely, "Yes."

"Maybe we should . . ." she began tentatively.

"No," Harry said, "really, I don't think I could . . ."

"I wasn't going to unbutton my blouse," she said, breaking into a giggle. "I was going to suggest a cup of coffee."

Her giggle, which charmed Harry and set him laughing, also brought him back to earth. "The coffee sounds good."

"I haven't been kissed like that since high school," Caedmon said when she returned with the coffee.

Harry was sitting in front of the sofa. "I can't remember that far back," he said. "Thank you for not suing me, or does that come later?"

She laughed and patted him on the head. "I was going to say, 'No hard feelings,' but that wouldn't be true, would it?"

"I'm taking the Fifth," he said.

The pat on the head had been a downer.

"New subject," she said, moving to the sofa. "Before I turn the hounds loose, I'm talking with GB—about an hour from now, in fact—any advice?"

"Yes," Harry said, "I would not tell him his wife has run away until the interview is over, if then."

"Wait until it's no longer open to denial."

"That would be my suggestion. He's very touchy on the subject. I think he'd rather be told she was dead than that she's left him."

"Not unusual," Caedmon said with a thin smile. "Thanks for the warning."

That wound it up. As they were walking toward the door, Harry tried to apologize, but Caedmon stopped him. "Are you going to tell me you didn't mean to kiss me?"

Harry still had enough phenylethylamine flowing through his

system to sense her anger although she had not raised her voice.

"I intended to do a lot more than that," he said, "but kissing you was a good beginning."

The tightness around her eyes vanished, to be replaced by lovely laugh lines.

"I could feel your interest increasing," she said, turning away and resuming their progress.

"As long as you're not angry with me."

"Go away, Harry," she said, pushing him out the door. "Try not to get run over."

As Harry left Ashbury Gardens, he admitted to having felt better than he did at that moment. No, it was worse than that. Of course, Caedmon's patting him on the head didn't necessarily mean what it usually means when a woman, especially a younger woman, pats you on the head. And being told not to get run over did not unquestionably mean he was too old and foolish to be outdoors without supervision.

Then his mind was flooded by the sensations of having her in his arms, kissing her while her arms tightened around his neck. His adrenalin mill roared into production, and Harry really should not have been driving. His cell shook him out of his trance and saved the other drivers of North Avola from a runaway silver Rover.

"Remember my mentioning a rumor Renata picked up in the courthouse about Breckenridge?"

Harry unscrambled his brain enough to recognize Jeff Smolkin's voice. "I remember."

"Get over to Harley Dillard's office. I think it came from there. I'm in front of Judge Cockburn for the defense in a larceny case Harley's prosecuting, and I can't risk calling his people on a fishing expedition."

"What's this about?"

"When we talked, I didn't know. Now I've heard more, but I'm not going to repeat it. I'll tell you this much: It's a tar baby. You should get over there and find out what's going on."

"And this definitely involves Breckenridge."

"Absolutely."

"But you're his lawyer, why can't you make the call?"

"I'm not his lawyer. He hired me to revise that Rivers contract for him, period. He was so wound up with the secrecy issue he didn't even trust his own attorneys to deal with it."

"Who are?"

"Lansdowne, Pollack, Minsk, and Frye. They have offices in Miami and Washington. Look, this involves you more than me."

Something's wrong here, Harry thought. *Lawyers don't do favors.*

"You're not doing this," he asked, "because I've . . . ?"

He was going to say, "asked Renata out to dinner," and changed his mind. She would probably not want Jeff knowing about their date, if that's what it was. And he felt much too guilty about it to want Jeff to know what he'd done.

"I'm trying to do you a favor here," Jeff said, showing some edge. "And what Renata does with her spare time is her business, but I will say this, I'm disappointed. I thought she had better taste."

Harry found himself listening to the emptiness and put his phone away.

It doesn't take much sand to spoil a salad. And so far today, not only had he sexually assaulted Caedmon Rivers on their second meeting, but now his cover was blown on dinner with Renata. He groaned, expecting to hear it reported on the *Guys and Gals* segment of the local evening news.

Oyster Street twisted through the old section of Avola, which meant that the street was narrow, traffic flow minimal, and no building was more than three stories high. Red tile roofs prevailed, and coconut palms and stately ficus gave grace and shade to the area.

The state's attorney's offices occupied the entire fourth floor of the Goodnight Building, a cream-colored stucco structure with gleaming glass and a red tile roof. The building was banked with pink and white oleander and its narrow lawns were studded with beds of orange and white impatiens.

Once out of the Rover, Harry stepped into a fresh Gulf breeze and shifting dappled shade and sunlight filtering through the gently swaying trees. They were only two blocks from the beach and laughing gulls were circling over the building, calling cheerfully, but Harry climbed the wide stairs to the smoked glass doors, lost to everything but his own gloomy thoughts.

Harley Dillard was a large, powerfully built man with a square jaw and heavy face with a permanent beard shadow. Harry's hand vanished in Harley's grip but emerged undamaged. The state's attorney, like a whale that has little to fear, was a mild and gentle man, except when he had a malefactor in his sights in a courtroom where his physical presence was potent testimony to the might and majesty of the law.

"It's good to see you, Harry," Harley said, beaming down on his visitor. "What brings you into this quiet backwater?"

"You, too, Harley. I don't see you nearly enough," Harry replied honestly. He liked the big man and knew for a fact that he presided over something closer to a snake pit than a backwater. Harley needed every bit of his strength and intelligence to keep the legal work of District 21 and its five-county court systems meting out justice smoothly, honorably, and efficiently.

Harley was a passionate bass fisherman, and Harry asked if he'd been on the water lately. Harley scowled in disgust at his lack of time, and they talked about places they had fished together and where Harley was planning to fish in the coming months.

"I'm having too much fun and the damned clock's ticking," Dillard finally said.

"And I'm in search of clarification," Harry said. "The word on the street is that your office is preparing some kind of action against Gregory Breckenridge. I'm working for him, and I'd appreciate a heads-up if something is brewing."

"Is his wife missing?" Dillard asked, suddenly all business.

"I don't know," Harry answered, "but he's hired me to find her."

"Meaning you think she walked?"

"What I don't think," Harry answered, "is that she's the victim of foul play."

"Are you working alone?"

"No. Breckenridge wants her found before the media discovers that she's missing, and he's hired Caedmon Rivers to track her down."

Dillard's scowl deepened. "I thought you said he'd hired you for the job."

"That's right, but I soon found out I didn't have the horses for that kind of race. Jeff Smolkin recommended Rivers, and now she's working for Breckenridge, but most of the contact between them takes place through me."

"What's his problem?"

"He's the principal partner in Dominion Investments, a hedge fund, and he's convinced that publicity, particularly of the negative variety, will damage his fund by frightening off investors."

"He's probably right," Dillard said, shifting heavily in his chair and looking at the ceiling for a few moments while Harry tried and failed to guess what was coming next.

"Here's what I can tell you," Dillard said, bringing his attention back to Harry, "and what you don't hear, I can't tell you. The good news would be if you never heard anything more from me on the subject. How long has she been gone?"

"Two weeks. I gather you've learned she's missing."

"Not necessarily. Harry, I'm going to be very careful. You're not going to be satisfied, but it's the best I can do."

Dillard was right, and when he finished speaking, Harry was not satisfied, having learned nothing specific about what Dillard's people had found or what they were doing with it.

"You know something, but it's in the verification stage. Therefore, for now, it has no standing," Harry said, controlling his disgust.

"Right."

"And as a consequence, you don't know what, if anything, can or will be acted on."

"Right again."

"What do I tell Breckenridge?"

"It's your call. Any further response from me would tend to add credibility to one or another conclusion about what we're looking at."

"Assuming that you've just answered my question, it might be reasonable to conclude that little would be gained by adding to his anxiety, a case of 'least said, soonest mended.' "

"You might conclude that," Dillard said, his scowl dissolving in a grin.

Harry left the building feeling that, aside from seeing Dillard and lying about the size of the bass they had caught in ages past, he might as well have been on the Hammock helping Tucker to paint his barn, which had all the appeal of a pulled tendon. And as a result of his having gone to see Dillard, despite the man's advice, Harry felt he had to tell Breckenridge about the conversation. But not now. Caedmon was probably still with him.

9

It was Harry's opinion that no woman knew how to wear a little black dress until she was at least thirty-five. Up to then it was just another dress. After that, like a warrior's face, it conveyed all the scars of battles fought, experience gained, hopes fulfilled, dreams abandoned, and the price of all of them.

"Renata," Harry said with complete sincerity, "you are drop-dead gorgeous."

"Well, thank you, Harry," she said, passing him the key to lock her door. "I haven't had this black dress on for five years, and if I sneeze, every seam is going to explode."

"Until then," he said, returning her key, "you are going to set this town on fire."

"No more, Harry," she said as they walked down the single flight of outside stairs. "Two lies are all you're allowed."

The Rover was parked under the holly trees lining the association's streets, and as he opened the door for her, he said, "As God is my witness, Renata, no joking, no exaggeration, you are lovely."

"How are you getting along with Caedmon Rivers?" she asked as they drove toward Lafitte's.

Caedmon. Harry had managed to get her out of his mind since ringing Renata's doorbell. Now she came roaring back.

"Oh, fine," he said. "So far she's been easy to work with, very professional, very skilled at what she does."

"Strange work for a woman."

Harry was surprised by the comment. "I would have thought you would be the last person to say that."

"Because I'm a woman?" Renata asked.

"You're very independent and good at what you do. Very impressive, in fact."

"Thank you. Skip chasing is predatory," she said thoughtfully. "It's not that I don't think women are aggressive—good God, Harry, I run an office stuffed with them, and not one has fewer than three elbows."

Getting the Rover parked—a two-person job in downtown Avola—and making their way along a crowded sidewalk toward the bar briefly interrupted their conversation. Lafitte's was a sprawling, open-fronted, low-ceilinged, bamboo and hardwood structure with a U-shaped bar and a random scattering of tables, most of which went unoccupied because the clientele, heavily under thirty, favored crowding around the bar six deep or wandering with their drinks into the equally crowded and narrow pedestrian street outside and pretending to talk in the serious uproar of Black Sabbath and shouted scraps of conversation.

The hostess took in Renata and Harry at a glance and, running interference past the bar, led them to a remote table under one of Lafitte's signature paddle fans that slowly beat the outer heat and the arctic air-conditioning into a fairly comfortable mixture.

"Do you feel we might be getting a little beyond this?" Renata, slightly out of breath, asked once they were out of the crush.

"A case could be made for it," Harry said, holding her chair while she rearranged her dress, "but isn't this where the movers and shakers drink?"

"After the children have gone to bed," she said, slipping into her chair. "At least that's what I'm told. I'm usually asleep by then."

"Tonight," Harry said, "we have miles to go before we sleep. What are we drinking?"

A waitress with black fingernails, freak hair, and the face of a Botticelli Madonna appeared at the table, carrying the menus as if she was looking for a trash can.

"Anything without an umbrella in it," Renata said, smiling at the waif, who remained unmoved.

"Can we go wrong with gin and tonic?"

"You asking me?" the waitress said, watching some young man in the street.

"Do you have an opinion?" Harry asked.

"Sure. In this place it could come with a rat in it."

"Let's risk it," Renata said.

"I'm with you," Harry said.

The waitress trailed off, having successfully avoided looking at them.

"How will she find us again?" Renata asked.

"She may not," Harry replied.

But she did, and having taken that first, life-enhancing sip, they finally smiled at one another.

"When you gave me Caedmon's card, why did you say I was on my own with this one?" Harry asked, not fully aware of why he was asking the question.

"Oh," Renata responded in a mock-cheerful voice, "it's Caedmon now."

"Don't blame me," Harry said, seeing his error too late. "It's her name, an odd one I admit. Probably a family name, wouldn't you think?"

"I didn't know sharks had names," Renata said with a sweet smile.

"My question is answered," Harry said, and unable to stop talking about her added, "she seems to be living alone and doesn't wear a shoo-fly ring."

"Why give yourself a handicap?" Renata asked, already halfway through her drink. "The last I knew she was sharpening her teeth on the golf pro at the Beach and Fairway Club."

"Then you figure I'm safe," Harry said, bearing up well under the blow.

"No, I think the lady's quantum of wantum is unlimited."

"You read Samuel Beckett?" Harry asked, determined to get off the subject of Caedmon Rivers.

"I've read him."

"And?"

"Too cerebral," she said and emptied her glass.

Harry realized that there was a catastrophe in the making here and set out to derail it. "Is it OK to talk business?" he asked.

"If you have to," she said, staring at her empty glass.

"I don't. Is it you, me, or the booze?"

For a long moment she seemed to go very far inside herself. Then she came back with a straightened spine and a clear, hard expression on her face. "Harry," she said. "What's going on here?"

Well, he'd asked for it, but admitting it didn't make the question any easier to answer.

"First, Lafitte's is a mistake. My fault. I don't know about you," he continued, looking around, "but I feel like a chaperone."

"Do you want to leave?" she asked, still stiff-faced.

"Yes."

"So do I."

When they had struggled free from the crowd in front of Lafitte's and gotten far enough away to be able to talk without shouting, Renata took Harry's arm and said, "It's too early for the restaurant. How about a walk?"

"The beach and back?" he asked.

"Good, if we go down Orchid Street, look at the moon on the water, and come back on Coral, I'll bet we won't see more than half a dozen cars the whole way."

"Done," Harry said, "but I want to leave my blazer in the Rover."

"And I'll shed this mantilla."

It being Southwest Florida, there was no need for them to comment on the warmth of the evening. Orchid was a narrow street flanked by low stucco buildings, devoted to shops and the occasional restaurant. Only a few shops were open, and Harry and Renata had the sidewalk almost entirely to themselves. The tree branches nearly met over the street, and in the gaps between the trees, moonlight mingled with the scattered light from the street lamps, shining through the leaves.

"Back to my question," Renata said.

"I'm enjoying myself," Harry said. "Are you?"

"Oddly enough, yes," she said, followed by a soft laugh that suggested to Harry that, at least, she was no longer angry. "But keep going."

"Why did I ask you to go out with me?"

"Yes, and I warn you, it matters to me."

"Something has happened to wake me up," he said. "And when I woke up, I decided I wanted more out of life than working and living alone on the Hammock."

"And did you see me as a doorway leading to a new and happier world?"

She was still holding his arm, and Harry broke away from her.

"Actually," he said, "I saw you more as a bicycle with training wheels."

"I've made you angry."

"No, puzzled. Out with it. Why this cross-examination?"

Renata recovered his arm. For a few moments they went on

walking, watching the moon. She seemed to him to be lost in her own thoughts.

"I've always liked you, Harry," she said suddenly, "even if the way you've conducted your life has not always won my admiration."

"I often find myself wanting," he replied. "Two wives and one or two others have also."

She did not respond at once and seemed contented to walk in the scattered moonlight, leaving her comment where it was, but her criticism of the way he conducted his life still rankled, and Harry felt compelled to pursue it.

"Before I break into a *mea maxima culpa*," he said, "what, exactly, don't you like about my life?"

"It's too fringey," she said, giving his arm a squeeze.

"On the fringe of what?" Harry asked, genuinely puzzled.

"Disaster," she said.

They had crossed the last street and stepped between the palms onto the white sand. The breeze was fresh and free from the taint of red tide. In the moonlight, the dark water of the Gulf glistened and bubbled as the smooth waves broke, darkening the sand, then slipped back into the oncoming wave. Pulling off their shoes, they walked down the beach, sending ghost crabs skittering into their burrows.

"It's been months since I was last here," Renata said, stopping at the water's edge.

"When I first moved to Avola, I spent hours and hours on the north end of this beach. Now, I seldom come near it."

"The same with me," she said. "I don't know why."

"Life happens," Harry said, not liking the thought and determined to bury it. "Are you as hungry as I am?"

"A very cynical observation," Renata said with a sigh, "but, yes, I'm starved."

★ ★ ★ ★ ★

Waterside was built on pilings driven into the bed of the Seminole River, and the southern wall of the restaurant was mostly glass, giving diners the feeling of being on a ship. There was an open deck with tables at the east end of the room, accessible through double French doors, but by May the heat and humidity discouraged all but the hardiest from eating out there.

"In or out?" Harry asked Renata as they approached the *maitre d'*, who loomed at the top of the stairs.

"In," she said, "and I'm glad I brought the mantilla."

The dining area was nearly full, and the murmur of conversation, the gleam of white linen, the flickering lamps and glinting flatware on the tables restored Harry's good spirits.

"You must know someone," Renata said when they were seated at a table beside the window. "I'm impressed."

"Good," Harry said. "Let's hope it's not the chef's night off."

"I haven't been here for a while," she said, leaving the menu where the waiter had placed it. "What's the report?"

"This is secondhand, but it's supposed to have pulled its socks up. Shall we stick with gin?" he asked in response to the beverage query.

"A Chardonnay, I think, for me," Renata said. "I don't want to be carried out of here."

Harry let the waiter persuade him to order a bottle.

"Harry," she said as soon as the hovering was temporarily over, "why are you and I walking together in the moonlight, preparing to eat and drink together, and moving toward the overwhelming question . . ."

"Now I am impressed," Harry said, delighted with her. "You're quoting Eliot at me."

"Eliot who?"

"Thomas Stearns Eliot."

"Oh, nonsense," Renata protested, leaning back as the ritual of the bottle began.

Harry tasted and approved. Their glasses charged, he said, lifting his, "To 'The Love Song of J. Alfred Prufrock,' may he rest in peace, and to you."

"Can we leave Freshman English now?" she asked, putting down her glass, sounding to Harry more serious than he had thought.

"Does this overwhelming question have anything to do with sex?"

"This wine is really not bad. No, it has everything to do with it. Stop being silly."

The waiter appeared, prepared to take their order, and was rebuffed.

"They no sooner get you seated than they begin trying to get you out," Renata said, showing a little ruffle.

"You're very odd," Harry said, somewhat at a loss and trying not to show it. "Attractive, but definitely different."

"It's because I'm scared to death," she said, holding up her empty glass.

A waiter appeared and filled it.

"Why?" Harry asked, concerned.

"What are we going to do, when it's time to say goodnight?"

Harry saw at once that he was in a tight corner. If he said something like, *That might be two or three o'clock tomorrow morning, and all we'd have to do is close our eyes,* Renata might think he had taken her out just to shag her. The consequences would not be pretty.

On the other hand if he said, *It's been a fun evening. Maybe we can do it again sometime,* she might conclude she was not attractive to him, and that would be 1) not true and 2) very unkind. Then he remembered Tucker once saying, "When you're at the end of your rope, tie it to another."

"What would you like us to do?" he asked.

"We've walked arm in arm once tonight," she said, having taken a sustaining swallow of her wine. "So that's out. We've known each other long enough to be brother and sister. How would that work out?"

"What if we're descendants of Egyptian royalty?"

"Be serious, Harry. This is not funny."

"When in doubt, procrastinate," Harry said as the waiter swooped down again from his branch.

They consulted the menus and ordered like two people in their right minds. Before leaving, the waiter filled Renata's glass.

"Be honest, then. What's worrying you?" he asked.

"Me. You."

"Are you feeling guilty about something or, more to the point, someone?"

That was cutting pretty close to the bone, but Harry decided something had to settle her down or very probably she was going to have to be carried out of the restaurant.

Renata pushed her wine glass away and sat with her hands folded, staring at him with a pained expression. "I've been in love with him for years," she said, her eyes misting.

Harry did not have to ask who. "And?"

"Nothing."

"Oh, dear woman," he said, startled by that single word, "I'm really sorry."

"Thank you," she said, "and Harry, I don't know what's wrong with me."

Harry understood at once.

"Clear the decks," he said. "Prepare for action. There's nothing wrong with you, Renata. You're a beautiful, desirable woman."

"I'm waiting for the *but*," she said.

Harry wanted to say, *So am I*, then squelched the impulse as being too crass even for him. "How long have we known one another?"

"It must be nearly ten years."

"The first day I saw you, I wanted to take all your clothes off, open a jar of body cream, and . . ."

"Why didn't you?" she demanded, too loudly.

"The setting was a little awkward," he said.

Their food arrived, giving Harry time to recall an old saw that went something like . . . "Wine on gin,/Leads to sin." He didn't think he had the couplet quite right but let it go.

Upset or not, Renata set to with gusto and Harry followed suit. They finished the meal with crème brûlée, and Renata said, holding Harry's arm as they descended the stairs, "I feel like Marie Antoinette heading for her tumbrel."

"Do you expect to lose your head?" Harry asked.

"No, I'm afraid I won't."

"You will," he told her, and she did, and so did he.

It turned out to be such a pleasant surprise for both of them that they saw no reason to stop. Neither said, "Goodnight." At some point words dissolved into sighs, inarticulate murmurs, and then silence.

10

At ten-thirty the next morning, Harry got a call from Frank Hodges, asking him if he could stop by the office.

"Why aren't you still in the hospital?" Harry asked, surprised to hear his voice.

"Aside from having my arm strapped to my side and my head wrapped in a bandage, I'm feeling pretty good. Something's got the captain stirred up," Hodges complained, "and whatever it is, he's not sharing it with me."

"Probably only wants to go through it once," Harry said. "Are you in pain?"

"The arm aches like hell," Hodges said, "and operating left-handed is a bummer. For example, trying to . . ."

"Right," Harry said quickly. "Tell Jim I'm on my way."

Driving into town, he allowed himself to reflect on how he felt about sleeping with Renata and whether or not it had done anything to lessen his fixation on Caedmon. His reflections along those lines lasted about thirty seconds and consisted entirely of disturbingly vivid images of Renata *redivivus* before being obliterated by scenes of her anxiety when they woke to the day and she saw that she was going to be late for work.

"There's coffee and eggs," she told him, fresh from the shower, as she rushed around the bedroom, blow-drying her hair with one hand and pulling bits of clothing from drawers with the other before vanishing into her walk-in closet and emerging moments later, zipping and buttoning. "Number One has a fit if I'm not there when he arrives," she gasped. "Christ! Look at the time."

Harry watched all this from the bed, and when she suddenly rushed at it, shouting, "Sit up! Sit up!" he did.

She dropped her shoes and her briefcase on the bed, bent over and caught his head in her hands, kissed him repeatedly and rapid fire, more or less on the mouth, grabbed up her things, and sprinted for the door.

"Blessings on you, Barefoot Boy," she called over her shoulder and was gone.

At that point he asked himself several questions that went unanswered and lingered to plague him: *What do I do now? Send her flowers? Pretend nothing has happened? Call later and compare notes on the evening? Invite her to the Hammock for a weekend? Send her a non-stick frying pan for cooking scrambled eggs?*

"Jesus wept," he said out loud, turning off CR 29 into Avola, thoroughly disgusted with himself.

Twenty-four hours later, the truth was he had no idea what to do.

"All right, I'll call her," he broke out suddenly as if he had been engaged in a fiery argument with one of his avatars. "I'll say something sensible if I can, but not right now."

Jim Snyder *was* worked up. He was pacing around behind his desk, waving his arms and stopping occasionally to criticize Hodges, who was sitting beside Harry, beaming merrily. With his head swathed in bandages, he looked alternately happy and insane.

"It is the craziest thing I've ever heard of," Jim said, finally coming to a halt and dropping into his swivel chair, which creaked miserably and skated backward into the wall.

"Jim," Harry said, waving down Hodges' laughter. "Just tell me what's happened."

"Harley Dillard, laughing up his sleeve, has stuck us with a ridiculous mess," Jim said, picking up a file from his desk and dropping it again as if it had bitten him.

"It's the voice from the grave," Hodges broke in, grinning, "that's got the captain in such a snit."

"Read it!" Jim said, picking up the file and stretching a long arm over the desk toward Harry.

"Start with the letter," Hodges said.

The letter was folded inside a cream-colored envelope, addressed in longhand to State's Attorney Harley Dillard. As Harry extracted it from the envelope, he caught the fleeting scent of a perfume that for a blissful instant chained his mind. Then Hodges' voice broke the spell. As far as Harry could tell, the paper on which the letter was written was the same color and weight as the envelope, and he thought the same hand that had addressed the envelope had written the letter, which was dated.

Dear State's Attorney Dillard, the letter began. *If you find when you receive this letter that I am missing, you will know my husband has killed me. Shortly before Christmas, I learned that he was sleeping with another woman. Her name is Beatrice Frazer.*

Harry skipped to the end. It was signed *Afton Breckenridge.* Harry quickly read the section of the letter he had skipped and found that Breckenridge and Beatrice Frazer had spent Christmas together in the Bahamas, that Afton had made several attempts following their return to Virginia to discuss the situation with Gregory, and that he had refused. She then told him she wanted a divorce, and he had refused to consider it. She had not as yet sought the advice of a lawyer but intended to do so and file for divorce. She had told her husband of her intention, and his anger over her decision had led her to write the letter.

For a moment, Harry stared at the letter in silence, then said,

"The lying bastard."

Jim passed over the evaluation. "You know what this means. Don't you?" he demanded, and quickly provided his own answer. "With the department short-handed and down to its last nickel, I'm being told to go on a long and expensive search for Afton Breckenridge unless Breckenridge is willing to tell me where she is, which he probably can't or won't."

"You're half right," Harry said, gathering his thoughts sufficiently to answer. "He doesn't know."

"How would you know that?" Hodges asked.

"Because he hired me to find her."

"Lord, Lord, Lord," Jim intoned, raising his eyes to the ceiling.

Harry thought he'd never heard Jim sounding so burdened.

"How did you come to be working for Breckenridge?" Hodges asked.

"Jeff Smolkin gave him my name," Harry said, "and he came out to the Hammock to interview me."

Harry was amused to see Hodges settle back, cross his legs, and give what was being said his full attention. There was nothing, outside of pig hunting and his wife's key lime pie, that Hodges loved as much as a story. He collected gossip the way sticky-paper collected flies, and with any or no encouragement, he would share his hoard, talking as long as anyone would listen.

"How did Smolkin come across him?" Hodges asked. "It don't seem they'd have much occasion to meet."

"No, they don't," Harry said, keeping his eye on Jim, eager to see how long he would let this go on. "But Breckenridge was so afraid that people would find out his wife was missing, he wouldn't even tell his own lawyers she was gone and went to Jeff Smolkin, hoping to keep it a secret."

"Why did Smolkin send him to you?" Hodges asked.

"Harry," Jim said loudly, apparently abandoning his search

for divine intervention. "Have you had any success in finding her?"

Hodges opened his mouth, apparently to protest, then glanced at Jim and thought better of it.

"No," Harry said. "I gave up trying almost as soon as I started."

"How did Breckenridge take that?" Hodges asked, his eyes widening.

"Frank! Shut up!" Jim roared in an outbreak so unlike him that Harry and Hodges sank back in their chairs, staring at him in astonished silence.

"Jim," Harry said, deciding he had to do something to ease the captain's mind, "I'm working with a skip tracer, who specializes in missing persons. She's just getting started."

"Who is she?" Hodges asked, bearding the lion.

"Caedmon Rivers," Harry said.

"I've heard that name," Jim said, dropping his shoulders a bit and opening his fists.

"She lives in Ashbury Gardens."

"Northeast Avola," Hodges said. "I didn't think there were any office buildings in that association."

"She works out of her house," Harry said. "It's got enough electronics in it to run an airport. I'm really impressed with her."

Mentioning Caedmon's name had flooded his mind with her image, and he stopped talking to focus on her.

"Harry," Jim said impatiently, "are you all right?"

"Sorry, yes, where was I?"

"How long will it take to find this Breckenridge woman?"

"Who says she's alive?" Hodges asked.

"Well, she may not be," Jim conceded.

"This Rivers any good at catching ghosts?" Hodges asked in a loud voice, followed by louder laughter.

Jim's ears started getting red again, and Harry said quickly, "Caedmon thinks from what she's seen so far that Afton Breckenridge or someone else has been erasing all traces of her." He had not fully absorbed the possibility that Afton Breckenridge was dead and that her husband had killed her.

"What does that mean?" Jim demanded, shifting his attention away from Hodges.

"I'm not too clear, but there's no record of any recent telephone calls made from her cell phone, no recent charges against her credit cards. More may be missing."

"If we have the letter, doesn't it mean she's dead?" Hodges said, as if he was stating the obvious.

"That's even worse," Jim said.

"No body," Hodges said.

"It's probably going to take time and effort just to determine whether she's alive or dead," Harry added, not sure whether Hodges had to be right or not.

That in turn shifted the focus of his thinking to Gregory Breckenridge.

The three men sat quietly for a few moments, Harry struggling to come to terms with the possibility that Breckenridge might be a murderer. Whether he was or not, he was certainly a liar, and Harry did not like being lied to. Then Jim sighed, threw the pen he had been fiddling with onto the desk, and rubbed his head vigorously, a certain sign of stress.

"Maria Fuegos came in," he said, sounding as if calamities came in threes, the third always being Hodges.

Harry, half his mind still on Breckenridge, was slow in grasping the significance of Jim's comment. Then he made the connection. "Then she's not an illegal."

"No, full citizenship. She's more than a cut above, if I'm any judge."

"What does she do for Ogilvie?"

"She wasn't very specific, but I concluded she's Gwen Ogilvie's secretary and general factotum."

"Did she accuse Ogilvie of stealing paintings?"

"Not in so many words," Jim said, planting his elbows on his desk, "but she claims to have seen several of the shipments being unpacked and, according to her, each time, she has watched Mr. Ogilvie take unframed paintings out of the packaging and quickly carry them away."

"Why would she have been present when the pictures were being unpacked?" Harry asked.

"Mrs. Ogilvie is responsible for the paperwork, and that means Maria Fuegos does the actual work while her boss supervises."

"There must be at least one man besides Ogilvie there to open the crates."

"Not according to Fuegos. Ogilvie handles that part of it."

"Rowena told me that Roswell and Hart handled the crating and shipping of Ogilvie's paintings."

"That's part right," Hodges said quickly, "but Ogilvie and his missus send out some and receive some on their own."

"According to Fuegos, he gets one of these shipments every two or three months," Jim added.

"If you've questioned Roswell and Hart's people, Ogilvie probably knows by now he's become a subject of interest to the department," Harry said with a sinking feeling.

"I sent Lieutenant Jones and one of his sergeants over there to talk with Philip Scruggs, the gallery manager," Jim said a bit defensively. "Millard said he made it clear Scruggs was to say nothing about their visit."

"Millard said he leaned on him pretty hard," Hodges added.

"Too bad the manager wasn't a woman," Harry said sourly. "She would have done all the leaning for him."

Hodges gave a shout of laughter and began slapping his knee. Women found Millard Jones irresistible, but he had never married. Jim's mentioning his name caused Harry to recall, to his annoyance, that even Katherine, his second wife, who never had any trouble controlling her enthusiasm for men, began blushing and smoothing her dress whenever they met.

"I could never understand it," Jim said reflectively. "I asked Kathleen about it once, but all she did was turn red and break out in an odd little smile and change the subject. It's not that he's anything much to look at. He can't be more than five eight. His hair is thinning, and I never did like that miserable mustache."

"Someone besides the manager is bound to have seen the head of the Crime Scene Unit and one of his officers in the gallery," Harry said, anxious to change the subject.

"They wouldn't know why they were there," Hodges said, having wiped his eyes and blown his nose.

"I take your point," Jim agreed, "but why would they bother to say anything to Ogilvie about it?"

Harry had a rule about how far he would go in offering advice and comment on Jim's operations, and he decided he had reached that limit. "Good luck with the investigation," he said, getting to his feet.

"I want to talk to you later about Breckenridge," Jim said.

"Let me talk to him first—if it can wait."

Jim said it could, and Harry left, deciding to talk with Caedmon before seeing Breckenridge. He didn't even bother to find a reason.

11

"I suppose it means she's dead if Jim has the letter," Harry said after telling Caedmon what had happened.

She was sitting on the sofa with her legs crossed, swinging her foot and obviously thinking. He was on his chair, watching her. She had brought them coffee, but both had set the cups down in order to focus on the news.

"Not necessarily," Caedmon said after a while, then fell silent again and went on staring at the window beside the sofa.

She was dressed in a light blue sundress and had fastened her hair back in a gold circlet. Harry thought she looked ravishing and would have been content to just sit looking at her in silence, but he forced himself to respond.

"Why not?"

She looked back at him and smiled, her dark eyes regarding him with an amused expression.

"What's funny?" he asked.

"You," she answered, her smile widening, "but funny in a nice way."

"Good," Harry said, drifting in her eyes like a rudderless boat but thinking about the golf pro and what there was or had been between them.

"What?" she asked.

"The golf pro."

"None of your business, but I'll tell you anyway. He plays with the other group."

"Thanks," he said, wanting to break into song but controlling himself.

"You have a face like a book, Harry," she said, grinning. Then in a more businesslike voice, "Pay attention to what I'm going to tell you. You'll have to convey this to Breckenridge, and I want you to get it right."

"I'm listening," Harry said, gathering all his resources and forcing himself to stop dreaming over her like a lovesick adolescent. He wasn't entirely successful, but he pretended to be.

"Let's suppose you were Afton Breckenridge," Caedmon said, "and you wanted to disappear, leaving everyone thinking you were dead, and you had written the letter she wrote. How would you get it delivered?"

"I have an idea it's going to be difficult to tell him anything for a while. But as for your question, I could ask a lawyer or even a friend to mail it," he said.

"You could do that, but consider the complications."

"Which are?"

Caedmon was on her feet, having tried the coffee and made a face. "Fresh coffee all around," she said, gathering up Harry's cup and striding out of the room, talking as she went. Harry followed like a moth in pursuit of a flame.

"A friend is a friend, and that's a mixed blessing."

"Why in this case?" Harry asked, walking into a spotless white kitchen.

"Friends ask questions."

"Do you do anything in this kitchen except make coffee?" he asked.

"What do you have in mind?" She rested a hip against the counter while the coffee maker bubbled.

"I meant do you ever cook in here?"

The thoughts that came up with some other answers made

his knees wobbly.

"Sometimes," she told him, the smile returning.

"What kind of questions?" he asked, trying to slow his heart rate.

The coffee maker having performed its alchemy, Caedmon filled their cups. She passed very close to him on her way back to where they had been sitting, engulfing him with her scent. For a moment his head spun and his vision blurred, but he managed to get back to his chair without further debilitating symptoms.

"Drink some coffee," she told him. "It may help."

"What do you mean?" Harry demanded, suddenly angry with himself and her for the way he was feeling.

"Ouch!" she said. "I mean you're not thinking. This *friend* is going to want to know why she's been given the letter, or worse, she may even guess. Being a friend, she probably knows your relationship with your husband is rocky at best. Then there are the police, who will come asking questions once the letter has been delivered."

"And a local postal stamp may intensify the attention," Harry agreed. Listening had calmed him enough to allow him to be civil.

"*Will* intensify it," Caedmon said. "Why were you angry with me?"

"The devil made me do it."

"My ass," she snapped, scowling.

"That too," he said.

Her responding laughter released Harry from whatever spell had chained him to his chair. Not entirely sure what he was going to say or do, but determined to end the uproar churning his emotions, he crossed the space separating them and sat down beside her. She turned toward him, watching him with interest.

"Caedmon, there's something I've got to tell you," he said,

and stuck there.

"Is it something I don't know?"

"You've already said I was laughable, so perhaps not."

"Wrong. I said you were funny in a nice way."

"Not much difference."

He was losing his courage very rapidly and started to get up, but she pressed her hand against his shoulder and said, "Don't. Finish what you started to say."

He dropped back, feeling a total idiot, but gathering the shards of his self-confidence, he said, "I'm in love with you. I know what you're going to say. I shouldn't have said it, but . . ."

He was already halfway to his feet and she rose with him, and when they were standing, pulled him around to face her.

"Don't spoil it," she said sharply. "I'm very flattered. It's lovely to be looked at as if one was a pearl beyond price, especially if the man lying to you is attractive."

"Believe me, Caedmon," Harry said, "I'm not lying. I'm being totally unprofessional, but I'm not lying."

"I'm glad to hear it," she said. "You might try kissing me and see how that goes."

It went very well.

As they were recovering their breath, Caedmon gasped, "My God, you have been in the woods a long time. Let's move this show to the bedroom. I'm too old for floors and sofas."

So that's what they did, and tried their best to wreck the place. The limitations of age notwithstanding, they fell off the bed and clambered back as if they had fallen into shark-infested waters.

"I've just gone to heaven without all the trouble and expense of dying," Harry said somewhat later in a raddled voice as he lay sprawled on a rumpled sheet.

"Save a place for me," Caedmon croaked as she crawled onto

him and with a groan dropped her head onto his chest as if she might never move again.

"As I was saying before the interregnum," Caedmon observed, popping the last strawberry in her bowl into her mouth, "giving the letter to a lawyer, who, never having trusted his mother—especially not his mother—would want to know more than your friend."

They were sitting at her kitchen table, finishing their cereal and strawberries, Caedmon having overridden Harry's complaint that one breakfast a day was enough.

"You had one more strawberry than me," he said, watching her chew.

"Tough luck," she said, pushing back her chair. "Time to work again."

"Then what's the answer?" Harry asked when they were back in the living room.

"Postal drops," she said firmly, "that is, businesses that will receive your mail, hold it, forward it, or keep it until you pick it up."

"In any city in the country," Harry said, awaking to the possibilities.

"Not so easy," she said, "because you will have to provide legitimate identification to open the account. But because all this will be set up ahead of your leaving, once you are gone, if anyone looking for you locates your mail drop and manages to weasel information like an address or telephone number out of the company, they will no longer be valid."

"So I should leave my letter at my mail drop with instructions to mail it on a certain date."

"Right. There's a lot more I've got to tell you, but I'll wait until I've done more work on AB. Then Disappearing 101 will make more sense."

Caedmon paused and gave Harry a serious, appraising look. "By the way, are you feeling better?"

"Yes, Doctor, but I suspect the improvement is temporary. How are things with you?"

Harry wasn't sure whether or not her question amused him more than it angered him.

"Okay—nothing that Muscle Rub won't take care of. Let's get to what you're going to tell Breckenridge."

When that was settled, Caedmon walked Harry to the door.

"Harry," she asked after kissing him, "does it matter that I'm not in love with you?"

"I've heard better news."

"Does that mean we're scrubbing the calisthenics?"

"Only if I drown in the shower."

Once back in the Rover, Harry called Breckenridge and through Ernan arranged a meeting. He had eaten only the cornflake and strawberry pick-me-up since breakfast, and it was now almost three. He had an hour before his appointment with Breckenridge, time he knew he should give to talking with Jeff Smolkin. But also shining brightly was his awareness that doing that would mean talking with Renata, and considering what he had just done with Caedmon, he was well short of having enough moxie for that encounter.

Yes, he would have to talk with her, but not now.

In fact he grew pale and his stomach tried to go somewhere else at the thought, and he instantly abandoned it. As he sat at the bar in the Avola Club, rumored to recycle road kills, he was uncertain whether the white streak forming in his thinning hair or the yellow streak inching down his back had the greater claim on his attention.

Over the ensuing days shame and guilt, those two angels of darkness, struggled intermittently for control of his anguish monitor. Nonetheless, he continued to eat heartily and sleep deeply, conflicting indicators.

"Has anyone from the police department called you?" Harry asked as soon as Ernan led him into Gregory Breckenridge's office.

Harry intended to keep this conversation on a civil note, but with the letter Jim had shown him fresh in his mind he would have liked very much to tell Breckenridge to look for another dogsbody. In fact, he had a strong impulse to do just that. However, before Breckenridge could answer, Ernan opened the door and said, "I apologize, sir, for the interruption, but Captain Snyder from the Tequesta Sheriff's Department is calling, and he insists on being put through to you."

Scowling and swearing, Breckenridge snatched up the phone. When Ernan had completed the connection, he said, "Breckenridge." After that he just listened, then said, "Fine," and slammed down the phone.

"Snyder is coming over here," he said sourly and glowered at Harry. "What the hell is going on?"

"I'm not sure, but our conversation had better wait until you've talked with Jim," he said.

"Who the hell is Jim?"

"The man you were just talking to. He's an old friend."

"What does this Snyder want with me? If he's trying to raise money, I'll have his balls."

"I'd cool off if I were you," Harry said, "and start thinking prudently. His visit has to do with your wife's disappearance."

"How the hell does he know about that?" Breckenridge demanded, a look of alarm replacing his scowl. "Have you told him . . . ?"

"No," Harry said. "Harley Dillard, the state's attorney, sent him some documents that may have come from her."

Harry was not dodging his responsibilities. He had thought

carefully about what he was doing, and it now seemed to him quite possible that Afton Breckenridge had not sent that letter. And even if she had, there was, as Caedmon had suggested, the possibility she was alive. He hadn't half thought through all the contingencies surrounding the events named or hinted at in the letter, but he wanted to hear what Jim had to say to Breckenridge before deciding whether or not to sever connections with the man.

"You may as well hear what I've learned from Caedmon," Harry said, avoiding an awkward silence as they waited.

Breckenridge was frowning and staring at his clenched fists as if contemplating mayhem.

Caught where he thought he was safe, Harry concluded, *and if I were a gambler, I'd bet he was wondering if Harley knew about Beatrice Frazer.*

"Is it going to make me feel any better?" Breckenridge demanded.

"That's up to you," Harry said. "Do you want to hear it or not?"

Breckenridge flung himself out from behind his desk and made a couple of circles of the room, came back, dragged his chair back in place, and sat down, elbows planted on the desk. "What's he got?"

"Additional confirmation that Mrs. Breckenridge or someone else is erasing all traces of her."

They were interrupted by Ernan.

"Captain Snyder and Sergeant Hodges are here, sir."

The introductions went very quickly. Jim was polite but unsmiling. Breckenridge looked at Hodges as if the sergeant was a dangerous escapee from a mental institution. Everyone sat down.

"This conversation will be recorded," Jim said, nodding at Hodges, who placed the small black recorder on the desk in front of Breckenridge and switched it on, then gave the date, address, time, and the names of those present.

"This is Captain James Snyder, Sheriff's Department," Jim began. "Am I speaking with Gregory Breckenridge?"

Breckenridge nodded. Then, without having to be prompted, he said, "Yes, and before I go any farther with this, I want to know why you're here; and if I'm not told, I will refuse to answer any questions without my lawyer being present."

"We can do this two ways," Jim said. "The sergeant and I can handcuff you and take you to headquarters, put you in a detention cell while I try to get in touch with Harley Dillard, the state's attorney, who is very busy and sometimes can't be reached for hours, and ask for further instructions. Having heard back from him, I will try to question you. At that time, if you choose to, you can call your attorney. After some further delays you will be released. But it will be noted that you refused to cooperate with this investigation."

"And Mr. Breckenridge," Hodges added, "that's a bad way to begin with what looks to me like a long and drawn-out business."

"Are you threatening me?" Breckenridge demanded, lifting himself half out of his chair.

"Do you feel threatened?" Jim asked in the same level voice he had used throughout.

"I don't tolerate threats."

"The other alternative," Jim said, ignoring the boast, "is that if you cooperate, we can get you through this unpleasantness as quickly and as painlessly as possible. You may stop cooperating whenever you wish, call a lawyer whenever you wish, but my very best advice to you is to let this interrogation go forward. You have Mr. Brock as a witness to whatever goes on here."

Breckenridge dropped back into his chair. "Let's see where it goes," he said.

"Thank you," Jim said. "Is Afton Breckenridge your wife?"

"Yes."

"Where is she?"

"I don't know."

"When did you last see her?"

"Three weeks before last Christmas."

"Where were you at that time?"

"In our house in Virginia."

Jim read off the address and asked Breckenridge if the address was the correct one, and was told it was.

"Did she leave the house?"

"Yes. She came down here. I think she left on December the fifteenth."

"Why did she leave?"

"She said she was tired of the cold and wanted to spend what remained of the winter here."

"By *here*, you mean this house."

"Yes."

"Have you been in contact with your wife since that time?"

"Yes, in March she called me in Rome, to ask if I would visit our son on his birthday." Breckenridge then explained why his son was in Italy.

"And you have had no contact with her since?"

"No."

"And you have no idea where she is?"

"No."

"Have you made an effort to locate her?"

"Yes." Breckenridge then explained that he had hired Harry and Caedmon Rivers to search for her. For the record this time, Harry confirmed the statement.

"With what results?"

At that point Breckenridge looked at Harry.

"Ms. Rivers has been unable to locate Mrs. Breckenridge,"

Harry said. "It's her professional opinion that either Mrs. Breckenridge or someone else is systematically erasing all traces of
her."

"Can you be more precise?" Jim asked.

Harry repeated what Caedmon had told him.

"All right," Jim said. "Mr. Breckenridge, when did you
discover your wife was missing?"

"April eighteenth," he answered and explained that he had
called Ernan to say he was coming down for a few weeks and
found she had left that morning for Miami, leaving him a phone
number.

"Did you call the number?"

"Yes, it was the Miami Seaquarium."

Hodges started to laugh, was glared at by Jim, and pretended
he was coughing. Hodges, Harry thought, struggling to keep his
own face straight, was as skilled at subterfuge as a rhinoceros,
and the struggle caused him to look even wilder than before.

"Does she have friends in Miami?" Jim asked.

"Yes," Breckenridge said, watching Hodges with obvious
concern, "and Ernan called everyone listed in the house phone's
telephone address book, living in Florida and in Virginia. She
had not talked with any of them recently."

"What do you think has happened, Mr. Breckenridge?" Jim
asked.

"I have no idea, and it is very worrisome."

Harry wondered if Breckenridge's answer was truthful. If it
wasn't, he was a very good liar, which he might be.

Jim's response was another question. "Today is May sixteenth,
which means Mrs. Breckenridge has been missing for almost a
month. Why haven't you notified the police?"

12

For the first time since the questioning began, Breckenridge looked seriously troubled. There was an extended silence, during which he sat staring over the heads of the men in front of him.

"I exist, Captain, on my credibility and trustworthiness," he said at last in a voice lacking any force. "If it becomes known that my wife is missing, for whatever reason, my hedge fund may be seriously impacted. If my investors become uneasy and start bailing out, a lot of people, including myself, stand to lose a great deal of money."

Hearing the answer a second time, Harry thought it still sounded truthful, as far as it went. The trouble was that it said nothing about him and his wife. Was the story about financial risk deliberately concocted to deflect attention from Breckenridge and his wife? He watched with interest as Jim leaned over and took from the folder laying beside his chair the envelope containing Afton Breckenridge's letter. He placed it on the desk where Breckenridge could easily reach it.

"This letter arrived at the state's attorney's office yesterday. A copy was sent to me this morning. Please read it."

Breckenridge, now stony-faced and with obvious reluctance, opened and read the letter. As he read, his face drained of color and he shrunk back until he was holding it almost at arm's length.

"What are you trying to do to me?" he asked in a cracking voice.

"Did Mrs. Breckenridge's leaving Greenfields and coming to Avola just before Christmas have anything to do with your relationship with Beatrice Frazer?"

"How dare you make such an accusation?" Breckenridge demanded, color flooding back into his face.

"Were you with Ms. Frazer in the Bahamas over the Christmas holidays?"

"My lawyers will make you pay for this," Breckenridge grated, slamming the letter onto his desk. "And unless you are going to arrest me, get out of here."

"Did he throw you out along with Snyder and Hodges?" Caedmon asked.

"No," Harry said, "but it was a while before Ernan and I got him calmed down enough to talk sensibly."

By the time Harry got to Caedmon's house, the heat of day was diminishing, and at Harry's urging she had agreed to hear his report on their way to look at an occupied bald eagle nest— located, astonishingly, in a tall slash pine in the center of Ashbury Gardens.

She had changed into white shorts and a pale blue halter top, and having put on her straw hat and her sunglasses and pushed him toward the door, she said, "Do you know what? You're more trouble than a kid."

Harry was ridiculously pleased by her complaint. As for the nest, neither of them had seen it, and she had never heard of it. He was learning that the great outdoors did not hold many charms for her. Her assessment of the beach, one of Southwest Florida's glories, was that, "It was a great place to step on a stingray and get sand in your underwear."

"In payment," he said once they were out of the house, "I'll explain how eagles do it and fly."

"So why the hell can't I?" she asked. "And the answer is . . . ?"

"We fall out of bed?"

She gave one of her good laughs, put her arm under his, and in a sudden shift asked, "Are we out of a job?"

"No. Once Jim and Hodges were gone and Breckenridge had vented enough to be rational, one of the first things he said was, 'I want that woman found. How much longer will it take?' "

"What did you say?"

"Caedmon's doing her best, but it's going to take time."

"Good," she said, "because it will."

"Will you have to add Beatrice Frazer to your list?"

"Probably not, but we'll see. When are you going to interview her?"

"As soon as I can, and that may not be soon enough."

"Meaning what?"

"Breckenridge's lawyers will stop her from being interviewed by anyone without one of them present."

"Wouldn't she be better off with her own lawyers?" Caedmon asked.

"Yes," Harry said. "If Breckenridge is charged with murder, she is at risk of being turned into an accomplice by his lawyers and given the lion's share of the blame. By the way, do you know where we are?"

They had been walking and talking, and Harry had not been keeping track of the streets.

"Sure," she said. "When I moved in here, I was given a map of the place and memorized it."

"How large is this association?"

"There are six hundred and seventy-three houses in here," she told him, pulling on his arm. "Come on, we're wasting time."

"And you've memorized all the streets."

"Yes. I stuck the map on the john door, and within a couple of months I had them down."

"Most people read or reflect on life during those interludes."

"I do the *Times* crossword. Now, can we get out of the can? Do you think GB killed his wife?"

"I don't know, but who do you think is erasing her tracks?"

"She's not using her credit cards. She's not using her cell phone. As far as I've been able to tell, she's not registered in her own name in any hotel in Miami, and in the last month her name doesn't appear on any flight manifest in or out of here, Miami, or Orlando."

"Car rentals?"

"I looked and came up dry. If her car had been found by the police, GB would have heard by now."

"Hospitals?"

"She hasn't been admitted to any hospital in the state, and she hasn't been arrested."

"Gone like the birds of winter," Harry said.

"Very poetic, but possibly accurate." Caedmon paused to look around and said, "The next street is ours."

"What do you think's happened to her?" Harry asked as they turned down the street.

"There are only four options. She's dead. She's been kidnapped, she's hiding, or she's living openly somewhere with a new identity. If it's the last possibility, she's been planning this for some time."

"How long does it take to plan a successful disappearance?"

"If I were doing it, I'd want two or three months."

Harry looked up.

"There it is," he said.

The pine was standing on a small lawn in front of a pale green house that was dwarfed by the huge tree. The nest, constructed of sticks and decorated here and there with hanks of cloth and pieces of colored plastic, was built against the trunk some thirty feet above the ground and supported by two heavy branches, making the tree look as if it existed to be a nest site.

"My God!" Caedmon exclaimed, holding her hat on with one hand as she craned her neck, staring at the huge structure. "Look at the size of that thing!"

"It's about five feet deep and six or seven feet wide," Harry said, "and it will grow larger with every passing year."

"Where are the eagles?" she asked, giving up staring and rubbing the back of her neck.

"One of them, probably the male, is away hunting," Harry said, grinning at her look of astonishment. "Listen," he said, having heard the mewing call of very young chicks.

"What is it?" she asked.

"The babies. Keep watching the nest," he said, having guessed what had roused them.

"My neck is . . ."

Her complaint was cut off by the sudden rush of wings as the female eagle passed over their heads. For a moment the big bird hovered over the edge of the nest nearest them, wings fully extended, a large mullet gripped in her talons, then dropped onto the nest.

"My God, she's huge!" Caedmon cried, falling back against Harry.

"Her wingspan's between seven and eight feet," Harry said, his arms around her.

"Will she attack us?" Caedmon asked in a not quite steady voice.

"No," Harry said, "we're not threatening her chicks, and we're too big to eat. Seen enough?"

"Yes. I can't see her anyway. I had no idea, Harry. She's

magnificent. Did you see her bill?"

"All the better to eat you with, my dear."

"Not funny."

They walked away, with Caedmon looking back every few yards until the nest was lost to sight.

For the next two days, Harry waded around in the Stickpen Preserve counting wood stork nests for the Fish and Game Commission. After dinner on the second day, he was working online at his computer, filing his report, when his house phone rang.

"I'm worried," Rowena Farnham said, and sounded it. "Maria Fuegos' daughter, Theresa, just called me to say that her mother has not come home from work and is not answering her cell phone."

Harry glanced at his watch. "What time does she usually come home?"

"Theresa says that Wednesdays she comes home at four."

"Four hours late," Harry said. "How old is the girl?"

"Twenty-two. She's in her last year at the University."

"At Florida Gulf Coast U.?"

"Yes, and she would not be calling me unless she was genuinely concerned."

"Does she know about her mother's going to talk with Jim?"

"I wondered the same thing, but I didn't dare to ask."

"No. Has she called the Ogilvies?"

"Yes, the butler said Maria left at three-thirty."

"Does she ever do things like go to an early movie on these Wednesdays?"

"Never. Theresa says she always comes home and paints. I didn't know exactly what she meant, but she says her mother has painted botanicals for years."

"It's highly specialized work," Harry said. "Artists working in botanicals usually paint flowers and grasses, although those who do illustrations for books and journals may be drawing and painting anything from mushrooms to trees. Some of the work is extremely beautiful."

"Theresa says that she has galleries in New York calling her all the time with assignments but that Maria doesn't take half of them, preferring to paint what interests her."

"She's got to be very good," Harry said. "Is there a man in her life?"

"What a question! I don't know, but I think Theresa would have known and checked."

"Are you concerned enough to have me call Jim's office and ask if she has been talking with anyone there today?"

"I think so. Theresa seemed quite upset. And after what you said the other day, I'm worried too."

"It's late, and they may not tell me anyway, but I can try."

"And why would you be calling me?" Lieutenant Maureen O'Reilly demanded, sounding as if had Harry been in her office, she would have cut out his liver and eaten it.

Maureen O'Reilly looked down on the world from an elevation without heels of more than six feet, with blazing green eyes, flaming red hair, a body that might have just stepped off a marble pedestal, and a fearsome reputation for mayhem. But Harry, who had to look up when talking to her, had won her indulgence if not her heart by ignoring her Celtic scowls and dark threats and telling her he had only one goal in life, which was to die on her breast, a protestation that invariably sent her into gales of laughter.

"To hear your voice. Why are you still in the office?" he said.

"Short-handed and far behind. What do you want?"

"You know what I want," he told her, adding a heavy sigh.

"Oh, you randy devil," she said, her voice breaking toward

laughter. "Have you no shame at all?"

"Not where you're concerned, my little darling."

This went on for a while. Then he asked her what he wanted to know.

"Fuegos has not been in since the day she talked with Himself," O'Reilly said, having made the necessary inquiries. "Is there something I should know?"

"This is unofficial, but Fuegos did not come home from work this afternoon. Her daughter says she's usually home by four and never varies."

"Is it the Reverend Farnham then who told you this?"

"Yes, but neither of us thought it right to ask if she knows that her mother talked with Jim."

"Give me the daughter's name," O'Reilly said without hesitation. "I'll call her."

"I'm not sure . . ." Harry began.

"I am. There's no time to be lost. She must file a missing persons report with no more fiddling."

Harry tried to break in again, to no avail.

"Will you listen!" O'Reilly snapped. "I'll tell her no more than she has to know, and there'll be no Ogilvie in it. Go on now! Your 'little darlin'' has work . . ."

She couldn't finish the sentence because she couldn't speak for laughing. Harry hung up the phone, grinning like the Cheshire cat.

At ten the next morning, Harry, who had been parked for the past hour on a shady section of Bowline Drive, finally had his patience, which had worn very thin, rewarded. Thirty yards in front of him on the opposite side of the street, a slender blonde woman in tennis whites and wearing red-rimmed sunglasses came out a pedestrian gate in the stucco wall of the Turtle Beach Association and walked briskly along the sidewalk toward him, her black toy poodle trotting in front of her on a red leash.

Harry leaned back in his seat, raised the compact camcorder he had been holding in his lap, and filmed her as she approached and passed the Rover. She was holding a phone to her ear, and had not even glanced at him.

"She made a serious mistake," Harry said, stepping back from the outside wall of the tool shed to study the section of lapstrake wooden wall he had just stained. *I like that dark wood color,* he thought. *It would look good on my barn.*

"And she was suing Rideau Cleaners for half a million dollars," Tucker said, going on painting as he talked.

"That's right," Harry replied, returning to his task. "She was claiming permanent back pain that prevented her from walking without a cane."

"One of their delivery trucks did hit her, as I recall."

"Backed into her, according to her testimony. No one saw it happen. The driver heard a woman scream, jammed on his brakes, and leaped out of the truck. She was lying on the street, yelling her head off."

"Seems as if modern medical technology should be able to tell if she really was injured."

"It's the pain that can't be registered," Harry said.

"So what will happen now? By the way, you might talk and paint at the same time. That way, we won't still be painting here after the sun goes down."

"You're pretty critical for a man who's not even paying minimum wage."

"Stop complaining. What's happening with your skip tracer?"

Harry pulled a stained rag out of his back pocket, swearing loudly at the brush, and wiped a dribble of stain off his arm.

"With stain, you've got to wipe both sides of the brush on the edge of the pail," Tucker said. "It's thinner than paint. I thought you knew that."

"I forgot."

"You also forgot that you were going to live a life free of entanglements with women," Tucker said, working steadily.

"Now wait," Harry said. "That's not fair. I told you what had happened with Caedmon, and you've used it against me."

"Have you talked with Renata yet?"

"Jiminy Cricket," Harry complained, not wanting to be reminded of his foot-dragging.

"That's a *no*," Tucker said, pausing to frown at Harry. "She deserves better. Keep working."

"Yes, she does," Harry admitted, "and I'll talk with her as soon as I can decide how to tell her I can't go on seeing her."

Harry began putting some shoulder into his work and rapidly caught up with Tucker. The blazing sun had climbed high enough to strike the men's backs, and Harry noticed that Tucker was slowing in the heat. The front of his old and faded blue shirt, in addition to being spotted with stain, was dark with his sweat.

"This wall's almost done," he said. "Why don't you let me finish up while you get a head start on the cleanup?"

"All right," the old farmer said. "Come along as soon as you're done."

A few minutes later they were seated in the deep shade of Tucker's back stoop with glasses of cold cider in their hands.

"Go easy with that cider," Tucker said. "It's got a stick in it. Yesterday afternoon when I came in from the garden, Oh, Brother! and I had a couple of glasses of it—Sanchez is a teetotaler and won't touch it. The next thing I knew, I'd slept in this rocker right through to supper time. Sanchez complained that Oh, Brother! had been making silly jokes and was now stretched out in the barn asleep."

Harry decided to let that pass and said, "Maria Fuegos is missing."

"How long?"

"Maureen called Fuegos' daughter last night, to tell her she had to file a missing persons report. I haven't heard anything since."

"I hope the rule of three doesn't come into play," Tucker said.

"Meaning?"

"There are now two women missing by my count."

"Hadn't thought of that," Harry said just as Jane Bunting, Tucker's cat, appeared out of the woods, her bushy tail held high. She was followed by Frederica and Aurelius, her two full-grown kittens, both of whom were larger than their mother and had marked tufts of very dark hair on their ears, suggesting their father was a bobcat.

On their first meeting, Jane Bunting had shredded Harry's shirt, leaving him looking as if he had run into a thorn plum in the dark, but they had patched up a truce. By its terms, when they met, Jane Bunting would rub once against Harry's leg in greeting and he would scratch her briefly behind the ears. Frederica, however, had fallen in love with Harry as a kitten. Whenever he came for a visit, she would run straight at him and leap into his arms.

"Oh, God," Harry said, quickly putting down his glass. "Here she comes!"

And come she did, flying the final eight feet through the air and landing squarely on his chest. And because she weighed somewhere between twenty-five and thirty pounds, she landed like a hairy rocket. Fortunately for Harry, she kept her claws sheathed, but he and the rocker were knocked back almost to the tipping point.

"How do you suppose they keep from being coyote meat?"

Harry asked, once his purring, kneading armful of very affectionate cat had settled on his lap, loudly enjoying a thorough head and back scratch.

"Vigilance," Tucker said as Jane Bunting made her mandatory three full circles on his lap before curling up and apparently going instantly to sleep. "When they come out of the woods and onto the stoop, they're never more than two jumps from a tree."

"Does Aurelius ever get to sit in your lap?" Harry asked. "I remember that time he tried it on his own and Jane Bunting almost skinned him."

"That was a mistake he never repeated," Tucker said with a grin, "but I pick him up two or three times a day. If I do it, she doesn't seem to mind."

"Speaking of your animals, where are Sanchez and Oh, Brother!?"

Tucker's face clouded at the question.

"Out looking for that panther," he said gloomily. "I haven't been able to convince them that she's dangerous."

"One thing in their favor," Harry said, sorry he'd asked the question, "is that panthers are afraid of dogs, even a little one, which Sanchez isn't, and I think Oh, Brother!'s way too big for her to tackle."

"Have you seen her lately?" Tucker asked, showing no sign of having his mind eased by what Harry had said.

"Last week," Harry said. "She was up in the northeast corner of the Hammock. If she is going to have cubs, she's chosen a place as far away from us as she can get."

"Good," Tucker said. "I hope she stays just as far away from the road."

As Harry was leaving, Tucker said, "Good luck with Renata," spoiling all the good effects of the cider.

13

Harry got home to find a cryptic message from Caedmon saying she needed to see him. It was approaching noon, and Harry's first impulse was to call her and suggest lunch. But Tucker's reminder that it was necessary now and then to behave with some degree of decency tightened his cinch. Shaking inside like a poplar leaf, Harry dialed Jeff Smolkin's office instead, knowing he'd reach Renata.

"Will Number One let you out of your cage long enough to have lunch?" he asked when she answered.

"Do I know you?" she asked.

"In the Biblical sense you do," he said. "It's about the only way you do, but it's a start."

"Nasty," she said. "Are you suffering from snake bite?"

"Cider hangover," he said, "and I'm sorry. Let me try this again. If you can get away, I'd like to take you to lunch."

"Yes, but I'll only have an hour. Things are crazier here than usual."

"We could get takeout and eat while we were . . ."

To his relief, she laughed. "I'll be ready by the time you get here."

She was waiting outside for him.

"Where can we get a grouper sandwich that doesn't taste like yesterday's bait?" she asked, scrambling into the Rover before Harry had actually stopped.

"The Lagoon," he said, remembering too late that it was

where he used to take Soñadora Asturias, a woman who'd traded him in for a mountain village full of poverty-stricken people and a young priest who reminded her of her father. Harry had been trying for a long time to convince himself, with little success, that history did not strike twice in the same place.

"I've heard of it," she said. "What's happening with Breckenridge?"

"How much do you know?" Harry asked. Her question surprised him, having expected a grilling on his not having called following their all-night dinner date.

"Not much. Number One mentioned that he might be in trouble with the police."

"He is. Harley Dillard got a letter from Afton Breckenridge, saying that if she was missing when Harley got this letter, she would be dead, and her husband was the person who killed her."

Renata gave a low whistle. "Is she still missing?"

"The people looking for her can't find her, but that's different from saying she's missing."

"But it's a fairly strong hint," Renata suggested, her mouth twitching.

Harry laughed. "You have a sense of humor," he said.

"About a lot of things."

"Ahh," Harry said, "I expected this sooner."

"Well, you're not getting it on an empty stomach."

"My God," Renata said, her mouth half full, "this is awesome."

"There's juice on your chin," Harry said.

"Who cares?"

Harry watched as she took a second bite. "Maybe I should ask if anyone in here does the Heimlich maneuver," he said, "just to be prepared."

She put down her sandwich, chewed, swallowed, wiped her

chin with her napkin, and said, "Eat your damned sandwich. You're not getting any of mine, but if you're not finished when I am, I may fight you for what's left of yours."

Harry thought she might do that and concentrated on eating.

When they were finished, Harry said, "My father told me that his freshman year in college was the year WWII ended and the G.I. Bill was put into operation. He roomed with a man who had survived the Bataan Death March. If my father's description was accurate, the man ate the way you do, without speaking and without stopping until everything on his plate was gone."

While he talked, Renata was wetting the end of her finger on her tongue. She picked up all the remaining crumbs on her plate and put them in her mouth.

"Heartbreaking," she said and checked her watch when the crumbs were gone. "Let's go."

"First," she said when they were in the Rover and Harry was backing out of the parking space, "thank you. That was the best grouper sandwich I ever ate in my life, no comparison."

"You're welcome. You seemed to enjoy it."

He did not get the laugh he had expected, nor had he delayed Renata's agenda.

"What comes now is a lot less pleasant," she said.

"Renata," Harry began, "I'm sorry I didn't call you. There's no excuse . . ."

"That's right, Harry," she said in a conversational voice. "There isn't. I have every reason to be insulted and angry, and you're lucky I'm not Lorena Bobbitt."

"That bad," Harry said.

"Worse. You're sleeping with Caedmon Rivers, aren't you?"

"I wasn't when you and I . . ."

"I'm glad to hear it," Renata said. "Now, here's a confession from this side of the aisle. I went out with you for the same reason you went out with me."

"Not quite," Harry said.

"No, not quite," Renata said quietly, turning her head away to look out her side window. "I've been in love with Number One since God's dog was a pup. You were falling in love with Rivers and thought shagging me might break your fall."

"How did you guess?" Harry asked.

Renata fished a tissue out of her purse, wiped her eyes and blew her nose, and turned back to look at Harry.

"I've known you a long time, Harry. You had to have guessed about Number One and me, although I'm betting you thought I was his outside woman. Well, I wasn't, and, luckily for you, I found out that much as I like you and enjoyed our night together, I wasn't going to be able to go on with it."

"It was a wonderful night," Harry said, glad that he didn't have to lie.

"Thank you. That really helps. I knew that your losing Soñadora had knocked you way back on your heels. So it wasn't hard for me, when I thought about it, to see that you must have taken a dive over Rivers and it had scared you."

"That's about it," Harry said, reaching over and squeezing her hand.

They sat looking at one another for awhile without speaking. Then she said, "Maybe the next time around, Harry."

"I should be so lucky," he said, and meant it.

"You're not paying attention, Harry," Caedmon said, a slight frown line forming between her eyes.

"Sorry," Harry said.

Ever since leaving Renata at her office, he had been trying to understand why in the short time he and Renata had talked about their dinner and what followed, he had come to feel closer to her than he had in all the hours they had spent together drinking, walking, talking, eating, and making love.

He couldn't seem to get his mind off it.

"Is something troubling you?" Caedmon asked with less edge.

"No," Harry said. "No, go ahead."

Caedmon leaned forward on the couch and said, "I don't know what it means, and it may mean nothing, but this morning while I was talking with Ernan, he said that Mrs. Breckenridge and Gwen Ogilvie are very close friends. Is this new information for you?"

"It certainly is. Breckenridge never mentioned their relationship," Harry said, "but he's never said much of anything about his wife."

"No animosity?"

"None. According to him they never quarreled."

"Have you taken note of the fact that now two people connected with the Ogilvies have disappeared?"

"I think I might have gotten there," Harry said, stung.

"Don't be sore, chum. I've been chewing on this for several hours."

"Did you find out anything else from Ernan?"

"Nothing else half as interesting as what I've just told you. Are you going to talk to her?"

"Maybe," Harry said, considering the possibility.

Caedmon got up, dropped the file she had been holding on the couch, and walked over to stand in front of him, hands on her hips. "Are we eating out or in tonight?" she asked, as if the fate of nations hung on the answer.

Harry got up, smiling at the thought. She was wearing a sleeveless, lavender sundress. With her hair pulled back, Harry thought she was breathtaking. He told her so.

"Flatterer," she told him, suppressing a smile. "Here's another question, answering is optional. Who did you have lunch with?"

"Renata Holland, Jeff Smolkin's Good Woman Friday and

every other day of the week, except Sunday."

"Do I detect some bitterness?"

"Yes. He runs her off her feet and treats her as if she was a piece of furniture."

"You mean he's not doing her."

"Right."

"Are you?"

Harry felt his face burn.

"Of course not!"

"Would you like to?"

Harry put his hands on her waist and drew her to him, but she put her hands on his chest, to hold herself back.

"That's not an answer."

"You shouldn't be asking me that."

"Don't change the subject."

"Over the years the thought has passed through my mind."

"Why haven't you?"

"Perhaps I have."

"But although she's not wearing a ring, she's already taken."

"That's about it," Harry said rather sadly.

"I know," she said, sliding her arms around his neck. "After I'd been with them ten minutes I saw it. Sad, really."

"Yes, it is. About tonight. How about having dinner at my place?"

"You're not planning to serve alligator or bear or some other exotic entrée, are you?"

"I was thinking of grilled red snapper, roasted peppers, and a potato salad. Before we eat, we'll take a walk and listen to the symphony."

"What symphony?"

"It's a surprise."

"Okay. Oh, my goodness! Two surprises!"

★　★　★　★　★

By the time Harry—with Caedmon's help—had made the salad, sliced the yellow, orange, and the green peppers, and readied the snappers for the grill, the sun was backlighting the top half of the live oaks surrounding the house and casting dense shadows across the lawn and sandy road.

"I still don't see why I have to wear slacks," Caedmon complained. "It's still hot as hell. And sneakers instead of sandals! Do you have a clothes fetish you haven't told me about?"

"Your feet excite me, and I didn't want to be distracted while I was making dinner. Let's go before we lose the light."

Harry had been thinking for several minutes how extraordinarily pleasant it was having a woman in his house, especially this one, but the feeling was tinged with an elusive sadness brought by memories he would rather not be having. Shaking off his reflections, he dropped a small pair of binoculars, a can of Deep Woods Off, and the sweater she had draped on a chair into his shoulder sack and led Caedmon out of the house onto the sandy lawn.

"This is much nicer than I expected," Caedmon said, looking around with obvious interest, "and your house is whistle clean."

"So is yours," Harry said.

"I wasn't being condescending," Caedmon protested. "I like order and cleanliness. I also like not having to hold my nose when I kiss you."

Harry laughed.

"You're a picture no artist could paint," he said.

"Where did you hear that old-fashioned expression?"

"Probably in Maine. We're going this way," Harry said when they reached the road, and pointed them deeper into the Hammock with the dark water of Puc Puggy Creek sliding along on their right.

"This is much cooler," Caedmon said, rubbing her arms, as they walked out of the broken sunlight that fell through the oaks and into the deeper shade of the unthinned woods.

"It's the height of the trees that does it," Harry said, fishing the cardigan out of his shoulder sack and draping it across her shoulders. "It's usually ten degrees cooler out here than in town and cooler than that at night."

Pausing to adjust the sweater, Caedmon actually looked through the bushes on her right to where the creek water flashed and bubbled softly. A small fish broke silver and sparkling through the surface, glistened briefly in the light, then dove back into the water with a distinct plop.

"What's the name of this little river?" she asked.

"Puc Puggy Creek," he said. "It's named after the botanist John Bartram, who according to legend passed through here in the early eighteenth century."

"What does it mean?"

"Flower Hunter, a name the Indians gave him."

"You said it was legend, but the name's here."

"Very sharp. He never did come this far south and spent most of his time wandering in the St. John's River area in the northeastern part of the state, but the name stuck."

As the sun sank lower behind the trees, the white sand of the narrow road looked more and more white. A breeze began to stir the leaves and whisper in the branches, stirring the damp feral smell of the forest.

"That's a wonderful smell," Caedmon said, moving a bit closer to Harry, "but is it all right to be walking out here?"

"Absolutely," Harry said.

He had been watching two male cardinals, glowing a brilliant red and flickering from branch to branch in a gum tree, screaming threats at one another. He was about to call Caedmon's attention to them when she broke her silence.

"Oh," she said, pointing up the road. "Look. There's two yellow dogs off their leashes."

"They're not dogs," Harry said quietly, stopping her by putting his hand on her arm.

"What are they?" she whispered.

"Coyotes," he replied.

The two golden brown animals were standing in the road, caught in a soft beam of light that had penetrated the canopy. Heads up and ears pricked, they stared at the two humans, displaying interest but no obvious fear.

"They're beautiful," Caedmon said.

"Yes, they are," Harry said.

Then a vagary of the wind carried their scent to the two animals. Together, they vanished silently into the undergrowth.

"I thought coyotes lived in Arizona," Caedmon said, still speaking in a whisper.

"And in every other state with the possible exception of Delaware," Harry said, then laughed.

As they went on walking and talking in the slowly fading light, the clouds over the road and the wide and treeless swamp east of the creek turned pink from the sunset, giving the white road a faint rose glow.

"You live in a weird place, Harry Brock," Caedmon said, slipping a hand under his arm and gazing at the towering thunderheads to the east, awash in reflected colors, "but it's beautiful."

"It's not really weird," he said quietly. "It is profoundly integrated, which should appeal to you. Everything is exactly where it should be. If it weren't, it wouldn't be there."

"Is this another version of, 'His eye is on the sparrow'?" she asked with a slightly mocking smile.

"No, it's more about the sparrow's eye being exactly as it must be."

The light dropped further. Caedmon gave Harry a puzzled

look. "Nothing changes? I don't believe that."

"You shouldn't. Everything changes."

They had begun walking again, Caedmon frowning, apparently considering Harry's response. Then suddenly they were engulfed by the sound of a multitude of tiny silver bells chiming. The ringing grew louder, sustained itself for several seconds, and then slid away into silence.

"What in the world?" Caedmon asked, turning to Harry, her eyes widening.

"The orchestra is warming up," Harry told her, stopping and taking the insect repellent out of his sack. "Close your eyes," he told her, having felt the first needles of midge bites on his neck.

"What for?"

"Midges and mosquitoes that come out every night to enjoy the music and drink blood."

"Ouch, spray my arms," she said, holding them out. "They feel as if they were on fire."

While the ceremony of spraying one another went forward, section after section of the woods and swamp began to ring with chimes and bells and harsher sounds.

"What's doing it?" Caedmon asked as Harry turned them back toward the house.

"Frogs, colony frogs, and no two colonies sound just alike."

"Why not?"

Harry laughed. "It's all about sex. It's a general announcement by the males of the colonies that they're ready to have it. The females are attracted by the piping of the males in their own colony, and the rest is what you think it is, except that when the male clambers onto the female's back and clasps her with his front and rear legs, she lays her eggs, and he covers them with sperm as they emerge."

"You mean they never get to really do it?" Caedmon demanded in an offended voice.

"That's right. It's all external."

"Disgusting," she said. "Don't tell me any more."

"It works for the frogs," Harry said.

"Yeah, great! He has a premature ejaculation, and she lays eggs. How lucky can you get?"

Caedmon dropped his arm and showed every sign of being angry. Worked up as she was, she began walking faster, and had gotten slightly ahead of him when she sudden gave a loud yell, broke into a sort of dance, and flung herself back against Harry.

"I think I stepped on a snake!" she cried. "A God-awful, great big thing!"

In the swiftly advancing darkness, Harry had seen it too late to warn her.

"It's OK," Harry said, catching her in his arms and preventing her from sprinting back up the road. "It doesn't bite."

"It was huge, Harry. It stretched all the way across the road, and I put my foot on it, and it squirmed!"

"It didn't like being stepped on any more than you enjoyed stepping on it. It's all right. It's gone."

"What was it?" Caedmon asked, regaining most of her composure.

"An indigo snake," Harry said. "It was enjoying the leftover warmth in the sand. I wish the sun had been shining. Its skin is the darkest, most beautiful brilliant blue you have ever seen."

"Oh, God! What if I'd been barefoot?"

"It would have been an even more exciting experience."

By now the frogs were in full chorus, and they walked home hand in hand. Caedmon had fallen silent, and Harry left her to herself. He thought he knew what was happening. The Hammock tended to awaken those parts of the mind dealing with sensory experience and dampen cognitive thought.

"Why didn't the snake bite me?" Caedmon asked as they began to eat.

"It knew it couldn't swallow you," Harry said.

"You think you're being funny," she said, but smiled. "I still think you live in a weird place."

"Do you like it?"

"Yes, I think I do, please pass the butter."

Long after midnight, she wakened Harry, whispering in his ear, "Wake up, wake up."

"What's wrong?"

"Listen."

A moment later he heard the booming call of an owl.

"It's a barred owl," he told her. "A pair is nesting in the oaks behind the barn. Did it wake you?"

"Yes. Would you mind holding me? I feel a little too close to . . . things. Why is he making such a racket?"

"They have nestlings," Harry said, putting his arms around her. "This one, which sounds like the female, is hunting for mice and rabbits. Does this feel better?"

"Much better. Look how the moonlight is falling across the bed."

"One should never waste moonlight," Harry said, kissing her forehead.

"Mmm. Just what I was thinking."

After they had made love Harry lay awake, watching the moon in the window, feeling her heart beating against him. His mind should have been at rest and it was, almost, but for the cold trickle of dread set in motion by the unwelcome thought that everything does indeed change.

14

"Rivers is certain?" Breckenridge demanded.

"Yes," Harry said. "Mrs. Breckenridge or someone with access to her accounts has cashed out all assets and wired the money to Panama."

The two men were on the dock in front of Breckenridge's house, preparing to take the dinghy out to Breckenridge's day sailer, a shining bright, white Catalina 250, bobbing its bow in the ripples of the outgoing tide. At the news, Breckenridge dropped more than set down the cooler and wicker lunch basket he was holding. Harry was standing in the dinghy, waiting to stow them between the seats.

"Are you telling me *everything* she had is gone?" he asked, his face paling under its tan.

"That's what Caedmon says."

"Where's it gone?"

"She thinks probably into an anonymous corporation account in Panama," Harry said. "An anonymous corporation—"

"I don't need to be told what a fucking anonymous corporation account is," Breckenridge grated and suddenly began shoving things from the dock at Harry, his face still pale and stripped of expression. When he was finished, he nearly dumped them both into the river while clambering into the dinghy.

"Start the engine, Brock," he said when he managed to land on the bow seat. "Get us out of here, and I wish to God I was going to China."

Harry unfastened the last line, tossed it onto the dock, switched on the little electric outboard, and got them quietly under way. Breckenridge sat, his elbows resting on his knees, holding his head in his hands like a man *in extremis*.

Harry left him to his own thoughts for a couple of minutes, then said, "There may be an upside to this. Caedmon hasn't yet been able to establish for certain that it is Mrs. Breckenridge who has made the transfers. If she can, it would mean that your wife was alive when the transactions occurred."

Breckenridge straightened up and rubbed his face, then turned to look at the Catalina.

"Come up on the lee side of her," he said, then added, "I suppose I should take some comfort from that, but I don't."

He stood up and caught the side of the boat. It struck Harry as a fine irony, to see as they drew closer that the boat's name was *Afton*. Breckenridge dragged himself awkwardly onto the sailboat, leaving Harry to unload the dinghy. That done, Harry tied the dinghy to the mooring buoy and waited for Breckenridge to start the inboard motor while he finished preparations to cast off.

"Let's go," Breckenridge shouted, flaunting proprieties. Harry freed the *Afton*'s mooring line, tossed it aboard, and grabbed the swimming ladder as Breckenridge slammed the engine into forward gear.

Harry wasn't an ardent sailor and harbored no hankerings to go to sea, but his heart beat a little higher whenever he stepped into the cockpit of a good boat and felt it come to life under his feet, and heard the hum of the wind in the rigging, even if it was only the boat's quiet inboard and not the sails that propelled them out into the channel.

"Why wouldn't it help to know your wife is still alive?" he asked from the comfort of one of the observation chairs as they slid through Snook Pass and into Avola Bay.

Breckenridge was handling the wheel skillfully, easing Harry's concerns about the man's competence on the water, but he was withholding final judgment until the sails were hoisted.

"She owns a very sizeable chunk of Dominion Investments. If she has run off, and if she decides to divorce me, those shares may bite me in the ass."

"Was that why you refused to divorce her when she found out about Beatrice Frazer?"

"She's known about my relationship with Frazer for more than a year."

Not really an answer, Harry thought as they passed the final channel marker and turned north. Breckenridge cut the motor and quickly winched up the mainsail.

"Very handy having the halyards managed from the cockpit," Harry said.

"This is a pretty good pocket sailer. I bought her when I was just getting the fund under way. I've got an Antares Lagoon 421 in the town docks, but it's too big for this kind of use."

"A blue water catamaran," Harry said, impressed. "Have you done any cruising?"

"Nova Scotia last summer," Breckenridge said, and ran up the jib. "Afton doesn't like sailing. She's afraid of the water."

Harry assumed that Beatrice Frazer had been his companion on the trip.

The Catalina responded quickly to the brisk southwest breeze and was soon running through the water with a bright, purling sound that lifted Harry's spirits. Breckenridge tied off the wheel and sat down in the second observation chair.

"I'd live out here if I could," he said.

There was, Harry thought, no posturing, no bullying, no manipulation in the statement, but he could hear the pain clearly enough. *Serves you right,* he thought, then checked himself, recalling the adjuration about casting the first stone. He probably didn't qualify.

"Where do you stand with Harley Dillard?" Harry asked.

"I put it in the hands of my attorneys," Breckenridge said. "It's too crazy for me to deal with."

"What do you think is going on here?"

Breckenridge glanced at the sails, got up and brought the boat into the wind a few degrees, bringing her starboard scupper closer to the water, and increased her speed. A fine little boat, Harry thought.

"I don't know," Breckenridge said, scowling again. "I know you think Afton's run off with somebody, taking all her cash with her, and the sheriff's people may actually think I killed her. They're dumb enough to believe that."

"I don't think your wife has run off with someone, but it's one of the options. That she ran off alone is another, that someone kidnapped her and is systematically emptying her accounts is another."

Harry paused to see how Breckenridge responded to the corrections. Seeing nothing but the same stubborn scowl, he went on. "It would be a serious strategic mistake for you to misjudge the competence of Jim Snyder and his staff. There may be some hayseed in their hair, but it's on display as camouflage. Don't be taken in."

Breckenridge snorted, possibly in derision. "Prepare to come about," he said.

That maneuver accomplished, he put the boat on a port tack and sat down again.

"One of the things I like about sailing," he said, his scowl fading, "is the simplicity. A limited number of options. You choose one and either execute it correctly or you don't. Limited gray areas. You, the boat, the water, and the weather."

"You left out the waterlogged tree trunk drifting just under the surface, the rogue wave, and the uncharted reef," Harry said, revealing more of himself, perhaps, than he had intended.

His codicil got a laugh from Breckenridge. "Or the fatal heart attack," he said in a surprisingly cheerful voice. Harry's comment seemed to have buoyed his spirits.

"Do you know Peter and Gwen Ogilvie?" Harry asked, hoping to elicit an unguarded answer.

"Not well," Breckenridge replied, his eyes on an approaching jet skier. "Afton saw more of them than I did. I think she and Gwen are friends."

The skier shot across their wake close enough to have slapped the boat's stern had Breckenridge leaned back and extended his hand.

"Stupid son-of-a-bitch!" Breckenridge shouted, half rising from his chair and staring after the rider.

The roar of the jet ski's engine as it blasted apart the quiet sounds of their own passage through the water left Harry jarred and vaguely angry as well. The disruption also momentarily drove out of his mind his reaction to Breckenridge's use of the present tense when speaking of his wife. Was it a positive indicator? Uncertain—depending on whether or not the use was calculated.

"Flaming youth," Harry said with a wry expression, once their visitor had gone bouncing and bucking away in a cloud of flying spray and stinking exhaust.

"What made you ask?" Breckenridge gave Harry a sharp look.

"Someone remembered having seen them together, and I was wondering whether or not it was worthwhile talking to Mrs. Ogilvie."

"Can't hurt," Breckenridge said, apparently losing interest. "But I'll make a side bet with you that you won't get much from the effort—and it will take some effort to get near her."

He grinned at Harry. "Once she finds out what you do for a living, I doubt that you'll see her at all."

"Comes with the country," Harry said. "Why do you think Mrs. Ogilvie won't tell me much?"

"Two things. She may not want to say anything about Afton, and I've always found Afton very unforthcoming with information about herself. I've never known a third of what's going on in her head. It's been like getting to know a tree."

Harry noted the bitterness but moved on, deciding to think about it later.

"Here's a question for you," Breckenridge said, stretching in his chair as if trying to relax. "Where do *you* think that wonk Dillard is going with Afton's accusation?"

"It can be determined pretty easily whether or not she wrote it. And even if she did, there's still the possibility that she wrote it under pressure. Dillard's aware of all that, and I'm sure he's going to proceed very carefully."

"You mean this could be dragged out until they find her?"

"Or until they're satisfied they're not going to find her," Harry said, "in which case they may or may not indict you."

"Couldn't it just become a cold case?"

"Yes," Harry agreed, "but neither the state's attorney's office nor the police like open files. They're constant reminders of failures and fodder for their critics, as well as being like bad investments."

"Are you saying I might be tried for murder just to close a file?"

"I'm afraid so."

"All that damned publicity!" Breckenridge cried.

"There's a good side to it," Harry put in. "If you didn't kill her, they probably won't be able to convict you. In which case, you walk away safe, free of any taint."

Harry didn't really believe that, but there was some truth in what he had said. Of course, he knew that unless she was found alive, there would always be the possibility in people's minds that he had gotten away with murder.

"What the hell's that?" Breckenridge shouted, grasping the wheel and turning the boat into the wind, leaving the sails to snap and ripple futilely.

"Turtle," Harry said, having sprung to his feet to see what Breckenridge was looking at.

Their forward motion had carried them past the turtle and toward the shore; but Breckenridge quickly furled the mainsail and the jib, started the engine, and brought the boat around to the lee side of the floating animal.

"That's a big turtle," Breckenridge said as they idled, the wind holding them about five yards from the black head and large, soulful eyes watching them. The animal's shell was awash, the large flippers extended and at rest.

"It's a female," Harry said. "I'd guess she weighs about three hundred pounds."

"She'd make a lot of soup," Breckenridge said with a grin. "What kind is it?"

"Loggerhead," Harry said. "She's late, but she's probably already made a couple of nests; and she's resting out here, getting ready to dig her final nest for the year."

"How do you know it's a female?"

"Her size. Male loggerheads are much smaller."

Breckenridge, still watching the turtle, grunted and pushed the throttle ahead.

"Screwing must be damned difficult," he said as the boat gathered speed.

Jim had pulled off his hat and was standing at the top of the bank, staring into the water and rubbing his head. The afternoon sun was brutal, but Harry knew it was useless to remind him that he burned from exposure to a flashlight. Frank Hodges was helping the ambulance people get their gurney down the steep incline to where the crime scene team was photographing and making a record of the body, tangled in weeds and spread-eagled, face down in the water.

Harry had noticed a vulture drawing lazy circles high above their heads, and thought that there was always someone watching, waiting their turn, confident it would come. Then Jim's voice pulled him back to earth.

"I'd like to know why," Jim said peevishly, replacing his hat as if it had offended him, "when someone is killed, they have to be thrown into the Luther Faubus Canal."

"It's a tradition," Harry said, "and it gives the place a certain cachet."

"Very funny."

Just then Hodges, who was struggling red-faced up the bank toward them, called out, "It's a woman, Hispanic, shot once in the back of the head."

He tried to say more but had run out of breath and was gasping when he reached them.

"Frank," Jim said in a concerned voice, "you've got to do something about your weight. A man your age ought not to get winded climbing a thirty-foot bank."

"It's a lot more than thirty feet," Hodges protested, getting the words out between gasps. "And it's steep as a cliff."

Harry knew where this was going and intervened. "What do you think the chances are it's Maria Fuegos?" he asked.

The question caught both men's attention. They forgot their argument and turned to watch the activities at the water's edge, which from a distance looked like an arcane baptismal ceremony.

"Lord in heaven!" Jim exploded. "Where has my head been?" With that he plunged down the bank.

"Don't bag her!" he shouted as the ambulance team, two men and a woman all dressed in blue coveralls, blue caps, and face masks, were wrestling the body out of the water and into a large, blue body bag.

"Is this a style statement?" Harry wondered aloud as he strode after Jim.

"And that's just who it is," Jim said to Harry when he joined the little group, standing around the dead woman.

"You recognize her, Captain?" the lieutenant in charge of the crime scene team asked, sloshing through the water toward them.

"Yes," Jim said, without looking away from the body. "Zip her up, Judy," he told the woman and immediately turned away, looking across the canal to the empty sweep of saw-grass swamp.

Harry knew that Jim, despite his years of dealing with death and the human toll of violence and mayhem, found having to look at dead people deeply distressing. He could not watch an autopsy without becoming sick.

"Her name's Maria Fuegos, Lieutenant," he said in a low voice. "I'll add the details to your report later."

"Fine, Captain," the officer said, and splashed back to his people, who were working with cameras, sketchbooks, and measuring tapes and taking water and soil samples, and bagging the weeds from Fuegos' body and labeling everything.

"You OK, Jim?" Harry asked quietly.

"Not really, but there's nothing to do about it." He paused, shook his head, and said, "What a terrible mess we've made of this beautiful world."

"Good or bad," Harry said, in an effort to get his friend's mind off Fuegos, "we've still got to climb this bank or live permanently with the alligators."

"You're getting as bad as Frank," Jim said with a frown and waded up through the grass and weeds toward the road where Hodges was waiting for them, mopping his face with a red and white bandana.

"And this is only May!" he complained when Harry reached

him. Jim had gone straight to the cruiser and was making a call.

"Did you hear?" Harry asked.

"And I saw him looking at the body, too," Hodges said in an undertone. "How bad is it?"

"About medium, I'd say."

"I suppose he had to look at her, now or later," Hodges said, then added, "This business about his wife ain't helping him none."

"He told me the other day that trouble Kathleen had over finding herself pregnant and the depression after the baby came was all behind them. He said she was happy."

"Wishful thinking," Hodges said, "but you know, she's not really been right since."

"Are they talking to one another?"

"Pass the salt. Let the cat out."

"As bad as that."

"And all over his taking that new deputy out to lunch," Hodges said with obvious disgust. "All he was doing was making her feel welcome."

"Apparently, Kathleen thinks there's more to it."

"Can you see the captain sneaking around, lying, renting rooms so he and that blonde kid can have a nooner? I'd sooner believe he was screwing goats."

"What have you got against goats?" Harry asked, provoking a bellow of laughter from Hodges that was cut short by Jim's arrival.

"Fuegos was in to see you, wasn't she, Captain?" Hodges asked, making a fast recovery.

"Last week," Jim said. "Harry, I've got to get back to the office. Thanks for coming out. Frank, let's go."

"Wait," Harry said, startled at the oversight, "we're forgetting Theresa."

"Who?" Jim demanded impatiently.

144

"Maria's daughter."

"Oh, my God!" Jim exploded. "Did they live together?"

"Yes."

"Then she's as much at risk of being shot as her mother."

"Rowena knows her. There's Haven House."

"The battered women's safe house, run by St. Jude's."

"That's the one."

"How old is she?"

"Twenty-two. She's a day student at FGCU."

"I'll have Maureen locate her. Then I'll break the news. If she's in any shape to listen, I'll tell her she should leave the house. Is there family?"

"I don't think so, not in Avola anyway."

"Maybe Rowena Farnham can talk with her."

"Maybe. There's something I've got to tell you," Harry said.

Jim stopped. "Make it short."

He knows we were talking about him, Harry thought, looking at the lawman's pale and lined face and thinking how long he and Kathleen had waited to make a family, and what a miserable mistake it had been so far.

"Afton Breckenridge and Gwen Ogilvie have been friends for some time," he said. "How close they were probably depends on who you ask. I thought you ought to know."

"You were right. Who told you this?"

"Caedmon. She learned about the connection while talking with Ernan, Breckenridge's butler. He mentioned it as though it were common knowledge. I asked Breckenridge if he knew the Ogilvies, and he said slightly, but he thought Afton and Gwen were friends."

"Did he say anything else?"

"I asked if anything would be gained by my talking with Gwen Ogilvie about Afton's whereabouts. I found his answer interesting."

"Harry, you do not keep Lieutenant O'Reilly waiting."

Harry smiled. "I'm glad to see you haven't lost your sense of humor."

"Harry."

"Breckenridge said he thought I wouldn't learn anything from Ogilvie because there was a good chance she wouldn't talk to me; and if she did, she wouldn't know anything because Afton didn't tell anyone what she was thinking. He added that penetrating his wife's reserve was like getting to know a tree."

He did not say he intended to interview Gwen Ogilvie, thus avoiding being told the department had first dibs on her.

"Has he said other negative things about his wife?"

"Captain!" Hodges called from the cruiser. "It's the O'Reilly again."

"Lord, there truly is no rest for the weary," Jim groaned. "And I've got to tell the Fuegos girl we've found her mother. We'll talk later."

Harry watched Jim hurry toward the cruiser, and thought of Rowena Farnham and how she would take the news. Then he thought of Caedmon.

15

To Harry's surprise, Gwen Ogilvie returned his call and, after a short and crisp conversation, agreed to see him. She was not what he expected. He had, of course, seen grainy pictures of her in the *Banner* and among the glossy portraits of the vain and vulgar ephemera published in *AVOLA* Magazine. But he found her neither vain nor vulgar.

"Please sit down, Mr. Brock," she said, having shaken hands with him. "I wish this meeting were on a more pleasant subject."

He had been met at the door by a young, uniformed maid, whose only words during their long walk were, "This way, please." The maid had met his attempts at conversation with stony silence, leading Harry to conclude that *This way, please* was all the English she knew. But the long walk was far from dull. The hallways and stairwell he traversed, as well as the walls of the several rooms he looked into while following his guide, were hung with stunning paintings. Many were the Dutch genre paintings he recognized, but many others were early twentieth-century American Impressionist works: New England gardens, women in sun hats and flowing summer dresses, and glimpses of the sea.

Located on the second floor of a large, rambling, cream-colored house in South Avola, set sixty yards back from the tree-lined avenue on spacious grounds with mature trees and shrubs, intermingled with flower beds and manicured lawns, the house was completely screened from the street and other houses.

The two west-facing French doors in the Ogilvies' second-floor study opened onto a balcony beyond which fifty yards of emerald-green lawn ended at a gated iron fence. Beyond the fence stretched the white beach and the green Gulf, glittering in the afternoon sun.

"Did you know Mrs. Breckenridge well?" Harry asked.

"I like to think so," Gwen Ogilvie said, dropping into a chair. "She's a friend. Why did you use the past tense in referring her?"

Gwen Ogilvie was short, slim, and decisive in her movements. Harry guessed she was in her fifties and was also aware that her gray eyes had been steadily weighing him. She was dressed unapologetically in tennis whites and sneakers. The sneakers were worn and grass stained, and her short, lightly streaked brown hair needed brushing. Harry thought she might have just come off the court, although she did not appear to be perspiring. She wore no makeup except for the sunscreen that made her nose shiny.

Her question stopped him for a moment. "I was not aware I had," he said. "I hope I haven't upset you."

"Do you think she's dead?" Ogilvie asked, showing no signs of distress.

"There are several possibilities," Harry replied, "and one of them is that she has been killed. The state's attorney's office, through the Sheriff's Department, is working on the problem. I'm also trying to find her—without much success."

"Which means Gregory has told you that he doesn't know where she is."

Harry tried to decide whether or not she was trying to mislead him. He decided he would assume she wasn't and see what happened. "Do you have any idea of her whereabouts?"

"No. Doesn't it strike you as unlikely that he doesn't know where his own wife is?"

"When was the last time you saw Mrs. Breckenridge?"

"Why haven't you answered my question?"

"It suggests Mr. Breckenridge is lying. Do you think he's lying?"

"I'm not in a position to say."

"Neither am I."

They sat for a moment in silence, Harry waiting for her to answer the question. One of the French doors was open and somewhere close by a cardinal was singing. The bird's clear, sharp notes burst around them in the still room like silver bubbles.

"I don't recall, exactly," she said. "Maria kept my appointment book, and at the moment I don't know where it is. Her death has rattled me. I hadn't realized how much I depended on her."

For all the grief her voice conveyed, Harry thought Ogilvie might have been talking about losing her Blackberry. "Had she worked for you long?"

"Six years. I will miss her, and replacing her will be a daunting task. I dread it." She gave a slight shudder, braced her back, and said, "I don't think there's much more I can tell you, Mr. Brock. I'm afraid I haven't been much help."

Harry took a calculated gamble that might get him thrown out. "Did Mrs. Breckenridge ever discuss her husband's affair with you?"

"You've crossed a boundary, Mr. Brock," she told him in a cold voice.

"Yes," Harry said evenly, "but your friend, if she's still alive, may be in serious trouble. If we are to find her, knowing her state of mind—angry, despairing—could help us to learn what she's done, where she's gone, what may have been done to her."

He paused and, seeing no relenting in Ogilvie's expression, added, "The relationship with Beatrice Frazer is already public

149

knowledge. The media hasn't found it yet, but they will very soon; so nothing's to be gained by pretending Afton Breckenridge's privacy has been violated."

"I see that I'm going to have to revise my opinion of you, Mr. Brock," Ogilvie said in the same cold, detached voice.

Harry waited while the wheels turned; and having had about all he wanted of Gwen Ogilvie's company, didn't give a damn whether she threw him out or not.

"Of course, I had guessed that Gregory was having an affair," Ogilvie said after a pause, during which she seemed to be listening to the cardinal, "but Afton never said word one about her relationship with Gregory. It was odd, really. I tried once to get her to say something about it, but I saw by her reaction that if I persisted I would lose a friend."

"Can you say anything about her state of mind the last time you saw her?"

"She seemed much as she always was, pleasant, conversational, and self-contained."

"Thank you," Harry said, standing up. "Everything you've said corroborates everything else I've been able to learn about Mrs. Breckenridge, which is very little. But I have one final question, and it's off the record. Your answer will not be for attribution. Do you think you knew her well?"

"The past tense again," Ogilvie said with a thin smile.

She had risen with Harry and seemed to be at ease with him again.

"Mr. Breckenridge said to me that getting to know Afton was like getting to know a tree," Harry said.

Ogilvie looked away briefly, then said quietly, "I think he got it about right, but she's delightful company, well-read, intelligent, and possesses a wickedly mordant wit."

"Too mordant, possibly," Harry said, thinking of the letter in Harley Dillard's possession.

"Maria Fuegos is dead," Rowena said in a shattered voice.

"Yes, I'm sorry. How are you?"

"We killed her, Harry," she said. "I don't yet know how I will be able to live with that knowledge."

"We didn't kill her, Rowena. It was done by someone with a gun."

"Don't be so superficial, Harry," she told him, anger boiling up suddenly in her voice.

Harry was not surprised by the outburst. Close contact with violent death, he had learned, stripped even the most centered people of their sense of control, leaving them emotionally naked and frightened and at some point angry.

"The moment she told you what she suspected about the Ogilvies, she put herself in harm's way."

"But if we hadn't . . ."

"I've talked with Gwen Ogilvie," Harry said firmly, "about her relationship with Afton Breckenridge. She's sharp as the proverbial razor. If Maria gave Gwen any indication that she had guessed what was going on, Gwen would have seen it instantly."

"And what does that mean?"

"It means," Harry said without drama, "that plans to get rid of her may have been in process when she spoke to you."

"Then you do think that it was the Ogilvies who killed her."

"I don't know who killed her, but they would be on my short list."

"Harry, I just feel so absolutely wretched about this. I've talked with Theresa, and of course she's devastated."

"I'm not surprised, but that's not the worst of it. She's in danger. If she will listen to you, put her in Haven House as

151

quickly as possible, and don't tell anyone."

"I hadn't thought of her being at risk," Rowena said, "but now that you've mentioned it, it seems obvious. Have you discussed this with Jim Snyder?"

"Very briefly. He was considering sending her to stay with relatives. I told him I wasn't sure she had any."

While he spoke, Harry was also trying to assess Rowena's exposure to the same risk and decided it was low but it could not be entirely dismissed.

"I'm sure she has relatives in the area."

"Probably," he agreed, "but it's the first place someone hunting her would look. It would be more difficult to connect her with you and with Haven House."

"All right," Rowena said, sounding steady and practical again, "I'll get right on this."

"Stay away from her house. Do the planning on the phone, and have one of your people from Haven House do the driving. Do it late at night or very early in the morning."

"Wait!" Rowena said. "If there is family in Mexico, what about sending her to them?"

"Good idea, but someone should drive her to Tampa or Orlando for the flight out of the state. She may want to leave from Southwest Florida International and take an airport limo or drive herself. Don't let her."

"What about the Sheriff's Department? Are they going to want to keep her here?"

"Let's not cross that bridge until we have to."

"The bullet came through that window," Hodges said loudly, pointing to the window on the right of the chair where Harry usually sat when talking with Caedmon, "and hit a piece of framing in that wall."

Hodges had swung around as if he was directing traffic and

indicated the place where a section of wall beyond the last row of files had been cut away to expose the upright. Two crime scene officers were chiseling the slug out of the stud where it had lodged.

"That whole wall will have to be refinished," Caedmon complained, "and the window and the curtain replaced." Then in a sudden shift, fists planted on her hips, she said, "I don't know what all the fuss is about. It was two o'clock in the morning, for God's sake. Who else but kids drinking beer and raising hell would be on this street at that hour?"

She had found the hole in the window at six o'clock and called Harry. Harry had called the Sheriff's Department. Then Hodges had called him, asking Harry to meet him at Caedmon's house. It was now nearly nine.

Harry and Hodges glanced at one another, neither prepared to answer her.

"Well?" Caedmon demanded, glaring first at Hodges and then at Harry.

"It might not be kids, Caedmon," Harry said, trying hard to sound reasonable without being dismissive.

"You ever have anything like this happen before?" Hodges asked.

"I've never been shot at, if that's what you're asking," she replied.

"Anybody ever try to kill you?"

"Why are you asking me this?"

Harry was thinking hard of some way to keep Hodges from being scalped. "Maybe . . ." he began and was cut off.

"Actually," Caedmon said, grinning at Hodges, "someone did try to run over me once. It was the husband of a woman who'd hired me to find out where all their money was going. Turned out he was spending it on another woman. When I told his wife, he decided, I guess as a public service, to get rid of me."

Hodges leaned back and broke out in an uproarious laugh.

"Well! There it is," he told her when he had managed to get his breath back and wipe his eyes with a red and white checked handkerchief, half the size of a dish towel, which he carried in his sling. "You just might have got somebody else riled. You find any other men lately with outside women?"

Harry expected another explosion, but it didn't come. Instead, she looked thoughtful. Pushing her hands into her jeans pockets, she said, "Harry and I are working on a project, but I can't see any way the people involved would want to harm either one of us. Do you agree, Harry?"

"Sergeant Hodges knows about Breckenridge and the letter," he said, not wanting to disagree with her. Neither did he want to say to her that whoever had put that bullet into her wall was certainly not a kid.

"Got it," one of the detectives at the wall said.

A moment later they took pictures of the studding with the bullet in it and then pried it free.

"Handgun, 9mm," the man who had spoken earlier said.

"Serious stuff," Hodges said, all traces of humor drained from his voice.

The two officers bagged the slug, made notes, took another picture, and left.

"I'd better get back," Hodges said. "Nice meeting you, Ma'am."

His large hand engulfed hers, and she had to catch her balance when he shook it.

"Thank you for your help, Sergeant," she replied.

"All part of the service," Hodges said, giving her a wide smile.

Just before leaving, he turned to Harry, serious again. "You and Ms. Rivers better have a serious talk, Harry. You hear?"

"I hear," Harry said, not looking forward to it.

"What did he mean by that?" Caedmon asked, as soon as the

door shut behind Hodges. She was rubbing her shoulder.

"It wasn't hell-raising kids who put that bullet in your wall."

"How do you know that?" She went on rubbing her shoulder while she spoke.

"Some guy who had trouble sleeping was walking his dog and saw the shooter," Harry said, "and called it in."

"Why didn't the sergeant tell me that?" she demanded.

"To protect the man who gave them the information," Harry told her, deciding to get it over with quickly. "The shooter was driving with his lights off. He stopped in front of your house, got out, and fired one shot over the roof of his car and through your window—he was using a silencer on his weapon—then drove away."

She stared at Harry in silence for a moment, then said, "Why would anyone want to kill me?"

"I don't think anyone was trying to kill you."

"What then?"

"I think it was a warning."

"Harry, you're trying to frighten me, and if it's a joke, I don't think it's funny."

"Caedmon," Harry said, "it's not a joke, and I'm not telling you this to frighten you."

"It can't be true."

Harry took her hands and held them as though he expected her to take wing. "There's a remote chance it wasn't meant for you, that someone made a mistake. Wrong address. What isn't wrong is the message. The bullet through the window was a warning."

"About what? I don't know anyone who shoots out people's windows. What kind of person do you think I am?"

"The kind of person who was almost run over once?"

"Good try, Harry, but I'm not in a joking mood."

She snatched her hands out of his and stalked into the

kitchen. He watched her go, angry and, he guessed, frightened, but unwilling to admit it. Harry followed. They needed to talk it through, work out what should be done. Be realistic. Good luck.

She was making coffee.

"You've scared someone," Harry told her, pulling a chair out from the table and sitting down. "They want you to know it."

He waited. When she made no response, he continued.

"We've never talked about your other clients. I think we'd better do that now."

She went on with what she was doing as if she hadn't heard him.

"I'm trying to find a woman's estranged brother she hasn't seen or heard from for ten years," Caedmon said at last in a hard, angry voice. "Last week I completed a trace on a guy who had vanished with most of the funds from a business partnership. He's in police custody, and the money's gone. So is the woman he spent it on. And there's Afton Breckenridge."

She turned from the counter and said, "Take your pick."

"Is that coffee ready?" Harry asked.

"Christ! Is that all you can say?"

"Pour the coffee for both of us," Harry said quietly. "Bring it over here. If you're as smart as I think you are, you'll sit down and stop being a pain in the neck so we can talk about this."

"All right," she said, to Harry's surprise.

Hearing Harry out, Caedmon said, "Then you're telling me that Afton Breckenridge might have hired someone to drive out here and put a bullet though my window."

"It's a possibility if not quite a probability."

"How could she have found out I'm working for her husband?"

"There are two ways," Harry said. "Either she hasn't left Avola and has been spying on Breckenridge, which doesn't sound at all likely, or she has an informant in the house."

"Ernan," she said.

"Possibly," Harry replied.

Half an hour later and after a lot of persuasion on Harry's part, she agreed to have some serious security installed in the house.

"And while that and the repairs are being done," he told her, "you're going to stay with me."

"OK, but two of my computers are coming with me," she told him, turning toward her bedroom.

Harry quailed, then rallied. "Need any help packing?"

She stopped, turned around slowly, and pointed at the door.

16

When Harry had recovered from carrying Caedmon's suitcases and computers into the house, he found her in the dining room, converting it into a work station, and some of the connections were not cooperating. He asked her if she needed any help. She stopped swearing long enough to say, "Go away."

"Then I'll make a call," he said. "If you need me, just holler."

There was no response to that. Under the weight of a second rejection and feeling like an unwanted visitor, Harry went into his study and punched in the Breckenridge number. Ernan answered.

"Hello, Mr. Brock," Ernan said. "Mr. Breckenridge is not available. Would you like to leave a message or make an appointment?"

"No, Ernan. Do you have a few minutes to talk with me?"

"Yes, of course," he replied, the warmth draining out of his voice.

"What can you tell me about the relationship between Mrs. Breckenridge and Mrs. Ogilvie?"

There was a blank space in which Harry listened to that vast silence that asserts itself when voices cease. He had decided to go on behaving toward Ernan as if he and Caedmon had not agreed that if there was an informant in the Breckenridge house, Ernan was the most likely candidate.

"I'm afraid there is nothing I can tell you, Mr. Brock."

"Is it because you feel it would be improper to say anything infringing on your employer's privacy?"

"There is that, but I have nothing to tell. From time to time, Mrs. Breckenridge would ask me to call Mrs. Ogilvie. Invariably, Maria Fuegos would take the call, and I would convey to her whatever message I had been given."

"These messages were all to arrange a meeting?"

"Yes."

"Lunch, shopping, drinks, that sort of meeting?"

"Usually."

"But there were exceptions?"

"Occasionally."

"Messages about what?"

"I would have to speak with Mr. Breckenridge before saying anything more."

"Ernan," Harry said, "do you know that Maria Fuegos is dead?"

"No, and I am very sorry to hear it. Our contacts were always most cordial. She seemed to be a very nice person."

"She was murdered."

"A terrible thing, Mr. Brock."

"Yes," Harry said in a flat voice. "The police will talk with you again. They will ask the same questions I'm asking and many more. If you pull the same kind of crap with them that you're pulling with me, you will find yourself in an interrogation room."

Harry knew very well what he was doing, and although he disliked frightening people, he knew it was an effective way to get information that he couldn't get any other way.

"But why talk to me about the woman's death?" Ernan demanded in an unsteady voice. "I know nothing."

"You know the answer to my question."

"The messages were always to make appointments to meet with Mrs. Ogilvie at her house."

"Frequently?"

"Two or three times a month."

"Did Mrs. Ogilvie call her?"

"Not to my knowledge. Of course, calls may have come on Mrs. Breckenridge's cell phone."

"And she never told you what the meetings were about?"

"Never."

"OK, I'll tell Captain Snyder what you've told me and that it's all you know about their relationship. Is it really all you know?"

"Yes."

"Then don't worry."

"I learned long ago it is wise to worry if the police are involved," Ernan said in the same shaky voice.

"I can understand why," Harry said, putting some sympathy in his response, "but if you've told me the truth, you're safe."

Harry broke the connection, wondering why Afton Breckenridge would have been meeting with Gwen Ogilvie two or three times a month if not to have lunch or go shopping. On the other hand, why not? Maybe they played tennis together.

His conclusions may have been reasonable, but they left him unsatisfied.

Possibly, he thought, it was just a bad conscience from what he had done to Ernan. Frightening foreigners with the police was pretty shabby behavior.

Harry wandered back into the dining room to find Caedmon standing, hands on hips, looking at the computers humming on the table with a pleased smile on her face.

"You see?" she asked brightly. "You just have to show them who's in charge."

"Did anyone ever tell you that you are a tad aggressive?"

"I've been pursued all my life by a tiresome Greek chorus

thrusting that information at me."

She grinned at Harry. "I gather you've joined the company," she said in a challenging tone.

"Oh, no," Harry said. "I've always found you meek and mild as cottage cheese. Are you finished here?"

"Are you quoting again?"

"Yes. Are you finished here?"

"Why?"

"There's someone I want you to meet."

"I really ought to do some work," she said, looking back at the computers, her shoulders slumping a little.

"This won't take long," he said, his nose growing a bit longer, "and we can walk."

"You have neighbors?"

"I do. Find your sun hat, and let's go."

"Am I OK in these shorts and top?"

"You're far better than OK," Harry said, putting his arms around her.

She kissed him and asked, "Are we postponing the visit?"

"I have a feeling we're going to be asked to lunch. Then, when we come back, perhaps we could sit and read to one another for a while."

"Sounds delightful," she said, kissing him again. "Let's go."

They had almost reached the turnoff to Tucker's farm when Caedmon stopped, grasping Harry's arm.

"Oh, my God!" she said. "Look what's in the road. Should we run?"

"It's our welcoming committee," Harry said, suppressing his delight at seeing Sanchez and Oh, Brother! waiting for them.

She was still holding onto his arm. "How would a horse and a dog know we were coming?" she demanded, followed by a derisive laugh.

Harry stopped, turned her to face her, and began speaking in a low, hurried but urgent voice. "That's a mule. His name is Oh, Brother! The dog's name is Sanchez. Never, ever call Oh, Brother! a horse. It upsets him, and don't laugh at his hat. I mean it."

Caedmon was staring at him as if he'd lost his mind.

"Finally, assume they understand what you're saying,"

The two large animals had been hurrying toward them, and Harry turned quickly to greet them. Once he had grasped Sanchez by the sides of his head and given him a good shake and stroked Oh, Brother!'s neck and complimented him on the new anhinga feather in his hat band, Harry introduced them to Caedmon.

Oh, Brother! stepped forward, pressed his nose against her chest, and blew softly.

"Oh, my," she said, her face flaming, "How extraordinary, but really . . ."

She looked at Harry for guidance as the big mule gently moved his nose against her.

"Stroke him," Harry said. "He likes you. It's remarkable. He's usually much more reserved with strangers."

"He's beautiful," she said, having found the courage to stroke his head and then his neck. "Look how his coat shines."

"Say hello to Sanchez," Harry told her.

She turned and found the tall hound's head on a level with her belt. He was grinning at her, an experience that people often found chilling.

"Harry," she asked in alarm, "is he going to bite me?"

"No," Harry said quickly, "He's smiling at you. Grab him behind the ears and really dig in. He'll know you like him."

She bent forward and a bit tentatively began to scratch his neck. To encourage her, Sanchez lifted his head and gave her a warm, damp lick that started at her cleavage and went all the way to her chin.

Taken by surprise, Caedmon shot up straight with an ambiguous, "Oh!"

Sanchez then demonstrated his approval by giving her a firm boost in the crotch with his nose, an action that brought a loud cry from Caedmon.

"Congratulations," Harry said, "you've been given the Sanchez stamp of approval. You've now got a lifetime membership in the dog fraternity and a friend to go with it."

Caedmon flushed, gave a small nervous chuckle, and said, "It's the first introduction by foreplay I've ever experienced," and then gave way to delighted laughter.

"Oh, Brother! would be very pleased if you'd ride him the rest of the way," Harry said. "You'd be safe as houses on his back."

"With this crew," she said, "I'm surprised not to be asked to ride naked."

"You'd make a beautiful Godiva," Harry said encouragingly, "but you can keep your clothes on."

"How would I get on him? He's tall as a tree."

"Your left foot in my cupped hands like this and up you go, easy as stairs."

Sanchez barked in approval and Oh, Brother! nodded his head.

"They can't really be telling me to do this," she said, looking speculatively at the two animals.

"I wouldn't bet on it," Harry said.

Caedmon declined, but she gave Sanchez another good head shake and insisted on walking beside Oh, Brother! as they set off for the house, with one hand on his shoulder, the other hand on Sanchez's head. Harry trailed along as best he could, concluding he had lost his woman to a mule and a blue tick hound.

They had spent most of the time between Harry's house and

Tucker's place talking about the shooting and where Caedmon was in her efforts to trace Afton Breckenridge. The discussion of the shooting was brief and inconclusive. Caedmon was still not admitting that she had actually been threatened, and Harry, unable to offer conclusive proof to the contrary, let the subject drop before they reached the arguing stage.

She was more interested in talking about Afton Breckenridge. "I'm just about ready to say that unless we're dealing with a magician, no one but Afton could have done all the things that have been done with her credit cards, investments, bank accounts, cell phone, mailing addresses, and all the other threads of connection that attach the rest of us to our world."

Caedmon had been ticking the items off on her fingers as she talked. When she was done, Harry was ready with a question.

"How can she function with all of these things shut down?" he asked, thinking that her list suggested someone had indeed found a way to strip Afton of everything; and that she was probably dead.

"Do you think she's dead?" Caedmon responded.

"After listening to you, I'm considering the possibility."

"She'd like that because it's just what she wants you think. What she's done isn't easy, but it can be done. Here's how."

Caedmon then reeled off a string of alternatives ranging from prepaid phones bought in a supermarket, to prepaid credit cards, credit cards with false names, private mail drops, and duplicate social security numbers and driver's licenses.

"Of course, as I've already told you, she's transferred her assets to Panama, where you can become a citizen of the country just by keeping a certain amount of money in a Panamanian bank and paying the government a monthly fee. The name on her Panamanian documents will not be Afton Breckenridge, but she will be able to travel to most countries in the world, including this one, on them."

Harry whistled. "A person who's done that would become invisible."

"Almost," Caedmon agreed.

It was a five-minute walk from the road to Tucker's vegetable garden, the first sign of cultivation a visitor to Tucker's farm encountered.

"It's beautiful," Caedmon said, stopping to stare at the rows of corn and beans and peppers and hills of pumpkins, gourds, and squash, their vines all in bloom. "And look at the flowers!"

"Marigolds," Harry said. "He claims they're a natural bug repellent."

"Better than insecticides," a voice said from among the corn stalks.

A moment later, Tucker, wearing his shining white collarless shirt and ironed overalls, stepped into view.

"I love it!" Caedmon said.

"So do I," Tucker said, walking toward them with his hand out. "My name's Tucker. What's yours?"

"Caedmon, Caedmon Rivers, and I'm pleased to meet you. Harry can't get through a sentence without mentioning your name. It makes me quite jealous."

"You needn't worry, Miss Rivers," Tucker said, taking her hand and holding it while he added, "Harry told me you were beautiful, but I see now that he failed to do you justice. It's a pleasure to meet you."

"Why thank you, Mr. LaBeau. Please call me Caedmon."

"Gladly. I see you've met Oh, Brother! and Sanchez. Did they behave themselves?"

"Perfect gentlemen," she said, coloring.

"Good, let's get you out of this sun. There's some cold lemonade at the house. Harry, you know the way. Lead off and go by way of the henhouse; I want to talk with Caedmon. I have

165

some catching up to do."

Harry protested mildly at the transparent gambit to get Caedmon to himself, but Caedmon was already beaming, her hand under Tucker's arm, leaving Harry to the company of the animals.

They were met at the henhouse by Tucker's big Plymouth Rock rooster, who began crowing lustily and flapping his wings in a great display of welcome as soon as they came in sight. As usual, the hens all began to squawk and race around their run until Longstreet settled down and expressed his feelings more calmly by strutting and clucking in a dignified fashion.

"This is General Longstreet," Tucker said to Caedmon, taking a handful of cracked corn out of his overalls pocket and scattering it among the hens, which ended their rushing about. "He's a lot more level-headed than his predecessor. General P.G.T. Beauregard was flighty and headstrong, which led to his ending up in the stomachs of Bonnie and Clyde."

"Surely not . . . ?" Caedmon began, eyes widening.

"Oh, no," Tucker said with a laugh. "I'm inclined to forget not everyone knows them. They're neighbors of mine, a pair of larcenous gray foxes. They tend to confuse this henhouse with a grocery store, much the way their namesakes confused their money and the bank's."

That led to more laughter in which Harry did not fully participate, his nose being somewhat out of joint by the way Caedmon was hanging on Tucker's every word and if not flirting, then making it very plain how much she liked him.

"But before we go," Tucker said, "I want you to see something. Come over here."

He led the group, including Sanchez and Oh, Brother!, around the fenced run to the shadiest corner, where he had installed a wire enclosure about four feet square and one foot high. Within the enclosure were a dozen black and white chicks, slightly smaller than tennis balls, peeping and chasing one another.

"How delightful!" Caedmon exclaimed, dropping to her heels to be closer to them.

From another pocket Tucker took a small handful of finely ground feed and tossed it into their run. The chicks put out their tiny wings and rushed about in excitement until their huge mother, clucking protectively, dropped in among them and began to peck at the feed, which led them to do the same.

"I thought all baby chickens were yellow," Caedmon said as they were leaving the run.

"Some are," Tucker said, "but barred breeds like these— Barred Rocks were developed in Massachusetts in the nineteenth century—are gray and white or black and white."

"What are you going to do with them?" Harry asked. "Isn't it a departure for you to leave eggs under one of the hens?"

"I'm considering taking the best of them to the county fair in October. The mother of those chicks is an outstanding bird, and Longstreet comes from show stock."

"And the rest?" Caedmon asked.

"Fryers," Tucker said.

17

Caedmon was subdued by the "fryers" comment, but by the time Tucker seated them on the back stoop and produced the lemonade, she had recovered her spirits. Conversation became general again, helped along by the appearance of Jane Bunting and her huge kittens, Aurelius and Frederica.

"I suspect she feels her prerogatives have been trodden on," Tucker said by way of apology when Jane Bunting narrowed her eyes at Caedmon and hissed, refusing Tucker's attempts at reconciliation.

Caedmon could not really give her full attention to Jane Bunting's hostility because Aurelius had trotted straight to her and jumped into her lap, purring loudly, and immediately began licking her face.

"This cat weighs a ton," Caedmon said, trying to lift him away from her face and settle him in her lap.

"Twenty-eight pounds," Harry said, "and still growing." He was having his own struggle with Frederica, who was doing her best to smother him, kneading his chest as if it was a tree trunk.

"By the way," Tucker said when they had finished their lemonade, "there's a ham in the oven, a potato salad in the refrigerator, and a raspberry tart cooling on the sideboard. I think we can make a lunch out of that, and I've got a jug of plum brandy I've just opened that is the best of the batch. I figure it will help that raspberry tart go down. What do you think?"

"I look forward to the test," Harry said.

"I've never drunk plum brandy," Caedmon said a bit warily.

"Gentle as mother's milk," Tucker assured her.

Once they were eating, Tucker asked Caedmon how her search for Afton Breckenridge was progressing. She glanced at Harry, who nodded.

"I've told Harry that I'm now almost certain she has skipped and is probably alive. This ham is wonderful," Caedmon said, eagerly accepting Tucker's offer of another slice.

"Thank you. A friend of mine smokes his own," Tucker replied. "How can you be sure you're right?"

Caedmon ran quickly through the answer she had given Harry and added, "When you do this work of tracing someone, a moment comes when you can almost see the person. I reached that point with Afton Breckenridge a week or so ago. I can see what she's doing. I can almost tell you what she'll do next."

"And what will that be?" Tucker asked.

"I've never seen a skipper as thorough as she's been," Caedmon said, obviously following her own train of thought.

Harry was listening closely, and not wanting to distract her made no comment, although he thought the business about seeing Breckenridge was a bit far-fetched.

"How do you mean?" Tucker put in.

"I'll give you odds," she said, laying down her fork, "that she's got it all—a mail drop where she's storing her new lease and insurances. I'd even bet that she's got an apartment, a car, credit cards, a whole new identity."

"In Panama?" Harry asked.

"Before you answer," Tucker said, "let me give you some more potato salad. How about more lemonade? And don't stop eating."

"Okay," she said, picking up her fork. "My God, I'm going to gain pounds and pounds if I go on."

"It will only add to your charms," Tucker told her.

Caedmon broke into laughter. "I've never heard them called charms."

"You must forgive me. I didn't think," Tucker said, a comment Harry considered a shameless untruth. "I didn't mean to embarrass you."

"You didn't," she told him with a smile, then speared a piece of potato drenched in dressing. "As for your question," she continued, turning to Harry, "it might be Panama, but knowing a little about how her mind works, I'd say her money's in Panama, she's got a Panamanian passport, but she's probably living in Belize or some other country in the area."

"Why?" Tucker asked.

"To put another wall between herself and whoever is looking for her. She will assume her husband will try to trace her."

"Will you find her?"

Caedmon went on eating for a couple of moments before answering.

"Only if she makes a mistake," she said at last. "You know, thinking more about it, I wouldn't be surprised to find out she's made all these arrangements and then come back here."

"Why would she have done that?" Harry asked, startled by her statement.

"To watch the fireworks," she said. "Tucker, could I persuade you to give me the recipe for this salad?"

"Yes," Tucker said, "I'll write it out for you. By the way, Harry, the female coyote has a six-inch gash in her right hip. I'm thinking she got careless around that panther. I don't know what else could have cut her that cleanly."

They talked about the coyotes and the panther until it was time for Tucker to serve the tart. That done, he poured the plum brandy.

"Now for the test," he said, sitting down and lifting his glass.

The test appeared to be a success, judging from the laughter that soon sprang up among them like desert flowers after a rain. Sometime later, Harry and Caedmon reached home in a mellow plum haze, and after some difficulty with buttons and zippers, accompanied by considerable laughter, they helped one another climb into bed. Much later, they fell asleep.

The next morning Harry rousted an old friend out of bed with an early call.

"Hello, Ernesto," Harry said. "Are you alone?"

"Why would I be alone?" a very tired voice responded.

Harry heard a woman's voice murmuring drowsy complaints in Spanish. "Increasing your *responsabilidades?*" Harry asked.

Ernesto Piedra was a long-time friend with whom he had occasionally worked and who was Harry's eyes and ears in the county's criminal world. Ernesto had begun life as one of that faceless host of immigrant workers, a few of whom were legals, that makes Florida's agribusiness profitable. He was very intelligent but barely literate, and he quickly saw that life in the bean fields had no promise. His options for making a conventional living being limited, he decided to become a burglar.

For him, it had worked out well, and he regarded it as an art form as well as a craft, taking pride in work that for him had never been violent. Over time, he had become a specialist and something of an authority on antique silver. It was solitary work, but it suited him. A remarkably handsome man with a thick shock of black curly hair, now streaked with gray, and large, soulful brown eyes, his success with women was legendary. Never married, he had a dozen children, which he referred to as his *responsabilidades,* and their mothers, who were to him collectively *Las Madres.* His labors supported all of them.

Between the children and the mothers, whose demands on him were insistent and, even had he wanted to, difficult to turn

171

down, he seldom had a daylight hour to himself when he was not sleeping. "They are so lovely," he had recently told Harry sadly, "but I am no longer a young man."

"Well?" Harry said.

"It is not even ten o'clock!" Ernesto protested in a shocked voice, apparently having checked his watch.

"I need to talk with you. Today. It's important. Where can we meet?"

It was one of the difficulties that beset their relationship. Being seen together by someone with police connections who knew both of them would be very inconvenient.

"Somewhere I can eat."

"Where did you and Soñadora eat? I've forgotten the name. The place with the one-eyed cat."

"La Gallina."

"In an hour."

"This is business?"

"Yes," Harry said, understanding that his *yes* meant that he would be helping out with Ernesto's *responsabilidades*.

The restaurant was located in a dusty, out-of-the-way corner of East Avola. Many of the narrow streets were lined with *tiendas,* selling clothes, vegetables, jewelry, shoes, freshly killed and dressed fowls, and chilies and tortillas. Among the shops were warehouses, surrounded by chain-link fences topped with razor wire. *La Gallina* was at the end of a tiny cul-de-sac, and Harry's Rover, parked as close to the restaurant as he could get it, looked like an elephant in a cow barn.

Ernesto was standing outside the door, talking with an old man wearing a ragged brown serape, who hurried away at the sight of Harry.

"You look tired," Harry said, expressing genuine concern as they shook hands.

"Because I am," Ernesto said. "The life is becoming more and more difficult."

They were led to a tiny wooden table beside an open window. There was no air-conditioning. Harry breathed deeply. "What smells so good?"

"Everything," Ernesto said.

"Where's the cat?"

A young waitress in a black and red skirt and white blouse came as soon as they were seated and passed them a menu inside a cracked plastic cover. Ernesto spoke to her in rapid Spanish that left Harry far behind. Before leaving, she gave Harry a blinding smile.

"The cat is dead," Ernesto said, looking offended, "and the owner has decided against replacing him, for reasons of cleanliness."

Because Ernesto did not laugh, neither did Harry, but he wanted to. Then he looked around, taking his time. "The place is spotless," he said. "Change of management?"

"The daughter has taken over from the father, who only comes in on the weekend," Ernesto said, examining the menu. "She recommends the *chalupas* and the pork green *chile.*"

"Will they be flaming when they arrive?"

"I told her the *gringo* will need help with the chilies. The cook will take pity."

"Have you forgotten this is your breakfast?" Harry asked.

"I do not eat breakfasts."

"Sorry, I forgot. I'll have the *chalupas.*"

"I've already ordered it for you, and the black bean soup. You have never eaten bean soup until you have eaten it here. I'm having the chili and, like you, the soup. Why am I here?"

Their food arrived. The waitress with dancing eyes said something to Harry and treated him to another smile before hurrying away.

"Why does she keep smiling at me?" Harry asked. "And what are these things?"

"I told her you made movies, and they are *teleras*, Mexican flatbread rolls."

"An oxymoron."

"Moron or not, you will need them. When fire breaks out, do not drink the water. Eat from the roll."

"You didn't really tell her I was a producer."

"Yes, I did. It will excite her and make her day brighter. Didn't you see how pretty she is when she smiles?"

Harry did not answer because he had begun to eat the *chalupas* and was now eagerly chewing on the *teleras*.

"Both dishes you are eating are very ancient dishes. How do you like them?"

"Excellent," Harry gasped, wiping his eyes before picking up his fork again.

Now that he could speak, he ate more carefully and began explaining his problem to Ernesto. The waitress brought another plate of *teleras* and put it down in front of Harry. This time he smiled first.

"She is very pretty," Harry said, turning to look at her walking away with her head up and a swing in her stride that had not been there when they arrived.

"I also said you left large tips."

"That, I can believe. So you see what the situation is. I'm betting it's a professional who shot out the window. I want you to use your connections to find out if we have an East Coast gun in town."

"I will try, but the problem is that there is always a gun or two in town, usually waiting for the heat in the other place to grow smaller. What is in this for me?"

"Five hundred, but there's more for you to do."

"I had not dared to believe my good fortune. Now I do. What is it?"

Harry pushed a photograph, face down, across the table. Ernesto glanced at it and slid it into his shirt pocket.

"She is the woman who has disappeared?"

"That's right. Her name is Afton Breckenridge, the wife of the man who hired me, only don't mention the name because she will not be using it."

"A name you don't know."

"Right."

Ernesto leaned back with a sigh, to wipe his mouth on the paper napkin and to rest from the pork green chili. "And you do have another name?"

"No."

"But you suspect that she is hiding under your noses?"

"I'm not at all sure, but I'm trying to eliminate possibilities."

"As I do when I visit a new property to assess the *posibilidades*," Ernesto remarked with a nod of approval.

"*Potentials* would be a better word," Harry said, feeling slightly uneasy that he was encouraging Ernesto in his criminal career.

"Thank you," Ernesto said. "Is she more likely to be in one place than another?"

"She might be where the less well off tourists are more than where the rich ones congregate to mingle with the local gentry."

"*Gentry?*" Ernesto asked.

"Rich people. Do you work in the south section of town, towards the Seminole River?" Harry asked.

"She will not be there," Ernesto said without committing himself.

"No."

"Hotel rather than furnished apartment?"

"I'd guess apartment, but it's only a guess."

"There is maid service in both."

"I follow your thinking."

Harry passed Ernesto a small, brown envelope, which vanished instantly.

"How long will this take?"

"My older *responsabilidades* are reliable. I will have the photo copied by an equally reliable person," Ernesto said. "I would say a week for the picture, possibly less. On the shooter, three days at most."

"Good," Harry said.

The bill arrived, and Harry paid for it in cash and separately gave the waitress a heavy tip. In exchange for which she spoke seriously to him for a moment, smiled, and left.

"She thanked you for coming, hoped you enjoyed the food, and asked you please to tell your friends that we are here."

"I'll leave first," Harry said after settling the bill and shaking Ernesto's hand. "Before you leave, please tell the waitress that I will be glad to tell my friends the food at the *La Gallina* is excellent. And one more thing, Ernesto, I saw how you were looking at her. She is far too young to be creating *responsabilidades.* "

"Not too young, Harry," Ernesto said, shaking his head sadly, "but too married."

18

While waiting for Ernesto's responses, Harry was not idle. Neither was Caedmon. In an unusual show of civility Breckenridge agreed to see Harry and Caedmon together for a briefing on their progress. But Harry knew that Harley Dillard was close to convening a grand jury, which meant Breckenridge would probably be charged with murdering his wife. One look at Breckenridge's face after Ernan had ushered them into his study told Harry that Breckenridge had also heard the news.

"What fucking use are you?" was Breckenridge's initial greeting, shouted at them from behind his desk.

He was wearing a pair of sand chinos, a red short-sleeved shirt, and a pair of high gloss loafers. Harry thought he might be striding back and forth in front of his desk to keep from freezing to death. In concert with the air-conditioning, the ceiling fans were setting up a brisk breeze of the sort a traveler in Labrador might encounter.

"Breckenridge," Caedmon said in a calm, cold voice, advancing toward him steadily, "a long time ago, I made it a policy not to be sworn at by foul-mouthed assholes like you. So you can clean up your act or you will have my contract back with a bill attached to it that might even get *your* attention."

Breckenridge stopped in front of Caedmon, glaring at her as if he might bite her face off. Harry was about to intervene, because Caedmon was glaring back.

"My apologies, Miss Rivers," Breckenridge said calmly, defusing the situation. "What's about to happen to me is in no way your fault. I'm fairly seriously distressed, however."

"You've heard from Dillard?" Harry asked.

"My lawyers," Breckenridge said, waving them toward heavy cherry wood chairs fitted with black leather upholstery, anchored by brass studs, which gave the place the look of an updated Viking mead hall.

Harry watched Caedmon uneasily, not sure what she might say or do.

She turned and sat down beside Harry and gave Breckenridge a grim smile. "Apology accepted," she said. "I seem to be lacking information."

"Harley's convening a grand jury," Harry said. "He's almost certainly going to charge Mr. Breckenridge with killing his wife."

"Then he'll be premature," Caedmon said flatly, rummaging in her bag and pulling out a small leatherbound notebook and quickly flipping its pages.

Breckenridge had pulled a third chair around to sit facing her and Harry. "What do you mean?"

She looked up from her book and said to Breckenridge, "Answer a question for me. When did Dillard receive that letter from your wife?"

"May thirteenth."

"That confirms what I have for the date."

"And?" Breckenridge demanded.

"I'm as close to certain as I can be that Mrs. Breckenridge was alive when that letter was delivered."

"Then let's get this information to Dillard right now," Breckenridge burst out, jumping up.

By now they were all on their feet. "Give it to your lawyers," Harry said. "It's way premature to talk to Dillard."

"Harry," she said as if she was quieting a restless child, "you don't have to worry. I'm really on solid ground here."

"I'm not questioning your conclusions, Caedmon," Harry said, while struggling to find a way to stop Breckenridge from making a bad strategic mistake. "Please, let's all sit down, quiet down, and listen to what I have to say."

"Does it apply?" Breckenridge said loudly.

"Of course it applies," Harry barked back. "Why else are you paying me all this money?"

Harry hadn't realized how much force he had put into his little speech until both of his listeners suddenly dropped back into their chairs as if they'd been pole-axed.

"Go ahead," Caedmon said.

"First, Caedmon's information in its present form, important as it is, will not stop Harley from persuading the grand jury that he has probable cause to issue an arrest warrant and proceed to trial. The absence of Mrs. Breckenridge and Harley's receipt of her letter, assuming a handwriting expert will testify that the letter is written in her hand—and it's probably already verified or Harley wouldn't be convening a grand jury—will be enough for the jury to find probable cause."

"But if what Rivers says is true, the charge is baseless," Breckenridge said, slumping in his chair.

"Caedmon," Harry said, "can you prove that Mrs. Breckenridge is alive?"

Caedmon frowned and said, "No."

"Well, what do you have?" Breckenridge demanded.

"Probabilities," she answered. "That doesn't mean I'm wrong, but it does mean I can't prove I'm right."

"Try again," Breckenridge said.

"I've been tracking Mrs. Breckenridge's actions in her various accounts—credit card purchases, cell phone accounts, plane ticket purchases, withdrawals from her bank accounts, transfers, liquidation of assets—in short, any activity that would require her name. Since her disappearance, if you could believe your eyes, she hasn't made a phone call or bought a lipstick."

"Then maybe she is dead!" Breckenridge exploded.

Caedmon shook her head and waved him down. "All through the time that she wasn't in evidence, her money was being moved, accounts were closing, and funds were transferred. It's the only mistake she's made. It can, I suppose, be reasonably argued that this proves she's dead and that someone has managed to forge his or her way through all her financial holdings, but I don't believe it. You would have to do what I do or something like it to know how nearly impossible it is."

"There's identity theft all the time," Harry said.

"On a small scale, your credit cards, maybe your debit card, even a bank account," Caedmon insisted. "And cleaning up the mess can be trying, but doing the things Mrs. Breckenridge has been doing is almost impossible unless she's doing it."

"What did you mean by saying it was the only mistake she made?" Harry asked.

"She should have done those things first," Caedmon said, showing excitement for the first time since their conversation had begun, "but she didn't, and she's left a trace that I will exploit."

"One thing further," Harry said, directing his comment to Breckenridge, "if you take Caedmon's speculation to Dillard, his people will say that her work is inconclusive and later will use it against you."

"Then what am I supposed to do with it?" Breckenridge asked, looking more and more discouraged.

"Give it to your lawyers," Harry said without hesitation. "Let them go to work on it. Eventually, you will have to let Dillard see it, but they will make certain it's done in a way that minimizes the risk."

"And I'm still going to be working," Caedmon said. "I may reach the point when I can prove she's still alive."

They talked a little longer, with Harry and Caedmon doing their best to persuade Breckenridge that it was much too soon to give up hope.

"Do you believe that stuff we told him about a brighter tomorrow?" Caedmon asked Harry as they were driving away from the house.

"Don't tell me you're ready to give up," Harry said.

"Of course not!" Caedmon said.

"Good, but I don't know whether Afton Breckenridge is alive or not."

"Thanks for your support."

"The bullet through your window suggests to me that she is," Harry said, ignoring her sarcasm.

"And that she's trying to kill me," Caedmon said gloomily.

"Not yet."

Having checked her car to see that it was in good order, Caedmon led Harry into the house and found the place in a mess. The drapery people had taken away the damaged curtain, but the window crew had not yet arrived. The handyman crew, however, were cheerfully and loudly cutting away her work room wallboard in a cloud of white dust.

"Shit!" she said on walking into the room.

"Want to leave them to it?" Harry asked.

"No, I'm staying. I have work to do, and I was swearing because I'm going to have to cover the computers and the fax machines and my bookcases before I can start."

"Want any help?"

"No."

"OK, I've got some catching up to do with Jeff Smolkin and Rowena Farnham. How long will you be?"

"I have plenty to do. Pick me up when you're ready to go home."

Hearing Caedmon say *"home,"* meaning his place, when she was standing in her own home, gave Harry a strange feeling. He wasn't sure it carried any special meaning. But if it did, it meant at some level that she was beginning to think of the Hammock as home, his home as her home.

His cell began to vibrate, and Harry pulled off the road to answer it.

"Harry, it's Renata. Number One wants to see you."

"What number am I?"

"Twelve or thirteen. When can you come in?"

"I'm totally crushed. Do you want to check again and see if you've made a mistake?"

"Just a second. Nope, I was right. When can you come in?"

"How about right now?"

"Fine. Stop by when you get here. I've forgotten what you look like. I hate it when that happens. I never know when the ME is going to ask me to identify someone with a tag on his toe."

"I'm about to sign off. Any more compliments?"

"If your belly's showing between your shorts and your shirt, don't come in at all."

"Fill me in," Jeff Smolkin said. "Is Dillard really going to arrest Breckenridge? Rumors are flying."

Harry was sitting in Jeff's office, having avoided talking to Renata, but as usual the lawyer leaned over his desk, looking at a brief while questioning Harry.

Harry didn't answer, and eventually Smolkin looked up and tried to stifle his surprise at seeing Harry sitting in front of his desk.

"Who says you haven't got too much work to know what the hell you're doing?" Harry asked.

"You do," Smolkin said with a grin as he came around the

desk and sat down beside Harry, "and you might be right, but I'm listening."

Harry told him Caedmon had decided that Afton Breckenridge was probably alive, and that he had advised Breckenridge to take the information to his lawyers, not to Harley. "It was not easy, but I think I've convinced him."

"Can she prove it?"

"No."

"That's why you told him to go to the lawyers and not to Harley."

"Yes."

"You were right. How's he going to take being arrested?"

Harry felt a sinking feeling in his stomach and was surprised to find that the thought of Breckenridge's arrest troubled him.

"Not well," he said. "He developed some bad habits over the years, and living large and overreacting when he's crossed are only two of them."

"He's not going to like losing his belt and his shoelaces?" Smolkin asked with a grim smile.

"Losing his good name is going to hurt much worse. He's certain that if word of his wife's disappearance gets out, his business will tank. Imagine the catastrophe he'll see coming when he's arrested."

They talked a while longer about what the grand jury would probably do and how soon Harley would issue the warrant and whether or not Breckenridge's lawyers would be able to bail their client.

Finally, Harry said, "Why did you want to see me? A call would have gotten you this information."

"Two things," Jeff said. "Is there any chance that the shooting at Caedmon's house is linked to Maria Fuegos' murder?"

"I've thought about it and decided the only possible connection is too far-fetched to be rational."

Jeff glanced at his watch. "Is it a long story?"

"Not particularly."

"Go."

"Afton Breckenridge is/was a friend of Gwen Ogilvie. If she somehow became involved in their criminal activities and her disappearing is connected to that, then the Ogilvies or their running dogs may consider Caedmon's hunt for her a threat."

"Sure it's a stretch," Jeff put in, showing interest, "but what if Afton was going to vanish in order to put herself in a safer position to somehow help the Ogilvies expand their racket?"

"Your imagination is even more inflamed than mine," Harry said and laughed.

"That's probably true," Jeff agreed, "but if we're wrong, the only people with a motive to move Caedmon off the case are Breckenridge and his wife."

A sharp rap on the door was instantly followed by Renata, crisp in black and white, stepping into the room and saying, "Your appointment is in the conference room."

Then she looked at Harry as if he was the source of a bad smell and said, "Who let you in here?"

Before either man could answer, she turned and pulled the door shut after her, with the parting comment, "Heads will roll."

Jeff gave a deep sigh and looked at the closed door with a frown of worry or fear—Harry couldn't tell which—and said, "She likes you."

"Thank God she doesn't dislike me."

"She's the second thing I want to talk to you about," Jeff said and fell silent.

"Have you decided on a nap instead?" Harry asked after impatiently watching Smolkin stare at his shirt buttons for longer than it would have taken to count them.

"She's not happy, Harry," he said, looking up with a sigh.

"Can you shed any light on the situation?"

"First," Harry said with some urgency, "Renata and I have not been seeing one another. So I'm not the one providing the distraction, if that's what it is."

Smolkin shook his head vigorously. "It's not distraction, Harry. She's unhappy. Her coming in and taking some hide off you displayed more life than she's shown since you and she had dinner."

"That was some time ago."

Jeff's mentioning the dinner made Harry uneasy. The serpent of guilt stirred in its cave.

"Tell me about it."

Smolkin looked so miserable that Harry felt compelled to say something. "Have you talked with her about it?"

Smolkin jumped as if someone had jabbed him with a needle. "I can't do that. She's an employee, not a friend."

He hesitated over that final comment and amended it. "Well, yes, after all these years I suppose we are friends, but I still can't ask her a question like that."

"Why not?"

"She might expect me to do something about it, and where would that lead?"

"I don't know. Do you?"

"No, and I don't want to find out. But this office is no happier than Renata is, if you take my meaning."

"If Mama-san isn't happy . . . ?"

"That's about it. Could you talk to her, Harry? She likes you. She might . . ."

"Oh, no," Harry said firmly, getting up quickly.

"No, I can see why you wouldn't . . ." Smolkin said, looking too dispirited to finish his thought.

Harry left Smolkin, intending to ghost out of the office, but Renata was waiting for him in the hall.

"How are things in the geriatric group?" she asked, pointing to her office door.

"Keeping the toilet occupied," he said, making a sharp left when he reached her. "Why do people call this your den?"

"I'd like a list of their names," she answered, closing the door.

Trapped, Harry thought.

"How are you?" he asked, standing with his hands in his pockets.

"I've been better. What about you?"

"Taking nourishment."

Renata snorted with choked laughter. "You need it, considering what you're shagging."

"Not funny."

"No, but I don't feel very funny. What have you learned about the Maria Fuegos investigation? Number One doesn't seem to know a damned thing."

She was standing with her arms folded and one hip leaned against the front of her desk, and while she talked, Harry looked at her and saw that despite the immaculate turnout with no hair out of place, there were shadows under her eyes, and she looked tired. Ill? Not sleeping? *There's something*, he thought.

"Jim's people aren't making much progress," he said. "I've got some feelers out, but for now I doubt I know any more than you do."

"What about Afton Breckenridge? Is the whiz girl performing miracles—I don't mean in bed? That goes without saying."

"Renata," Harry said, breaking his vow of silence on the subject, "what's wrong?"

"Plenty," she replied sharply.

"Are you ill?"

The possibility made his stomach sink.

"Only in the head. Harry, I don't think I can go on working

here, being around him."

"What's changed?"

"I'm not sure, but it was our night out that did it."

"Are you pregnant?" he asked.

She grinned, and some of the old sparkle brightened her eyes. "No, but thanks for the compliment. What if I had said yes?"

"If you were happy, I would be too."

"Where do you keep your halo when it's not around your dick?"

"Jesus, Renata!"

"Sorry, it's become a habit. The thing is, I'm missing out on life, Harry. You brought it to my attention."

A buzzer on her desk sounded.

"Number One," she said, followed by a rueful laugh.

"If you want to talk some more about this . . ." he began, but she raised her hand and stopped him.

"It's okay," she said. "Thanks for the concern. I'll see you later."

With that, she stepped around him and left.

19

Harry left the building and stepped into the blinding light with a sore heart. He was not solipsistic enough to believe that he was the cause of Renata's pain, but he saw all too clearly that his selfish use of her had probably been the trigger that jolted her out of her resignation or whatever it was that had held her in bondage to Jeff all these years.

It was also true that she had been an enthusiastic participant in their midnight revels, and they had both risen from her bed pleased with themselves and one another. Harry found the attempt to hide the sepulcher of their night together under a white coat of self-justifying paint was a painful failure. The truth was that whatever pleasure and joy they had shared was quickly unhorsed by guilt for him and a sense of failure for her. But was that good or bad?

Silence followed as he turned the Rover into St. Jude's parking lot.

"Come in, Harry," Rowena said, ushering him into her vestry office. "I've got some good news."

"I could use it," Harry said.

"Are you and Caedmon on the outs?" she asked with a frown that flickered briefly over her face.

"No, but I was just talking with Renata Holland. She's fairly miserable."

"Jeff Smolkin's office manager?"

"Yes, do you know her?"

"Not well. She's been a volunteer at Haven House for several years, and we talk when we meet there. She doesn't wear a ring, but nowadays that doesn't necessarily signify."

"She's single. I don't think Jeff could function without her. It's a problem. What's your news?"

"If you don't want to talk about it," Rowena said with a smile, putting the tea tray between them before sitting down, "that's all right."

She poured the tea, and when they were settled, Harry tried it.

"Earl Grey?" he asked.

"Yes, day in and day out I find it remains my favorite," she said. "What about you?"

"The way you make it works for me."

"There are three things that need to be done. The tea must be kept tightly sealed, the water has to be at a rolling boil when you lift the kettle, and you have to show the pot the four corners of the room before you pour."

"Interesting," Harry said. "Now, your news."

"Theresa Fuegos, with my persuasion and that of a CID lieutenant, one of Jim Snyder's people, has agreed to go into Haven House for a while. She has a cousin about her own age, who's working for a real estate company in town. The cousin and her mother and father have agreed to move into Maria's house while Theresa is at Haven House. I must say, Theresa was very taken with the lieutenant."

"Let me guess. His name is Millard Jones."

"Yes, I think that is the name. Despite the fact she's still very much in mourning for her mother, she mentioned him several times while we talked and even blushed a little. I was quite surprised."

"I'm not," Harry said. "Millard Jones should be in the movies. He would have made a fortune as a romantic lead, if that's not too old-fashioned an expression."

Rowena's face grew a little pink. "I did meet him," she said in a failed attempt at coolness. "He's quite attractive."

"You could say that," Harry said, keeping a straight face.

Rowena and Harry suddenly collapsed in laughter. When she had blown her nose and wiped her eyes and Harry had sponged up the tea he had spilled, Rowena asked what progress had been made in locating Maria's killer.

"None, and I'm not surprised," Harry said, accepting a refill. "I'm fairly sure the murder was carried out by a professional, probably someone brought in from the East Coast."

"Does that make it more or less likely that the Ogilvies are involved?"

"I doubt they hired the killer, but I'm sure she was killed because of what she knew."

"Not a pleasant thought," Rowena said.

Harry wondered if she was worrying that she might have become someone's target of interest.

"I don't see you at risk here," he said. "There's nothing really to connect you to Fuegos, aside from the fact she was a member of your congregation."

"Actually, I was thinking about Theresa. Do you know that she's still going to classes and driving to the campus every day? That puts her on I-75 an hour and a half a day."

"I'm not surprised. Is any of that night driving?" Harry asked.

"I don't think so unless she stays on campus, to work in the library or attend an evening program."

Harry set down his cup and saucer. "Since she won't leave Avola," he said, "I don't think it's reasonable to expect her to give up school. Targeting her on the campus or on the highway in the daytime would expose her attacker to considerable risk."

"I suppose so," Rowena said, but didn't sound convinced. Then, accompanying him to the door, she asked, "By the way, how is Caedmon's living at the Hammock working out?"

"Did I tell you she had moved out there?"

They were standing at the door, letting in the calling of ring-neck doves and the warm Gulf breeze.

"No, but this place is a village. Actually, Millard Jones told me. Apparently, it has surprised nearly everyone in the department."

Harry did not like the news. "I would think adults had better things to do with their time than speculate about my private life." He paused to think and said, "I'd give you odds that Frank Hodges has been talking."

He was surprised to find he especially didn't like having Maureen O'Reilly knowing about it, but he avoided analyzing his reaction.

"Frank likes a good story," Rowena agreed. "How is it working out?"

"I took her out there thinking only a few people would know where she is," Harry complained. "Now I expect to see it in the newspaper."

"You didn't answer my question. Was that intentional? Is anything wrong?"

"No, when I see her growing uneasy with what she calls, 'excessive woods,' I take her to see Tucker. If the work on her apartment isn't finished soon, she may move in with him. He's major competition."

"A charming man and worth listening to," she said, "something that can't be said of many people, present company excepted."

"Where would Millard Jones fit in that multitude of the excluded?"

"A horse of a different color, Harry," she said briskly, but grew pink anyway. "Entirely different, wouldn't you say?"

★ ★ ★ ★ ★

Harry thought there was only one answer to that question and got away without giving it or telling Rowena how he and Caedmon were getting along. As far as he and Caedmon were concerned, he had no idea how they were "getting along." The question hadn't arisen. Coming on her unexpectedly still made his knees weaken and his heart do odd things.

She was very different from other women he had been intimate with. She was not particularly demonstrative, did not demand his attention except when it was obviously needed. And although she had a temper and did not go to great lengths to control it, she was not temperamental. She was extremely focused and had a kind of brilliance that was entirely different from his own way of thinking. She was beautiful but seemed unaffected by the fact.

Did he mind being in love with someone who was not in love with him? Caedmon was passionate, generous, caring, a good listener, and fair and forthright.

How could he even begin to answer the question?

As he was turning the Rover into Ashbury Gardens, Ernesto Piedra called him. He slowed down and took the call.

"Perhaps we should talk," Piedra said without fanfare.

"Where?" Harry said.

"Somewhere that people will not turn either to look at me or at you."

"There's the Green Tomato Bar on Fifth Street. But I'm tied up the rest of the day. Can you tell me now?"

"It is not a good idea. As for the bar, I know the place. Good choice. Tomorrow afternoon around two?"

Harry accepted Ernesto's insistence on meeting, going along with his friend's instincts, which over the years he had come to trust. "Okay," he said. "Two o'clock."

"Watch your back, Harry," Ernesto said and was gone.

Harry analyzed Ernesto's warning as he made his way to Caedmon's house. He had lived with warnings of one kind or another for enough years not to have his mind freeze at the prospect of danger. Instead, he began making a list of the possible sources of the threat. It was very unlikely Ernesto had learned that someone had a contract to kill him. So he put that possibility at the end of his list.

It was not improbable that Caedmon had been targeted for further harassment, and he left that possibility floating near the top of the list. He decided to assume until Ernesto said otherwise that the threat was coming from Afton Breckenridge. If it was, it meant either she was in a position to know firsthand that Harry and Caedmon were trying to learn her whereabouts, or it meant someone was an informant.

Harry's mind came to rest again on Ernan. It seemed increasingly likely that Afton had an informant in the house. Of course, it was possible that she and her husband were in this together, but Harry could find no way of giving that possibility legs.

"Things would be a lot more convenient if I could take my car," Caedmon said as Harry helped her carry out of the house the materials she had been working on in his absence.

She looked as if she had spent the time in a flour mill. It had done her disposition no good, and Harry was treading carefully. The men were still at work, but their radios were silent. They were talking in low voices, speaking only when they had to. No one was laughing.

"Yes, it would," Harry agreed. "The thing is, if your car disappears, whoever's watching the house will know you're not there and will come looking for you."

"Who gives a shit?" she demanded, throwing the two stuffed boxes she was carrying into the back seat of the Rover. She began rubbing her arms and legs and shaking herself, as if army ants had found her. Plaster dust rose around her in a white nimbus.

"You look like a goddess with that cloud around you," Harry said, hoping to make her feel better.

"I don't want any compliments on my ass or any other part of my anatomy," she told him, stopping her exotic dance, "no part of which is not dusted white, including my tongue from the taste. Are you going to just stand there, or are you going to put that stuff in the car and get us out of here?"

Normally, Harry enjoyed a quiet drive back to the Hammock, but today was different. Today it was the tense kind of quiet surrounding a hunting cat passing through the woods, and was not restful.

"I'm going to take a shower," she said as soon as the Rover came to a stop under the live oak.

Harry carried in the boxes and immediately set about making her a martini. Then he made one for himself, charity beginning at home and so on. Both were very large and very cold.

"Onion or olive?" he asked, carrying the tray with the drinks on it into the bedroom.

She was bent over drying her hair, a sight that still shortened his breath.

"What?" she demanded sharply, coming up for air.

He was standing in front of her bearing icy gifts. The scowl that had darkened her face vanished. She dropped the towel. Oh, happy day!

"Harry! How thoughtful. How did you guess?"

"Just washing away the dust wasn't going to do it."

"You were right. An olive, please. Just let me get my robe."

"I wouldn't bother."

"No, you're right," she said, lifting her glass, "it's too warm for a robe. Why don't you make yourself more comfortable?"

"First, a toast," Harry said, putting down the tray.

Their glasses touching made a bright, silvery sound.

"Oh, yes," she whispered a few moments later, "how thoughtful of you."

Despite its dim lights, aged wooden bar, old-fashioned mirror, and dark, high-backed booths, the Green Tomato bore a certain resemblance to an airport waiting area. All sorts of people passed through its bat-winged doors—executives and reporters from the newspaper offices two blocks away, boat owners and tourists on their way to the City Docks on the Seminole River, laborers from the boat yards, clerks from the shops on Anchor Avenue, and cops from the Central Precinct.

The principal draw was, of course, booze, but the food ran a close second. At lunch time the screened porch, standing on pilings over the Seminole River and fitted out with skimpy tables, red-checked table cloths, and bent tin flatware, was crowded and raucous. The ringing wail of Allegheny laments, backed by twanging guitars, sawing fiddles, and sweating schooners of beer, provided an elegant background for the mingling of titled English yachtsmen in starched whites and undocumented workers in stained dungarees.

"I had forgotten about the *policia*," Ernesto said, sliding into the chair across the table from Harry.

"They're off duty," Harry said. "Their minds are on hamburgers and fried onions. You're looking rested. How does this happen?"

"The storms kept me from working last night, and I slept alone," Ernesto said with a slightly superior air. "You, on the other hand, look wasted."

"That's because I work for a living," Harry said.

"I tried doing that when I was young," Ernesto said, holding the menu at arm's length as he scanned it.

"You need glasses," Harry said, making a production of putting on his before picking up the battered "Guide to Good Eating" that lay on the table in front of him. It was mostly show as he always had the house specialty, lobster salad.

"I see enough, as much as I want to and sometimes more," Ernesto said, bristling.

The waiter interrupted their colloquy. "What is it?" he asked in a surly voice.

"What will it be?" Ernesto protested, giving the waiter an offended look.

The man stared at him down a long, thin nose and said some something incomprehensible that Harry thought had the ring of "Fuck you."

All the waiters in the Green Tomato were Latvians. They were all tall, thin, dark-haired, insolent, and indifferent. Their aprons may once have been white, also their shirts. When the waiter had taken their orders, which at first he pretended not to understand, and left scowling and muttering under his breath, Ernesto watched him go and said, "When I first began to come in here, every time I would swear an oath never to return. But then I would forget. Now I no longer care. Why is that?"

"Same here, but they make the best lobster salad in Avola," Harry said with a shrug. "The good outweighs the bad in this case."

"Do you suppose they are refusing to speak English because they can't?"

"No."

"I think so, too. Shall I tell you what I have learned? Or shall we eat first?"

"Tell me."

"First, there was a professional, driving a rental, who came in and stayed where the guns from the East Coast always stay."

"The Grouper Club?"

"On the Bridge Road."

"Right."

"He left the Club a while after one A.M., came back a couple of hours later, and checked out the next morning. That's all the night manager knew."

"What was he driving?"

"A black Mercedes."

"It looks right," Harry said. "I'll see Jim gets this. What about the picture?"

"A disappointment," Ernesto said, frowning. "Several people said she looked familiar, but no one admitted to having seen her recently. I think she is not around or else she has changed her looks enough to fool people."

"Back where we started," Harry said.

"Not all the way back," Ernesto insisted. "Those who saw the picture still have it."

The waiter returned and banged their plates down on the table with more muttering.

"Before we start on these," Ernesto said, regarding the heaped food with apparent alarm, "I have more uncertainty to mention."

"All right. Do you think we can eat all of this?"

"We are not required. Here is the troubling thing. Two nights ago, a man came by cab from the airport, having arrived on a flight from New York. He did not go to the Grouper but to the bus station, where, it is thought but not verified, he took another cab to the place he was going."

"Not a tourist and not a businessman?"

"No, and too pale to be living here."

Harry thought a moment and then said, "I suppose even connected people take vacations."

"South Beach, maybe," Ernesto said, picking up his fork, "not Avola."

"Your informant is sure about him? My salad is excellent.

How's your pulled pork?"

"*Excelente!* He is not likely to be wrong about this."

They ate for a while, and Harry, lost in his salad, even forgot that Alison Krauss was singing with Union Station behind her, playing their hearts out.

"Are you at risk from your work?" Ernesto asked, leaning back in his chair and putting down an empty *Dos Equis*.

"I don't know," Harry said, falling back with Ernesto, acknowledging defeat. "I wouldn't think so, but it is impossible to know for certain."

"Ms. Rivers?"

"Possibly. A professional put a bullet through her window. I'm curious about something. Why do you keep such a large network of informants at your beck and call?"

"*Beck and call?*"

"Working for you."

Ernesto considered the question while eating more of the pork a pinch at a time.

"In my profession when trouble comes," he said quietly, wiping his fingers, "I cannot go to a lawyer or the police for help. I must attend to it myself. I protect myself by making it my business to know what the police know, where the bad people are, and what they are doing."

"I have never heard you mention this before," Harry said.

"No, I am a very peaceful man. I do not own a gun. But now and then someone comes who either wants my clients or a percentage of my earnings."

Harry fought hard and managed not to laugh at the mention of *clients*.

"Before these plans become a reality, I take steps to dissuade them."

"They disappear, in other words," Harry said in surprise, never before having seen this side of Ernesto.

"Not in the way you mean, no. They are persuaded that their plans expose them to risks it would be better not to take."

"I'm impressed," Harry said. "And so far your competitors have withdrawn quietly."

"Yes. I have been very lucky. I sleep well."

"When you sleep at all."

He gave Harry a brilliant smile. "A man must have some pleasure, or life is not worth living."

20

Harry had not responded to Ernesto's question as to whether or not Caedmon might be the reason the New York man was in town, but the man's presence worried him. At the same time, without arriving at a satisfactory answer, he had asked himself repeatedly in the past several days if Afton had sufficient reason to hire a professional gunman to fly here from the East Coast to put a bullet through Caedmon's window. It didn't, as Caedmon would say, "compute."

That Afton had now hired a New York–based assassin to kill her was even more difficult to believe. Feeling stymied, he decided to talk with Jim. When he got there, he found the Sheriff's Department in an uproar, or at least as close to an uproar as Harry had ever seen it. People were almost running along usually sedate corridors. On his way to Jim's office he nearly crashed into Lieutenant O'Reilly, charging around a corner like a Celtic warrior, her hair streaming behind her. Harry's heart gave a jump, partially in fear and partly because she looked so magnificent—what would she have been like with a sword in one hand and her shield on her shoulder?

He crowded against the wall, expecting she would rush past him. Instead, she pulled up short and grasped him by the shoulder. It took all his fortitude not to wince. Yanking him away from the wall, she bent down, her green eyes blazing, bringing her face close to his, and said, "I'll be having a word with you in a bit, Harry Brock, you black-hearted devil."

With that she thrust him back so hard his head banged against the wall and then dropped him as if he had been a sour apple. "Just you see if I don't!" she added over her shoulder, rushing away like a fury in pursuit of her victim.

Harry, regaining his balance, was standing, rubbing his head and watching her go, lost in mingled dread and admiration, when Hodges arrived.

"I saw some of that," Hodges said, wide-eyed and breathing heavily.

Harry guessed he too must have been hurrying somewhere. "What the hell is going on here?"

"Never mind that," Hodges said. "Why was the O'Reilly banging your head against the wall? Are you all right?"

"Yes," Harry said, wanting to change the subject, "but I'm in a lot of trouble."

"I noticed," Hodges said, followed by a wide grin.

"God," Harry said, "she's a wonder. I think she's wonderful, all six and a half feet of her."

"A holy terror is what she is," Hodges said, losing his grin. "If she's mad at you, you're in deeper shit than you can even begin to guess. Think about going away for two years, at least two years. Take the Rivers woman with you."

Hodges spoke with such feeling and energy that Harry couldn't help laughing.

"Where were you going in such a rush? What's happened to this place?"

"It's the Danton case," Hodges said, losing his happy face.

"That's the man who shot and wounded his wife and tried to kill her mother with his bare hands?"

"That's the one. You know, there's an odd twist to that story," Hodges said, leaning back a little to balance his belly, shoving his hands into his pockets and getting comfortable before going on. "For twenty years, Clyde Danton worked for the Tequesta

County Power and Light. He was a lineman, and from what we learned, a good worker. He was also a good family man . . ."

"Wait, Frank," Harry said. "This is too good to spoil by having to hurry it. Let's save it for later when we're not in such a rush. Just tell me what the problem is."

"Good idea," Hodges said. "The original record of Danton's interrogations and confession, conducted by the CID people, has gone missing. The state's attorney's office has put on its war paint, and that pounding you hear outside is a gallows going up for the hangings."

Hodges' glum expression faded as he developed his joke, and Harry laughed to help him along.

"Is Jim in his office?"

"He was, if the O'Reilly hasn't found him."

"How can an electronic recording be lost?"

"Well," Hodges said a little sheepishly, "the interrogations and the confessions were taped. We've been so strapped for money, we haven't got all switched over to the other thing."

Harry did not share his thoughts on that revelation, which was hardly credible but no doubt true. "Lost or misfiled?"

"We think they're in a drawer or locker in the Evidence Section or in the CID offices."

Edging away, Harry said, "But just in case, you're tossing the whole department. Look, you just go on, I've held you back, and I've got to talk to Jim."

Jim's office was a small area of calm, although Jim was not calm. In fact, as Harry could see, he was hopping mad.

"It's like living on a flood plain," he told Harry, pushing back in his chair and swinging his feet onto the corner of his desk— one of the ways, as Harry knew, he tried to relax. "At unpredictable intervals the river comes in your front door. We live on a loss plain. At unpredictable intervals some significant piece of evidence disappears. Of course, it's only when it's needed yesterday that I find out it's missing."

"Are there copies?"

"Half a dozen, but you know how that goes. The court and the defense attorneys want the originals."

"You don't seem overly concerned," Harry said.

"No, over time I've grown accustomed to this particular failure, but that doesn't mean that when evidence goes missing I don't put the stick in amongst those responsible for seeing to it that the chain of evidence is kept in one piece and that at all times we know where any particular piece of evidence is."

"Which accounts for the running in the corridors," Harry said.

"That's it," Jim said with a humorless smile.

Harry wanted to lay out for Jim his speculations about the possible connection between Afton and the Ogilvies, but he decided to let that wait in favor of pursuing something more pressing.

"On the other hand, you don't seem too cheerful," Harry said.

Jim let his feet crash to the floor. He picked up a pen and stared at it in the way that Harry thought Lady Macbeth must have looked at the knife that appeared before her.

"Maybe you'd better tell me," Harry said, hoping Jim's thoughts weren't as bloody as those of Lady Macbeth.

"Marriage," Jim said in a sepulchral voice, "is no bed of roses."

"Full of rocks," Harry responded.

"What?" Jim asked, looking puzzled and also irritated.

"It's often the bed that's strewn with rocks."

"I don't feel like jokes, especially those made at my expense."

Jim's face had darkened, and Harry hastened to mend the damage. "I'm not joking. Some years ago, I read in a 'Dear

Abby' column a letter from a reader, saying that her marriage was on the rocks. Abby's reply was that, 'When a marriage goes on the rocks, the rocks are usually in the bed.' "

"Why in God's name were you reading 'Dear Abby'?"

"I don't remember, but it may have been a case of any port in a storm. From time to time, the seas ran high in my marriages."

"I see you're struggling toward some point," Jim said testily. "As I don't have anything better to do, I'll just sit here and wait till you get there."

"You and Kathleen," Harry said. "If you don't want to talk about it, I'll get to what brought me here."

Jim dropped the pen as if it had grown too hot to hold and glowered at Harry, his long face still dark with some unexpressed emotion.

"All right," he said at last. "I do remember those troubles you had, and I recall your talking to me about them. Possibly, I'd better talk about this before it eats a hole in my innards. And I guess talking with you would be a place to start."

"I'll listen," Harry said. "Sometimes it helps just to have someone listen."

"I think Kathleen may leave me. That will be really bad."

Jim seemed to stick there, staring at the wall as if deciphering writing that Harry couldn't see. Harry knew well that strange suspension of will that comes when domestic pain reaches a critical level.

"Yes, it will," Harry said and waited.

"Losing Clara will also be bad. How bad, I don't want to consider."

Harry waited again. He knew what Jim was going through and gave him time to corral his emotions.

"For reasons I don't understand," Jim said, consulting the wall again, "the rocks got into the bed right after Clara was born. Now, there's not much bed left."

"What does Kathleen say about it?"

"We are not going to discuss that," Jim said grimly.

"That's all right," Harry said quickly.

"I mean," Jim said, shooting Harry an angry glance, "that's what she says about it."

"Ah! I'm sorry. You've probably tried the usual things—getting a babysitter, going out to dinner, maybe having a weekend away someplace nicer than you usually go to."

Harry heard himself and stopped talking. He was sounding like something off the grocery store magazine rack.

"A year ago, but nothing helped, not since the suspicions took root."

"That new deputy?"

"Her and half a dozen others. Things are stretched so tight that something's got to snap."

"Jim," Harry said, risking a rebuke, "I think that you and Kathleen have to talk with somebody. If she won't, you should go alone."

"A marriage counselor," Jim said in a dead voice.

"I'd move that up a grade," Harry said as gently as he could.

"Are you saying Kathleen's . . ." and he couldn't go on.

"As I recall," Harry said, "Kathleen had a hard time adjusting to being pregnant, then a hard time with the delivery, and more trouble adjusting to being a mother."

"But she loves Clara as much as I do, probably more," Jim protested, "and she's an excellent mother."

"Of course, but how are you and she getting along? And why the change?"

"I don't know."

"Needing help finding an answer and then accepting the help that comes after you've got it is nothing to be ashamed of, and it's better than letting your marriage collapse."

"I'll give it some thought. What brought you here?"

"One last thing," Harry said, knowing the discussion was over. Tearing a blank page out of his pocket notepad, he scribbled a name on the scrap of paper and passed it across the desk to Jim.

"Gloria Holinshed is the best," he said. "She's in the book. Katherine and I worked with her when we were having that trouble with Minna. Turned out Katherine and I needed the help more than our daughter."

Jim stared at the name as if it was written in hieroglyphics, but in the end he stuffed the paper into his shirt pocket and thanked Harry. "Now, let's move on."

Harry quickly summarized what he had learned about Afton's relationship with Gwen Ogilvie, their appointments and the phone calls that Ernan handled, and mentioned the possibility of cell phone calls and messaging.

"How likely do you think it is," Jim asked, "that Afton Breckenridge is involved in what the Ogilvies are doing—if they're doing anything illegal?"

"Anything you can tell me about the investigation?"

"There's nothing to tell, aside from repeating Attorney Dillard's warning not even to hint to the Ogilvies that they're being investigated."

"I suppose that means there's nothing new on the Fuegos murder."

"At a standstill."

"Not surprising. As for the likelihood that Afton's disappearance has any connection with the Ogilvies, there's no hard evidence to support it."

"But you thought it was worth bringing to me. Why?"

"I have satisfied myself that it was a professional brought in from the East Coast, presumably by Afton, who put a bullet through Caedmon's window to warn Caedmon to stop her investigation. That is serious overkill.

"Also, I've learned that another one has just come in from New York. There's no information on who hired him. Afton again? Why? To kill Caedmon? That is not reasonable, and if it is, there has to be more motive than I've found."

"I won't ask how you know all this because you won't tell me, but the target, if there is one, may not be Caedmon."

"Possibly not. Anyway, Caedmon no longer thinks Afton has disappeared just to make things miserable for her husband." Harry paused, then added, "She also says that's what lawyers are for. And it's true. With Breckenridge's infidelity an established fact, she could have used the courts to skin him."

"Good points," Jim said, still looking glum. "There's this as well. If she succeeds in having him convicted for her murder, she will lose everything that she hasn't taken with her, identity included. How reasonable is that?"

"If she's alive," Harry said, "and Caedmon says she is."

Harry left with no help from Jim as to whether or not the gunman from New York was a serious threat. The captain's lack of enthusiasm over the possibility that there was any criminal connection between Afton and the Ogilvies did not ease Harry's mind. He had already discounted the probability, but couldn't convince himself that probability ruled out possibility.

His uncertainty took him a step further, which led to his making another call on Breckenridge.

"Thanks for seeing me on such short notice," Harry said when Ernan had announced his arrival.

Breckenridge, dressed in shorts, polo shirt, and sandals, was on his balcony, sitting under a green canvas canopy, staring out over the river. Harry noticed that the opened notebook in his lap had been forgotten, its pages flipping quietly over in the light breeze.

"Have a seat," he said. "What can I do for you?"

"What's happening with Dillard?" Harry asked, knowing that the grand jury was convened and Dillard had begun making his case, but wanting a glimpse of Breckenridge's state of mind. Harry thought he looked as though he hadn't been sleeping much and was feeling miserable.

"I only know what my lawyers tell me. They don't tell me much and half of that is bullshit."

"In case you haven't been told, the grand jury is sitting. I think their deliberations will be brief."

"What will they decide?"

Harry thought the outcome was a certainty. They would give Dillard what he wanted. But Harry did not want to say so.

"It could go either way. I don't know what Dillard is taking to them."

"Afton's letter should be enough," Breckenridge said dully.

"Maybe," Harry said. "Grand juries are unpredictable. There are too many contingencies to anticipate their actions accurately. Look, something's come up regarding Mrs. Breckenridge. Do you feel up to talking about it?"

"It's a better offer than sitting here anticipating the joys of prison life."

"You may not find what I'm going to say pleasant or the questions easy to answer," Harry said honestly.

"Get to the point," Breckenridge said, showing some of his old edge.

The show of spirit encouraged Harry. "Caedmon and I have slowly come to the conclusion that your wife is probably alive."

"You two have already told me that," Breckenridge snapped.

"Yes, we have, and I've repeated it only because it lays the groundwork for what's coming."

Breckenridge muttered something about getting on with it and leaned back in his chair.

"If she is alive, her motives for doing what she's doing begin to look inadequate."

"She's angry with me because of Beatrice, and wants my head," Breckenridge said. "Christ, Brock, does it take two people to figure that out?"

"It's the first thing everyone, including the state's attorney, would think of, and it's such a good motive, why look for another?"

"I'm getting lost," Breckenridge said, beginning to show more interest.

"Let me back up. Caedmon has been following your wife's trail, and it's been a long and twisting journey," Harry said. "Every new revelation has made it clearer that Mrs. Breckenridge has been systematically deconstructing her life."

"So? She wants the police to think she's dead."

"Humpty Dumpty," Harry said.

"What do you mean?"

"She can't put it together again."

Breckenridge started to speak, stopped, and sat staring at Harry—and, Harry hoped, thinking about what he'd just heard. Several long moments passed while Harry waited, listening to the laughing gulls diving and screaming over the river.

Breckenridge finally stirred and said, "Okay, your point."

"If making you miserable had been her only goal, she could have, as Caedmon pointed out, left it to her lawyers."

Breckenridge still looked unconvinced.

"Think about it," Harry said. "She could have frog-marched you through a divorce court, kicking you hard every step of the way."

Breckenridge appeared to contemplate the event with deepening gloom.

"Instead," Harry said into Breckenridge's silence, "she's lost her identity, her homes, all possibility of returning to this country, and she's left with a future of running and hiding."

"And your question is, 'Why would she do it?' "

"That's right."

"She may not be as bad off as you two think," Breckenridge said, getting to his feet and shoving his hands into his pockets. "Afton wasn't born in this country. Her mother is American and her father was Swiss. She was born and raised in Switzerland. In fact, she doesn't particularly like this country."

"She has her American citizenship through her mother?"

"Yes, a dual citizenship. When Afton was eighteen, her mother and father divorced. Her mother returned to her family in northern Virginia. Afton completed her studies at the Sorbonne, then earned her law degree at the University of Virginia. She was working for a Washington, D.C. firm when I met her, although by then her father had died, leaving her a wealthy woman."

Harry was surprised by Breckenridge's sudden openness. Usually, getting information from him was like cracking a beechnut. Even so, he wasn't certain he understood what he had just been told.

"Then you mean that, for her, staying away from the U.S. wouldn't be a hardship."

Breckenridge gave a short, dismissive laugh. "I mean the money she's got stashed in private Zurich banks makes what she's cleaned out of her holdings in this country look like tips."

Harry noted the bitterness in Breckenridge's voice.

"I've just thought of something," Harry said.

"What?"

"Has she left a will?"

21

"What have you found out?" Caedmon asked, her excitement making her cheeks glow.

Harry had called her, told her he had talked with Breckenridge, and she was waiting for him on the lanai. The sun was back in the trees, throwing long shadows over the creek; the breeze was still moving the leaves and passing through the lanai with a restful sound, bringing with it cool air, and the redolent smell of earth and growing things.

"Wait!" she said, springing out of his embrace. "I almost forgot. There's gin!"

Harry was more surprised by Caedmon's enthusiasm and wifely attentions than he had been by what Breckenridge had told him. Since coming to the Hammock, she had never made anything but the coffee and that was done out of desperation.

"Here," she said, hurrying back, "sit down, drink some of this, and tell me everything."

Harry sat, drank, gasped, leaned back, closed his eyes, and let the gin work its magic.

"Harry," she said with more irritation than concern in her voice, "what's wrong?"

"I was thinking how good it is to come home and find you here," he said, suspecting he was risking something.

He was right.

"Don't be an idiot," she said. "What did Breckenridge tell you?"

Harry, mentally kicking himself for being so reckless, ran through his conversation with Breckenridge, and ended by telling her about the Swiss banks and the possibility Afton had a will.

"What was his response?" Caedmon asked.

"That she never mentioned one."

"If it exists, I'll wager it's with her Swiss bankers. The Devil himself couldn't get to it. Even God would have a struggle on his hands, especially if it's in a private bank such as Wegelin and Co."

"How important is it to you?" Harry asked.

"Well, my curiosity is aroused," she said, pausing to take a long drink. Then she surfaced, gasping. "My God!" she croaked, "That is strong! How's yours?"

Harry took the opportunity to have another hearty swig.

"Just right," he told her, his voice rising an octave as he struggled to breathe. "What's for dinner?"

"Whatever you're cooking."

"Chicken soup, pickled beets, sautéed onions, anise, and red peppers in olive oil and balsamic vinegar."

"We'll be eating at midnight!" she said.

"Wonders of the freezer," Harry said. "The broth is preserved."

"I usually have a salad for dinner."

"I'm trying to fatten you up."

"What for?"

"Use your imagination."

"I don't have to."

Their glasses were empty and she held hers out to him.

"Follow me into the kitchen," he told her, "and I'll show you how to defrost something."

"Forget it," she told him, sinking back in her seat. "Roughing it holds no attractions for me."

"You can't get up," he said.

"I can so," she protested and struggled to her feet. She took one step and stopped, swaying slightly. "Wow, that was a drink."

He held out his hand. "Let's try for the kitchen."

They missed the kitchen but made it to the bedroom.

Later, they made do, rather sleepily, with tuna salad sandwiches and sliced cucumbers and tomatoes in rice wine vinegar.

The following morning, Caedmon, glowing from her shower, insisted on a walk after breakfast. They had risen before the sun was up; Harry shut off the AC, then opened the windows and the door to the lanai, letting the last of the night wind into the house. It billowed the curtains and hummed in the screens as it went on its way. All around them the voices of the dawn chorus were waking and the night choristers sinking into sleep.

"This place is never quiet," Caedmon said, resting her hands on one of the window sills.

"Hymns of praise," Harry said. "Constant reminders."

"Of what?"

"The urgency of life lived fully," he said, a little surprised at himself.

"Is that what we're doing?" she asked, turning to look at him over her shoulder as he put away the last of the dishes.

"Only people have to ask that question," he said. "For the rest of creation, it's a given."

"Why?"

"Other creatures can't pause to ask. Come on," he urged. "Sneakers, slacks, hat. We're going into the trees."

"Snakes, ants, bugs, and plants with stickers," Caedmon complained, but Harry knew from the tone of her voice that it was a pro forma protest.

" 'Deep Woods' will protect you," he said, waving the can, "along with my strong right arm."

She was ready first.

"Put an arm around me and tell me you're happy," she said, stopping at the foot of the stairs to wait for him, holding her hat on with one hand as she watched him descend.

He set his backpack down long enough to embrace her, kiss her, and say, "I love you, Caedmon."

She gave him another kiss and said, "I'll settle for being loved."

That little exchange took some of the glow out of the morning. Why hadn't he simply told her that of course he was happy? Would it have been the truth? Not really. She had told him she didn't love him, and nothing she had said since gave him any hope that the situation had changed. Making an effort, he pushed aside the darkness of that reality and led them out the back door, pausing under the tree where the barred owls were nesting, to check on the owls, which were preparing their fledglings for their first flights.

"Why are owls thought to be wise?" Caedmon asked as they stared up through the branches at the messy nest.

"They're not, but the habit they have of sitting and staring makes them look thoughtful."

"Now I know," Caedmon replied with a sigh, "and it wasn't worth getting a sore neck for."

She walked behind him in silence, occasionally singing quietly, apparently lost in her own thoughts. "Why are we going this way?" she asked after a time.

Harry, brooding, welcomed her interruption. "I'm supposed to be keeping track of this hammock," he said, "and that means walking over all of it every now and then. I haven't been out here for a while. How do you like it so far?"

"I thought there'd be more bushes."

They were following a grassy path that twisted through a stand of heavily leafed trees. The trees formed a dense canopy far above their heads, shading them from the sun, which was already climbing steadily up the sky, gaining strength as it rose.

"This is a mature forest, or nearly so. No trees have been cut here for at least fifty years. There's only light enough for ferns and shade tolerant plants to grow down here."

"There's something really strange about it," she added. "I just noticed that it's quiet in here. Spooky."

"When it gets hot enough, the cicadas and locusts will tune up," Harry said.

A bit later he stopped and said, "Let's stop here. We've come almost two miles, and I want you to do something. Pretend you're just skin, eyes, nose, and ears. No thinking now. Just be those four senses and nothing else."

At first, Caedmon groaned, fidgeted, restlessly twisting her body, bored and showing it. Harry pretended not to notice, and gradually she grew still.

A few minutes later she whispered, without looking at Harry, "What is it I'm feeling?"

"The Hammock," he answered.

"Oh, my," she said and sighed. "I thought I was going to be afraid, but then I wasn't."

"Are you OK?"

"Yes," she said. "Different. Is it alive?"

"I think so."

"I thought all that Gaia stuff was crap."

"Not entirely."

As they went on, the big trees gave way to smaller trees and denser undergrowth. The sun edged through the leaves, the grass grew taller and sharper edged, and the bugs found them. But Caedmon remained quiet. It wasn't until Harry had sprayed them both that she broke her silence.

"There were moments when I thought I might lose myself. I don't know if I was afraid or not. I've never felt that way before."

"Haven't you been so focused while you were working that everything else fell away?"

"Yes, I guess I have, and sometimes making love," she said, "but this was different and somehow . . . more spacious."

"Explain."

"The inside and the outside began to blur."

"Was it pleasant?"

"Yes."

They began walking again, and Harry asked her no more questions. Not wanting her to reduce the experience to words, he began pointing silently at things and spoke only in response to her questions. Reaching a place where their path was less impeded by thrusting branches and tall grasses, Harry increased the pace a little.

Their subdued conversation stuttered to a stop, and Harry, looking back now and then, was pleased to see that Caedmon appeared to be moving freely and at ease in their silence. They had just moved into a clearing, dotted with saw palmettos and knee-high bunch grass, and he was congratulating himself when the gentle, sunny hum and buzz of the surrounding woods was interrupted by a sudden, loud clamor, followed by half a dozen very dark, broad-winged birds beating their way upward through a tangle of stopper saplings. They cried raucously and crashed through the smaller branches in their haste, sending down a shower of twigs and leaves.

"Harry!" Caedmon said, her voice rising. "What are they?"

"It's all right," he said, putting a hand on her arm but not taking his eyes off the place where the commotion was occurring. "They're turkey vultures. Something has frightened them. Keep your voice low."

He did not say they had been feeding on a carcass when

something bigger than they were had jumped them into panicked flight. Instead, he spoke very quietly, gently shaking her arm to hold her attention, which kept shifting to the vultures, now above the brush and climbing heavily upward toward the top of the canopy.

"Don't talk," he told her. "Just back up, slowly and quietly. Hold onto me if you want to. I'll back up too. Slowly now, stay on the path, here we go."

They had moved perhaps thirty feet when Harry stopped abruptly.

"Don't move," he said.

Harry's gaze was fixed on the far edge of the clearing where the vultures had been feeding.

"Watch," he said as she moved up beside him, "but don't say anything and don't move. Don't move."

A moment later, a long, sleek animal, powerful muscles rippling under her tawny coat, trotted silently out of the bushes and came to a stop in a sunny patch of belly-high grass, her thick tail switching. She fixed them with brilliant yellow eyes, a deep growl rumbling in her chest.

The cat stood motionless except for its tail, and Harry made a decision.

"Don't take your eyes off her," he said quietly. "When I say, 'go,' begin backing away. Move very slowly. I'll go with you. Slowly. Go."

At their first movement, the cat tensed, her tail stiffening.

"Keep going," Harry said. "Slowly, slowly. Keep watching her."

The cat took a step toward them. Then another.

"You're doing well," Harry said. "Keep moving. Whatever happens, don't run."

Harry made a short, silent prayer of hope that wherever it was, her den wasn't behind them.

The cat took two more quick steps toward them and then stopped, and Harry saw her relax. A moment later, she turned and in two long, graceful bounds vanished into the undergrowth.

"I think that's enough zoology for the day," Harry said, turning to Caedmon, who was still looking at the spot where the cat had been standing. "What do you think?"

"I think she was magnificent," Caedmon said in a steady voice, her eyes wide with the intensity of what they had experienced, "and I don't even like cats. How do you know it was a *she?*"

"First, I think we should begin putting a little more distance between her and us. She let us go because she decided that was what we wanted to do. Let's not disappoint her."

He turned and put his hands on her shoulders and said, "You were great. Let's go."

"Two things," Caedmon said over her shoulder. "First, how do you know it's a female. Second, was there any chance she might have attacked us?"

"Her breasts are full. She's got kittens. Yes, there was a moment when she was seriously considering it. Those vultures were probably on a deer she had killed and dragged into those stopper shrubs. Having just charged into them as we were stepping into the clearing, she might have thought we wanted her groceries."

"What would you have done if she had attacked us?"

"Pulled off my backpack and tried to fend her off."

"Could you have done it?"

"Probably not."

"Harry, I'm not satisfied with that answer."

"Neither am I."

22

The next morning, Harry repaid an overdue favor by agreeing to try to trace a stolen, Rockport-rebuilt Dark Harbor 17 sailboat, the owner's substitute for a savings account. Harry did not have a high opinion of boats. He began with the boat dealerships in Avola, a depressing activity because he knew when he started that the thief would avoid such places like the plague. His next effort had a slightly better chance of success. Boat rentals and repair. There was the possibility that the thief had removed all identification numbers from the boat, then shopped it around for a quick sale or a new paint job.

The last boatyard owner clasped Harry by the shoulder for support when he heard what Harry was trying to do. "Here's some free advice," the man said when he had stopped laughing, "you're chasing water spouts. Ninety percent of boats stolen in Avola are either trailered or sailed to the Keys or around the bend to the East Coast and resold and re-licensed with bogus papers. Quit while there's some of your day left."

"What happens to the remaining ten percent?" Harry asked, trying to save some face.

"Shipped to the islands on smugglers' boats or sold off the back of a truck on the panhandle."

Harry drove back to the Hammock in a sour mood, which was not improved when Caedmon did not return his greeting or appear on the lanai. *Maybe she's gone to see Tucker,* he thought, trying for a positive attitude.

That vanished the moment he looked into the dining room and saw that the computers were gone. Their cords lay tangled on the table. Not waiting for the dread to freeze him, Harry dove back into the kitchen and called Caedmon. Her phone rang in the dining room. Harry found it under the table. It was only then that he noticed the stack of expandable files was missing from its corner.

"Someone's got her," Harry said as soon as he reached Jim. He had to repeat himself twice, using Caedmon's name, before Jim fully grasped what he'd been told.

"Don't move, don't touch a thing," Jim told him. "We're on our way."

Harry made one more call, this time to Caedmon's house, but there was no answer. He found he couldn't stay in the house with her not in it. With his pistol in his hand, he walked along the road, searching without success for clear tracks in the loose sand until the wail of sirens broke through his misery.

"I don't want to make things worse," Hodges said, once he had persuaded Harry to do the waiting on the lanai while Jim and the CID team were scouring the rest of the house for anything that might help them understand what had happened to Caedmon, "but I suppose there's no chance she could have called a taxi and bailed out?"

Harry was too shaken to find the energy to be offended. "Frank, I suppose it's possible," he said, "but her car's at her place in town, and I can't even begin to explain why she would have done such a thing."

"We had her house checked," Hodges said. "The car's there along with two painters. We checked on them, and they're for real. They hadn't seen or heard from her."

Hodges got up and left, and Harry heard him rummaging in the kitchen. A moment later he reappeared with a tall, sweating glass of ice water. He had also found the crullers.

"I made the call. Is this OK?" he asked, holding up one already half eaten. "I was late getting up this morning and didn't really have a breakfast, just a couple of fried egg and bacon sandwiches."

The anguish Harry was feeling from the rush of his mind creating horror stories of what might be happening or already have happened to Caedmon was almost overshadowed by the pain of having to sit and do nothing, at least until Jim and his teams had finished their work. It did not make it more endurable to know that for the moment there really was nothing he could do.

"As far as Millard Jones and his people can tell," Jim said, "there's not so much as a hair of evidence here to tell us what happened, no sign of a struggle, nothing."

"And now that we've driven in from the road," Harry said, "there are no tire tracks to use."

"Not that we'd have got much in that loose sand," Hodges said, earning a scowl from Jim.

Harry let it ride. A short time later, after Hodges had called in a missing-persons report on Caedmon, Jim and his people gathered their gear and left. Jim was the last to go, but not before talking privately with Harry. "I'm sorry about this," he said, his long face etched deeply with worry lines, his voice heavy with concern. "You're going to want to find whoever took her and cut his balls off."

Harry was so startled to hear Jim using that kind of language, the mental fog that was dulling his mind lifted enough for him to take in what his old friend was telling him.

"Don't do it," Jim repeated with slow emphasis. "Don't even think of doing it. For the same reason surgeons shouldn't operate on someone in their family, you shouldn't go hunting the son-of-a-bitch who did this. Do all the sleuthing you want, but leave the hunting to us. Otherwise, some innocent person may get killed."

"Do you really expect me to just sit out here and do nothing?" Harry demanded.

"Sleuthing isn't doing *nothing*, Harry."

They were standing on the lanai, close to the screen door. Jim paused and looked out through the screen as if he was listening to the mockingbird sing in the wisteria vine at the south end of the lanai.

"There's something you know about yourself, Harry," he added after a short wait, as if reaching a decision that had required some effort, "you're not like most people in one respect."

He halted again. Harry had listened enough. "If you're going to say it, say it."

"You can kill people," Jim said quietly, bringing his gaze back to Harry and bending slightly as he spoke. "You and I can do it. It doesn't mean we like it, but we can do it. I don't want you doing it in the kind of anger you're experiencing now. I don't want this to be a revenge killing."

"You want whoever did this alive."

"Yes. That way we might find out who put up the money."

"You're sure then that it's not Afton Breckenridge who's done this." Harry could feel anger plunging through his body like a wrecking ball.

"No. But if she's behind it, a professional is doing the heavy lifting."

"Probably so," Harry agreed, chaining his rage, "but I doubt it is Afton."

"Ogilvies?"

"We may have been wrong about why Afton has gone into hiding," Harry said. "We've all been thinking she did it to harass her husband. When that didn't add up the way we wanted it to,

we decided she was involved in whatever the Ogilvies are doing."

"I don't see what else it could be," Jim said, looking puzzled.

"What if they hadn't brought her into their operation? What
if she somehow found out what the Ogilvies were doing and
went to earth to escape from them?"

"And it's the Ogilvies who are trying to stop Caedmon from
finding her?" Jim asked doubtfully.

"Yes."

"Why on earth would they want to do that?"

"So that they can find her first. If Caedmon locates her,
wherever she is, it's likely the police will talk with her, which is
the last thing they would want."

"Let's say you're right," Jim said, "and I'm a long way from
thinking you are. Your theory seems shaky, to be charitable." He
took time to pull off his hat and rub his head. "But saying you
are, it means Mrs. Breckenridge isn't in Avola."

"Remember 'The Purloined Letter,' " Harry said.

"That's the one about the letter being hidden in plain sight,
right?"

"Yes."

"Why kidnap Caedmon? It would be a lot less risky just to
kill her."

Jim's blunt appraisal shook Harry, but he knew Jim had
spoken the truth.

"Yes," he said, "but let's hope they have some reason for
keeping her alive."

When Jim left, Harry went to the phone and called Breckenridge. Ernan answered.

"Caedmon Rivers has been kidnapped, Ernan," Harry said.
"I've called to tell Mr. Breckenridge, but first, I want to ask you
a question."

"Of course, Mr. Brock. What terrible news. Do you or the police have any idea who took her?"

"No, not yet."

While he dealt with Ernan's question, he also reflected on the man's poise. Given the strained nature of their last talk, involving Afton Breckenridge's phone calls, Harry would not have been surprised to hear resentment, even dislike, in the man's voice. But he sounded as he always had.

"I want to make use of your memory again, Ernan," Harry said, having added some information so as to lengthen his answer.

"What is it you wish to know?"

"Did Mrs. Ogilvie call Mrs. Breckenridge after she had left for Miami?"

Following a short pause, Ernan said, "Only once. I suppose she must not have known Mrs. Breckenridge was going away. To my knowledge, she has not called since."

"When did she call?"

"It was only a day or two after Mrs. Breckenridge had left."

"And she never called again?"

"Not to my knowledge. Of course, she may have called Mr. Breckenridge."

"I'm not sure I ever asked him," Harry said, his mind already on the fact that Gwen Ogilvie had not called since that first call. "Did you tell her where Mrs. Breckenridge was going or for how long she was going to be away?"

"Interesting question, Mr. Brock. I think I understand the reason for your asking. Yes, I said Mrs. Breckenridge was visiting friends in Miami and had not told me when she was returning, which was the truth and also not at all unusual. Mrs. Breckenridge frequently withheld from me the times of her coming and going."

Harry noted the past tense.

"You have, as always, been very helpful, Ernan. Thank you."

"You're welcome, Mr. Brock. I conclude you find significant Mrs. Ogilvie's not calling more than once."

"It may be, but it's too soon for me to say for sure. I think I'd better talk to Mr. Breckenridge."

Breckenridge was on his terrace, sitting at his table, facing the river over the usual stacks of papers and folders and notebooks. In late afternoon the terrace was shaded by the house, and with a breeze sweeping in from the Gulf, Harry found it cool and welcoming, although nothing lifted his anxiety-laced gloom brought on by Caedmon's disappearance.

"Welcome to the group!" Breckenridge shouted, scrambling to his feet at Ernan's announcement that Harry had arrived. He came toward Harry, hand outstretched. "I hope Dillard doesn't call accusing you of killing her."

Harry winced but supposed that would be as close as Breckenridge could get to saying he was sorry, then immediately wondered whether he was concerned about Caedmon or the loss of her computers.

"I suppose someone wants her shut down," Breckenridge said, leading Harry to a chair.

Harry immediately felt small for having thought him incapable of finding interest in anyone other than himself.

"The sun is pretty close to the yardarm. What about a drink?" Breckenridge said.

"I could use one."

"So could I. What's yours? I'm having a Macallan."

"Gin and tonic."

By the time Breckenridge had put down the phone and finished swearing about the tax problems Afton's absence was causing, Ernan arrived with the drinks.

"Have you any idea who grabbed her, if that's what's happened?" Breckenridge asked as soon as he had taken a healthy swallow of his single malt and Ernan had gone.

"I really don't," Harry said, thinking a bit wistfully that the gin in his drink hadn't come from the supermarket. "But I have a question to ask you that might help clarify something."

"Ask away."

"Have you had any calls from Gwen or Peter Ogilvie since your wife left?"

"That's easy," Breckenridge answered, holding his whiskey up to the light and studying it critically. "I've never had any calls from either of them. Why are you asking?"

"Unless Gwen Ogilvie called her cell phone—and I don't think she did, because Caedmon could find no evidence that her cell phone was used to make or receive calls after she left here on April eighteenth—Ogilvie called only once after your wife left. Ernan took the call and told her that Mrs. Breckenridge had driven to Miami to visit friends and had not given the day of her return. Ogilvie never called again."

"Probably thought Afton would call her when she came back," Breckenridge said, recharging his glass from the bottle Ernan had left on the tray.

"Possibly," Harry said, "but these women talked to one another at least once a week. Doesn't it strike you as odd that Ogilvie wouldn't have called again after a week or so, to ask if she had returned?"

"Who knows why women do or don't do things?" Breckenridge demanded in a surly voice. "Maybe Caedmon wasn't snatched. Maybe she just pulled stakes and left."

"On foot? Carrying two computers, one a desktop, two printers, and a fax machine?" Harry asked, rankled by Breckenridge's return to being his uncivil self.

Breckenridge threw up his hands in a gesture of hopeless confusion, tossing eight dollars' worth of whiskey into the air.

Without turning a hair, he banged the glass onto his desk and refilled it. "Called a cab. Who knows? What's all this about Gwen Ogilvie? An ice maiden if you ask me."

Harry decided that, no matter how ridiculous the idea that Caedmon had left the Hammock by cab, he would check with the three or four Avola companies that were willing to send their cabs so far out of the city.

"In my experience, friends, especially women friends, check on one another," he said, unwilling to tell Breckenridge that the Ogilvies might be criminals and that Afton may have gotten herself involved in their activities. Formulating his theory that way while replying to Breckenridge's question, Harry began to doubt there was any truth in it. The recognition left him feeling empty and helpless. Afton, the Ogilvies, Caedmon—they all seemed suddenly caught up in actions and events beyond his ability to either understand or control.

"In my experience," Breckenridge said with almost palpable bitterness, "they do what they want to do and fuck the consequences."

"Isn't that what you do?" Harry asked, his hopelessness turning quickly into anger.

"You mean Beatrice," Breckenridge replied without obvious rancor. "Not really. I spent weeks looking at the possible consequences before deciding that no matter what I did, things between Afton and me were not going to get any better."

"Why not ask for a divorce?"

"Partly from cowardice and partly because I may have hoped she would ask me for one before she found out about Beatrice, and partly because I thought a divorce would sink my ship."

"Your ship being your hedge fund."

"That and the money she's invested in the fund—were she to pull it, which so far she hasn't. Has all of Rivers' work gone with her?"

227

"I don't think so. She's said more than once that she had herself backed up four ways from Sunday."

"But if her computers are all missing . . ."

"Not the end," Harry said, interrupting. "She is backed up in at least one company and probably two or three. Whether there's any way of finding that out from what's in her computers, I don't know."

"The point would be to make them untraceable internally," Breckenridge said in an approving voice. "I make use of similar protection, not that I believe all they tell me about being the electronic world's Fort Knox. I could probably walk into Fort Knox on a red carpet for twenty-five thousand bucks put into the right hands."

"But you know where Fort Knox is," Harry said, trying to hold onto some shred of hope.

"Good point. What do we do?"

"Find Caedmon," Harry said. "Without her, we've got nothing."

23

The time came that afternoon when Harry had no one left to inform, question, or just talk to. Jim and his people were deploying their assets, limited and oversubscribed as they were, in an effort to find some trace of Caedmon. Harry had talked with Ernesto Piedra and had his promise to alert his underground and report as soon as he had any information.

Rowena Farnham had done what she could to buck up his flagging spirits, but she was herself so shaken by the news that Harry had found it necessary to pour the second round of tea and insist she eat at least half a buttered scone to bolster her flagging spirits. Jeff Smolkin was concerned to learn Caedmon was missing and, having commiserated briefly with Harry, asked what was being done to find her.

When he found out there were no clues as yet, no obvious suspects, and no one to sue, he quickly lost interest. Renata made a good show of being sorry to hear what had happened, and she even managed to tell Harry she hoped Caedmon was found all in one piece. But Renata had obvious difficulty maintaining even that level of cold comfort. And when her buzzer sounded, she jumped guiltily, gave Harry a quick, dry kiss on the cheek, and bolted, calling over her shoulder, "Number One needs me! Try not to worry," leaving Harry feeling that he had been thrown overboard and left to tread water as his ship sailed over the horizon.

It was in a mood of considerable despair that he clattered

over the humpbacked bridge onto the Hammock, dreading having to face his empty house, still harboring the remnants of Caedmon's equipment and a closet full of clothes. He was so absorbed in his misery that he drove past the body lying in the weeds beside the narrow road. Then his wandering wits gathered themselves and shouted at him.

Jamming on the brakes, he reversed, then jerked to a stop in a cloud of white dust. He jumped out of the Rover and threw himself onto his hands and knees, silently repeating Caedmon's name as he swiftly brushed the broken weeds off her naked body. Her breathing was so shallow that at first Harry could not discern it, but there was a froth oozing from the corner of her mouth, and bubbles were forming and breaking in it. He was still searching for a pulse when her body twitched briefly, then grew still. She groaned faintly.

Harry thrust an arm under her shoulders and pulled her up against him, telling her over and over to hang on. Still gasping instructions, he struggled to his feet, carried her to the Rover, and laid her across the back seat. Once on CR19, he called the hospital and had Esther Benson paged. She was an old friend and several years ago had helped to put his eleven-year-old daughter back together after a foiled sexual assault had left her almost catatonic.

"What happened to her?" Benson demanded of Harry as the ER team was lifting Caedmon out of the Rover and onto a gurney.

Benson was a slim woman in her late forties with large black eyes, thick graying dark hair, and the voice of a drill sergeant. She did not suffer fools gladly, and her manner suggested that Harry fit in that category, but he was prepared for it. It was how she had always treated him.

"I don't know," he began, but that was as far as he got.

"For God's sake, Harry," she snapped, striding along beside

the gurney, pressing her stethoscope against Caedmon's neck and chest, "get hold of yourself."

Harry was doing a walk trot, trying to keep up. "She was kidnapped," he said. "I found her beside the road near the house half an hour ago. She didn't appear to be bleeding. She was unconscious."

"Look at her face, you damned idiot! She's been beaten half to death. She hasn't got as much pulse as a mosquito. Is this your doing?"

"Of course not," Harry protested. "I've been half out of my head . . ."

By this time they were inside the doors and rushing Caedmon toward the examination room.

"You were born in that state, Brock. What's her name?"

"Caedmon Rivers. She's . . ."

"I know. Your personal trainer."

"She was kidnapped. I thought she was dead."

"She's close. Wait out here. Try not to cause any trouble. When I know something, I'll tell you."

With that parting encouragement, she, the attendants, and the gurney with its silent occupant shot through the automatic doors, leaving Harry in the cold and empty corridor.

"In four-letter words," Harry muttered, feeling enormous relief that Caedmon was in Esther Benson's hands.

He found a waiting room and sat down. He tried to read a year-old *Time* magazine and couldn't understand a thing; the words darted across the page like a school of small black fish. He gave up and walked up and down the corridor. Nurses, doctors, interns, and candy stripers rushed past him. People in johnnies and blue cotton bathrobes, pushing IVs on a wheeled pole, scuffed along, their eyes fixed on some distant goal, ignoring him.

Before Benson appeared, Harry had adequate time to review

all the ways in which it was his fault that Caedmon had been kidnapped. And if she was beyond help, all the things he should have asked her about herself, all the things he should have told her about himself. It was not a shining hour.

Benson came down the corridor toward him at her usual headlong pace, her white coat unbuttoned and billowing behind her like a cloak. "I think she'll live," she said. Before Harry could respond, she asked, "Is she an addict?"

"God, no. She doesn't even smoke. Why do you ask?"

"She has enough heroin in her to make a horse take wing. I found the injection point."

"Those bastards," Harry said.

Then he had a terrible thought. "Will she wake up addicted?"

"I don't know. Some people are hooked from the first injection. Some may take a week."

To Harry's surprise, Benson tucked her clipboard under her arm, took him by the hand, and led him at a near run to the waiting room. Choosing an unoccupied corner, she took him to it, put his hand on the arm of a chair, and said, "Sit."

"Am I drooling?" Harry asked, giddy with relief from knowing Caedmon was going to live.

"If you are, it wouldn't surprise me," Benson said. "Listen up. Don't knock the bung out of the cider barrel just yet," she added. "Are you listening?"

"To the full extent of my capacities to hear and absorb information. Will that do?"

"It will have to."

Benson said these things with a face so straight only the initiated knew whether she was amusing herself or firing off insults. It was Harry's belief that making Esther Benson a doctor had cheated the world of a champion poker player.

"I've administered naloxone. It's a drug usually given in the presence of an opioid overdose. It works to counteract any life-threatening depression of the respiratory and central nervous systems, which often occurs in an overdose such as this. It seems to be working. Her vital signs have strengthened, but there's some cardiovascular instability I'd like not to be seeing."

"Is that all there is to worry about now, leaving out the possibility of addiction?"

"Sorry, Harry. It's not all there is. The naloxone is making her violently ill. And there's still the possibility of a pulmonary edema, but I'm counting on the oxygen feed to prevent that from developing."

She paused to take a breath and look at Harry as if she was trying to determine how much of this he could take.

"And the rest?" he asked, not wanting her to step too far out of her role. He needed her sharp tongue to keep him on his feet.

"She has a fracture in her right cheekbone, two cracked ribs— I'd guess she was kicked—and she's got blood in her urine, which means one or both of her kidneys have been damaged. We'll get to all that later. And here's the icing on the cake. She's been raped. I'd say repeatedly. We've got that all cleaned out and kept the semen. The police will have the DNA."

"Christ," Harry said. "HIV?"

"And all his disciples. Too soon to tell, but yes, it's a possibility. As soon as she stops vomiting and can keep anything in her stomach, we will begin a regimen of PEP . . ."

"What?" Harry asked.

"Post-exposure prophylaxis. The usual drugs administered are AZT and 3TC. If we determine more than one person raped her, we'll add Crixivan, a protease inhibitor, which prevents T-cells infected with HIV from producing more infected cells. But we've got to be able to talk with her before we begin the PEP."

"Will these drugs work?" Harry asked doubtfully.

"They will reduce significantly the chances of infection if the victim begins taking them within twenty-four to thirty-six hours of the assault. They decline in effectiveness up to seventy-two hours, after which it's too late. The lab tells us she was raped within our window of maximum opportunity. Stay hopeful."

With that, Benson slapped him hard on the nearest leg and stood up. "Have you called the police?"

"No," Harry said, getting up with her, "and Jim Snyder is not going to be happy when I do."

"Kidnapping, rape, aggravated assault, attempted murder, use of a controlled substance in the commission of a crime," she said. "That should give his people excuse enough to turn over a few rocks."

"Right, and I royally screwed up his crime scene."

"Smart move, Harry," Benson said. "If you had waited for the EMS, she would now be wearing a tag on her toe."

"Thanks for the snapshot," Harry said. "I'll treasure it. When can I see her?"

"Try us tomorrow morning, and now go away."

24

After Benson had left in her usual driving stride, Harry called the sheriff's headquarters, which was shedding the day shift. The dispatcher couldn't locate Jim, and without asking Harry, gave him to Maureen O'Reilly.

"And what would you be wanting with me, Harry Brock?" she demanded in a contralto voice that rattled the glass in the windows.

"Maureen," Harry said, feeling too rotten to play games, "I tried to speak to Jim, but he couldn't be found. A couple of hours ago I found Caedmon Rivers beside the Hammock road, stripped, unconscious, badly bruised, and barely alive. I took her to the hospital where she is now. Dr. Benson's been working on her. She says Caedmon was administered a nearly lethal dose of heroin and may or may not survive."

"Jesus, Mary, and Joseph," Maureen said, lowering the volume, "and has she been interfered with?"

"Yes, so if she lives, there's the HIV issue, for which Benson plans to begin PEP as soon as she is conscious and can keep something down."

"It will be the naloxone that's causing the upchucking," Maureen said. "And, praise be to God, it's saved many a wretched soul teetering on the very brink. The colleen is in good hands with Esther Benson."

"Yes, thank you for saying so."

"Then you'll be wanting me to write the report."

"I will," Harry said, then caught himself and added, "I'll give you the time and so on."

For the next few minutes Harry answered O'Reilly's questions and waited while she ripped into her keyboard. Listening, he felt as if he was hanging in some gray, windowless, and ghostly place, twisting in misery. He felt drenched in pain and incapable of anything but answering O'Reilly's questions.

"Done," O'Reilly said finally. "Where are you?"

"At the hospital."

"Are you thinking of going home?"

"I can't see her until tomorrow morning," Harry said, having hardly heard the question. "But I expect I'll stay here tonight." He hesitated. "Just in case."

He didn't say in case of what, but Maureen apparently didn't need the information.

"Stay where you are," she said. "I will be there in fifteen minutes. Are you fit to be alone until then?"

Through his private fog bank, Harry thought about what she had said.

"Maureen," he said, mustering his faculties, "there's no need. I'm all right."

"You and the drowning cat," she said firmly. "Fifteen minutes. Have you heard me now?"

"Yes," he answered.

Half an hour later, he was sitting in Maureen O'Reilly's apartment with a bottle of Jameson Special Reserve on the coffee table in front of him, half a large glass of it beside the bottle, and O'Reilly hovering over him, her heavy red hair set free from its cap and falling in a tumble of waves over her shoulders as she sliced a thick wedge of cheese and piled crackers on a cut glass plate. Then she picked up her glass, came around the coffee table, and sat down beside Harry.

"Glasses off the table," she said to him, and when he had his in his hand, she touched his glass with hers and said *"Sláinte!"*

"Sláinte," Harry repeated.

"And to Caedmon," she said.

Then they drank. The whiskey streamed through Harry like molten gold, burning away his fog. O'Reilly was still wearing her uniform skirt and white blouse, but she had shed the jacket. Harry thought on the heels of the whiskey that she must have showered because she smelled of—what else?—Irish Spring.

"Another toast," O'Reilly said, jumping up again.

Harry scrambled to his feet.

"This one to the memory of that darlin' man John Jameson, who gave us this heavenly whiskey," she said, lifting her glass toward Harry. *"Sine metu!"* Clicking his glass and emptying hers.

Harry said, *"Sine metu"* and followed her lead. When he got his breath back, he asked, "What is whatever it was you said?"

"Sine metu, without fear," she said seriously. "The motto of John Jameson's people all the way back to the fifteen hundreds and on past his lamented departure for the next two hundred and fifty years, give or take a decade or two. We have long since forgiven him for being born in Scotland."

"Triple distilled," Harry said.

"Fine whiskey that will pull up your stockings and no mistake," she said. "Sit down and we'll talk a bit, and then we will eat."

She picked up the bottle and nearly filled his glass, being equally generous with her own.

"I'll never get off this couch if I drink this," Harry protested, fearing she might be offended if he left it sitting.

"Go as easy as you like, but keep going," she said. "You're sailing into foul weather with a falling barometer. It's no time to become a teetotaler."

It was true he was feeling marginally better. Reflecting on

that, Harry took another, smaller drink.

"Who do you think kidnapped her?" he said.

"Ah, Harry-love," she answered with a sigh, "it's a puzzle and no mistake. The captain says you think it may have been engineered by the Ogilvies. Do you still think that?"

"It seems a more realistic possibility than making Afton Breckenridge the perp."

"I haven't thought much about it. I've been too busy with other wretchedness the captain has set me to work on. Now then, our supper is calling. Are you ready?"

Harry was becoming increasingly aware of a wonderful medley of cooking odors emanating from the kitchen. "Maureen," he began, trying to think of a way to tell her that eating was the last thing he wanted to do, "I really don't want . . ."

"Will you walk or be carried?"

He was also afraid he would have to sit on a cushion. The sofa was as big as a tanker. When he leaned back, his feet came off the floor. The chairs would all hold two of him. Everything in the house was king-plus size. Groaning inwardly, he stood up.

"And don't be forgetting your glass. There's a bottle waiting on the table."

He followed in O'Reilly's wake but not rejoicing as a strong man to run a race.

"It's nothing fancy," she said after they were seated, "but a stew that will stick to your ribs and buck you up, which, it's clear, needs doing."

Leaning forward, she lifted the lid off a black Dutch oven, releasing a gush of steam and wonderful odors.

"Shall I serve you?" she asked, flourishing a large ladle. Without waiting for an answer, she filled his plate, set it in front of him and then served herself. Rolls and butter followed.

"Glasses up," she said, raising her own. "A toast. Confusion and grim reaping to the black-hearted divils who did this to Caedmon Rivers. May their livers rot, their guts shrivel, and their graves be strewn with salt!"

Harry joined in with what enthusiasm he could muster, and when he lowered his glass, the room began to move around him in a stately but disconcerting circle.

O'Reilly frowned at him and said, "Eat, you will not flourish on an empty stomach."

Harry began to eat. In a few minutes the room settled into its wonted place, making Harry feel enough better to eat with more attention to the food.

"Maureen," he said, "this is delicious. You're a wonderful cook."

"There's precious little time I have for practice," she said, coloring at his compliment, and quickly changing the subject. "What are you going to do with Caedmon Rivers when they release her from the hospital?"

"Unless she requires more care than I can give, I'll take her back to the Hammock."

"And give those hooligans a second chance?" she asked, tearing one of her crusty dinner rolls in half as though she had one of her *divils* in her hands.

"It's either there or back to her house," Harry said, somewhat angered by the question.

Still trying to come to terms with what had happened to Caedmon, he did not want to think beyond that event and its immediate aftermath. He found being asked to consider the future an insult. What was Maureen thinking of?

She finished buttering her roll in silence and in silence replenished their glasses.

"Drink up," she said. "I told you the sea was rising."

Angry, Harry took a larger swallow than he had intended and was left struggling for breath.

"Will you want a tap on the back?" she asked in concern.

"No, no!" Harry gasped, having a vision of being knocked face down in his plate.

O'Reilly leaned over the corner of the table and gave his shoulder a moderate shake that made the room spin briefly.

"You're a dear man, Harry Brock," she said smiling, "but you need a minder, and that's God's truth. Now, will you have more stew?"

He did not have time to answer before his plate was recharged.

"You're very beautiful when you smile," Harry said, feeling tears stinging in his eyes.

A small voice in some dim corner of his mind told him to stop whatever it was he was doing; but because the stew was so good and the whiskey even better, he decided to get on with those.

"It's kind of you to say so, love," she told him. "Have you space for a bit of pie? Apple, is it?"

Harry was never able to remember with any clarity what followed. There were brief flashes of light, but the images, wondrously magnified and fleeting, redolent with warm, abundant flesh, were too blurred for positive identification. For a few moments after he woke, struggling into the light, he was unable to say where he was. The first familiar thing was the smell of coffee and O'Reilly coming into the room with a tray, loaded with a coffee pot, mugs, the butter dish, and a plate piled with toast.

"Is your head ferocious?" she asked, setting down the tray on a folding table beside the sofa and pulling a barrel chair up to the table for herself. She was wearing a pale blue wrapper that made her look more than ever like a Greek goddess.

"Was I . . . ? Did I . . . ?" he began hoarsely and gave up, utterly distracted by the realization that he was naked and knew where he was.

"You were a bit wobbly on your legs, but a gentleman throughout," she said with a straight face.

"Throughout what?" he asked in dread, pulling the blanket more tightly around himself.

"The evening," she said, pouring his coffee and then giving him a warm smile. "There's a hair of the dog that bit us in it," she added, holding up the pot, "just as the doctor ordered."

That was all that was said regarding the night, a large chunk of which was missing for Harry, but sipping his coffee, he was obliged to notice that his shorts, shirt, and underwear had been folded neatly and placed in a small pile at the far end of the sofa. By whom was never revealed, but Harry thought it unlikely that he had put them there. Who had taken them off him also remained a matter of conjecture.

"I called the hospital last night and again this morning," O'Reilly told him amiably while buttering his toast. "She is stronger and with all her working parts in good order. They are moving her out of the IC. For both our sakes, Harry dear, you might have made it clearer how close she was to shutting the door. But on second thoughts, it was probably the Benson who saw as well as I that you were altogether out of rope and had better not be told the whole thing."

"Probably not," Harry said, now sitting upright in his Gandhi outfit, his legs dangling, gazing at O'Reilly over his coffee in wild surmise.

25

It was after nine when O'Reilly, crisp as a new dollar, delivered Harry to the hospital doors.

"Thank you, Maureen," Harry said, having stepped out of her cruiser. "If there is ever anything I can do to make it up to you, I will."

"You're a darlin' man, Harry Brock, and you owe me nothing. Now, off you go. I'm fearfully late, and the Captain James Jefferson Snyder will have the hide off my back."

With that, she reached across the seat, pulled the door shut, and shot away, tires smoking.

"God in heaven," Harry whispered, watching her streak away. Pulling into the street, she gave a blast on her siren. Harry raised his arm in a farewell salute and went into the hospital.

The hair of the dog must have been a long one, because Harry walked into the hospital with a clear head. Benson was not available, but the duty nurse on Caedmon's floor—a short, stout woman with a face that said humor was not on offer—regarded Harry with distaste. Harry took a step back from the desk, concluding that the hair was barking.

"Can I see Caedmon Rivers?"

"No, she's being worked on. Come back this afternoon."

"How is she?"

The nurse looked at him as if he was wanting. "The miracle is that she's alive."

"Yes," Harry said a little brusquely, "I know. Is she conscious?

Does she know where she is? Have the sheriff's people talked with her?"

"Are you a reporter?"

"No, I'm Harry Brock, a friend."

"Ah," she said, glancing at a list. "She's been asking for you. No, Dr. Benson has refused to give them access. You might try again this afternoon. She'll still be sedated. But seeing you may ease her mind. She's afraid you're dead."

The last comment was spoken in a way to suggest the loss would not be great.

"It's wishful thinking," Harry said, surrendering to frustration and his dark side, and left.

Still not willing to go home, Harry drove past his house and went on to Tucker's place. The old farmer was working with his bees when Harry found him, having been guided by Sanchez and Oh, Brother!, who had been waiting for him when he arrived.

"I expected you yesterday," Tucker said, stepping out of a cloud of bees carrying a frame, filled with honeycomb. "How is Caedmon?"

"She's out of intensive care," Harry said, raising his voice because he and his companions had stopped a healthy distance from the hives.

"That's good news," Tucker replied, motioning Harry toward him. "You don't have to stand way out there. I've smoked the bees. They won't sting."

"I'm not getting any closer," Harry said, "and, please note, neither is Sanchez nor Oh, Brother!"

"Ye of little faith," Tucker said, following the quote with a wide grin.

A moment before, bees in their hundreds had been crawling over him, apparently without malign intent because none had stung him. By the time he reached Harry, the last of the bees had flown back to the hive, except for those crawling over the frame.

"I didn't get here because Maureen O'Reilly picked me up at the hospital after Caedmon came out of the O.R., took me to her place, gave me dinner and a place to sleep."

"What was wrong with your own bed?" Tucker asked, failing to conceal his surprise.

"It's a long story," Harry said, trusting to his friend's discretion.

"All right, let's go to the honey house. I want to separate this honey," Tucker replied, seemingly untroubled by the rebuff. "Have you seen Caedmon this morning?"

"No, I haven't," Harry complained. "The last time I saw her, Benson was wheeling her into the O.R. This morning, I was told to come back in the afternoon. I'm pretty damned disgusted, not that it serves any useful purpose."

"It never does. I suggest you spend the time here with us. There's nothing to take you home, is there?"

"Only empty rooms," Harry said, suddenly feeling sorry for himself.

"Your mockingbirds can look in on them now and then. Give me a hand here."

The honey house was a small, square building with stained shakes on the outside and pine planks and studding on the inside. Two large, screened windows gave light to the working space. Screens on the windows and the door were always populated by bees, trying to get their own back, and all the other nectar-loving bugs in Southwest Florida searching for a way in. Harry liked the room, and he was especially partial to its permanent smell of spicy pine pitch mingled with wild honey. He thought that stepping into the room was something close to what Dutch sailors must have experienced when first reaching the Spice Islands.

"First, I want to uncap these cells," Tucker said, walking to a section of the wide bench that ran around three walls of the room and held all the equipment and jars and caps necessary to move the honey from the frames to the jars.

With the frame positioned over a wide plastic pan with deep sides, Tucker said, "Do you remember how these combs are uncapped?"

"Yes," Harry said, picking up the scraper beside the bowl and setting to work freeing the honey cells of their wax caps.

"I'll gladly hear anything you want to say about Caedmon, what happened to her and so on," Tucker said in a quiet voice. "Of course, if you'd rather not talk about it, that's all right, too."

Harry found it a relief to tell Tucker what had happened to her and how he had gotten her to the hospital and what had happened then. It also helped to have the simple work of uncapping the cells and tipping them into the bowl while he talked. "How did you hear about Caedmon's being in the hospital?"

"One of my old friends, who like me doesn't have anything much to occupy his time, has a granddaughter who's a nurse. She mentioned Caedmon's name to her mother, who called her father because the girl had also mentioned that Dr. Benson and the man who brought Caedmon in had words, and wanted to know if the name Brock meant anything to him."

While he talked, Tucker walked over to another spot on the bench that supported a large machine with a crank protruding from its side. Harry trailed along after him, thinking that the national intelligence agencies should consult with Tucker.

"Are you up to turning the crank on this extractor?" Tucker asked as he fitted the frame into the machine and tightened down the cover.

"I can try," Harry said, having over the years become accustomed to spinning the extractor, often for extended periods of time when Tucker was stripping his hives.

Tucker had a few more details to add to the information he had been given and said—hoping Harry didn't mind—that it was probably Harry Brock who had taken Caedmon Rivers to the hospital, but his granddaughter made a mistake about Harry and Dr. Benson quarreling. He and the doctor were old friends and always talked to one another that way. "I'm not sure I convinced him," Tucker added between chuckles. "He said his granddaughter said that the doctor was really ripping into you."

"Very funny," Harry said, trying not to sound out of breath.

In the next few minutes they opened the tap on the separator and strained enough honey to fill and cap a couple of jars of what was now heavy, dark golden liquid. Once the equipment they had been using was cleaned and ready for the next batch, Tucker led them out into the late morning sun.

"This time of day, I usually like to sit a while in the citrus grove," Tucker said. "I tell myself it's a healthy meditative practice, but the truth is that having been up and active since five, I need a rest."

"Sounds good to me," Harry said, failing to mention that turning the crank had set his head slowly revolving in honor of "Glasses off the table."

Recalling those moments, as well as he could and imperfectly, an awful fascination drew him back to wondering what had actually happened during those vague and troubling hours he could not recover. A tumult of mingled awe, astonishment, rejoicing, comfort and joy, and shame-laced guilt took hold of him and shook him like a terrier shaking a rat.

"Are you all right?" Tucker asked, having turned to wait for Harry to come out of the honey house. "You're white as skim milk."

Oh, Brother! and Sanchez trotted out of the cool barn to

rejoin them.

"I'm a bit light-headed for some reason," Harry said.

"Probably the whiskey," Tucker said complacently, setting off on the path to the orchard.

"How did you know about that?" Harry blurted before he could stop himself.

"And what else would the lieutenant be serving you, it being leagues too far from the Liffey to be drinking Guinness?"

The arrow, feathered with implication and mockery, went home. Harry actually staggered slightly, his head adding a lurch to the spin. "All right," he said, "she drank me under the table and God knows where else."

"You blacked out."

"That about sums it up."

Tucker suddenly stopped and, turning to Harry, demanded, "You didn't sleep with her, did you?"

"I want to sit down," Harry said, pushing past Tucker, heading for the split log bench with its bentwood back, sunk into a grassy bank under the shade of a large orange tree, which was now in sight. He reached it and sank onto it with a groan, his delayed hangover claiming him for her own.

"When you feel capable of speech, I'm prepared to listen," Tucker said.

Sitting down in the cool, dappled shade, the smell of the lemon and the orange trees drifting on the mild breeze, Harry gradually steadied. When he found the strength to open his eyes, he saw Oh, Brother!, Sanchez, and Tucker standing in a half circle in front of him, gazing at him as if they had stumbled on something extraordinary.

"What's this for?" Harry demanded, feeling as if the jury had reached a verdict he was not going to like.

"You did, didn't you?" Tucker said in a voice dense with pity and condemnation.

"I don't think so," Harry said, being careful not to shake his head.

Had he said he didn't know—that would at least have been honest. He did not in truth think he hadn't. He didn't know, but having the small pile of neatly folded clothes, including his underwear, clearly in his mind, he thought he had.

"No!" he said. "Forget that. I don't know. I remember, dimly, eating a piece of apple pie, followed by a swallow of whiskey. Then, all is darkness."

"Very dramatic, but you have all the outward trappings, the shifting eye, the excessive protestations, of a guilty man."

"The worst part is, Tucker," Harry said, abandoning pretense, "that I wish I could remember. And although I ought to be hoping against hope that I didn't, I don't wish that. Quite the opposite. What a glorious thing, to have slept with a goddess and lived to tell the tale, especially one as beautiful as and on the scale of Maureen O'Reilly."

"Where does Caedmon come into it?"

The question deflated Harry's gas balloon. "Well," he said earnestly, "I hope to God she doesn't."

"Speaking of God," Tucker said in a lighter tone of voice, "do you have any idea at all of who might have kidnapped her?"

"What has God got to do with Caedmon's kidnappers?" Harry countered.

"About as much as he or she does with your shagging Lieutenant O'Reilly. Answer the question."

"I have a suspicion, but not a smidgen of supporting evidence," Harry said.

"Care to share it with me?"

"I already have, pretty much. As I said, it involves the Ogilvies. Jim doesn't give the idea house room even though he pretends to listen."

"He's usually level-headed. Are you sure this idea isn't the product of frustration?"

"It may be. The core of it is that I don't think the attack on Caedmon has anything to do with the struggle going on between Gregory and Afton Breckenridge."

"Supporting evidence?"

"For this part, if it had been focused there, I would have been attacked as well. Also, why the savagery of the attack? It was all out of proportion to the offense."

"Two things: They might have been trying to make a point. If you had been home, they might have taken both of you or taken her and shot you."

Harry had no stomach for dwelling on that possibility. "Caedmon was beaten, kicked, and raped, repeatedly according to Benson, then injected with what would have been, if I hadn't come along when I did, a fatal dose of heroin," he said, some of his initial rage returning. He quelled it with difficulty.

Suddenly an outburst of yelping at the southeast corner of the orchard brought Harry to his feet. "Something's got Sanchez," he said, starting in the direction of the uproar.

"Come back. Sit down," Tucker said, stretching out his legs and fanning himself with his straw hat. "Sanchez is a slow learner when it comes to mother woodchucks. One is now giving him instructions on deportment in the presence of young woodchucks."

Harry grinned and settled down beside Tucker on the bench. "What's gotten him into trouble?"

"She reluctantly tolerates her youngsters chasing Oh, Brother!, while he pretends to be fleeing in terror, but draws the line at Sanchez's trying to pick one of them up in his mouth and taking it for a lap around the orchard."

"Does he really do that?"

"He tries to and when she was being careless he actually got away with it a couple of times. But if she sees him reach for one of them, she lands on his head and begins chewing. Hence the yelping. She doesn't hold back. It all has to do with ancient enmities, some of which are bred in the bone. That she tolerates his playing with them at all is a wonder. Go on with what you were saying."

"The level of damage," Harry said, "was more than excessive. Where is there anything in Afton Breckenridge's history that would account for this level of brutality?"

"I take it you feel fairly confident that you do know enough about her to make that assessment?"

"Thanks to Caedmon, yes," Harry said. "One of the first things Caedmon did . . ."

Thinking of Caedmon in the days when they were getting to know one another choked Harry, and he had to turn his head away from Tucker, to stare with blurred eyes at the orchard.

Without speaking, Tucker put his hand on Harry's shoulder and kept it there until, his composure restored, Harry was able to go on talking.

"She worked up a bio on Afton that corroborated what Breckenridge had told me and confirms that he did meet her in Washington where she was working for a law firm."

"We have visitors," Tucker said, pointing slowly into the dappled green light of the orchard.

It took Harry a few moments to see the deer, a doe and a fawn several weeks old, its spots almost blended by its new coat of soft brown. Thirty yards away, the two were feeding quietly on the grass under the trees and switching their short tails.

"Peaceful scene," Harry said quietly.

"Yes, deceptively so," Tucker said.

A moment later, two brownish streaks, flowing silently under the trees, hurled themselves at the deer. As if lifted by a magic carpet, the two grazers suddenly sprang without apparent effort into flight, the younger deer matching its mother's speed, leaping with her, long stride for long stride. But the two coyotes were gaining.

"The doe's holding back for the fawn," Harry said.

"She'll have to fight them," Tucker said. "She saw them too late."

At that moment, coming in from the side, cutting behind the deer and turning straight into the path of the coyotes, came Sanchez, belling loudly. The coyotes braked and then split to go around the big hound, but Sanchez had accomplished his task. The two animals had lost their advantage and knew it. Tongues lolling, they slowed and turned to look at their tormentor briefly, then loped back the way they had come. Sanchez stood watching them go, growls rumbling in his chest.

"Not bad for an old dog," Harry said admiringly.

"I'm glad he didn't decide to chase them," Tucker said. "Even together he'd be too much for them in a serious fight, but being long in the deviltry suit they might have decided to trust to their speed, tangle with him briefly, and cut him up a little before he could get his teeth into one of them."

Oh, Brother! appeared from the direction in which the deer had vanished, trotting along, head up, ears pricked.

"Second line of defense," Tucker said, getting to his feet. "Come along. We'll have some lunch. Then you can drive in to see Caedmon. And I take your point about Mrs. Breckenridge. She doesn't make a convincing murderer."

26

"I thought they might be lying to me," Caedmon said in a hoarse whisper.

"I'm alive and so are you," Harry said, leaning down and carefully kissing very lightly one of the places on her face that wasn't bruised or bandaged.

Caedmon was lying propped on a pile of pillows with an IV in her right arm, her left arm in a sling, and bandages covering most of her face. "I'm not sure I am," she croaked. "This may be Hell. Is it?"

"I don't think so," Harry said, pulling the gray folding chair up to the bed, sitting down, and gingerly taking her hand.

"Don't," she said.

Around her left eye and the remaining visible part of her face, the skin was stained several shades of red and purple. The eye was nearly swollen shut.

"All right. Someone's brushed your hair," Harry said. "It's beautiful spread out on the pillow that way, very Burne-Jones."

"Not funny."

"I wasn't making a joke. I was paying you a compliment."

"Harry, Dr. Benson says you saved my life."

"She saved your life. All I did was get you to her."

"And don't you forget it," an unmistakable voice said from behind him. Benson put her hand on Harry's shoulder. "Is he making a nuisance of himself?"

"Not yet."

"He will. How are you feeling?"

"About the way I look."

"Still nauseous?"

"A lot less."

Benson slapped Harry's hand away and began taking Caedmon's pulse, frowned, made an ambiguous sound, and snatched a blood pressure cuff off the wall. Wrapping the cuff around Caedmon's arm, she pumped it up and watched the monitor as the pressure sighed away. Then, still frowning, she put on her stethoscope and pressed it under Caedmon's left breast, making Caedmon gasp.

"Sorry," Benson said, moving the chest piece around while she listened. "You'll do," she said at last, hanging the stethoscope around her neck.

"HIV," Caedmon said.

"Clean so far," Benson said.

"More testing?" Harry asked.

"Are you at risk, or is it ridiculous to doubt it?"

Caedmon began to laugh and ended groaning.

"See?" Benson said to Harry, giving him a whack on the arm with the back of her fist. "Wherever you are, there's trouble. Leave, wait for me in the hall. I want some privacy with my patient."

"Sadist," Harry said.

A few minutes later, Benson came out of the room. "You can go back in when I'm done with you, but don't stay long. She's running on a very low battery and needs every moment of rest she can get. The good news is her kidneys are all right. The bleeding's stopped. The bruising will heal, the bone in her left forearm will mend."

"Good news," Harry said.

"Don't begin the celebration. She's been through a terrible ordeal, and either she's blocked her memories of it or is refus-

253

ing to say what happened. Either way, she's going to have to talk about it, probably with a professional, or the aftereffects are likely to be very bad."

"Is there anything I can do?" Harry said.

"Listen when she wants to talk, don't press her, urge her very gently to trust the people working with her. Most of all, be gentle and patient, but don't smother her. She needs a lot of space."

"What about urging her to see Gloria Holinshed?"

Benson tapped her chin with a finger and looked at Harry speculatively. "You and Katherine took Minna to her, didn't you?"

"Yes," Harry said, "best thing we did in that mess."

"I remember. I'm surprised she didn't have you committed."

"Was that why you recommended her?"

Benson started to grin, then cut it off by giving him a medium jab in the midriff with a corner of her clipboard.

"I don't see why . . ." Harry began, rubbing his stomach.

"Shut up and listen," Benson said. "Were you two in a sexual relationship?"

"Why are you asking?"

"Don't go coy on me, Harry."

"All right, yes. Why the past tense?"

"Because it will be over for a while. If she's one of the unlucky ones, permanently."

"I'm not going to . . ."

"No, of course you aren't, but know this: For an indefinite period of time, having sex for her will almost certainly be very painful, physically, mentally, and emotionally. And before the issue even rises, no pun intended, you may find her remote and unresponsive. Are you with me?"

"I remember Minna went through a period of withdrawal."

"Yes, but she was a barely out of childhood, and Caedmon is

an adult. Her problems will be different and more complex. And because she's older, she may require more time to recover. Are you ready to take on the responsibility of getting her through what's coming?"

He started to speak, but Benson laid her hand on his chest. Speaking softly but with force, she said, "Think about this, Harry. Take your time."

"I've taken all the time I need," he said, putting his hand over hers. "I'm going to do it. Now what about Holinshed?"

"I'll ask her to see Caedmon today or tomorrow. With luck, she will agree to go on seeing her. She may want to talk to you as well. No, not *may*, she will."

"She's a fine therapist," Harry said. "She'll help Caedmon recover if anyone can."

"Let's hope so."

27

Caedmon liked Holinshed and agreed to begin working with her. But before any of that could happen, Caedmon had to deal with being questioned and prepared for her testimony to the grand jury, which the state's attorney's office was assembling as a preliminary to bringing a charge of kidnapping, attempted murder, and aggravated rape against a person or persons at the moment unknown.

Benson had not exaggerated. For the first week after Harry took her home to the Hammock, she had to be carried everywhere. She also had to be taken to the hospital for physical therapy and to have her bandages changed.

"Couldn't Harry do this?" Caedmon had asked Benson on her first visit to Caedmon's office after leaving the hospital.

"I'd rather trust you to a chimp," Benson told her.

Harry, sitting behind them, managed not to respond. Benson glanced at him over her shoulder and asked if his brain had ceased functioning altogether.

"You told me to sit down and keep quiet," Harry said.

"I should have known that following a two-part request would overtax your brain."

"Stop this," Caedmon pleaded, holding her side. "Even trying not to laugh hurts."

By the second week Caedmon was shuffling around and spending most of the day out of bed. Since coming out of the hospital, she had been sleeping in the second bedroom, leaving

Harry alone to ruminate in his own bed. Following the churnings of his mind through the dark hours, he began to suspect that Benson's assessment of his mental capacities was accurate.

When he could force himself to stop thinking about Caedmon and the shocking state of her mind and her body, he immediately slid into pondering the difficulties of trying to find Afton Breckenridge—an impossible task with Caedmon out of action—and tracking down Caedmon's assailants.

Every turn of his thinking led to a blank wall. The longer he thought about it, the more difficult the task appeared. Finding who had kidnapped and assaulted Caedmon had taken on the appearance of a quest without an end. More than once, tossing and turning, rolling his sheets into knots, Harry thought of Browning's "Childe Roland to the Dark Tower Came" and the windowless, doorless, impermeable, heart-breaking black pile that confronted Roland at the end of his journey. The one pale, flickering conviction that Harry found to cling to was that the answer to part of the riddle lay with Afton Breckenridge, who had efficiently and effectively vanished.

One morning two weeks later, Caedmon said to Harry, "Computers. I'll make a list."

In general, Harry gave Benson's assessment of his mental capacities little attention. But regarding Caedmon's behavior, she had been painfully accurate. Since leaving the hospital, Caedmon had become increasingly morose and withdrawn, shrank from his touch, seldom looked at him, and said as little as possible when she spoke at all.

Harry had been giving her whatever space she needed, but he was also obliged to help her with daily exercises, assigned by her physical therapist, all of which involved touching her. Feeling her shrink away and hearing her stifle a gasp when his fingers touched her flesh distressed him and also, to his alarm and shame, sent bolts of anger and resentment rocketing through him, churning his stomach and making him grit his teeth.

To counter these reactions while he worked on her, he resorted to telling her edited stories about his early life as a warden, keeping his mind as far away from what he was doing and how she was reacting to it as possible. The ploy helped to reduce his unwanted responses, but it also lessened his sense of closeness to her and dimmed his awareness of her physical presence, something that falling in love with her had made incandescent and a vital part of being in love with her.

Also, he was aware that his carefully constructed defenses, raised to protect him from the knowledge that she didn't love him, could not hide her revulsion, and all the reasoning he could muster could not protect him from the pain of that awareness.

"I'll go in town this afternoon," he said, "and I'm really glad you're ready to go back to work. Just promise me that when you begin to feel tired, you'll stop and rest. Benson said . . ."

"I've heard enough from Benson and from you on that subject," Caedmon replied coldly. "I don't want a lecture every time I ask you to do something for me."

"No," Harry said. "Of course you don't. Forget it. I'll be very pleased to buy what you need to get started again."

To that, she made no response other than to hobble out of the kitchen onto the lanai. Harry reminded himself that this was what Benson said would happen, and he had promised to be patient, even long-suffering if need be. But every angry attack was a ding, whether he knew it or not, in the hitherto pristine surface of his still strong love for her.

She made the list, gave it to Harry, and said, "If there's anything you don't understand, call me. And, Harry, I'm sorry, but I can't seem to help myself."

"It's OK," Harry said, desperately wanting to put his arms around her but knowing if he did she might break down crying or fly into a rage. "I'll be back with this stuff as soon as I can," he added with mock cheerfulness, waving the list as he left.

He returned to find four cars in his yard, not counting Caedmon's BMW. Jim's cruiser was among them. A young woman in a white blouse and black skirt came out of the house to meet Harry, who had jumped out of the Rover and was running toward the lanai door.

"It's all right," she said, holding out the palms of her hands toward him, her voice rising in alarm at the speed of Harry's approach. "Attorney Dillard called a meeting for out here so that Ms. Rivers would not have to travel."

Harry slowed to a walk, laughing in relief, but instantly feeling his fear transmogrify into anger.

"I'm Penelope Whittier," the young woman said, a little short of breath. "I'm a lawyer, recently assigned to Attorney Dillard's office."

She was very young, Harry thought, and with her dark hair cut in a bob and large brown eyes, she looked far too young to be out of college—certainly too young and inexperienced to be shouted at.

"I'm Harry Brock," he said. "I'm sorry if I frightened you. After what's happened, I'm . . ."

He let that drop and took the hand she held out to him. "I'm pleased to meet you. How's Caedmon taking this?"

"Very well, considering," Whittier said, stepping into the lanai and holding the door for Harry.

"Is she responding to what's said to her?"

"Some of the time. Three of the four people from our office are women," Whittier said. "She's sitting on the sofa. One of us is on each side of her and I'm on a kitchen chair in front of her. Mr. Dillard and Captain Snyder are seated at a distance from her."

"Why all the cars?"

"Coming from different locations. I drove from the airport. I can understand why you would be upset at seeing cars all over your lawn."

"No, you can't," he said quietly, forcing himself to smile. "Let's go in."

Jim met them in the kitchen. His hat lay on the table, suggesting to Harry he'd been waiting a while.

"Miss Whittier," he said, "would you please excuse us? I want to talk with Mr. Brock for a bit."

"Of course," she said, coloring slightly, and hurried toward the living room.

"What's all this about?" Harry asked. "Why in hell did Harley bring all of you out here? Any one of his people could have dealt with the grand jury issues or the question of charges."

Harry's anger was coming to a boil again. Jim sighed and rubbed his head.

"He seems to think that surrounding her with his people is going to make her feel cared for and protected. I tried to tell him, but as you know, Harley's a little pig-headed."

"How's she taking it?"

"Pretty well, so far as I can tell. Having the women on both sides of her on the settee seems to have helped. I suspect, however, she's getting tired. She's beginning to close her eyes a lot."

"They're leaving right now," Harry barked, starting for the living room.

"Hold on," Jim said, one of his long arms snaking out and grasping Harry by the shoulder. "I've got something to tell you."

"Make it quick."

"We've picked up a rumor that Afton Breckenridge is back in the country. A sometimes-reliable informant said he saw somebody arriving at Miami International who had the wrong hair color and was wearing sunglasses but still looked like her. I wouldn't put a plugged nickel on that horse, but for what it's worth, it's the first report we've had, which is almighty unusual. The report came in yesterday. I've got to go. The sheriff wants to see me."

"Is he still wearing that silly mustache?"

"I'm afraid so. It makes him look like a preacher selling raffle tickets."

Harry managed a grin, then said, "Thanks for the news."

"I won't be holding my breath. Go easy in there."

Listening to Jim had cooled Harry's ire enough for him to see that any ruckus he caused would only frighten Caedmon more than protect her. He went in quietly and found them all except Caedmon on their feet. The three lawyers were gathered around Caedmon, saying their goodbyes.

"She's a trouper," Harley Dillard said, picking up his hat from the chair and turning to Harry. "I hope what we've done here helps. Let me know. If it has, we'll plan more sessions."

"Did Jim tell you about the sighting?" Harry asked, not trusting himself to talk about what had just taken place.

"He did. I doubt it's reliable," he said, shaking his head and turning his hat in his hands. "Even if it is, how much farther ahead are we?"

"Why didn't you tell me you were going to do this, Harley?" Harry asked, deciding he could do it without swearing.

"Because you'd have met us with a shotgun." He grinned at Harry, then turned to the women and called out in a stagey voice, "Come along, you minions of the court, we have a world to save."

Harry saw them out and came back to find Caedmon curled up on her side like a wounded animal, which, he thought, was what she was.

"How bad is it?" he asked.

Surprisingly, she swung herself into a sitting position, rubbed her face with her free hand, and managed a wintry smile. "I'm dead with exhaustion," she said with a creaky laugh, "but otherwise, I enjoyed myself. Dillard is a funny guy. I hadn't expected that."

"One of the few remaining good old boys," Harry said with relief and a twinge of jealousy.

"Bring in the goodies," she said, pushing to her feet. "I'll be the door opener."

After a two-hour rest and then with Harry's help, Caedmon worked one-handed, reprogramming the computers and restoring her memory banks from the hidden files where she had secreted them.

"How did you keep this stuff out of their hands?" Harry asked, standing behind her as she worked.

"I had flash files, which they found, and one company offering storage, which they also found, and a second they could not find."

"Which is where this material is coming from?" Harry asked, watching the streaming monitors.

"Yes, and I also have everything of value on disks in a bank vault, which I renew every week. They did not locate them either because I have no bank vault in my name."

Harry was going to ask her how she managed that, then changed his mind. In answering the questions he had already asked, her voice told him clearly that she resented the inquisition.

The unintended result of the hours of work she put in was that she was unable to sleep. Sometime around midnight, Harry was wakened by bumping sounds from her room. But when he went in and found her slowly dragging a chair across the floor with one hand and offered to help, she told him that when she wanted his help, she would ask for it.

"Until then, leave me alone," she snapped, sending him a savage look.

He did, but he did not sleep any more than she did. However, at some point in the night he must have dozed off, because when she came down to breakfast, she asked him to take her to Avola. He had already asked if she had slept at all and been snapped at.

So his response, "Where are we going?" was intended as a peace offering.

"God," she said irritably, "I'll be glad when I can drive. Holinshed's office."

It was, he knew, not a day for her regular appointments, which meant she must have made a call in the night or early this morning. She had told him nothing about her sessions, and Holinshed had talked to him once, immediately after Caedmon's first meeting. It had consisted of a brief conversation from which he learned nothing, or so he thought, that Benson hadn't already told him. All the same, in the following days one of her comments kept intruding on his thoughts. At the time, he thought she had somehow wandered off track or confused him for a moment with another patient.

She had been bringing their conversation to a close by shutting her notebook and pushing back her chair. At first, he thought he was remembering it only because it was so bizarrely off the point. "Harry, in the aftermath of catastrophes there are often surprises that may or may not be consequences of the event. I hope you will keep that in mind."

He had made some anodyne comment in response and dismissed her remark as having no particular application to Caedmon's situation. But whenever it surfaced, it dragged up from the depths a disturbing chill of dread.

When Caedmon's session ended, Holinshed, looking tired and unhappy, accompanied her into the waiting room.

"She wants to talk with you," Caedmon said grimly. "Give me the keys. I'll be in the Rover."

Harry guessed that she had not wanted him talking to Holinshed and lost the argument. He gave her the keys and followed the therapist into her office.

"Sit down," she said and pointed at one of the chairs.

Her office was decorated in quiet blues and grays, except for the walls, which were painted a subdued rose. Holinshed, Harry knew from experience, seldom sat behind her desk, usually choosing one of the upholstered chairs. With Minna she often sat beside the girl on the sofa. After Harry was seated, she took the chair facing him.

"How are you and Caedmon getting along?" she asked.

"Like a cat and a dog forced to share the same space."

Before she could respond, he held up his hand. "No, wait," he said. "That's not what I need to say. Everything you and Esther Benson told me about what to expect has been all too accurate."

"I'm sorry," Holinshed said. "How is she treating you?"

"*With loathing* comes to mind."

"Yes," she said, "that's what I was afraid of."

She paused, tapping her pen on the unopened notebook in her lap.

"Harry, you may find this very painful, as it was for Caedmon, but it has to be said."

"Fire away."

"She has to find another place to live," Holinshed said, leaving his question unanswered.

The statement left Harry speechless for a moment. But after the initial hit, he found he wasn't surprised. Lack of surprise didn't lessen the pain.

"If it's because she can't stand my touching her, we can arrange for someone to come in," Harry said, leaning forward as he spoke. "I know just the person. Doreen Clampett. Remember? She looked after Tucker that time he was ill. And she probably saved Minna's life."

"Yes," Holinshed said with a sudden grin. "Larger than life, as I remember."

"Yes," Harry said. "She hugged me once. I'll never forget it."

"Would you like to talk about it?" she asked with a straight face.

"Not right now," Harry said, unable to stifle a laugh.

"Then back to Caedmon," she said, serious again. "It won't do, Harry. I'm thinking she needs a clinical setting for at least six or eight weeks."

Harry suddenly felt as if all the air had been sucked out of the room.

"Buxton?" he asked when he found his voice.

"To be realistically frank, Caedmon's in need of professional care of the sort that Buxton Regional can give her. And Harry, people come out of BR all the time. It's not a detention center. It's a hospital where people are healed."

Harry heard Holinshed's effort to reassure him, but he was too focused on Caedmon to respond. "Is she a danger to herself?"

"I'm not sure."

"Can she be left alone safely?"

"For now, yes, but the difficulty is that I can't predict whether her condition will improve or degrade."

Harry sat back in his chair, struggling to fend off a sense of utter defeat. "What have I been doing wrong?" he asked.

"Wrong question, Harry!" Holinshed said brusquely. "This isn't about you. It's about Caedmon and how she feels about you."

"You probably know this, but I'll tell you anyway," Harry replied, trying to hide the bitterness. "I love her, but she doesn't love me, and that's probably the nub of the problem."

"Whether she loves you or not is both speculative and irrelevant," Holinshed insisted. "I'm failing to make it clear that it's not about you or your relationship with her before the kidnapping and its attendant horrors. How she feels about you, how she responds to you, is due entirely to the mélange of emotions being generated by what she's been through. What she feels at any given moment shifts in the next, and all of the changes take place in a matrix of fear, rage, and mental anguish."

At that moment the door to the waiting area was thrust open and Caedmon limped in, her face white with some powerful feeling. Harry held his breath.

"Both of you listen to me," she snapped in a gravelly voice, "I'm not going to Buxton. I'm not going to cut my throat. I'm staying where I am as long as Harry can stand me. I can work again. I can put three sentences together, all on the same subject. I'm going to get through this. *Capisce?*"

Harry grinned despite himself and wanted to cheer. She sounded so much like the old Caedmon that he jumped up and, taking hold of her shoulders, kissed her on her forehead, the first time he had kissed her since her return to the Hammock.

"Jesus, Harry!" she croaked, pushing at him with her good arm. "Get off me!"

Harry stepped back, turned to Holinshed, and asked, "With a little help from her friends?"

"Maybe," she said, looking doubtful.

28

Harry took a silent Caedmon back to the Hammock, slumped in her seat, staring out her side window, leaving him to construct his own theories about what had happened between her and Holinshed beyond Holinshed's suggestion she consider spending some time in Buxton. Beyond assuming that they had clashed over her need for more intensive care, he was left to conjecture.

They were crossing the humpbacked bridge when Harry's phone rang. Harry waited until they were over the rattling plank before he answered.

"It's Harley. Your client's in jail. Jim's people have told him he's charged with murdering his wife, read him his rights, and taken him to the county lockup. You and Rivers can see him if you want to, although his lawyers may not want him talking to anyone at this point."

"Jim says an informant reported seeing her in the Orlando airport only a few days ago," Harry said.

At that, Caedmon gave a start and pushed herself up in her seat, showing marked interest.

"Harry," Harley said, "this office gets a dozen of them a week. It's smoke."

"When is the arraignment?"

"Four this afternoon. His lawyers are already making a stink about not having been warned of the impending arrest. I told

Kinley Roby

them I wasn't interested in finding the house empty when we got there."

Harry could hear the pleasure in Dillard's voice.

"Harley, no one is going to believe that this is anything but an accusation," Harry said, trying for more information. "Why are you bothering?"

"Good try, Harry. We'll see how it goes. How's Rivers?"

"Making good progress," Harry said, glancing at Caedmon, who gave a disgusted snort.

"Glad to hear it," Dillard said. "Watch your back."

"They finally got there, did they?" Caedmon asked sourly as the Rover slipped quietly along the white sand road. She had lowered her window, letting in a warm breeze, redolent with soft smells of creek water and ferns and the dry wire grass beside the roadway.

"Yes," Harry said, "you heard me ask Dillard why he's gone forward with such skimpy evidence. Of course he didn't answer, but I imagine he was hoping that, after the experience of being arrested, booked, and cooling his heels in a cell for a few hours, Jim's people might be able to pry something out of Breckenridge before the lawyers arrive."

"I don't think they'll get squat out of him," Caedmon said as Harry pulled into his parking place under the live oak.

"Neither do I," Harry agreed, "but it must work often enough so that Dillard's willing to spend the money it takes to get the accused to trial."

As he was pushing open his door, he paused and asked Caedmon if she wanted any help.

"Don't be a pain in the ass," was his answer.

Caedmon went straight to her bedroom and slammed the door. Harry decided to catch up on some insurance reports, but he spent more time thinking, to no purpose, about what Holinshed had told him than actually writing. By eleven-thirty, he had finished only one report. With relief, he sent it, printed a hard copy, signed and filed it, and committed himself to thinking about lunch.

He was just walking into the kitchen, wondering if Caedmon was sleeping, when a white BMW sedan, followed by a swirling cloud of silvery dust, turned off the road and stopped beside the Rover. Harry did not recognize the car or the tall, slender woman, dressed in a tropic-weight tan pantsuit, who got out of it. She wore sunglasses, the kind, he recalled, that Jacqueline Kennedy wore so frequently. In fact, she carried herself with that remarkable woman's physical grace.

Harry watched with interest as she paused, turning slowly, first right then left. Harry wondered what she found so interesting in the house, the barn, the woods, the creek, and the expanse of swamp beyond that she was studying so carefully.

His speculations were interrupted by her abruptly hooking her right thumb under the strap of her shoulder bag and breaking into a long-legged stride toward the lanai door. Harry hurried to make sure he reached it before she did. When Harry opened the door, she hesitated only long enough to pull off her glasses, squint in the glare, and say, "Harry Brock?" and for him to answer, "Yes," before striding past him straight into the kitchen. Reaching the table, she turned and waited for him to catch up with her. At close quarters, and even before she said anything more, Harry felt the weight of her personality. Her dark eyes were particularly arresting and seemed at odds with the bobbed, dark blonde hair.

"Are you lost?" he asked, that being the usual reason strangers reached his house.

She was giving him the same close scrutiny she had given the house, and the intensity of her gaze made him a little uneasy. She was not a beautiful woman, but there was enough character there to more than make up for it.

"Most people who find their way here are," he said, trying to dispel whatever was keeping her from speaking.

"No," she said with a flicker of a smile, "I'm dead, or at least I'm supposed to be."

The duck came down from the ceiling.

"Afton Breckenridge," he said.

"No longer," she said, "but it will do for present purposes."

"And what would that be? To finish the job?" Caedmon asked.

Harry turned to see her standing in the dining room doorway, dressed in pajamas, holding in her right hand a Smith & Wesson .38 Special, pointed at Afton's head.

"Drop that bag on the table," she said icily. "Do it very slowly."

Afton did as she was told.

"Now pull one of those chairs away from the table," Caedmon said, moving further into the room, the revolver tracking Afton's movements. "Keep going. All right, sit on it."

"Caedmon," Harry said quietly, "this is Afton Breckenridge. You were right. She's not dead. It's all right. You can put the gun down."

Although Caedmon's physical healing had gone forward as Benson had hoped, her face was still streaked with the purple and yellow remnants of her bruises, her left arm was still in its sling, and she still half dragged her right leg. But Harry saw that the hand holding the gun neither wavered nor trembled.

"Harry," Caedmon said, "there's a gun in her bag. Take it out."

He had seen too many people in confrontations in which somebody was holding a gun not to know whether that person was likely to use it. He saw at once by looking at Caedmon's face and listening to her voice that, finding the slightest additional excuse, she would blow Afton's head off. Given the distance between Caedmon and her target, it would be nearly impossible for her to miss.

"Okay, stay calm. I'll open the bag," he said, glancing at Afton, who was watching Caedmon closely but showed no signs of fear.

He unzipped the bag and emptied it onto the table. "No gun."

"How do you like your handiwork?" Caedmon demanded, her eyes never leaving Afton's face.

"You've made a mistake," Afton said. "I'm very sorry about what happened to you, but I had nothing to do with it."

"Then how do you know what's happened to me?"

"The same way you learn things, and for the record, in case you decide to shoot me anyway, I decided to return when I learned what had happened to you. Oh, another thing, there have been several times in the past weeks when I've wanted to wring your neck, but it's never gotten past the wanting stage. You're very good, you know."

"Is it possible she's telling the truth?" Caedmon asked, glancing at Harry. Some of the tension went out of her stance, but the gun remained trained on Afton.

"I think so," Harry said, trying at first to watch both Afton and Caedmon at the same time, then concentrating on Caedmon.

Afton was remarkably composed, sitting erect on the chair, legs crossed, her left hand resting on her knee, the forefinger of her right hand lightly touching her chin. He wondered in admiration if in the same situation he would have as much command of himself as she had displayed.

"Are the Ogilvies looking for you?" Caedmon asked, slowly lowering her gun.

"It's another reason I came back," Afton said. "They're trying to kill me."

★ ★ ★ ★ ★

As if her adrenalin pump had switched off, Caedmon slumped into the chair Harry had pulled out for her. "The safety's on," she said, laying her gun on the table.

"Secrets," Harry said, pointing at the weapon and carefully masking his relief.

"I'm very good with it, actually," she said, wearily but with a touch of pride.

"How long do I have to sit out here in the middle of the floor?" Afton asked.

"Your choice," Caedmon said.

While Afton was lifting her chair back toward the table, Harry said, "How about some coffee?"

"Oh no, Harry!" Caedmon said, shaking her head. "Tea. Make tea."

"I assume coffee's not your drink," Afton said. "I'm seriously addicted to it."

"Do you want to break the habit?" Caedmon asked, considering Afton with what appeared to be a new interest.

"Not really."

"Then you don't want to drink Harry's coffee."

"It's not that bad!" Harry protested, turning on the kettle.

"It's much worse," Caedmon said to Afton in a voice heavy with sincerity.

"Not to be rude," Afton said, "but do you always greet unannounced guests with a gun? Or is it because you live in a forest?"

"I made a special effort, knowing it was you."

"I hope you're convinced that it was not I who was responsible for whisking you away."

"Not entirely," Caedmon said, "but enough not to shoot you, at least not yet."

"Very sporting of you," Afton said, smiling at Caedmon.

A few minutes later with steaming mugs in front of them, the tea ceremony completed, Harry, eager to hear her answer, turned to Afton and said, "Why are the Ogilvies trying to kill you?"

"Because," she said without hesitation, "up until the time I left, they thought I had become a part of their enterprise. With my Swiss and U.S. citizenships, bank connections, and property in both countries, they thought they were securing an ideal way to move money in and out of Europe while laundering it in the process."

"Did you get cold feet?" Caedmon asked.

As Afton looked confused, Harry added, "Caedmon means they must have had a good reason to believe you were coming in with them." He watched Afton closely. "You must have done more than express a casual interest in their enterprise."

"Sorry," Afton said, speaking with energy and emphasis, "I'm being a bit slow. I worked effing hard at convincing them I was fully committed. That said, I did such a good job of it that if they'd been nobbled, I would probably have gone to jail."

"*Nobbled?*" Caedmon asked.

"Pinched," Harry said.

"Spot on," Afton responded. "And I tell you, it wasn't easy."

"Why did you skip?" Caedmon said, persisting.

"Ah! That's a smidgen more complicated," Afton said, a smile tugging at the corners of her mouth.

"I think you had more than one reason," Harry offered by way of encouragement when Afton leaned back in her chair and seemed reluctant to go on.

She lifted her hand in what might have been a dismissive gesture, turning her face away from them and looking out the door.

"I had and still have a pressing reason and a convenient reason," she said after a small pause, concluding with a tight smile, which Harry was sure contained no humor. "My principal reason was to save my life."

"I know I'm not thinking as well as I was," Caedmon said, with obvious irritation, "but are you saying that your husband threatened to kill you?"

"Heavens, no!" Afton protested. "If you squash a spider in Gregory's presence, he grows pale as Marley's ghost. It's the Ogilvies who give *me* the willies."

"But you just told us you had agreed to join them in their crooked doings. What am I missing?"

"I'm guessing," Harry said quietly, watching Afton with interest, "you thought the Ogilvies weren't convinced by your protestations."

"Not quite. What I did believe, once I'd put my mind to work, was that they had no reason to cut me into their very profitable thievery."

"Why did they do it in the first place?" Caedmon asked.

"Because of a fluke. One afternoon, shortly after the New Year, I stopped by their house to see Gwen. Maria, her secretary, the one who was murdered, happened to be in the foyer when the butler let me in and said, 'I'll take Mrs. Breckenridge upstairs. I have something to ask Mrs. Ogilvie.'

"I thought the butler looked strange, but didn't pay much attention. He was always stiff as an old gate, whereas Maria was charming, and I liked her very much. Anyway, we walked straight into Gwen's parlor, the door being partway open. There the two of them were, holding between them at arm's length and studying intently an unframed, medium-sized Flemish painting I'd never seen before. The canvas had obviously been travelling in the tube, but there was neither an address nor stamps on it. A framed painting by Pieter de Hooch, which I knew was in their collection, was leaning against the table, its newly opened shipping crate on the floor beside it."

Harry wanted time to think about what he had just heard. He interrupted Afton's narrative to pour more tea all around and noticed that Afton had not touched hers. Caedmon made no response.

"How could you be sure the canvas had been *travelling?*" he asked as he was sitting down.

"One, I had never seen it before. Two, because it was obvious that they had just taken the canvas out of a Plasticine tube, which was lying on Gwen's work table on top of some of the packing materials, strips of foam padding and corrugated board, wood framing, cardboard squares, and so on."

"That doesn't really answer my question," Caedmon said. "After offering you a role in their enterprise and your accepting it, why did you suddenly conclude they were planning to kill you?"

Harry expected Afton to bristle at the challenge, but she didn't.

"Well done," she said, giving Caedmon a warm smile. "It actually took me a while to admit there was a fetid odor surrounding the deal. Why, I asked myself, should those two sharks first reveal to me, which they had done at once after Maria left the room, that they were smuggling stolen or contraband art into the country and then offer me a share of their business just because I saw them unpacking a seventeenth-century Dutch genre painting I had never seen before?"

"Did you think Maria Fuegos knew what they were doing?"

"I assumed she didn't and had probably become accustomed to having paintings and other *objets d'art* coming in and out of the house. After all, buying and selling paintings was what they did."

"When did you learn Maria was murdered?" Harry asked.

"Almost as soon as it happened."

"I suppose you're not going to tell us how you found out,"

Caedmon said wryly.

"I read the *Banner* online like everyone else," she replied calmly.

"Good save," Caedmon said.

This time it was she who smiled. Harry watched the exchange with interest and was surprised to discover that the two women were beginning to like each other. He would have enjoyed thinking about that but forced his mind back to Afton and the Ogilvies.

"Did reading about her death confirm your suspicions?" he asked.

"I was actually convinced long before."

"Does that mean," Caedmon asked, "that you concluded they had asked you join them, to control you until they could kill you?"

"Precisely."

"When did you decide to disappear?" Harry asked.

"Much earlier than that."

Perhaps it was her self-confidence. Perhaps it was Harry's knowing how miserable Breckenridge was, but just when the conversation should have been over, he asked, "How do you feel about your husband cooling his heels in jail?"

"Tickled pink," she answered with a happy smile.

29

Harry had not learned from Afton all he wanted to know, but he had adjusted his thinking to accommodate the fact of Afton's return and more or less accept as fact that it was the Ogilvies who had tried to kill Caedmon.

"I don't think I'm fully convinced yet by that yarn she spun," Caedmon said, sipping her gin and tonic and resting her head against the back of the lounge chair.

When Afton left, Caedmon had been too tired to do anything but laboriously climb the stairs and put herself to bed, where she remained until Harry brought her lunch on a tray. When she came downstairs much later, there had been a transformation. She had washed her hair, put on her makeup and a new, pale green sundress, looking, despite the sling and her limp, like a new woman.

"Do I look like a recovering dead person?" she asked bravely.

"Not the words I would have chosen," Harry said, having gotten up from his desk when she spoke. "Appealing, fresh as a spring morning, gorgeous," he said. "And restored to life. What accounts for the stunning transformation?"

"Afton Breckenridge. I'm staying in the game."

Harry did not have to ask what she meant. He had only to look at the energy she put into leaving him and making for the dining room, where she planted herself in front of one of her computers and, having powered it up, set to work. She went on working until Harry started dinner.

"Is there any gin in the house?" she asked, coming into the kitchen. She pulled open the refrigerator door and stared inside as if she was contemplating a mystery.

"Enough to float a rowboat," Harry replied. "There are limes in the vegetable tray and tonic behind the orange juice, top shelf. The gin is in the bottom door rack."

When all the ingredients except for the ice were grouped on the sideboard, she said, "Stop whatever you're doing and make us drinks. Is there anything for a snack? I'm starved."

"You're in good hands with Harry Brock," he said, hoping for a laugh.

"Feeble," she said, moving, quite rapidly for her, toward the lanai. "Make enough for seconds."

That was how for the first time in weeks they came to be on the lanai together at about five-thirty in the afternoon with the sun already in the tops of the oaks behind the house, the first cool breeze of evening whispering in its passage through the screens, and the dark water in Puc Puggy Creek flickering moodily as it slid past the house.

When Harry came onto the lanai, carrying a tray laden with a pitcher of gin in an ice bucket, a bottle of tonic, crackers, cheese, carrot sticks, onion and chive dip, and a cut glass bowl filled with giant green olives, the first flocks of white ibis were winging toward their roosts in the Stickpen. As he was setting down the tray, one of the barred owls coasted silently across the lawn.

"I was looking out my front bedroom window the other night," Caedmon said, leaning forward to take the glass Harry passed her, "and saw one of them pick a rabbit right out of those green frondy things growing at the edge of the woods."

"Ferns."

"What?"

"The *frondy things* are ferns."

"Those birds are assassins, and fuck the ferns."

"Not on one drink."

Out of the corner of his eye he saw her grin. It was a little lopsided, but his heart soared.

"What makes you think Afton's lying?" Harry asked, settling back for a long, slow drink.

"Everything she says strings together beautifully, but where's the support structure?"

"Meaning?"

"Where's evidence that any of it is true?"

Harry chose a carrot stick, thrust it into the dip and ate it, savoring the flavor and delighting in the crunch.

"Should I give you some privacy when you get to the olives?" Caedmon asked, staring at him over her drink.

He put a slice of cheese on a cracker and passed it to her.

"Try it," he said. "Then we'll see what happens."

"Celery stick and dip," she said, brushing the crumbs off her sling when she'd finished the cheese and cracker.

"There isn't any evidence so far," he said, filling her order and passing her a freighted celery stick, "but in the absence of any other plausible narrative, I think that for the present it makes sense to go with what she's told us."

Caedmon chewed noisily, then looked at him and said, obviously surprised, "That was good. Why didn't we hear more about the elephant?"

"Good question. I thought she handled the avoidance pretty skillfully. Why didn't you call her on it?"

"I was ready to do it three or four times, but each time I thought, No, I'll wait. I want to hear what she's saying."

"Same here," Harry said. "Also, it occurred to me that she might be saving Breckenridge for next time."

"Is there going to be a next time? I thought that where she was going after she left us, when we were going to see her again, what she was going to do, what if anything she wanted us to do, was left pretty vague."

Harry got up and freshened their drinks, the ice in the pitcher making a cheerful rattle as he poured. "Are you really feeling a little better?" he asked as he bent over her.

She looked up and met his eyes with a smile.

"Yes, Harry," she said. "I can see land."

"The lost swimmer?"

"Something like that."

"Welcome home, sailor."

"I'm not there yet."

"You will be."

He put the pitcher back in the ice bucket and sat down, thinking his words expressed more certainty than he dared allow himself to believe, but her smile was like the first swallow of spring. He tried not to think that it might be a long wait for summer.

"Mentioning elephants, is she wanted by the police?" Caedmon asked.

"There's no arrest warrant outstanding," Harry said, "but if Harley Dillard knew she was in Avola, he would be trampling children to get to her."

"Charging her with what?"

"I'm not sure she's committed a crime, but she's already cost the state a bundle of money," Harry said with an olive still in his mouth. "My guess? If nothing else, they want what she knows about the Ogilvies."

"I knew I should have left the room," Caedmon said. "Where does that leave us with the law? If I get caught on the wrong side of the fence, my career goes up in smoke."

"It wouldn't do mine much good either," Harry said, "but I suggest we hold off telling anyone until we've heard everything she has to tell us."

"Meanwhile, the man who's paying us to find her cools his heels in jail."

"I don't think this can go on for more than a couple of days. When it's over and we send in our final bills, we can leave out the time we knew about Afton."

"You're being very generous with my money."

A couple of days passed during which Harry avoided Jim Snyder's office. But on the second day, he forced himself to visit Breckenridge in the county jail, a setting in which the hedge fund manager was not exactly flourishing. The cell block where he was assigned did not offer the amenities of home, and he was not dealing well with the deprivation.

"It's not as if I'd killed her," he complained to Harry. "It's not as if I'd done anything warranting my being kept in this rat refuge."

"Don't give up," Harry answered, feeling seriously guilty. "Help is coming. This is all going to go away."

"Not soon enough," Breckenridge said, sitting slumped in his baggy, orange jumpsuit. "I'm trying to run my business from in here, and Ernan is doing what he can to help, but my clients don't understand why they can't call and get me. Another thing," he said in an offended voice, "I was going to bring Beatrice down, but my goddamned lawyers killed that plan. I'm beginning to feel like that guy in the book who didn't have any country."

"They're giving you phone access?"

"Not enough. My lawyers have negotiated Dillard into letting me come in here with a guard and take and make calls an hour a day."

"Better than nothing. You're using your cell?"

"Yes. Is Rivers working yet?"

"She is," Harry said, glad of the opportunity to give him

some good news. "You know she traced at least some of Mrs. Breckenridge's money to a bank in Panama. Now she's trying to discover where it went next. She's sure it went somewhere."

"Can't the authorities help?"

"Not really. Everything Mrs. Breckenridge has done with her money is entirely legal. Panamanian law makes it relatively easy to move private money through its banks without much official supervision. Also, the government is not interested in answering questions about people's investments in its financial systems unless they can be shown to be engaged in criminal activities."

"Accusing me of murder ought to be criminal enough," Breckenridge protested loudly, prompting a "Keep it down!" from the guard.

"Because Mrs. Breckenridge isn't charged with anything at the moment," Harry said, "they wouldn't be interested."

"Time's up," the guard said, closing his magazine.

Harry got out of the jail, feeling as if he was the criminal.

Later, to pry her loose from the computers, Harry persuaded Caedmon to try walking to Tucker's. "If you get tired," he told her, "I'll go back and get the Rover."

At Benson's suggestion she had begun leaving the sling off for short periods, but for the walk, she cradled her arm in it again. "Just in case I have to fend off snakes," she said.

Harry had chosen well. It was one of those rare, early summer days in Southwest Florida when a cold front, pushing down the peninsula overnight, was holding the afternoon temperatures in the low eighties and easing the humidity. Thundershowers had raced ahead of the front, leaving the world bright and sparkling.

"Everything looks happy," Caedmon said with a laugh once they were on the road, and she had found she was actually going to be able to walk without pain.

"Including you," Harry said, delighted by her good cheer.

"Looks mislead," she said but took his hand, to Harry's silent delight.

Sanchez and Oh, Brother! were waiting for them at the end of Tucker's road, and Caedmon had visited Tucker often enough not to be surprised to see them.

Greetings over, the four walked to the house, Sanchez leading the way, and Caedmon resting her right hand on Oh, Brother!'s shoulder, telling him about the two foxes she had seen from the dining room window that morning as she sat working and their suddenly chasing and catching a rabbit and how mixed her feelings were about it.

Harry watched with bemused interest as Oh, Brother! from time to time turned his head to look at her, ears cocked attentively, especially when she mentioned feeling bad about the rabbit's being killed. It would be easy to believe he really understood what she was saying, Harry thought with mixed feelings of his own.

"I wonder why I told him all that?" Caedmon said, having stroked the mule's shining black neck and then turning back to speak to Harry.

"He's a good listener," Harry replied, rewarded by a laugh from Caedmon.

Then she said, "You can't fool me. You think he understands what I said to him. So do I, but you won't admit it."

Tucker was kneeling on the soft earth of his garden, sowing lettuce and radish seeds in a newly prepared bed, when they came upon him.

"This is pushing things," he said, sitting back on his heels.

"How so?" Caedmon asked.

"They're an early spring planting," Tucker told her. "I usually put the first batch in with the sweet peas at the end of February. If they make it, this will be the third crop. I'm thinking of putting a lattice over them to cut down on the sun. Think it will work?"

By now he was on his feet, pushing the seed packets into one of the side pockets of his overalls.

"My," he said to Caedmon without waiting for an answer, "you are looking lovely. Harry, what were you thinking of to let her walk all this way?"

"Thank you," Caedmon said, beaming. "But you are a shameless liar. As for the walk, I'm not even tired."

Harry thought that might be an exaggeration, but let it go. She really did seem pleased with her accomplishment.

"Let's not stand out here in the sun," Tucker said, pushing to his feet and giving his face a quick wipe with a large white handkerchief he had conjured out of one of his copious pockets. "I suggest we go down to the orchard. There'll be a breeze there."

He then asked Harry to fetch himself a folding chair, a thermos of lemonade, glasses and a wicker basket to put them in, and not to be too long because Caedmon was in need of shade and a cold drink. With that, he said, "Caedmon, unless you'd rather not, lean on this arm a little. That's right. Now, we'll go down and get comfortable in the shade while Harry takes care of the rest."

"Shall I harness Oh, Brother! and fasten him into the wagon?" Harry asked, hoping to make Caedmon laugh, but Tucker, pretending he'd been asked a serious question, said, "No need of that. Just make two trips if you have to."

Harry knew when he'd been bested and went off chewing on his serving of crow.

Once things had been settled to Tucker's satisfaction and he and Caedmon were seated on the bench with Harry on a canvas folding chair in easy reach of the lemonade cooler, they talked easily for a few minutes about the Hammock.

Caedmon leaned back on the bench with a sigh and said, "This place is magical. It's like being submerged in cool, pale green water."

"The light in the trees does it, and the space under them makes a chimney for the air to flow though. I sit here a lot."

Caedmon then told Tucker that two nights ago she had seen Bonnie and Clyde and later had seen an owl kill a rabbit. "I can't seem to reconcile myself to the violence of this place being all mixed in with its beauty," she said, as a wind-up to her story, sounding genuinely perplexed.

"Yes," Tucker said. "I've given it a good deal of thought over the years, and the best I can do is to suggest that the problem arises from our seeing the beauty and the violence as contradictory aspects of life here."

"Do you mean the killing is beautiful?" Caedmon demanded, bristling.

She's on the mend, Harry thought with satisfaction.

"We make distinctions through language that nature doesn't make," Tucker said quietly.

Caedmon did not look mollified.

"Remember René Magritte's painting of a pipe?" Harry asked her. "The artist painted a reminder under the pipe, *'Ceci n'est pas une pipe.'* "

"At the time it created quite a hubbub."

"Are you saying," Caedmon demanded, "my words describing what I saw out the window were not what I saw out the window?"

"I'm sure you saw what you say you did, but your words set the events in a context that existed only in the words," Tucker said, taking off his hat. The breeze lifted the fine, white hair above his ears until it circled his head like a halo.

"Unsatisfactory," Caedmon said, pulling a long face.

"I really don't know anyone who would disagree with you,"

Tucker replied. "Now, tell me how your work is going? You are working, aren't you?"

That led at once to Caedmon's saying that Afton Breckenridge had visited them. Of course, Tucker demanded details, which led to a spirited discussion of the whole tangled web of what her return meant, her link to the Ogilvies, and what Harry and Caedmon were supposed to do about it.

"One thing is certain," she said firmly, "we can't go on much longer keeping her presence to ourselves, or we will be boiled in oil when the state's attorney finds out what we've been hiding."

"The problem of her return," Harry said, "was very nearly solved because Caedmon came within the blink of an eye of shooting her."

"You see," Caedmon said, "when she showed at the house, I was still convinced she had arranged my kidnapping."

"Then you didn't buy into Harry's theory about the Ogilvies being responsible," Tucker said.

"No. It wasn't until she told us it was my being kidnapped that had brought her back that I began to believe her."

"She told us that her principal reason for leaving was to escape from the Ogilvies," Harry said.

"And you both believed her."

Tucker's statement was so neutral there were question marks all over it.

"She was very persuasive," Caedmon responded.

It took a few minutes for Harry, with Caedmon's additions, to explain to Tucker how Afton had stumbled on the Ogilvies and the unframed painting, their telling Afton what they had been doing and offering her a partnership in their enterprise, her acceptance and her belated realization that something was seriously wrong.

"Meaning," Tucker said, "that she finally woke up to the fact their admission and offer made no sense."

"Unless they intended to kill her," Caedmon said, "which, she concluded, was their intention."

"Did she explain why she accepted their offer in the first place?"

"She knew as soon as they told her what they were doing that she was in danger," Harry said. "Then, when they offered to bring her into the scheme, she accepted at once. Afton Breckenridge is a smart woman. Without much thought, she assumed they wanted to take advantage of her dual citizenship in the U.S. and Switzerland."

"Later," Caedmon said, "she began to see that even her addresses and bank affiliations in Switzerland and here were not enough to justify taking a third person into an operation of the sort they were running and that it could only mean they were making sure of her until they could kill her."

"Was that when she began planning her disappearance?" Tucker asked.

"No. I think she began planning that just before Christmas," Caedmon said.

"Why?"

"Because that was when she learned her husband was having an affair," Harry said, "but she was vague on that point. In fact we know very little about what happened between her and Breckenridge."

"I take it her plan to have him convicted of killing her is now on the compost pile," Tucker said.

"Not yet," Harry said, making a sour face.

"No?"

"Remember," Harry said, "the police don't know she's back."

"And what are your plans," Tucker asked, "for when they let you out of jail?"

"I thought I'd come back here," Harry said, "and start trading in alligator hides."

"And you?" Tucker asked, turning to Caedmon.

"I suppose," she said, grinning, "I could go on the street."

30

"Something's got to be done about this," Caedmon said over dinner that night.

"Here's the way I see it," Harry replied. "The only way we're going to find out how the Ogilvies run their smuggling operation is through Afton. As of now, we can't even reach her. So, I say we wait until she contacts us, listen to what she has to say, and then decide what to do."

"Tucker thinks time is not on our side."

"He's probably right, but what's our alternative?"

"There's a problem. If Afton's telling the truth, the moment the Ogilvies learn that she's in town, they will set their dogs on her. Thanks to you, I lived. She may not."

"Or she may learn in time that we've outed her and skip," Harry said, wanting to close the door on these speculations. "If that happens, the Ogilvies will probably escape detection."

"And if we go back to hunting her," Caedmon said, following her own train of thought, "they may come after me again. The only reason they haven't is that they know I haven't found her."

Her comment caught Harry's attention.

"Are you thinking now that they took you because they thought you had found her and not to prevent you from finding her?"

"It pretty much comes to the same thing," Caedmon said. "They probably knew I hadn't told the police that I'd found her. So they came for a look. Finding I hadn't located her, they decided to kill me, to stop me from continuing the search."

Harry thought she was right. What she hadn't mentioned was that if the Ogilvies had intended to stop the search, she was a target again. Until they were stopped or until they found Afton themselves, Caedmon would never be safe.

"We need her," Harry said. "She's our way out of this mess."

Afton Breckenridge came back the next morning, immaculately turned out as she had been on her earlier visit, although she had reduced her turnout to a yellow sundress, matching sandals, and a wide-brimmed straw hat with a crimson hat band, its ends trailing elegantly.

"And look at me," Caedmon grated, glancing down at her halter top and dungaree shorts and bare feet. "At least I'm not wearing my sling."

Harry and she were watching Afton walk toward the lanai from her car.

"In fighting trim, you look better than that," Harry said quietly and got a painful jab in the ribs for his effort.

"I had forgotten the heat," Afton said, smoothing her skirt across her knees, "but I've re-adapted."

Settled in a lounge chair, smiling easily, with a glass of iced tea at hand, Harry thought she looked entirely free from any kind of stress. But was she, and what did she want?

"I was nearly killed for trying to find you," Caedmon said. "Do you realize the same thing could happen to you?"

Afton pulled off her sunglasses, swung her feet back to the floor, and sat up.

"Caedmon," she said in a calm but firm voice, "please try not to be angry with me. Yes, I'm aware of the risk, but think of this. Unless the Ogilvies are stopped, I'll never be safe—nor, I suspect, will you. Maria's death and the attempt on your life made me confront the reality of my situation. I can't run far enough, can I, to escape them? Alive, I'm a threat to them, and as long as I'm flitting about, they won't stop looking."

"I see that," Caedmon agreed, but not sounding mollified.

"Afton," Harry said, interrupting, "intentionally or not, you've put us at further risk. If the Ogilvies find out you're here, they'll come at you and maybe through us. Also, by accusing your husband of murder, you have made yourself an object of intense interest to the police."

He paused, then decided to go on, lay it all out for her. "By not telling the authorities that you're alive and that we've been talking with you, we have risked ruining our professional reputations. Sitting here talking with you for a second time has compounded our breach of trust."

After awhile, Harry broke the ensuing silence. "Now, no more delays. You must have something in mind or you wouldn't have come looking for us. Tell us what it is."

"Fair enough," Afton said in a purposeful voice. "I was well along with my plans to disappear when I wandered into Peter and Gwen's little cottage industry. Maria seemed not to have noticed anything out of the ordinary, which I thought was very odd. But you will understand when I say, just then I was too busy pretending I hadn't noticed they were holding in their hands a seventeenth-century, unframed, museum-quality Flemish painting, to give any serious thought to Maria's lack of interest."

Afton paused, her frown deepening, appearing lost momentarily in the recollection, then went on. "And when Gwen did not say, 'Oh, Afton, darling, look what we've just bought for several hundred thousand euros!' but whipped it out of sight and popped it back into its tube, I knew for dead certain what I was looking at. Later, of course, I did think about Maria's apparent lack of interest, but concluded that finding her employers handling unframed paintings must have been a common occurrence. It also seemed reasonable that the unframed paintings meant nothing to Maria because she knew nothing about them and, after all, paintings were constantly arriving and leaving."

"By then," Harry said, "she had already guessed what was going on and taken her concern to Rowena Farnham. Rowena asked for my advice and I said that Fuegos should go at once to the police. She did and was murdered shortly after."

"So the Ogilvies have a mole in the Sheriff's Department," Afton said.

"It looks that way," Harry said. "Maria's murder was, or was made to look like, a professional killing, one twenty-two caliber bullet in the back of her head."

"And the killer or killers," Afton said quietly, "will not be found, and even if they are, it is probable that no link will be found between Maria's death and the Ogilvies."

"Something like that," Caedmon agreed, none too pleasantly. "How does your coming back change anything?"

"As far as Maria's death is concerned, it doesn't," Afton admitted, "but as for upsetting Gwen and Peter's art smuggling applecart, I think I know enough about their operation to make it happen."

For the next half hour, Afton laid out for them what she had learned in the weeks when the Ogilvies were taking her into their confidence.

"It's a beginning," Harry said when she was finished, "but they very carefully told you nothing that leads directly to hard evidence that they are actually buying and selling stolen works of art."

"But they have given me their Swiss and Belgian contacts and even the name of a London art dealer through whom the shipments are made," Afton protested.

"Yes," Harry said patiently, "but they are only names, and if the American, British, Swiss, and Belgian police could be organized to descend simultaneously on all of these people, if they exist, there is little likelihood that any stolen pieces of art would be found. Several of your names are those who organize the transportation on the Continent and in Britain. They are not even the carriers, and the likelihood of finding any stolen works of art at the art dealer's London address is vanishingly small.

"Finally," Harry continued, despite the glum expression on Afton's face, "there is no chance at all, based on your information, that any judge would approve a search warrant of the Ogilvies' house. And the state's attorney's office would not try to persuade federal authorities to put together an international team, based on what you've told us. It's a bummer, but there you are."

"Were you intending to talk to the police?" Caedmon asked in a much friendlier voice than the one she had been using.

"I'd have to be bonkers!" Afton retorted.

"You're right," Harry said, "and I'm afraid that's that."

"Oh dear," Afton said.

Caedmon chose a stronger four-letter word.

Three days later, Harry opened a manila envelope addressed to him and took out half a dozen stapled pages of printed material and another envelope addressed to Harley Dillard. He and Caedmon were standing on the humpbacked bridge, having just emptied the mailbox, a task he always approached with a slight tightening of stomach muscles ever since a client of his once had found a five-foot rattlesnake in her mailbox and called on Harry to take it out.

"From Afton?" Caedmon asked, leaning against him to see what he was taking out of the envelope.

Feeling her pressed against him for the first time in weeks cleared Harry's mind of snakes instantly, replacing them with rosy hopes of a brighter tomorrow, possibly even a brighter tonight. She was almost entirely free from her sling and was now walking with only a very slight limp. And her face was restored to its former configurations and no longer looked like a blue, purple, magenta, and Indian yellow abstract. The remaining damage was all inside.

Recalling that fact, Harry struggled back to reality.

"Yes, and I'd like to know what's inside the letter to Harley Dillard."

"What are all these printed sheets?"

"Let's find out."

Together, they read the pages. The last page was imprinted with a dated notary public's stamp and signed by the notary and by Afton. Under the signature was a very clear fingerprint in black ink.

"I'm betting that's Afton's," Caedmon said.

"I wonder if her fingerprint's on file?"

"Where?"

"FBI."

"Isn't everyone's?"

"No, for the most part only those who have been arrested and charged with a crime or who have worked in sensitive government jobs. Most of the rest of us have no such record."

"Then what good will this do?" Caedmon demanded, pointing at the print.

"The police can compare it with one taken from some personal belonging like a perfume bottle or her telephone."

"OK. Next, is there enough information in this account of what she learned about what the Ogilvies were doing to allow Dillard to ask for a warrant?" she asked.

"It's a thorough account of what they shared with her, but I can't give it more than a very tentative 'maybe.' "

Harry slid the pages and the letter to Dillard back into the envelope and gathered up the rest of the mail from the bridge railing while Caedmon stood staring at the dark water slipping and swirling along beneath them, lost in her own thoughts.

"Ready to go back?" he asked.

"She's gone, isn't she?" Caedmon asked as they started off together.

"I expect so," Harry said, with several conflicting feelings stirring up the emotional sediment. "The envelope probably went into a drop box soon after its single pickup time. That would give her twenty-two or -three hours. Then another forty-eight before delivery. My guess is she's already wherever she was going and moved on from there, having flown under at least two names and two passports."

"I've decided I like her, and I hope she's never found until she wants to be," Caedmon said, sounding as if she was flinging down a challenge.

"Whoa," Harry said. "I like her too. I don't want her caught. It was a righteous thing she did in coming back here at all. She's very brave."

"That's enough praise of sweet Afton," Caedmon said, sounding edgy. "It was bad enough being in the room with her and having you drawing comparisons."

"I wasn't making comparisons," Harry said, a little too quickly.

Caedmon gave a cynical laugh.

"And your owls don't slaughter rabbits," she said. "What I saw was a sloe-eyed, intelligent, elegant, beautiful, graceful woman, sitting across the table from another woman who looked as if she'd been rescued from a bombed building after being buried for three days in the rubble and you watching the sexy one like a starving cat staring at a mouse."

"That's a little over the top," Harry protested.

"I don't care," Caedmon said. "I wanted to say it. Now I

have. Why do you think she sent these papers to us instead of to Harley Dillard?"

Harry wisely left Caedmon's outburst where she'd dropped it and moved on, but leaving it wasn't the same as forgetting it. Her easy dismissal of her remarks hadn't misled him. She was carrying a large bag of pain.

"Let's think first about another issue," he said. "How are we going to explain to Harley our having this envelope?"

"How about if we put a large rock in the envelope and tossed it into the Puc Puggy?"

"That's one option. How seriously should we consider it?"

"OK, here's another: We forget we ever saw her—not that you're likely to—and tell him it just came in the mail."

"There are several references to us in the pages we read, and there may be more in whatever she's sent Harley."

"I'll need a few minutes to change," Caedmon replied. "Should I pack a toothbrush and a change of underwear?"

"I think they'll release us on our own recognizance."

Dillard listened to their story before opening his envelope. When he had read its contents, he passed the single sheet of paper across his desk without comment to Harry and Caedmon, who were sitting side by side in two of the dark leather chairs, arranged in an arc in front of him.

"I guess that frees up Breckenridge," Harry said when both of them had read it.

"Have you made copies of the other pages?" Dillard asked, breaking his long silence.

"It seemed the most responsible thing to do," Caedmon said.

"I'm surprised to hear you use that word," Dillard said, scowling darkly.

Caedmon shrank back a little in her chair, but Harry took up the challenge.

"We were in a bad place, Harley," he said. "Afton came back, to do whatever she could to get the Ogilvies off her back and ours as well. It took her two visits to get to the place where she could tell us what she knew about them and their operation. Then she wrote it down and wrote to you and sent what she'd written to us."

"Why to you?"

"I don't know," Harry said.

"I think I do," Caedmon said. "I think she was afraid if she sent it directly to you, it would end in the circular file. She wanted to be sure you knew that two other people knew what she'd told you, and we would testify to her being who she said she was. Harry even took a picture of her, as you can see."

Dillard picked up the photo of Afton and walked around the desk, sitting down next to them, still scowling.

"Not very flattering, is it?" he asked, his gloomy expression fading.

"The picture?" Harry asked.

"No, Ms. Rivers assuming I wouldn't believe what was in the letter."

"Well," Caedmon said, "I don't think you would have."

"No, probably not," Dillard said, staring at the picture as if he expected the sober-faced woman staring back at him to speak. "On the other hand," he said more cheerfully, "I wasn't looking forward to trying Breckenridge for murder with no body and no provable motive. He didn't need her money. His having a mistress in these times doesn't mean he needed to kill his wife."

"You might have made it stick," Harry said. "That letter Afton sent you would have weighed heavily with the jury."

"Maybe," Caedmon said, "but remember, I can prove she was still shifting money out of her accounts after you received the letter accusing her husband of killing her."

"But," Harley said, "you can't prove who was doing it."

"No, but you could."

"*Maybe* back at you," Dillard replied, "but think of the cost. And the feds would have to be brought in. That's Heartburn House, not even counting the costs of doing all the things they would want done."

"So how high are you going to hang us?" Harry asked.

Dillard gave them his hangman's smile.

"It hurts me to do it, but I'm forgetting you did anything but take these papers and my letter from her hand, take her picture at her request, and deliver it all to me."

"Breckenridge walks?" Harry asked.

"He walks."

"Harry," Caedmon said earnestly, "let's get out of here before he changes his mind."

"Not so fast," Dillard said, holding up a very large hand. "And by the way, you're welcome. There's the little matter of the Ogilvies still in the room."

"Looking like an elephant," Harry said, "and thank you."

"Thank you," Caedmon said coldly. "Harry doesn't think you have enough evidence to do anything with the Ogilvies, despite the fact they undoubtedly killed Maria Fuegos and nearly killed me."

She paused and Harry, risking a rebuff, reached over and put his hand over hers, clasped tightly in her lap. She sat staring straight ahead. Whatever she was staring at with such intensity, Harry knew it wasn't Harley Dillard's desk.

"The pain," she said in a near-whisper. "The nightmares."

She unknotted her hands, gripped Harry's in both of hers, and broke off her gaze to glance quickly at and away from Harry's and Dillard's faces.

"I'm sorry," she said. "I interrupted you."

"Perhaps we don't need to talk about the Ogilvies now," Dillard said.

"Yes, we do," Caedmon said sharply. "Afton is right. She and I will never be safe as long as they're free to pursue us."

"Harley's right," Harry said, "we can do this another time. He and I can do it without you."

He drew back his hand, which she had quite gently released on the arm of her chair.

"I told you, Harry," she said firmly. "I'm back in the game."

"All right, then I'll begin," Dillard said briskly. "Harry's partly right. I don't, even now, have enough to establish probable cause and convince a judge to issue an arrest warrant naming them."

"Then what's the use . . ." Caedmon began angrily.

"Wait," Harry said, "I think there's a *but* coming. Is there, Harley?"

"Yes. Up until now, Jim Snyder, having been warned that these two people are political dynamite because of their money and connections, has been tiptoeing around that pair, and so carefully that I don't think they're in the least worried."

"They were willing to have Maria killed," Harry said, seeing no reason to name Caedmon again.

"And me," Caedmon put in firmly.

"And Caedmon," Harry continued.

"This is not going to go forward without risks," Dillard said somewhat tentatively, looking at Caedmon. "You might begin thinking about doing a disappearing act yourself. I have contacts with people in the witness protection program who could offer some help."

"That's generous," Caedmon said without hesitation, "but I have no intention of running, especially not from the Ogilvies."

"Let's move on, Harley," Harry said. "How can you act without warrants?"

"There are a dozen different ways, from calling the people in the Avola art world connected with them through business or charities and asking questions. We can place their house under surveillance. And when they complain, which they will, I can assure them we're doing it for their safety. That's only the beginning. They will squeal, and people will begin coming to their rescue. I can make those efforts very public, all of which will put them in a spotlight."

"To what purpose?" Caedmon asked.

"Hopefully" Dillard said, "to pressure them into making mistakes."

"That spotlight," Harry said to Caedmon, "will also make it less likely they will come after you again."

"Maybe," she responded in a voice that suggested they were dreaming.

31

After their meeting with Dillard, Harry and Caedmon debriefed one another and agreed they had come out of the encounter better than expected. But Caedmon remained subdued. Harry tried to get her to talk about the nightmares, which he had heard about for the first time in Dillard's office, but she refused to discuss them and would not say whether or not she was taking them up with Holinshed. Harry did not press her and waited in vain for her to take his hand again.

On the morning of the day Breckenridge was released from jail, they met him with umbrellas in the heaviest thunderstorm of the season. Despite the umbrellas, they were soaked to the waist by the time they reached the Rover. Attempts at conversation failed in the cacophonous roar of the thunder and pounding rain, and the lightning, dancing around them like fiery fiends, made thinking about anything else very difficult. But by the time they drove under Breckenridge's porte-cochère, the storm had gone bellowing off toward the east like a herd of wild cattle.

"Then she really came back," Breckenridge said once they had gathered on the balcony, having been met at the door by Ernan, who, warned of their imminent arrival, had marshaled two maids with towels and white cotton robes and hurried the drenched arrivals into separate bedrooms to shed their still-dripping clothes, towel themselves dry, and put on the robes.

When they reached the balcony in borrowed sandals, Ernan

was waiting for them at a table laid with a linen cloth, plates, cups and saucers, silverware, a large pot of coffee, and breakfast muffins under a napkin.

"Ernan," Breckenridge called out, striding toward the table, "brandy! Anyone else?"

He got no takers, but that did nothing to dim his increasingly bright spirits. "I want the taste of that jail thoroughly dispelled, and coffee alone won't do it."

The brandy came. Breckenridge threw back a substantial drink while Ernan dealt with the coffee, then poured another into his crystal snifter and sat back with a sigh.

"So she came back, did she," Breckenridge said, repeating himself with bitter intensity.

"Yes," Harry said.

"The coffee is wonderful," Caedmon said. "Harry's is varnish remover, and mine varies between poor and wretched. How was the jail coffee?"

"I used it to clean the toilet bowl. How was she looking?"

"We had nothing to compare it with," Caedmon said, "but she is very beautiful, at least I think so."

"She appeared to be in good spirits," Harry said, skirting the quicksand, "but I think the Ogilvies have frightened her. She's sure they'll be relentless in their pursuit."

"Then she ran off because she thought she was going to be killed?" Breckenridge asked.

Harry decided to answer the real question Breckenridge was asking.

"She said she had begun her plans to go before she stumbled onto what the Ogilvies were doing."

"You're going to have to fill me in. It's obvious my lawyers didn't have all the information."

Being careful not to reveal anything that the assistant state's attorney would call evidence, Harry quickly described why Afton had decided that she had no choice other than to leave as quickly as she could and vanish.

"Then it was the Ogilvies who had you kidnapped," Breckenridge said to Caedmon, "and Afton had nothing to do with it."

"I came very close to shooting her before I was convinced of that," Caedmon said, "but I don't think there's any doubt that she had nothing to do with it."

"I'm very glad," Breckenridge said.

He paused for a moment, his happiness at being released from jail rapidly draining away, and said, "Why in God's name didn't she just divorce me?"

"I guess you'd have to ask her," Harry said, determined not to characterize Afton's behavior—not, at least, to Gregory Breckenridge.

Apparently Caedmon felt less constrained. "She was, and I think still is, a very angry woman," she said.

"With me," Breckenridge responded in a tight voice.

"Oh, yes," Caedmon said.

Breckenridge made no verbal response but turned away from her, looking suddenly exhausted, and appeared to be gazing at the boats on the river. Harry thought he could have given odds and won that Breckenridge didn't even see the boats.

"I think it's decision time regarding Caedmon and me," he said.

Although his opinion of Breckenridge had grown less critical over time, he was no admirer of the man. Not that he was particularly offended by Breckenridge's sexual sidebar, who he slept with being his own business. But Harry still thought, despite moments of doubt and even pain, that the man saw the world and whatever was in it, including people, as potential investment opportunities from which he might collect dividends.

He had invested heavily in Afton and lost. That had hurt his pride, even saddened him, but like all bad investments he would discard it as quickly as he could. In fact, he had already invested in another, younger company and might even be more careful with this one, take better care of his investment. But Harry thought that before long he would begin hedging this more recent bet, anticipating a future loss.

"I suppose so," Breckenridge said wearily, turning his attention back to them.

He gave a dry, humorless laugh. "The way this has turned out, I could have saved the money."

"Not so," Harry said, rage rising in him like molten magma. "If you had not hired Caedmon to find your wife, you might at this moment be on a train ride to prison instead of sitting on this patio a free man. And, in case it's slipped your mind, saving your neck nearly cost Caedmon hers, you solipsistic son-of-a-bitch."

Harry was on his feet with his fists balled. Breckenridge lost what little color he'd regained and was staring at Harry, bug-eyed and open-mouthed.

"Harry!" Caedmon said, grasping Harry's arm. "Harry, stop! That's enough, sit down, *sit* down."

By now she was standing between Harry and the still-seated Breckenridge, both hands on his chest, trying to push him back into his chair. After a long moment, he looked at her, his body beginning to relax, and sat down.

"Jesus, Harry," Breckenridge croaked. "I'm sorry." Then, strength coming back into his voice, he said, "Caedmon I've never forgotten what you've done for me. I don't know exactly how it happened, but I do know the pressure you put on her in your pursuit had a lot to do with her coming back."

"She said she came back because of what happened to me," Caedmon said.

"And because when she learned what had been done to Caedmon," Harry said, his anger still roiling in him but under control again, "she knew that she would never be safe until the Ogilvies were under lock and key."

"That sounds less generous than what I said," Caedmon said, keeping her eyes on Harry as if she still expected him to explode, "but I think she was genuinely concerned about me."

"Harry," Breckenridge said, standing up as if he was preparing to make a speech, "I'm really sorry. I sounded like a shit, probably because that's what I am. Caedmon, I apologize for not pausing to think how my comment about wasting money was going to sound to you. And, Harry, you were right to call me on it. I apologize to both of you."

"And I'm sorry I swore at you," Harry said, getting to his feet, an action that caused Breckenridge to take a step back. "Will you shake hands?"

The two men shook hands a bit awkwardly, but their grips were solid.

"I can hardly wait for dark," Caedmon said, watching the ceremony with interest.

Both men looked at her.

"Why?" Breckenridge asked, getting in first.

"Because I expect to see a new star in the East. I've heard in the same day two men say they were sorry."

That broke the ice, allowing them all to laugh and begin to put the unpleasantness behind them.

"I have something to show you," Breckenridge said, pulling a damp and bedraggled envelope out of a pocket in his robe. "They gave it to me along with my personal belongings as I was leaving the jail and I didn't get a chance to read it until I was changing out of my wet things."

He passed the envelope to Harry. Because the dampness had soaked through the note inside, he had some difficulty extracting it without tearing it. The note was handwritten and the ink had run, but the message was clear and cold. When he had read it, he passed it to Caedmon.

"Will taking her deposition in a foreign country be enough?" Breckenridge asked while Caedmon was still reading. "Is it even possible to do such a thing?"

"Afton seems to think so," Harry said. "She's said what she was willing to do and how she would do it."

"Mr. Breckenridge," Caedmon said, looking at him quizzically while holding up the letter and waving it gently like a flag, "what did you think when you read this?"

"That she's a hell of a woman, but I couldn't live with her. No more questions about that, please."

"You're just letting her go."

Caedmon passed Harry the letter.

"That's right, but I've learned my lesson. If I'd been more honest with her, I might not have gotten myself into this mess."

"I'm not sure what I would do in her place," Harry said, having asked himself the question while reading her letter. Hearing Caedmon's question reminded him of it.

He started to give the letter back to Breckenridge, but he waved it away. "Keep it. Give it to Harley. He's the one who will need it."

"What did you mean, Harry?" Caedmon asked, obviously still thinking about Harry's comment on the letter.

"Nothing very profound," Harry said, "but I might be tempted to stay as deeply tucked away as I could until the Ogilvies were safely in prison. She's being a good citizen, but it's a risk."

"How much danger are you still in?" Breckenridge asked Caedmon.

"I don't really know," she replied in a subdued voice. "I don't think I'm of any interest to the Ogilvies now. They know everything I know, which is less than I could wish."

"Which brings us," Harry said, not wanting her to begin

brooding again on what had happened to her, "to the question, Mr. Breckenridge, of what you want from us."

"I really don't want to pursue Afton anymore," he answered, shoving his feet out and plunging his hands into the pockets of his robe. "She deserves to be left alone. And if the Ogilvies really are hunting her, I don't want to turn up information revealing where she is."

"Sounds right," Harry said. "How about it, Caedmon?"

"I think my job's finished. What little I've done most recently has been mostly confirming what I've already given to you." She paused, waiting for Breckenridge to respond. When he didn't, she said, "If you really wanted me to, I could take the search a stage further and begin tracking her rather than her money. But that could become very expensive, and as you say, there's no reason to pursue her that I can see."

"No," Breckenridge agreed, "my lawyers assure me the assistant state's attorney is not going to bring in the federal authorities and launch a manhunt. It's a great relief to me to know that."

He sat up in his chair and yanked his hands out of his pockets.

"Then let's call it quits," he said, managing a faded smile. "Thanks to both of you for work well done. Send me your bills, and may both of you prosper."

Once on their feet, they shook hands.

"Your clothes will be dry by now," Breckenridge said. "Ernan will show you where you can change. Goodbye."

When they reached the balcony door, Harry and Caedmon paused briefly for a last look at the river. Breckenridge was on the phone talking animatedly.

"Broker or lover?" Caedmon asked quietly.

"Broker," Harry said.

"Wrong," she said with certainty.

"Why?"

"Who would you most need/want to talk with if you were in his shoes?"

"You expect me to say Beatrice Frazer, but you're forgetting something that I've just remembered."

"What?"

"He's still married. He may be talking to a divorce lawyer."

Over the ensuing week, Caedmon closed out her Breckenridge account, transferred her work to two of her new storage services, having stored daily with the third one, and cleared her drives of the Afton Breckenridge files. That done, she filed her final bill with Breckenridge. Three days later, she had a delivery requiring her signature. She opened the envelope on the lanai as the nervous driver, who had said he had no idea people actually lived this deep in the Everglades, banged his truck over the loose plank in the humpbacked bridge in his flight toward County Road 19.

"Harry!" she shouted. "Come down here!"

Harry pounded down the stairs, his pistol in his hand. She met him at the foot of the stairs, hopping with excitement. "Look what Breckenridge sent me!"

With that, she whipped a check from behind her back and pushed it toward his face. Harry caught her hand to hold the check steady and whistled.

"Five thousand!" she cried. "That's just the bonus."

"Very generous," Harry said, trying to be enthusiastic, all the while thinking with barely contained amusement that Breckenridge's conscience must have been dragging him through the thorn plums.

Her eyes were so bright and her smile was so wide that Harry shoved the pistol under his belt and reached out for her. But when he pulled her to him, to kiss her, the smile vanished, and her hands thrust against his chest, the check fluttering to the floor.

"I'm sorry," he said, releasing her and reaching down to retrieve the check.

"Why did you do that?" she demanded, her face drained of color and her eyes haunted with shadows that Harry recognized but could not read. "How could you forget?"

"I'm sorry, Caedmon. I haven't forgotten anything, but in that moment you looked so happy and looking at you made me feel so happy that I wanted to kiss you. I simply acted on impulse—without thinking."

"There's nothing simple about it, Harry," she said coldly, snatching the check from his hand.

Her eyes filled with tears, and she turned away, stiff-backed with hurt and anger.

Harry watched her go, knowing from experience that there was nothing he could do but let her work through the pain herself. He wanted to pursue her, try to convince her that he had meant no harm, that she must know he would never do anything deliberately to hurt her. But in the middle of that line of thought, he felt the stirring of his own anger—or, perhaps, resentment that everything he had done up to that moment meant nothing to her.

Then, too, there was her immediate and fierce rejection of any affectionate gesture, even one as anodyne as stroking her hair or placing her hand on his face, not even mentioning making love. Of course, he knew what lay behind her responses and was deeply troubled by her suffering, but for those moments while she was hurrying away from him, he floundered in his own pain. She had fled to the lanai where he could hear her half-stifled sobbing. Shaking his head, he turned and walked back up the stairs.

★　★　★　★　★

At sunset, Caedmon came down from her room and found Harry sitting on the lanai, wondering if he should go to her and ask if she wanted any dinner.

"Can we talk?" she asked, calm now but reserved.

"Of course," he said, not particularly encouraged by her demeanor.

She pulled the chaise lounge nearest to him away slightly and sat down. The implication of that gambit did not escape him. On the other hand, she had gone to some trouble for this conversation, whatever it turned out to be. Her hair was carefully brushed, and she was wearing the burgundy suit she had been wearing the first time he met her. She had looked beautiful in it then, and she looked beautiful now although still drawn and subdued in spirit.

"First, I want to say I regret what happened after I called you downstairs to look at the check," she began, her voice steady but lacking the warmth it usually had when they were talking. "It was ugly, and I was as much at fault as you. Will that do for an apology? I've already had yours. There's no need to repeat it."

"All right," Harry said, "and, yes, it's more than adequate." He struggled with competing desires to swear, laugh, and howl with frustration, then curbed his impulses, and leaned back to listen.

"Good. At Holinshed's suggestion, I haven't told you much about what's been going on in my therapy. Of course, you already know that, but I wanted to say it myself."

"Okay."

"Being touched makes me want to scream, Harry," she said. "And I can't describe the revulsion I feel at having physical contact of any kind with you or anyone. I can barely let you and Benson put your hands on me, and having you grasp me by the arms the way you did . . ."

She turned her head away as if she could no longer bear to look at him.

Her death grip on the arms of her lounge chair told Harry this conversation wasn't the most fun she'd ever had, and he assumed that her stress came from having to talk about what had happened to her.

"Are you sure you want to go on with this?" Harry asked.

"It must be said, Harry." She spoke fiercely, snapping back to face him. "I have to say it, and you have to listen."

"I'm listening."

All right, he thought, *I've got it, the less I say the smoother this is going to go*—smooth *being a relative term here.*

"Good," she said. "First, the way I feel now, it would be impossible for me to make love."

A long pause followed while Caedmon was very clearly struggling to keep from bursting into tears.

"Tissues, please," she said through her hands.

Harry brought them. She wiped her face and with an effort began speaking again, looking at him with more tenderness than she had yet displayed.

"Harry, I have no idea when it will be possible for me even to contemplate having sex with any feelings of pleasure. Harry, it is terrible."

Her voice began to tremble and her breath choked. "Not only was I beaten, humiliated, and raped, I was robbed of half my life. I'm a shell, Harry, a wretched, ugly shell."

With that, she broke down entirely. By that point Harry was half kneeling in front of her, desperately wanting to take her in his arms but not daring to so much as touch her. He had never felt so helpless in his life.

"Caedmon," he said into her tears, "I love you. I'll help you in any way I can. Please don't give up. You are healing. Your

311

body is healing. Perhaps with my help, whatever is broken will mend and you will recover that lost part of yourself."

He stopped, having run out of words. After a few more painful minutes, she blew her nose and mopped her eyes. "I feel as if the road you mentioned stretches all around the world, and I'll die before I reach the end of it."

"You won't. A few days ago, you put your hand on mine. Do you remember doing it?"

"Harry, that's not true."

"It was right after Harley Dillard mentioned the Ogilvies," he said gently. "You were sitting beside me with your hands clasped in your lap. You became a little upset and mentioned your nightmares, and I reached over and put my hand over yours. You freed one of your hands and made a sandwich of mine. Then the conversation moved on, and you released me."

"Yes, I was so focused on what he was saying, I forgot myself. Are you sure I held your hand?"

"For a moment or two, yes."

"I must have done it unconsciously," she said, giving him an odd look—one that Harry couldn't decipher and took no comfort from.

"The point is, you did it, knowingly or not. I'm certain you will reach the point at which you can do it whenever you want to."

"You help me with my exercises," she said, "and Benson treats me like pizza dough. But you can't begin to know what a relief it is when you stop."

Later, when Harry was making dinner, he allowed himself to read the *odd* look she had given him. She had looked at him as if he was a stranger.

32

The next morning Caedmon was up before Harry. Hearing her go down the stairs with that still-uneven tread, he thought with a sinking feeling that she must have had another bad night. He went to his door and opened it to ask her how she was feeling, but changed his mind. The question itself would suggest she wasn't feeling good. He turned back into the room, defeated. Somewhere in back of the house the scrub jays were screeching hysterically.

Snake, Harry thought, *in the tree where they're nesting, too bad they don't know the thing can't hear them.* He had just finished dressing when Caedmon called up the stairs to him.

"Sanchez is standing outside the lanai door, wagging his tail and looking expectant. What does he want?"

"A Milk Bone. Let him in."

A moment later, he heard Caedmon give a yelp, followed by embarrassed laughter.

"Did you get the honorary dog greeting?" he asked her, coming into the kitchen and nearly being bowled over by the big hound's enthusiastic welcome.

"Yes," Caedmon said, her face reddening, "and when I grabbed his head, I almost got lifted onto the table. He's got something in his kerchief."

"It will be a note from Tucker," Harry said, lifting the Milk Bone sack and Sanchez's water dish out of the back of the sink cupboard, "but first things first."

313

While the dog was eating, Harry filled his water dish.

"Untie the kerchief," he told her. "The note will be rolled up inside it. Tell me what it says."

"It's an invitation to lunch, both of us."

She dropped the kerchief and the note on the counter and said, "I'm sorry, Harry, I can't go. I've got an appointment in town with a potential client."

Harry bristled, started to ask why she hadn't told him about this new client, then thought better of it. "I'm glad you're feeling strong enough to get back to full-time work," he said.

"As one of the huddled masses, I have to earn my keep," she said with a smile.

"No you don't," he said, "not until you're fully recovered. Have you cleared this with Benson and Holinshed?"

The smile instantly vanished. "You've probably noticed that I'm a full-grown woman—at least I used to be. I plan to be one again. Invalid status doesn't suit me and infantilism holds no appeal."

"Is not telling me when you're planning major changes in your life part of your restoration plans?"

That got out before Harry had time to think it through.

"Are you my keeper?"

The question was asked in a deceptively gentle tone of voice, but Harry was not deceived. He knew at once that he had skated onto black ice and swore silently.

"Your friend, your lover, the man who would marry you if you'd have him," he replied.

Items one and two he had intended to say. Three was an add-on that slipped out.

"The act of a desperate man, attempting to escape his own hanging," she said, obviously amused, "but no thanks."

"How much is included in the rejection?"

"I'm just lifting you off the hook of the proposal."

"I don't want to be lifted off it."

"Let's not add being shackled to our new-found joy."

"Where are we, Caedmon?" he said, "And I don't mean the parts that are involved with your recovery. I mean you and me, separate from all the seaweed."

"Bad timing, Harry," she said. "There is no Caedmon separate from what's happened and is still happening to her. I don't love you, Harry. Right now, I don't even feel attracted to you. If that's a deal breaker, I'll pack and leave right now."

Harry took a while to respond. He spent most of that time stifling hurtful and belligerent responses.

"First, I don't think of our relationship as a deal, and I don't think it's the time for me to try to characterize it for you. Next, if I wanted you to go, I would have said so. Finally, if you want to leave, that's a choice you're free to make, but I hope you don't and you won't."

"Great save," she said in a voice devoid of anger. "I won't apologize for not telling you my plans, but Holinshed, in trying to stitch me back together, said the pattern calls for me to make independent decisions."

"Sounds sensible to me," Harry said, recognizing the olive branch.

And that's where they left it. Caedmon departed for town and her appointment. Harry finished some work at his desk, keeping Sanchez with him for company. Then, after driving the dog to Tucker's road with a note in his kerchief, telling Tucker he and Caedmon were going to be in town, he left for Avola himself.

Harry and Caedmon had parted on good terms, but their quarrel had revealed a deep division between them, the depth of which Harry chose not to acknowledge or couldn't.

Before leaving CR 19, Harry had a call from Ernesto Piedra.

"I have some troubling information," he said, skipping his usual polite inquiries into Harry's health and activities.

Harry pulled off the road. When Ernesto was troubled, except about his *Las Madras,* Harry knew he meant it. "I'm listening," he said.

"Two men have come into town. They are, I think, *mucho peligroso.* They are not on holiday. They did not come by plane. They are driving a large, black Mercedes with Florida plates. But like the car, they are probably stolen."

"And your informants have no idea why they're here?"

"No, and there is more. For the moment, none of the *pandillas* are at war with each other."

"Gangs?" Harry asked.

"Yes. No one has heard of any major theft being planned. And, Harry, these are not men who are employed to steal things. They are brought in to end things."

Harry smiled at the verbal flourish, but nothing else he had heard made him feel like smiling. "Where are they, Ernesto?"

"Sadly, I don't know. Last night they were at a motel, but they left early this morning, and the night clerk did not know where they were going."

"How long before you know whether they are still in town?"

"Perhaps two days. But, Harry, do not wait to find out before you and your friend take precautions."

"What makes you think that Caedmon and I are targets?"

"They did not kill her the first time. Now they will be more serious."

"I still don't hear why you think these two are after us."

"It is a matter of elimination. There is no one else, so far as I know, who would require such serious attention. And, you cannot prove they are not."

"Thanks for the call, Ernesto."

"Watch yourself, Harry."

The chilling message in Ernesto's goodbye stayed with Harry all the way to the sheriff's headquarters, despite his doubts that the Ogilvies, having gotten all the information in Caedmon's computers, had anything to gain by killing her that would justify the risk of making a second attempt. As for an attempt on his life, what could justify that risk? Nevertheless, he had no intention of ignoring Ernesto's warning.

"Is it possible," Hodges asked, "that someone recognized Afton Breckenridge while she was in town and told the Ogilvies?"

Harry, Hodges, and Jim Snyder were in Jim's office, Harry having decided that he had better share with Jim what he had heard from Ernesto without, of course, naming his source.

"Possibly," Harry said, "but she's been gone too long for their arriving now to make any sense."

"If she was the target," Jim said, lifting his feet off the corner of the desk and swinging around to rest his elbows on it.

"You're saying she's not," Harry replied.

"I'm not sure, but it came to mind."

"Have you told Rivers?" Hodges asked.

"No."

"Are you going to?"

"Frank," Jim said with a scowl. "Let's not wander off the subject."

"I think it matters," Hodges protested, his large face growing red. "It ties into what Harry's going to do about protecting himself and her if those two gorillas do turn up."

"It might help to have a deputy in a cruiser parked by the bridge for a couple of nights," Harry said, hoping to save the fifteen minutes Jim and Hodges would happily devote to wrangling over whether or not he should tell Caedmon and whether answering the question would contribute to solving his problem.

"Sorry," Jim said. "I haven't got a man to spare, and even if I did, the sheriff would break out in hives if he saw I'd spent county money chasing a rumor, because that's what we're dealing with here. We don't know who these men are, what they look like, or where they are."

"Ha, ha," Hodges broke in loudly, "and they're driving a black Mercedes. There's more black Mercedes in Avola than there are fire hydrants."

"OK," Harry said, getting to his feet, "I've been a conscientious citizen and told you what I heard. All I have to do now is to get on about my business."

"Hold on," Jim said. "I want to hear what you're going to do about this."

"I think I'll begin with trying to persuade Caedmon to leave town for a week or two. Then maybe I'll sleep somewhere other than in my bed for a while."

"The O'Reilly might take you in," Hodges suggested with a wide grin.

"Not funny, Frank," Jim complained. "Don't forget, she's a fellow officer and deserves our respect."

"Oh, I respect her all right, Captain. In fact, she scares the shit out of me." That was followed by a bellow of his own laughter.

Glowering at Hodges, Jim stood up, his ears flaming.

"Wait," Harry said, jumping up. "I'm leaving. I've got to see Jeff Smolkin. Thanks for your help."

"Don't even think of tackling those two gunmen," Jim said, deflected from his intention to give Hodges a ritual dressing-down, intended to put a stop to Hodges' use of profanity in the office and destined to failure.

"Keep the twelve-gauge pump close by," Hodges added helpfully, "and a couple of boxes of Number 4 buckshot shells. You can clear a lot of brush with that combo, especially when the light's bad."

"Do you want to get him killed?" Jim demanded angrily.

"Hell, no, I'm trying to improve his odds."

"Don't listen to him, Harry," Jim protested. "You get yourself and Ms. Rivers away from that place, and maybe take Tucker with you."

Harry got out the door and down the hall and had turned the corner when Maureen O'Reilly came striding out of her office and nearly flattened him. In fact, if she had not reached out with her free hand and caught him by the arm, he would have sat down hard.

"Harry," she said, with a mock frown that had no echo in her voice, having effortlessly stood him upright but maintaining her hold on him, "I was thinking you had dropped off the edge of the earth. Will you stay standing if I let you go?"

"Yes, but Lieutenant Maureen O'Reilly, if you would only promise to bump into me the way you just did, I would be standing outside your door every day."

"And what good would that do us, *muirnin?*" she asked, giving him a little shake that rattled his teeth, her green eyes full of laughter and something else.

"I missed that," Harry said. "What did you just call me?"

To Harry's surprise, she blushed. "It's only a little Irish term of endearment."

"Come on, Lieutenant. Out with it."

"I called you sweetheart, but don't let it go to your head, or I might take it off."

Harry tried to step closer to her, but with her still gripping his arm he made no progress. He said as warmly as he could while looking up at her, "Is that a promise?"

"Away with you," she said, trying to frown but not making it.

319

"Have you ever seen the likes of him?"

Then, suddenly serious, she let go of his arm and asked, "How is Caedmon Rivers? I hear mixed reports on the poor soul." Then a bit sourly, "She could have perished and gone to her Maker for all I hear from you."

"I'm sorry, Maureen, not to have called you," he said honestly. "But things have been fairly crazy since I last saw you. According to Benson, she is recovering physically very well. But in other ways, there hasn't been all that much improvement."

"Is she working, then?"

"She is going to make the effort. In fact, she's meeting with a new client today."

"Ah, the last bit sounds encouraging, but you look as if you'd just been dragged out of a bog."

"I'm ashamed to say that's how I feel," he replied, surprised to find that her words described well how he felt.

O'Reilly sighed and shook her head, regarding Harry with an expression that made him feel strangely comforted. She was, he thought, an oddly complicated woman.

"It will be the rape and what went with it that's done the damage, Harry," she said quietly. "It is something I've seen too many times. Try not to let it break your heart, but there is no certainty she will heal at all. No," she leaned toward him, laying her hand on his shoulder and bringing her face closer to his, "it's not quite that. It's that the woman who's with you now is not the same woman you knew before the calamity took her. God knows where she has gone, Harry, but she will not be coming back in the days of your life or mine."

She bent further and kissed Harry lightly on the cheek, then said, rising to her full height, "Mind how you go, Harry Brock, and let me hear from time to time that you're still putting one foot in front of the other."

With that, she brushed past him and was gone. Harry

watched her stride away, feeling strangely stirred, then brought himself back to earth, squared his shoulders, and left the station with her dark prediction for company.

33

Harry went from the Tequesta County sheriff's headquarters to Bubba Miller's Gun Shop, where he bought a fifty-round box of 9mm Winchester USA ammunition for his CZ and two boxes of twelve-gauge shells for his shotgun.

"You planning on starting a war, Harry?" Bubba, a patchy-haired refrigerator of a man, asked as he rang up the sale.

Bubba never smiled and would never see a svelte three hundred pounds again, but his weight gave him bottom. Where he planted his feet, they stayed, helping to make him—despite his small, narrow eyes—the best handgun shot in the county.

"I thought I saw a black helicopter over the 'Glades last week. If that was a reconnaissance flight, I'll be ready."

"You may laugh," the big man said.

"I'm not laughing, Bubba," Harry said, heading for the door. "I feel as though I might be done laughing."

Now why did I say anything that dumb? he asked himself, bouncing out of Bubba's dirt lot. No answer was forthcoming.

In the same gray frame of mind, he drove to Jeff Smolkin's office. He had been putting off the visit because he didn't want to meet Renata. Why, he wasn't sure, possibly because one woman in his life who didn't love him was enough. Of course, Harry hadn't thought it out that way, but his reluctance to talk with her was, in addition to knowing that she was helplessly in love with Jeff, working its magic.

"How's Caedmon?" she asked, standing outside her office, when he stepped into the hallway from the empty waiting room.

"As well as can be expected," Harry said, unwilling to go into details. "Do you know that you're as weird as Sanchez and Oh, Brother!? They're always waiting for me when I arrive at Tucker's place."

"Oh, good!" she said in a rising voice. "Now I'm being compared with a hound and a mule. Have you any more compliments to make before I bash you with this case file?"

Harry stepped back in an exaggerated display of fear. What he saw was dispiriting. Although she was turned out in a black skirt and an ivory blouse and her makeup and hair were in perfect order, she looked exhausted, with darkness under her eyes she couldn't hide and an aura of musty defeat hanging over her like smoke from a dump fire.

It jolted Harry. "You'll do," he said, forcing some conviction into his voice. "I'd say nine and a half."

"Liar," she responded with a bitter smile. "I look as if I'd just been taken out of a broom closet and you know it."

"You look as if you've been working too hard," Harry told her. "When did you last have a holiday?"

"I think it was when Noah put in at Cozumel, to give us all a chance to do some shopping."

"You and your fellow passengers."

"Right."

"Have you talked with anyone about this?"

"Such as Number One?"

"That wasn't who I had in mind."

"You'd better go in and see him," Renata said, taking his arm and starting him toward Jeff's office. "I told him you were coming."

"Look," he said, compelled to try to do something, but not knowing what, "maybe we could . . ."

"Forget it, Harry," she said, releasing his arm. "It's a lost cause."

Harry wasn't sure about the *its* referent and was, in any case, being propelled into Smolkin's office.

"I've been meaning to call," Smolkin said, closing the door behind Harry and beginning to carom about the room like a squash ball, "but the days have been running together, and . . ."

"What the hell are you doing to Renata?" Harry demanded, suddenly furious with him, although he was even more disgusted with himself and didn't know why.

"Don't start!" Smolkin said, coming to a halt and holding up his hands in appeal. "I feel as bad as you do. I tried my best to send her on an all-expenses-paid cruise of Scandinavia—her father was born and brought up in Norway, moved here when he was twenty—but you'd have thought I'd suggested a mushing holiday on the Greenland glacier. She nearly took my head off. It's wrecking my life."

Harry wanted to go on being angry, but he couldn't find a way to do it and still regard himself as someone with most of his marbles.

"She looks so damned miserable!" Harry said, dropping into a chair.

"I think she's trying to make me fire her," Smolkin said in a voice scarcely louder than a whisper.

He had come to perch beside Harry and made the statement leaning toward him like a co-conspirator, his eyes constantly darting toward the door.

"What?"

"Honor bright! She's making life miserable for everyone in the office, including me. Talking with her doesn't help. I'm about out of options. And if I don't do something that works, I'm going to start losing my paras. They've all been in here, saying they're about done taking her abuse."

324

"Don't you know why she's behaving like this?"

While Harry waited for Smolkin to stop holding his head in his hands, elbows on the knees, and answer the question, he tried to think of some way to wake Smolkin up in time to smell the bacon before it burned. But he came up dry.

"No," Smolkin said, sitting up with a despairing sigh.

"Why do you suppose she's worked for you so long and so hard? With her skills, she could have gone into management years ago and be running a Fortune 500 company today."

"No idea," he said, shaking his head gloomily.

"Well, I wish you luck and her too," Harry said, abandoning the effort, convinced that if he explained the situation to Smolkin, the man wouldn't be able to hear it. "I want to talk about Afton Breckenridge. Are you up for it?"

"Sure," Smolkin said, bouncing to his feet as if in relief at being freed from the problem. "I heard that Harley let Breckenridge out of jail. How is he?"

"He's all right."

"Any news of his wife?"

"She came back, briefly," Harry said. "Caedmon and I talked with her twice."

"Jesus, Harry," Smolkin burst out, "why didn't you tell me? This is huge! Does Harley know she's here?"

"She's gone, hopefully where no one can find her," Harry said.

Smolkin was on the move again. "Does Harley know she *was* here?"

Harry explained the visits and his subsequent trip to Harley's office.

"So she got Breckenridge off the hook and gave Harley enough to press ahead with the Ogilvie investigation," Smolkin said, dropping back into the chair beside Harry. "Somebody should write a book. Do you think she was telling the truth?"

"Yes. Can she really give a deposition in a foreign country?"

"Yeah," Smolkin said, "she can do that—if anyone can find her."

"She's made some kind of arrangement with Harley. When they need her, she'll surface."

"Risky, isn't it?" Smolkin demanded.

"I don't know. She seems to know what she's doing. She showed up on the Hammock before Caedmon could find her. When she left, she vanished like a puff of smoke."

"How is Caedmon? I should have asked as soon as you arrived."

"She's making progress, but she's not feeling very good. There are a lot of downs and not many lasting ups."

"I'm sorry the progress is so slow. Did she get to see Afton Breckenridge?"

Harry left out the gun episode and told Smolkin that the two women had gotten on very well.

"This is personal and difficult," Smolkin said, "but I've got to ask. How much danger are you two in?"

"From the Ogilvies?"

"If that's who's behind the attack on Caedmon."

"Not much," Harry said. "I can't see any compelling reason for them to want to come after us. What's to be gained?"

"You're sure they don't know Afton was in town?"

"I don't know," Harry told him, "but now it doesn't matter."

Harry's confidence in his answer lasted until he was out of Smolkin's building, at which point he acknowledged that he had not dealt with the question and neither had Caedmon. Along with that admission came another. Although he had bought extra ammunition and told Jim he was going to persuade Caedmon to leave the Hammock for a few weeks, he was not really convinced, even granting Ernesto's warning, that they were in any real danger.

Driving back to the Hammock, he tried to engage with the question, but two things prevented his making any progress. First, his mind kept drifting away from the subject, and then he found himself growing increasingly anxious about Caedmon. The oppressive feeling of foreboding intensified as soon as he turned onto CR19 and increased the closer he came to the Hammock. The speed at which he was driving also increased, and when he turned onto the Hammock, the Rover skidded on the sand and narrowly escaped going through the railing as it fishtailed onto the bridge.

He was so focused on getting home that none of his NASCAR antics made any impression on him. He leaped out of the Rover while it was still rolling and left the door swinging open.

"Caedmon!" he shouted, running hard across the lawn toward the lanai.

She thrust her head out her bedroom window and called down, "What's wrong?"

"Are you all right?" he shouted, coming to a stop, looking up at her, his heart still pounding.

"Yes, of course I am. Stop shouting. I'll be right down."

Harry, still shaken and somewhat shamefaced, met her in the kitchen.

"What's happened?" she demanded, hurrying toward him but stopping beyond his reach.

"I'm not going to touch you," he said, his fear converting to anger.

"Harry," she said sharply, "stop being silly. Tell me what's happened."

It took Harry a few moments to calm down, during which, to cover his agitation, he took a glass from the cupboard, filled it with water, and drank it.

"I talked with Jim Snyder and Jeff Smolkin," he said, putting down the glass and turning to face her. "Then, driving home, I became afraid something had happened to you. I'm sorry if I upset you."

"What did you think had happened to me?"

"I thought the Ogilvie's people had come after you again."

"Have you been drinking?"

"Be serious."

"All right, but I thought we'd agreed that the Ogilvies had no reason to pursue us."

Harry had quieted down and was leaning back against the counter. Caedmon was standing with her hands on her hips, regarding him with marked irritation. She had been dressing to go out and was wearing a pair of dress jeans, a light blue, short-sleeved blouse, and dark blue sandals. Harry thought she looked like a new woman and planned to say so. She had regained some weight, a healthy color had replaced the streaked bruise lines on her face, and her newly washed hair was regaining its luster.

"You look good," Harry said, deliberately keeping the compliment low key.

"Thanks," she said with no further response. "Back to the question."

"Coffee," Harry said, instantly deflated, and turned to find the pot.

"Oh, no!" she told him. "You sit down. I'll make the coffee. Talk."

Harry decided there was no use in shielding her from what he knew, not if he expected to put the plan that was beginning to take shape in his mind into operation. The fear that had skewered him driving home had broken through his denial. "Ernesto told me that two seriously bad guys have come to town. At first, I thought that was no concern of ours, but then

328

Jim and Frank Hodges and later Jeff Smolkin raised the possibility that the Ogilvies might have learned that Afton had come back."

Harry stopped there.

"Did you see Renata Holland?" she asked stiffly.

"I didn't know you knew her name."

"I hope you didn't stare at her breasts the way you just goggled at mine."

"Whoa, that's nasty."

"Yes, it is."

She remained quiet for a time, staring through him as if he wasn't there.

"Mine might as well be made of recycled rubber for all the good they're doing me," she said at last in a harsh voice. "I feel like a half-finished android that's been abandoned because her circuitry is all screwed up."

"I'm sorry, Caedmon," he said. "I can only imagine what you're going through. But you're not an android. You're a beautiful woman who's had a terrible thing happen, and you haven't been abandoned. I love you. I will not abandon you, and I absolutely believe you will recover."

"What makes them think the Ogilvies knew Afton was in town?"

They were sitting across the table from one another. The coffee had been poured and drunk. Harry's last comment had elicited no response from Caedmon, who appeared to have drifted into a long reverie. Harry was caught in compelling thoughts of his own, prompted by Caedmon's refusal to engage with him. When she spoke, the silence had extended to such a length that the sound of her voice actually startled him.

"Harry, I asked you a question," she said.

"I think it's just a floating fear. I'm feeling some of it myself. But before we go there, I want to say a couple of things."

"If it's about me, I don't want to hear it."

Harry switched off his sarcasm gene and said, "It involves you, but it's not about you. Can I go on?"

"Wise ass."

"I'll take that for a *yes*. There's no way I can know for sure whether those two goons I mentioned earlier are ticketed to take us out or not. But one thing is certain, it's a major mistake for us to stay here and wait to see. It's happened to me before. Believe me, being trapped in a house while someone is trying to kill you is not fun."

"So?"

"I'll suggest a couple things and then you chime in."

"What's this '*chime in*' shit?" she demanded. "Are you going through a personality change?"

"I didn't hear any of that," Harry said. "Just listen."

"That's marginally better."

"Good. We could go out to the Rover and leave town, go on a two-week vacation, telling no one but Jim Snyder and maybe not him. How about the Maldives?"

"No," she said. "Nothing personal, but I can't be that close to you. I have trouble being in this house with you. Forget it."

"Plan B," Harry said. "You leave town, having told no one where you're going. We could pick a destination while I'm driving you to the airport. You fly to Atlanta. Once there you buy another ticket for Chicago, not with the same carrier. You fly from Chicago on a new carrier to wherever you want to spend a couple of weeks. Once there you call me on your cell, using my cell number, telling me where you are."

Caedmon sat, arms folded on the table, lightly tapping a foot, and looking out a window. Her expression was strained, but Harry was left to guess what she was thinking.

"No," she said at last, speaking more briskly and with emphasis. "I can't put myself through that torment," hunching her shoulders as if experiencing the events. "If they want to shoot me, let them try." She nodded at her handbag on the end of the table. "I carry my gun now when I go out, and you can make money betting I no longer go to the door when I'm alone here and people knock."

Harry listened with a sinking heart, but he saw she meant it, and there was nothing to be gained by moving her back into her house in Ashbury Gardens. She would not be likely to ask him to stay with her. Here, they were together, allowing him to give her some protection.

"I guess that leaves Plan C. Go on as we are and see what happens."

"Good," she said, pushing back from the table and standing up.

He must have allowed some of his real feelings about Plan C affect his expression because, as she came around the table to grab her bag, she paused long enough beside him to touch him lightly on the shoulder.

"Thanks for trying, Harry," she said. "I appreciate your concern. Thank you for it, but the truth is I don't much care whether I go on living or not."

Harry went on sitting at the table until he heard the thump and clatter of the loose plank on the humpbacked bridge as she drove over it. He hadn't asked where she was going, but he thought it was probably to see Holinshed. Considering what he had just heard, he thought he'd better see her as well.

34

"I'm seeing Caedmon at three-thirty," Holinshed said, "and I can squeeze you in at one. But I'm not altogether easy about having a consultation with you without having cleared it with Caedmon."

"I'll be brief," he said.

"I'll have to tell her I talked with you."

"OK, I'll see you at one."

Caedmon called him at eleven, to say she would not be home until five as she had two appointments and planned to work the remaining time at her house. He assumed one of her appointments was with Holinshed and the other with her new client. Who her client was, Caedmon had not told him. He did not know whether it was a man or a woman, and he certainly didn't know what she was being asked to do.

"I live on a need-to-know basis," he said, "and so far as I can judge I have a security rating of one, ten being highest."

"Poor baby," Holinshed told him across her desk, her eyes sparkling with apparent amusement.

"Thanks a lot," Harry said, stung. "You should try living with someone who tells you he can't take a trip with you because he can barely stand being in the house with you, never mind an automobile or rubbing elbows with you in adjoining airplane seats."

"You look pretty good for a man living in Hell."

"If you're auditioning for Comedy Central, I'm not one of the judges."

"Why are you here, Harry?"

"This morning, Caedmon told me she didn't much care whether she lived or died."

"That frightened you."

"A mix of fear and alarm."

"I understand, but I'm not surprised or particularly worried. Neither should you be."

"Why not? Christ, Gloria," Harry said, becoming increasingly upset as he spoke, despite all his efforts to stay calm, "I'm reasonably sure she's being targeted again. The sheriff's people can't do anything to protect her. She refuses to go away, either with me or alone. And I know that without an army for protection, it's almost impossible to keep someone from being killed by a determined and skilled assassin. As you well know, killers have shot two presidents in our lifetimes."

"Fortunately," Holinshed said quietly, "only one died, but I understand your concern." She pushed back from her desk. "Look, Harry," she said, coming to sit beside him, "there's only so much either of us can do in a situation like this. Her disgust with her life, with herself, with a world that compelled her to go through what she's gone through, and with you for not having been able to stop it from happening, all these have combined to rob her of joy, even hope."

She paused and rearranged herself in her chair, recrossing her legs, adjusting the height of her white skirt, and pulling at the sleeves of her dark blue blazer, then hitching around so that she could look at him.

"Now," she said, "why did I just do that?"

"Only you and God know," Harry said, puzzled and irritated by the performance and the question.

"Let's leave God out of it. Things are sufficiently complicated as it is."

"You were trying to decide what to say next and weren't finding it easy."

"Not bad. How long do you think it would be before you exhausted all the possibilities?"

"I would run out of patience long before they were exhausted."

"What if I told you that you had to continue working on the problem although it might take you ten days."

"I'd consider shooting either you or myself."

"That's how Caedmon feels."

"Because she is trying to answer the question, 'Why did this happen to me?' "

"That and why has my life been destroyed? I hasten to add that from her perspective at this moment in time, she believes it has been irredeemably destroyed."

"She won't let me touch her."

"No."

"What do I do?"

"After those in your position endure long enough the rejection, abuse, hostility, rage—whatever the dominant and unpleasant reactions are—most end the relationship."

"I'm not going to do that. So how can I help?"

"Retain your composure. Return kind words for insult. Accept the total withdrawal of affection and sexual response. Take nothing personally. Wear the hair shirt with a smile."

"You're serious, aren't you?"

"Unfortunately, yes. If you wish, I can give you the name of a therapist. You may want some backup. Because Caedmon is my patient, I can't provide it. I think it might help, but it's up to you."

★ ★ ★ ★ ★

Once out of Holinshed's office, heavily burdened by what he had just heard, Harry decided to call on Rowena Farnham. Aside from a need for company, the visit was prompted, without his having articulated it, by concern for her safety. Ernesto's report of the *dos serpientes* had planted a seed of worry in Harry's mind that was growing vigorously.

"Harry!" Rowena said with a watery smile when she opened her office door. "Come in. I'm glad to see you."

Rowena was dressed for work in a Red Sox baseball cap, a shamefully ragged and faded blue sweatshirt, gray cotton warm-up pants with a comfort waistband, and Peter Rabbit slippers. Her office was, as usual, a chaos of books, pamphlets, reports, and church programs.

"This isn't an altogether social call," Harry said, looking for a chair that wasn't already occupied by printed matter.

"Just choose one," she said, following Harry's gaze, "and pile whatever's on it on the floor. It's the only way to find a place to sit in here," she added, implying some unseen agent of confusion had created the clutter. "That's what I'm going to do."

But before she cleared a space for herself, she said, "I've just opened a new tin of Earl Grey tea. What say we test it? There are also scones with raisins and, of course, butter and strawberry jam. You look as if you could use a pick-me-up. I know I could."

"There's something I've got to tell you, Harry," Rowena said from the sideboard, having switched on the electric kettle and the warming oven and gone on marshalling their "pick-me-up." "You won't like it any more than I do, but keeping it to myself is not going to help either of us."

"I'm listening," Harry said, the prospect of warm scones lifting his spirits, which were, as Rowena had noticed, down around his ankles.

"I've received two phone calls that have troubled me," she said. "Now, being a parson, I receive my share of crank calls, usually from recruiters from the Church of the Latter Day Saints, the Seventh Day Adventists, or converts to Roman Catholicism who urge me to come home."

The smell of warm scones accompanied Rowena, bearing a large silver tray, freighted with a silver tea service, a plate of scones under a white linen napkin, butter, sugar in a silver bowl, strawberry jam spooned into a Worcestershire sauce bowl, and two bone china cups and saucers.

"Whoops," Rowena said cheerfully. "Forgot the trolley. Harry, wheel it over here, will you? Thanks."

She set the tray down with a smile of satisfaction. "That ought to do it," she said, passing Harry a napkin. "Dig in. I'll pour the tea."

Lifting the pot, she showed it to the four corners of the room and then filled their cups. "Silly affectation," she said, stirring milk into her tea, "but it pleases me. My mother always did it, except when there was company."

"Does it have a practical origin?" Harry asked, buttering a scone and adding strawberry jam to the rapidly melting butter.

"Tea has to steep to gain its full flavor," Rowena replied. "Showing it to the room takes an additional moment or two, although that alone isn't enough. How is it?"

Harry finished swallowing his first bite of the scone and tried the tea.

"Excellent," he said, "What about these phone calls?"

"Threatening," Rowena said, putting down her cup and her scone as if she found them suddenly disgusting.

Harry stopped eating to focus on what she was saying. "Go on," he said.

"At least I found them so. They seemed to be warning me against doing something. The worst part was that they haven't specified what."

"How many have you had?"

"Three in the last couple of days."

"The same person each time?"

"I think so. It's a man. But from his accent I'd say not from around here."

"Where, then?"

"New York, New Jersey. Not much education but a rich vocabulary, chiefly expletives."

Harry felt a short, sharp stab of alarm. "Have you called Jim?"

"No, I more or less discounted the first two as the work of some nutcase, but the third call was just too menacing to ignore. It got my attention, Harry."

"When did you get it?"

"Last night."

"What was different about it?"

"The caller said I'd made a serious mistake. He said he knew I'd been talking to the police. And if I wanted to stay alive, I had better not do it again. He then said that if I did call the police about these calls or about anything else, it would be 'all over' for me."

Harry had forgotten about the tea and the scones.

"Rowena," he said, "I want you to do something for me. I want you to call Jim as soon as I leave. If you can't get him, ask for Millard Jones. If he's not in the office, ask for Maureen O'Reilly. Tell whoever answers that I said it was urgent. Will you do that?"

"All right, Harry, if you think it's that important, but I don't see . . ."

"I'll explain in a moment, but first there's something else. I want you to go to *Salvamento* tonight and stay there for a few days. Tell no one where you're going. Leave a message on your

answering service that you have been called out of town unexpectedly."

"That's Soñadora Asturias' safe house on Avola's most
dangerous neighborhood!" Rowena said in a voice full of
surprise, her eyes wide.

"It was. You've probably forgotten. Gabriela Rodriguez is
running it now."

Harry did not want to linger over the point. It had been painful enough to hear Soñadora's name.

"Why do you want me to go there—even if they would take
me in, which I doubt? If I were going anywhere—which I'm
not, I'd go to Haven House."

"First, I want you to go to *Salvamento* because I'm sure you're
in danger. Second, everyone knows the connection between St.
Jude's and Haven House. Third, it's almost certain whoever is
calling you is working for the Ogilvies. I'll make the arrangements. Gabriela has not forgotten how much you helped
Soñadora."

"If Maria had not been murdered," Rowena said, getting to
her feet, "I'd say you were mad as a March hare. Even knowing
about Maria, I find it scarcely credible."

"Have you forgotten what happened to Caedmon?"

"I'm sorry, Harry," Rowena said in a voice filled with contri-
tion. "Of course I haven't forgotten, but . . . Oh, what's the use!
What happened to her was so horrendous it seems outside of
any reality the rest of us can even conceive."

"It's real enough," Harry said, drawn by Rowena's words
back into the pain of Caedmon's affliction.

Rowena bent over Harry and put her hand on his shoulder.
"Forgive me, Harry," she said.

"Nothing to forgive, Rowena. I understand. Occasionally,
even I forget, but Caedmon doesn't."

"I'm sure she doesn't," Rowena said contritely.

Then in a sudden change of mood, she threw up her hands and cried, "If the sheriff's people know this is going on, why aren't the Ogilvies behind bars? It doesn't make sense!"

"Unfortunately, it does," Harry said. "The Ogilvies, as you know, are very influential people. Until Caedmon's attack, their standing in the county was enough to all but stifle any serious investigation of the charges Maria made against them."

Rowena stood in front of Harry, her fists planted on her hips, listening to him intently. "What will it take," she demanded, "for the police to break through that wall of money and influence?"

"Harley Dillard has decided that if he and the Sheriff's Department can't move the investigation forward, they will call in ICE and/or the FBI's art theft unit."

"*Ice?*"

"Sorry, it's U.S. Immigration and Customs Enforcement, an arm of Homeland Security. ICE and the FBI cooperate when necessary to investigate cases of stolen art smuggled into the country. The problem with calling them in is that local authority is pushed deep into the shade."

"Are they any good?"

"Once launched, they are unstoppable—unlimited resources, strong affiliation with major law enforcement agencies around the world, and very highly trained operatives. They are impressive."

"It sounds as though they should have been engaged from the moment Maria talked to Jim Snyder," Rowena said, clearly offended by the delay.

"Perhaps," Harry said, "but right now I want to hear that you are going to *Salvamento.*" Seeing her hesitation, he said, "Call what's his name, your assistant rector."

"Ron Buchwald."

"Tell him you have a family emergency and are leaving town

for a week. If he demands a number where he can reach you, make up one, and leave. I'm serious, Rowena."

"All right," she said, "but there are going to be some very offended people on my staff and in the congregation—committee chairmen, the entire Vestry. I'll never live it down."

"But you'll be alive to try," Harry said.

35

Having extracted a solemn promise from Rowena to hide out for a few days at *Salvamento,* Harry called Gabriela and made the necessary arrangements for Rowena to be picked up at the rectory by the bogus Acme Dry Cleaning van the safe house employed, and as discreetly as possible whisk her away. Although it was a painful struggle, he managed not to ask if she had heard recently from Soñadora. He drove back to the Hammock more slowly than usual, his mind alternately fighting off memories of Soñadora and trying to answer the question of how best to keep himself and Caedmon alive.

Once home and in no mood to go on wrestling with his mind's insistence on loitering in the graveyard of lost love, Harry decided to call on Tucker. Checking his watch and finding that Caedmon was probably sitting in Holinshed's waiting room, he decided to walk to Tucker's place even though the fiery heat of afternoon had silenced everything on the Hammock except the cicadas, locusts, and their fiddling backup in the upper-story symphony orchestra.

In the first weeks following his moving onto the Hammock, Harry was so broken in mind and spirit and so close to giving up the contest between himself and the ogre of living that his surroundings meant nothing. He had rented the house he now owned because it was so far from other people. He had no expectation of either remaining in the house or going anywhere else. Harry fully expected to die there and thought he would welcome the release.

However, the spirit of the Hammock had other ideas and a powerful assistant in Tucker LaBeau, who found him, and with the help of Oh, Brother! gradually led him out of his corrosive darkness and into the healing sun. Then, later, Tucker had acquired Sanchez, who according to Tucker, spent his puppy-hood speaking Spanish and when he was in certain moods still used that excuse for deliberately misunderstanding things said to him in English. Harry awakened into a family, and he had never forgotten the debt he owed them.

The big hound, his muzzle turning white, and Oh, Brother!, seemingly ageless, met him at Tucker's road. Greetings over, he walked between them, one hand on Sanchez's head and the other on the mule's shoulder, sharing with them the events of his day. Whether he knew it or not, in talking he unburdened himself. By the time they reached the garden where Tucker was picking green beans, his heart was lighter.

"Do you see this basket?" Tucker asked as if continuing a conversation they had been having a moment earlier, holding up the brimming container for Harry's examination. "I bought that from an Indian woman in a white doeskin skirt, red cotton blouse, and moccasins, all of which, aside from the blouse, she had made from scratch."

Harry studied the dark woven basket with interest. It was about a foot in diameter and a bit less than that deep, with a rounded bottom. The rectangular designs of alternating light and dark woven wood were exquisite.

"What's it made from?" Harry asked.

"Split wild cherry and stained with berry juices. I have the cover for it in the house. I've used this basket for one thing and another for thirty years," Tucker said, turning it slowly in his hands, gazing at it with obvious admiration. "I don't see why it shouldn't last another thirty years. I'm glad to see you. What brings you to this quiet corner of the planet?"

"First, I want to hear about this Indian woman," Harry said. "Were you thinking about her while you were working?"

"I was," Tucker admitted with a quiet smile and a look in his eyes that suggested that he could still see her.

He was quiet for a moment, then rested the basket on his hip and said in a livelier voice, "It's hard to talk with a dry throat. Let's go in out of this sun, and I'll see what I can find to wet our whistles."

The four made a small parade with Sanchez leading the way, Harry and Tucker walking side by side on the sandy path, talking quietly about the citrus grove, with Oh, Brother! covering their backs. Once settled on the stoop in the bentwood rockers with sweating glasses of cold lemonade in their hands, Harry said, "Get back to the Indian woman."

For Tucker to talk about the women in his life was a rare event, and Harry intended to keep the story unfolding as long as he could.

"She walked out of the woods one day in late October while I was splitting wood. I had worked up a sweat and had driven the axe into the block, then stepped back to wipe my face and take a breather. I don't know what it was, but something made me turn around, and there she was, standing just inside the shade line of the trees, watching me. I thought the nearest person to me was a good half day's walk away, and seeing her there startled me and no mistake.

" 'Hello,' I said when my Adam's apple went back where it belonged. 'Are you lost?'

" 'No,' she said and smiled as if I'd made a very good joke, 'thirsty.'

" 'Come in,' I said, walking toward the stoop, which I had just finished but not yet stained. I held the screen door open for her, but she wouldn't go into the house. So I carried a kitchen chair onto the stoop and asked her to sit down. She smiled at me again as if I had said something that amused her, but she slipped her pack off her back and set it on the floor as she eased onto the chair. I never saw her make an awkward movement. It was as if everything she did, she did to a music I couldn't hear."

Harry watched Tucker drift away again momentarily into his memory, then recover himself. He had emptied the basket into the sink and carried it back out onto the stoop after bringing them the lemonade. Now he reached down and picked up the basket and sat staring at it as if it was a crystal ball in which he could see the past.

"That was when I saw there was a little girl, about a year old, in her pack, which was woven like this basket. The knife in her belt and whatever else she had tucked into that backpack besides the baby and what she wore were all her worldly goods.

"I fetched her some water, which she drank. 'More?' I asked, but she only shook her head.

"While she was drinking, I had my first chance to take a close look at her. Two things I noticed at once were her skin and her hair. Her skin was beautiful, soft and glowing. I was also taken by her hair, jet black and fashioned into a heavy braid, worn draped over her shoulder and falling across her breast all the way to her lap and a bit more.

"But when she looked up and passed me the glass, I looked straight into her eyes and froze like a deer in a jacklight. It was as if all the darkness and mystery of night were in them. I'd never seen their equal, and never after, either.

"When I managed to stop staring, I noticed she was smiling again, and I believe I must have blushed because her smile widened.

" 'Why are you out here?' I asked, and she pointed toward the place where she had come out of the woods. Where she had been standing was a pile of a dozen or so baskets, strung together on a strangler fig vine.

" 'I wove them,' she said. 'Now I will sell them.' "

"What was her name?" Harry asked, breaking the long silence that had followed Tucker's last words.

"Willow," Tucker said. "She stayed with me six weeks. Then one day I had to drive into town. When I came back, she and her baskets were gone. All except for this one, which she had left on the kitchen table."

"Didn't you go looking for her?" Harry demanded, altogether unsatisfied with the way the story was ending.

"No," Tucker said, putting the basket back on the floor. "I let her go the way she had come. It would be what she wanted. I suppose she had commitments, responsibilities."

"And you never heard from her again?"

"No. Two years later I got married."

"But you kept the basket."

"Yes. By the way, that lady with the long tail has brought out her cubs. I was over in the northwest corner a few days ago and saw them. Fortunately, she didn't see me. You were right. She's got a den pretty close to where you and Caedmon saw her. So go carefully if you're out that way."

Walking home, Harry reviewed Tucker's story about Willow and had the uneasy feeling that he was missing something. Further reflection suggested that he had been listening to more than a story out of Tucker's past. In all the years he had known the old farmer, he could count on the fingers of one hand the times Tucker had regaled him with a story as personal as the one about Willow. And in every one of those tales from the past, there had been a message in it for him.

But what was the message here? Was there some parallel to events in his own life? Of course, Harry thought, experiencing instant gloom, Soñadora, but why remind him of that painful separation? No answer was forthcoming. Then he was missing the point. Could it possibly be Caedmon? But Caedmon wasn't going anywhere.

Enough, he told himself. He had more important things to worry about and, yes, Caedmon was the center of his concern.

She was sitting on the lanai with her feet up and a clinking Manhattan, heavy with cherries, on the table at her elbow. She had changed into white shorts, sandals, and a red tank top.

"If you ever mess with my therapy again, Harry," she said by way of greeting, "I'll disembowel you."

"No fair," Harry said, "you've got a drink, and I haven't."

"If you've been at Tucker's, I'm surprised you can walk. Between the cider, the plum brandy, and that home brew experiment of his, the farm is the reciprocal of a Betty Ford clinic."

"I'm sober as a hen," Harry protested.

"Why were you talking with Holinshed?"

"Didn't she tell you?"

"Don't be any dumber than you have to be."

"I resent the personal nature of that comment. In the eighth grade I was salutatorian."

"Answer the question, and stop trying to make me like you."

"I was worried about something you said. Only Holinshed could put my mind at ease."

She sat looking at him for a while with what he thought of as her Madame Defarge expression. He could hear the tumbrels rolling. But she surprised him.

"Do you worry a lot about me, Harry?" she asked.

"About as often as I worry about hurricanes."

"I'm not in a joking mood."

"Okay." Harry pulled a chaise around and sat on the leg rest, elbows on his knees.

"You're recovering from a terrible ordeal—faster than Benson or any of the other doctors thought possible," he said. "You

346

look even better than new to me. But you said something this morning that worried me."

"I told you that I didn't much care whether I went on living or not."

"Holinshed did tell you."

"No, she didn't, but I remember saying it. I shouldn't have."

"Did you tell her you'd said it?"

"None of your business."

"I understand what you tell Holinshed is confidential. But I'm not asking out of prurient curiosity or in an effort to increase my *schadenfreude*. So don't just swat me as if I was an annoying gnat interrupting your happy hour."

"All right! All right! Christ, Harry. I'm not sure what it means. I'm certainly not going to commit suicide, if that's what got you in a twist."

"Good. Because if you do, I'll hunt you down and make your life miserable."

"Make yourself a drink and mine strong."

She held out her glass to him as he got up.

"Did Tucker ever talk to you about a woman named Willow?" he asked when he came back with the drinks.

The sun was behind the trees by this time, and the breeze humming in the screens actually felt slightly cool. As he was sitting down again, the first flock of ibis lifted off the creek, heading for their roosts in the mangrove swamps at the mouth of the Seminole River. Then, getting an early start, some colony frogs in the cabbage palm on the creek bank a few dozen yards down the road toward the bridge began belling enthusiastically.

"Not that I recall. It's an unusual name."

"Did you ever see that small wicker basket he uses sometimes when he's picking beans?"

"Is that the one with the geometric designs?"

"That's the one. Willow wove that basket and gave it to him."

"Were they living together?"

"Yes," Harry said, "for a while."

"Very romantic," she said with no trace of interest in the story.

Just then, fish crows that been feeding beside the creek on the remains of an otter's bluegill feast exploded out of the bushes in loud and raucous alarm. Harry put his glass down, went to the screen, and stood staring out toward the road, listening as well as watching.

"What is it?" Caedmon asked, coming to stand beside Harry.

"Listen," he said.

"To what?"

"The frogs."

Harry was listening intently. Suddenly, they stopped singing.

"Come on," Harry said. "Someone's coming we don't want to see. Pull on your sneakers. We're getting out of here. Right now!"

Caedmon had started to protest, but at his "Right now!" she ran after him, grabbing her handbag off the kitchen table as she passed. Harry had dodged into his study and come back holding his shotgun, his CZ in its case, and a small bag with a leather strap slung over his shoulder.

"Where are we going?" she demanded as she kicked off her sandals and shoved her feet into her sneakers.

Harry was already moving toward the back door. "Into the woods. Don't let the door slam behind you, but once it's closed, run like hell, and don't talk."

Once they were through the oaks and onto the path, Harry stopped and, kneeling in the ferns, slid the CZ harness over his shoulder and fastened its straps across his chest.

"Here, with me," he said, reaching up and gently but firmly pulling her down beside him. "Watch the house. If you see anyone, don't speak but give me a nudge."

Harry turned his attention to the shotgun, jacked it open enough to see that there was a shell in the chamber, closed it, checked the safety, then drew the CZ, chambered a round, and was shoving it back into its holster when Caedmon gave a furious yell.

"You sons-of-bitches!" she shouted. "You fuckers!"

Before Harry could stop her, Caedmon had pulled her .38 out of her bag. She sprang to her feet and fired three times in rapid succession. Harry was up quickly enough to see two men in black suits, carrying short-barreled machine guns, diving for cover.

"Too bad you missed," Harry said. "Now's the time to leave."

"They were the ones, Harry," she cried. "Those bastards! I'm going to kill them. I'm doing it right now!"

Harry raised the shotgun and fired twice to keep them down in the grass. "Now," he said to her, spinning her around, "we run. Go before they kill us."

Her eyes lost their wildness and focused on him.

"We have ten seconds," he said. "Ten seconds to get away. If we don't, we're both going to die. Do you understand? Now," he said, pushing her down the path in front of him. "Run!"

He thought she might shoot him. She had looked angry enough to shoot her mother, but she suddenly broke into a full-out run, and Harry sprinted after her. Fortunately, the path made a sharp turn around the rotting remains of an old uprooted ficus.

They were no sooner past the tangle of thrusting roots, when there was an explosion of gunfire and the sizzle of bullets clipping leaves and branches over their heads, filling the air around them with shredded bits of twigs, leaves, and bark.

"Submachine guns. They're shooting high," Harry said, just loud enough for her to hear him. "Keep running."

They ran for another fifty yards before Caedmon slowed,

staggered, and dropped as if she'd been shot, but she was only exhausted. "I'm not as strong as I thought I was," she gasped, her face pressed into the leaf mold.

"Ants," Harry said, pulling her into a sitting position and brushing her face.

Then he tried to take the revolver out of her hand, but she said, "No!" and shoved it into her handbag. "The safety's on. What next?"

"Can you stand?" he asked.

"Yes. I think I'm feeling all right now. What next?"

"They'll follow, but fearing an ambush, much slower than we will—that is, if you can walk."

"I can walk, but why don't we just wait here until they catch up and then shoot them?" she asked.

They were in a stand of old growth slash pines and scattered saw palmetto. The pines were several yards apart and Harry did not like the thought of their running from one pine to another with two men with machine guns shooting at them.

"Not enough cover. It's thicker ahead. We were out here a while ago, remember?"

She nodded, but kept glancing back down the path.

"The panther has kittens. Tucker saw them. If she shows up, just get behind me. I'll walk us away from her. Okay?"

"Not really, but let's go."

"One more question," Harry said. "Are you sure they're the men who carried you away?"

"I don't know," Caedmon replied in a tight voice, "but seeing them triggered something. Thanks for stopping me from getting myself killed."

"No extra charge. Does this mean you want to live?"

"Christ, Harry, you're weird."

"Thank you. I'm going to call Jim. Then we'll go."

He made the call, spoke to the dispatcher, told her what was happening and where they were.

"We're on our way, Harry," she said, "as soon as I tell the captain. Watch yourself."

The pines fell away behind them, and the twisting path led them into wetter ground and thicker undergrowth with mahogany, wax myrtle, pigeon plum, bays, and Dahoon hollies, interspersed with small openings in which the last of the sun was casting long shadows over the grass.

"This looks familiar," Caedmon said, slowing and then stopping to stare around her.

"We saw the panther not too far from here."

"Are we going to keep going?" she asked, looking around uneasily.

"Yes, I want to get ourselves a little beyond where I think her den is located."

"I don't know if can keep up this pace much longer," she said.

"You won't have to. I'll go first now. No more talking. Grab me if you need me to look at you."

"I wonder if they're still following us?" Caedmon asked.

"Probably. They're not going to give up easily. They've failed at this once. I'm hoping they think we're running from them."

"Aren't we?" she asked.

"Not really. I'm hoping to give them a very unpleasant surprise."

They set off at a steady but moderate pace, their feet making almost no sound on the soft damp ground and sodden leaves. For a few minutes they walked with the rays of the setting sun in their eyes. Then it was gone and the evening sounds of the forest began to rise around them, led off by a poor-will's-widow, calling from a clearing in front of them.

36

By the time Harry called a halt and turned to look back along their path, tree frogs and crickets were tuning up and bats were swooping through the clearings, feeding on the insects, dancing in shifting clouds above the grass and bushes.

"Listen," he said quietly.

"For what?" Caedmon asked, turning to watch with him.

"For quiet places."

"There," she said, pointing back the way they had come.

"I agree," Harry said. "It's off to the south of the path, fifty yards or so.

"It's moving toward us," she said. "Is that possible?"

"Yes," he said, glancing quickly around him. "We're going to move off the path, being as quiet as we can, and hunker down behind that clump of saw palmetto."

"The quiet place is still moving this way," Caedmon said, giving him a worried look.

"I know," he said. "Quietly now."

Taking her arm, Harry led Caedmon through a belt-high stand of fiddlehead ferns and into a slight depression behind the saw palmetto.

"Lower yourself to your knees," he told her. "Good, can you see the place where the path comes out of those stopper bushes?"

"Yes," she said, peering through the palmetto fronds, "that's almost where the quiet started. You still haven't told me what's making things stop singing."

"It's the panther," Harry said. "She's following us. What do your ears tell you now?"

"The quiet place seems to be filling in."

"Good. She's stopped because we've stopped."

"Is she going to attack us?"

Caedmon had opened her bag, taken out a box of shells, and begun reloading her revolver.

"I don't think so," Harry answered, checking the shotgun, then the CZ.

Satisfied, he holstered the pistol, picked up the shotgun, and slowly pushed the barrel though the screen of branches, rattling the fronds as little as possible.

"Caedmon," he said, turning toward her, "promise me you won't jump up and start shooting."

"You mean I can't shoot one of those bastards if I get a chance?"

Harry could see the anger building.

"This is something I know a lot about," he said, carefully modulating his voice. "My first task is to get us out of here alive and uninjured. Are you with me?"

There was a pause, but she finally said, "Yes."

"OK. I want them to come about halfway from those stopper bushes to where we are. Then I want you to let me do the shooting."

"Isn't that awful close?"

"Yes, but the light is failing. It's brighter in the clearing, making it harder for them to see us here in the shadows. With any luck, we'll see them before they see us. With some more luck, they won't see us at all until it's too late."

"And I'm supposed to just 'hunker down' until it's all over?"

Harry knew what that question meant and set out to change her mind. "I need you for backup. If anything goes wrong, I'll say, 'Now' and you come up shooting."

"And if you can't say, 'Now'?"

"You're on your own. And I want to add, based on what I just heard, that you've been hanging around me too long."

She grinned, but the relief was brief. When Harry looked away from her to the path, there were two men standing at the edge of the clearing. The one ahead pointed to the right and then to the left. The second one nodded, and they began moving out along the edges of the clearing.

Harry swore silently. Depending on how wide they made their circle, they would either come back to the path behind them or walk up on them, one from each side.

"I've lost my man," Caedmon whispered.

"Stay alert. You'll see or hear him before he sees you," Harry replied. "They're circling the clearing, one on each side. Face left. Stay low, get as comfortable as you can, and if he comes, let him get as close as he can before you shoot. You'll only get one shot. Make it good."

"Right." She eased into a half turn to the left and braced herself, knees apart, settled down, and took a deep breath, releasing it slowly, her .38 held in both hands, resting on a half-rotted log.

"Come on, girl," Harry whispered.

"Where are we going?" Caedmon asked softly.

"Nowhere, I was praying," Harry said, drawing the shotgun out of the saw palmetto and laying it on the ground beside him, its barrel pointed to Harry's right.

"Are you attached to a female deity?"

"Right now I am."

As always happened to him when his life was in danger, all fear drained away, and he experienced a rush of adrenalin that brought with it an emotion close to anticipation. He drew his CZ and eased off the safety.

He could no longer see the man moving toward him, but he

could hear him. The brush was thick, and instead of picking his way through it, he was bulling his way through, snapping branches as he came. There was nothing to do but wait. As for the other man, there was nothing to indicate where he was.

"I can't see anything but leaves and branches," Caedmon complained in a whisper.

At that moment, there was a sudden rush of breaking branches and a snarling growl, followed by a loud yell and a scream.

"Good girl!" Harry said, wanting to jump up and shout, but holding himself in check.

"The panther?" Caedmon asked, swinging around.

"Yes," Harry said.

Howling bloody murder, the man staggered out of the bushes into the clearing. The panther, standing on her hind legs, gripped him from behind, her teeth sunk into his right shoulder. Harry could see he was struggling to pull his handgun out of its shoulder holster, but the big cat was throwing him from side to side, countering his efforts.

"I'm going to shoot him," Caedmon said, already halfway to her feet. Harry pulled her down, throwing himself on top of her.

The second man, racing into the clearing toward his partner, had seen Caedmon stand. He slowed, swung his gun and fired a burst at her, but Harry had pulled her down, and the slugs zinged and cut leaves over them.

"Lie still," Harry whispered in her ear before he rolled off her, shoved the CZ into its holster, and grabbed the shotgun.

A second volley of shots ripped through the top of the saw palmetto. Harry, still hugging the ground, waited for the shooting to stop. When it did, he scrambled to his feet. Caedmon had beaten him. The man, ignoring his partner's screams, was running straight at Harry and was not more than twenty feet away.

Caedmon and Harry fired at the same time. The man took the full charge in the chest.

It was as if he had been struck by a truck. Blown backward off his feet, his arms flung wide, he plowed into the grass, bounced once, and lay still.

"My God!" Caedmon said, her gun still pointed at the torn and bloody figure.

"Cover me," Harry said, dodging around the palmetto and racing toward the first man, on the ground now and being mauled by the furious cat. As Harry ran, he shouted and fired twice into the air. The roar of the shotgun and the shouting were too much for her. With a final snarl, she whirled, bounded into the brush, and was gone.

"He'll live," the leader of the medical team said as her team hoisted the gurney into the EMS ambulance, which had plowed along the path and was festooned with vines and branches and plastered with leaves and ferns.

"Who patched him up?" she asked as she pulled off her gloves and her cap, freeing a lot of thick, black hair that tumbled down the back of her orange coverall.

"She did," Harry said, turning to Caedmon.

"Good job," the woman said, glancing quickly at Harry and then at Caedmon. "His shirt?"

"Yes. Also what was left of the shooter's—and thank you," Caedmon said. "My first impulse was to strangle him. Harry talked me out of it."

"I'm glad you didn't," she said without smiling. "We get a bonus for bringing them in alive."

"Was she serious?" Caedmon asked as the woman clambered into the back of the ambulance, pulling the door shut as it started to move away.

"I don't think so."

"She's Indian, isn't she?"

"Probably from the reservation. More and more are working now in Avola and Miami."

"Is that good or bad?"

"Neither. How are you?"

"I don't know. I feel empty."

Harry, past caring for the consequences, took her hand and held it. She had leaves and bits of twigs tangled in her hair, a streak of mud across her left cheek, her shorts and top were torn and stained. Minus his shirt, Harry guessed he probably looked worse.

"The adrenalin's draining out of you," he said, surprised she had not pulled her hand away. "Are you tired?"

"Possibly. He can tell the police who hired him, but will he?"

"They electrocute people in this state. The chair they use doesn't always work right. Word gets around. Let's hope they were the two who kidnapped you."

"I'm going to have to think about that," she responded with a sound that might or might not have been a laugh.

By this time, Jim and Frank and the members of the Crime Scene squad were trailing back from both sides of the clearing. One of the men was carrying the dropped submachine gun. Two of the men had turned on their flashlights and were studying the grass as they walked.

"Looking for clues?" Caedmon asked.

"Snakes," Harry said.

"The cat ripped into that poor son-of-a-bitch pretty good," Hodges said loudly when he reached them, his red face streaming sweat. "There's blood everywhere. How did you manage to patch him up?"

He mopped his face with a blue bandanna and looked at Caedmon when he asked the question.

"Wherever the blood was pumping worst, I tied a rag around

it," Caedmon said. "I didn't really think beyond that. Harry helped me."

Jim came striding up and said to her, "You're going to ride back to the house. Let's get you going. Lieutenant O'Reilly is there. She's going to ask you some questions if that won't be too much for you."

He waited for an answer, and when she said she would be glad to tell what she could, he added, "I expect she'll have made some coffee, and if Harry's got anything stronger there, you might have a little of that."

"A lot," Caedmon said.

"Oh, I wouldn't," Jim said, sounding seriously concerned, "not on top of what you've just . . ."

"She's joking," Harry said, which set Hodges guffawing.

"Sergeant," Jim said, "put Ms. Rivers in that ATV and drive her back to Harry's place and try not to tell her any stories."

"Yes, sir," Hodges said, his broad face shining merrily as a rose-colored moon in the deepening twilight.

"Close call," Jim said to Harry as the two men watched the vehicle lurching away.

"I'm in debt to the buff-colored lady," he said.

"You knew where she was."

"Approximately."

"Good move. Let's get out of here while we can still see."

Falling into a rough line with Jim and Harry leading, the men started off, talking and calling to one another as they walked. Gradually over the next hundred yards, their voices died away until there was only the sound of the frogs, the insects, and the low call of a hunting owl. Jim mentioned the fact to Harry.

"It's the Hammock," Harry said.

"It was like this in the mountains," Jim said.

"Just feeling better being quiet?"

"I think that's about right."

For whatever reasons, those were the last words any of them spoke until they stepped into the clearing under the oaks behind Harry's house. Harry, breaking their lengthy silence, stopped to thank the men as they passed him in the moonlight, moving wearily toward their cruisers.

"Some of them are finishing their second shift of the day," Jim said, standing with Harry, watching them go. "The department's threadbare, and I can't hire until the next calendar year."

"Penny wise and pound foolish," Harry said.

"Like all bureaucracies," Jim said sourly when they reached the steps.

"She put on all the lights and then thanked me for being so helpful," Frank said in a loud voice, striding out of the brightly lit house and letting the screen door bang shut behind him. "Then she said she was going to bed, which was a good thing because she looked to me as if she was about to pass out."

"Dear Lord, give me strength," Jim said, possibly to himself, and more loudly, "Frank, keep your voice down."

"I've been creeping around in there like a mouse," Hodges protested.

"It's all right," Harry said, stepping forward and shaking his hand and then shaking Jim's. "You've both done good work tonight."

Peace restored, the two officers left for their cruiser, arguing in subdued voices as they left.

37

"Once in a while," Jim said, unfolding his length from behind his desk and pausing to stretch luxuriously, "the effort seems worth it."

The stretch was a certain sign, Harry thought with pleasure, that for the moment at least, the pressures had lifted, and his friend was not in pain. In this rare moment, he was not thinking about Kathleen.

The next two weeks passed quietly for Harry. Caedmon was working again. But in that week she had declined to talk with him about the shooting and had withdrawn further than ever from him, and all of his attempts to narrow the widening gap had been rebuffed.

"They're both in custody, retained as flight risks," the tall man continued. "Our Siberian émigré is basking in the warmth of the county jail, under a twenty-four-hour suicide watch, and singing like a meadow lark."

"Wrong part of the country," Harry said, hoping to provoke his friend.

No luck. Jim was obviously too full of contentment to be provoked.

"Is he really a suicide risk?"

"No," Jim said, coming around the desk to lean on it and looking down at Harry with the first frown Harry had seen from him since entering his office. "I told Harley that the Ogilvies are only slightly less dangerous in jail than out of it. Money runs between their bars like water."

"And Serge Rudakov is the only person who can testify to their being behind Maria Fuegos' murder and the assault on Caedmon," Harry said, feeling less comfortable for having said it.

"Yes, but don't forget, we now have access to Rudakov and his partner's bank accounts and access to the Ogilvies' accounts in this country. We have their accountant in jail, their broker as well. We're charging the accountant as an accessory to homicide—which won't stand up to judicial scrutiny. But we scared the hell out of him, and as the Brits say, he is assisting the police. What we want from the broker, and are almost certain to get, is the listing of the Ogilvies' overseas holdings."

"For that part," Harry said, "it doesn't hurt that the FBI has become involved, trailing their pack train of bullion behind them."

"No, the Ogilvies' money will lose its impact."

"That's right. So while it would be ideal to put Rudakov on the stand, we have his testimony, taken under oath. We have his and his partner's DNA, which is a match to that taken from Caedmon. I think we're going to make this stick."

"I prayerfully hope so," Harry said.

"How's Caedmon?" Jim asked, his attempt to make the inquiry sound casual failing.

Harry flinched. Suddenly being reminded of her was instant misery.

"At first, the shootout lifted her spirits," he said stoically, "and seemed to be bringing her down from her tree. Then she suddenly withdrew and is not even pretending to communicate."

"That's bad."

Jim scowled at the floor for a few seconds. Then, apparently finding inspiration from his study, he said, "Kathleen took a .38 slug out of what little was left of the dead man's chest. She thinks it had to have been in there when the buckshot hit him. Otherwise, it would have gone right through."

Harry knew she had ignored his telling her to stay down. He also had a very blurred memory of her standing beside him when he fired the shotgun, but no recollection at all of hearing the shot.

"How much of a part does that play in Kathleen's ME report?"

"A mention—the report assumes the buckshot killed him. Multiple pellets had ripped his heart apart," Jim said.

"I live in dread Harley will put her on the stand."

"It may happen," Jim said with a sigh of resignation.

"I don't think she could make it through a hard cross."

"Can't Holinshed and Benson be persuaded to pressure the judge to have her deposed?"

"I'm working on it, but Caedmon doesn't want me talking about anything concerning her to either woman."

"Doesn't she have a lawyer?" Jim asked, showing surprise.

"No, oddly enough, she's had no need of one. Her negotiations with her insurance company went without a hitch. Until now there's been no grounds for a civil case against anyone, although there may be one when the Ogilvies' trial is over."

"I think she should have somebody besides you advising her," Jim insisted.

Harry knew Jim too well to be offended, but the comment still stung.

"You're right, of course, but I don't have any hope of persuading her to hire a lawyer."

Jim frowned some more, then said, "How did she get along with Jeff Smolkin? What about asking him to call her and find some way to let her know she needs representation?"

The suggestion surprised Harry. First, because outside of trying to socialize Hodges, he'd never heard Jim give anyone any advice beyond reading them their rights or telling them that unless they put that gun down, he would blow their heads off. But thinking about it, he saw that it was worth a try.

"You're full of surprises," Harry said. "I'll give it a go."

"The sooner the better," Jim said, with a supporting hand dropped on Harry's shoulder.

The moment Harry entered Jeff Smolkin's office, he knew that something was wrong. Instead of the usual hum of activity, the staccato clatter of high heels signaling paras rushing at a near run along the corridor, and no one greeting him, there was a pervasive heaviness in the air that reminded Harry of a funeral parlor.

"Oh, Mr. Brock," Bernadette said, her smile faltering and then failing altogether.

He had found no one at Renata's desk. Even her assistant was missing. He had encountered Bernadette creeping along the corridor like a thief in the night.

"What's going on?" Harry asked. "I've attended internments more cheerful than this place."

"Oh, it's bad, Mr. Brock," the dark-haired young woman said, "and I'm afraid it's all our fault."

"Bernadette," Harry said, "is someone dead?"

"No, well, not yet, but I . . ."

Her voice failed, and her eyes filled and ran over.

"I'm really sorry to see you so miserable, but I thought Renata told me that paras who worked long for Number One lost the ability to cry."

His attempt to be funny only brought a keening sound out of Bernadette, who spun on a heel and ran with surprising speed back the way she had come and vanished around a corner. Harry felt as if he was standing with his mouth open. He wasn't, but he was becoming seriously irritated. Was this a law office or a halfway house?

"Hello, Harry," a dungeon voice said behind him.

He turned to see Smolkin standing outside his door, looking as if he was waiting to be hanged.

"What in God's name is wrong?" Harry demanded, hurrying toward him.

"Come in. Sit down. It's terrible, Harry. Terrible."

He sank into a chair in front of his desk, giving Harry the impression that he might never get up.

"Let's hear it," Harry said, sitting down.

"It's Renata," he said in a sepulchral voice.

"Is she ill? Christ, Jeff, what is it?"

"She's gone."

"Gone where?"

"Dallas, I think. Oh God, Harry. It's awful."

"What do you mean, *gone?*"

"She's gone, for Christ's sake. What part of *gone* don't you understand? She's skipped, flown the coop, run away, absconded. Don't you understand! She's left me!"

Smolkin had pushed himself half out of his chair, his face growing increasingly red as he shouted at Harry. Then he suddenly collapsed, head drooping. "I'm ruined," he said and groaned.

Harry squelched his impulse to laugh, the effort made increasingly easier by the very unpleasant sense of loss that was moving through him like a black and fetid tide.

"Is she coming back?" Harry asked lamely, all the while thinking of his and Renata's night together, no part of which did anything to make him feel better.

"She's definitely not coming back," Smolkin said in a more natural voice. "I'm only surprised the building's still standing and I'm still drawing breath."

"What was the final straw?" Harry asked without thinking.

"What do you mean?" Smolkin demanded, glaring at Harry. "Are you suggesting any of this is my fault?"

"Forget it, of course not. Why did she go?"

Smolkin stood up, shoved his hands into his pants pockets, and with shoulders hunched began pacing back and forth in front of his desk, the picture of despair.

"I suppose I should have seen it coming," he said. "She was getting impossible to live with."

"Live with?" Harry asked in surprise.

"What? Oh. Work with."

Having corrected the record, he then went back to staring at the rug and pacing. "The paras finally came to me in a group and said I could either rein her in or accept their resignations—no holdouts."

"And you talked to Renata."

"I had no more than said, 'We have a problem,' when she started. I'm surprised you couldn't hear her on the Hammock. I didn't understand it then, and I don't understand it now—none of it."

"You still don't know why she exploded?" Harry asked, awed by the Himalayan grandeur of Smolkin's failure.

"Well, all I can think of is that she might be starting menopause. My wife has signed up for a course in change of life," Smolkin began, frowning seriously. "Of course, she's way too young for that to happen. She's about Renata's age, but she says some women start early. She wants to be prepared. Do you suppose it could be that?"

"No, Jeff," Harry said with the certainty of a man who has just talked with Jesus, "I don't think it's that."

Eventually, Harry had recovered enough to get Smolkin off the drama of Renata's denunciation and departure, two classics in their own time apparently lost on Smolkin, but leaving his paras with a vocabulary of female fury and a standard of wrath unleashed that they drew on the rest of their lives. It was reported but unsubstantiated that some of them erected small shrines to her in their bedrooms, from which, once married, they drew inspiration when the need arose—as it invariably did.

Out of Smolkin's office, Harry was able to give more attention to what Renata's going meant to him. Thinking about it as he crossed the crushed shell parking area, he concluded that in addition to feeling sad, he had an unpleasant sensation of having lost something, of being diminished, damaged.

He got into the Rover and started the engine, immediately maxing the A.C. because, although the huge ficus had prevented all but flickering shafts of sunlight from striking the Rover, the cab was a flameless fire. The physical discomfort made him ask himself if he was in any way to blame for Renata's leaving. But he couldn't find any way to fall on his sword over her going. One thing was certain, though. He already missed her and knew he would go on missing her, which may in the end have been the best compliment he could have paid her.

38

When Harry reached the Hammock, the sun was slipping into the trees, and the shadows cast by the live oaks had reached the Puc Puggy. In the deepest shade on the creek's banks, the colony frogs were clearing their throats and tuning their instruments for their coming performance. Caedmon came out the lanai door and walked toward him as he was climbing out of the Rover. Her BMW, which she was driving again, was parked on the other side of the oak.

"Is anything wrong?" he asked, hurrying toward her.

That his sudden concern had anything to do with Renata's leaving did not occur to him. But by the time she had brushed the question away with a flick of her hand as if a fly was pestering her, his heart was beating heavily.

"Do we have time before dark to go out to where the panther has her kittens?" she asked.

Harry was short of breath because he had not been breathing. "Just about," he said, glancing at the sky while he puffed.

"If you don't want to go, Harry, just say so. There's no need to pretend I've been running you off your feet."

She looked so offended that Harry laughed in relief. "Yes, my day's been okay," he said. "What about yours?"

"Wonderful," she said, the sarcasm dripping like pitch.

"Just let me get my gun," Harry said. "Meet me in back of the house."

"Any further instructions?" she asked of his back.

In response, he waggled his fanny at her, which finally made her laugh.

"I just don't understand how the man could be so blind," Harry said, having told Caedmon the tale of Renata's going supernova and then blasting out of Smolkin's life.

Caedmon, walking in front of Harry, responded with a bark of laughter that had more vinegar than honey in it. "Why didn't she just tell the idiot she loved him and saved them both the hassle?" she demanded.

Harry decided to let the Renata story drop, but Caedmon wasn't finished with it.

"Just what was going on between you and her?" she asked.

"We've known each other for a long time," Harry said.

"An answer, please," she said.

"One brief period of intimacy, which she ended by saying it wouldn't work and goodbye. I guess we were friends."

"How upset are you over her leaving?"

"I'm not upset," Harry said, "but I hurt a little."

Caedmon stopped, turned, and said, "I'm sorry, Harry."

"Thanks," he said. "Now it's my turn to ask a question. What are we doing out here?"

"I want to see the place, stand in it for a while, check my memory with you about what happened, and go back to the house. OK?"

"OK," he said. "Lead on. In case we meet the lady of the house, remember the drill. You slip behind me and we back up slowly and quietly until I say, 'OK.' She may be a little touchy after what happened. Also, having tackled one person, she may be tempted to have another go."

"How worried about that are you?"

"Not at all worried. If we keep our heads, we'll be fine."

"Is that why you brought the shotgun?" Caedmon asked.

Harry grinned. "You have a fine instrument there, Caedmon,

and you play it beautifully."

"You may remember," she said with sudden bitterness, "that I have another one, but it's covered with cobwebs."

Harry could find no response to that, and as they walked along the path, his silence hung like a sword over his head.

"Why did you bring the shotgun?" she asked finally.

"It makes a lot of noise," he said, glad of the reprieve.

"I remember," she said. "You frightened her off the man she was chewing. I wish you'd let her work on him a while longer."

"I don't think he would have survived much more of her attention. I didn't tell you, but I saw him in the hospital a day or so after they finished working on him. There wasn't much of the top half of his body that wasn't bandaged, including his face."

"Good," she said. "I shot at the other one. I didn't think I could do it, but I did. I don't know whether or not I hit him because you fired right after me, and that sure as hell did."

Harry paused a moment to make up his mind and said, "You hit him. Kathleen found the slug in his chest." He left out the details.

"My contribution," she said and then fell silent, thinking, Harry supposed, but about what he didn't know and was content to leave her undisturbed.

It was early twilight when they reached the spot where the ambush had taken place. The night wind was feeling its way through the trees, and the crickets were trying out their saws, echoing the tree frogs. Overhead, mosquito hawks were feeding over the clearing, their wings thrumming loudly as they pulled out of their dives.

"Tell me where you and I were standing," Caedmon said in a subdued voice.

"Behind that saw palmetto with its top all shot up," Harry said, pointing.

Caedmon waded through the ferns to the spot where they

had stood and looked out across the opening. Harry followed close behind her, his head swiveling in search of any indication that the cat was also there. For the moment, he thought they might be alone.

"That's where she attacked him," Caedmon said, gesturing to her right, "and that's where the other one came from."

"That's right," Harry said.

She stood for a few moments scanning the area in front of her. Then she lifted her right arm, made a fist, turned it into a mock gun by pointing her first finger and raising her thumb, held the position for a long moment, then said, "Bang."

She turned to Harry and said in a defiant voice, "It feels almost as good doing it this time as it did then."

Harry had no time to respond because as soon as she finished speaking, the big cat burst out of the bushes directly across the opening from them and in deadly silence came straight at them in long, springing bounds.

"Company," Caedmon said, apparently without fear.

Harry slipped the safety off the gun and, pointing it so that she would see the muzzle blast but not be struck by the charge, he pulled the trigger. Her next bound, Harry knew, would put her right on top of them. He jacked another shell into the chamber.

At the very last instant, she braked with all four feet, tearing up the grass where her claws fought for purchase in the soft earth. Harry had the gun pointing at her head before she stopped skidding.

Then she took a step back, her head raised, her tail slashing, and her yellow eyes blazing. Caedmon stood absolutely still, so did Harry, so did the cat except for her tail. Harry held her gaze, hoping against hope she would back down. Then she shifted her eyes to Caedmon, held her gaze for a moment, growled once softly, and then with consummate grace and strength lifted her body to the left and in a single, long leap broke through the wall of leaves and was gone.

"I will remember her as long as I live," Caedmon said quietly.

Harry turned, listening intently, trying to locate her, but now all around the clearing the crickets were singing again. There was no moving circle of silence.

"Let's go home," he said.

That evening Caedmon was very quiet. Harry was not surprised. She was now often quiet, and he guessed that her encounter with the panther had taken more out of her than she realized. Twice in the night, Harry thought he heard her moving about in her room, but sporadic sleeplessness was another long-term gift her attackers had given her.

A little after five Harry came downstairs, having decided to make them pancakes for breakfast and intending to serve them to her, along with eggs and bacon, on a tray before she was out of bed. But he found her up and dressed, making coffee.

"Bad night?" he asked.

"I'm sorry if I disturbed you."

"You didn't. How about pancakes for breakfast?"

She turned to face him, an action that stopped his advance. A single look at her face wilted his smile as well.

"Harry," she said. "I'm moving into town. I've talked this over with Holinshed, and she agreed it was the right thing to do."

Harry moved forward, ready to argue, but then stopped. What could he say that hadn't already been said?

"I'm sorry to hear it. Are you going to tell me why?"

The coffee pot chimed.

"Over coffee," she said, returning to the sideboard and taking their mugs out of the cupboard.

Harry watched her going through the simple ritual of filling the mugs, carrying them to the table. She pulled out her chair and sat down. These, he thought, were the shared acts on which much of the happiness of domestic life was grounded. Trying to shake off the elegiac mood, he sat down and took a sip of the coffee.

"I'm ready as I ever will be," he said, forcing out a smile.

"There's no simple answer to your question, Harry," she said. "But it comes down to this. I have to learn how to live all over again, and I don't want to do it with you. I can't do it with you."

"Really," Harry said flatly.

If she had leaned across the table and slapped him, he wouldn't have been more shocked, hurt, angry. He struggled to sort out his feelings and failed.

"Try not to be angry," she said in the same level voice in which she had been addressing him since he walked into the kitchen. "I know it sounds brutal, even uncaring. Maybe it is, but if it is, it's because I can't do anything about it."

She sat looking at him in silence for a moment, then went on speaking.

"I'm deeply indebted to you, Harry, for everything you've done to help me, and I will never forget our time together before I was taken off, violated, then dumped naked beside a dirt road and left to die."

For a wild instant Harry wanted to ask if it would have helped if it had been a surfaced road, drank some coffee without tasting it, and drove the response back into its cage.

"But I don't love you, Harry," she told him. "The thought of having sex with you nauseates me. Living in this house with you, having you look at me, wanting me, is painful in a dozen ways. It has to be difficult for you as well, but that's not what we're talking about, is it?"

"No, I suppose it isn't. I'm sorry if I've added to your suffering."

"Don't try to make me feel guilty, Harry, for not wanting you. I'm beyond that game. Now and for a long time, I expect, my focus has to be on surviving. Holinshed keeps telling me it's worth the effort. I'm not so sure it is, but I have agreed to try."

"Then you're moving back to town," Harry said.

"Very temporarily. I've rented the house."

"Where will you go?"

Harry thought he was beyond being startled, but found he was wrong.

"Seattle," Caedmon said, without any particular emphasis that might have given him some sense of how she felt about the move.

"Why Seattle?" he asked.

"I've never been there. My client has been transferred to that area."

"Are you and he . . . ?"

"It's *she,* and haven't you heard anything I've said?"

"It feels as if I have," Harry said. "Were you packing last night?"

"Yes. I'll leave this morning, if you will help me put the computers and the other things in my car."

"Where will you take them?"

"I have movers in the house this morning, packing. They'll take most of my electronics. By the time my things reach Seattle, I'll have found a place to live."

"Your car?"

"I'm having it driven out there."

"You're flying."

"Yes. It will create a space for me."

"Like an ocean voyage."

"Possibly."

"You've been busy."

"Yes."

"What about Benson and Holinshed?"

He guessed he would not have to say more and he was right.

"My medical records will go to the Group Health Co-operative in Seattle. I have an internist, a woman, and a psychiatrist and a therapist, both women."

"I'm impressed."

"Don't be, Harry. There's nothing here to be impressed by. What you see is largely a mess."

By now Harry's emotional turmoil had subsided into a dull, aching sense of loss.

"What I see," he told her, "is a beautiful woman. I love her, and expect I always will."

"The woman you found beside the road is not the woman you loved, Harry. That part of me died miserably. Now, it's time for what's left to leave."

"Wait," Harry said. "I've forgotten. What about the trial?"

"I've been deposed," she answered, carrying her mug to the sink and rinsing it.

Harry watched her turn the mug over and set it on the drying rack. Almost without volition, he heard himself reciting a verse he had memorized as an adolescent, " 'And when like her, oh, Saki, / You shall pass, / Among the Guests, Star-scatter'd on the grass, / And in your joyous errand reach the spot / Where I made one—turn down an empty Glass.' "

Caedmon had turned quickly at the sound of his voice and listened without moving until he was finished.

"Harry," she said without smiling, "that was a coffee mug, not a wine glass, I was rinsing."

The clarification braced Harry, and he got up and said, "Do you want to leave now or eat first?"

"I'm ready to go," she replied. "It's going to be a long day."

"Yes, I think it will be," he said.

And it was.

But as he told Tucker much later, "It ended better than it began."

At sunset he found that staying in the house and cooking dinner was more than he could face and took a long walk along Puc Puggy Creek. When he returned home and, steeling himself, walked into the kitchen, he found the message light blinking on his phone. He punched a button and Maureen O'Reilly's rich voice, brogue and all, disturbed the grim silence of the room.

"You'll be forgiving the intrusion, Harry. I've heard, and I'm thinking this might be the night when Irish stew, John Jameson—the saintly man—and myself would be welcome alternatives to an empty house."

Dear Reader, he went.

ABOUT THE AUTHOR

Kinley Roby lives in Virginia with his wife, writer and editor Mary Linn Roby.